I0687116

A Question of Evil
The Imperial Chronicles

Nicholas Samuel Stember

Published by Rogue Phoenix Press. LLP
Copyright © Nicholas Samuel Stember 2025

Names, characters and incidents depicted in this book are products of the author's imagination or are used fictitiously. Any resemblance to actual events, locales, organizations, or persons, living or dead, is entirely coincidental and beyond the intent of the author or the publisher. No part of this book may be reproduced or transmitted in any form or by any means, electronic or mechanical, including photocopying, recording, or by any information storage and retrieval system, without permission in writing from the publisher.

ISBN: 978-1-62420-886-7

Credits
Cover Artist: Design by Ms G
Editor: Sherry Derr-Wille

Dedication

For my grandchildren,
Olaf Sonny, Boas, and Dorthea Jóhanna

Reflections
The Dream

Deep red starlight filtered through the spherical cathedral window of her luxurious chambers. The bedroom, cast in shadows the color of blood, was silent and peaceful. Usually, this was one of the few places she could rest but not tonight.

With a jolt, she sat upright in her grand bed, her scarlet satin sheets damp with sweat. She expectantly glanced to her left and parted her softly curved lips as if to speak. Her words died with a short breath as the realization came that she was alone. She had forgotten, of course she was alone. However, her unremembered solitude wasn't what disturbed her, for the dream returned. A dream which had been absent for many years, and she'd hoped would never come back.

Control, her thoughts drilled in his voice, *never let yourself lose control.* She drew a full, deep breath and felt the red in her delicate tanned cheeks smolder down. The torrents of the Cosmic Aura, invisible to most, were forced into a tranquil wave in her mind as she slowly soothed her emotions down. "Damn him," she whispered with a warm smile, "even when he's not here, he is."

She let herself melt back onto the bed, tiny curling wisps of steam escaping the heavy silken mass of black hair which rested against the pillow. Unconsciously, her brow furrowed as her thoughts drifted.

How long has it been since I dreamed that? Years? A decade? Even though she wasn't sure of how long, she was certain of the trigger that started it all. *Oh yes,* she recalled as she stared up at the window above her, the years melting away in her mind. *The Rehabilitation Center, that was when this all started…*

Chapter One
Justice

Angel let out a loud yawn as she tried to shut out her rehab counselor's monotonous speech on self-improvement, and the better way of living in peace and harmony inside the 'wonderful' and 'benevolent' United Star Alliance.

"Wonderful" and "benevolent", the young woman mused with a mixture of irony and fury. *If that was so true, then why am I here? What did I do that was so terrible that I deserved to be locked up in this Alliance Rehabilitation Colony? Seriously?*

For a moment, she struggled to block out the memories of her brief time with the Red Star Pirates, the fleeting thoughts enough to force her to admit some level of guilt. She absently rubbed the deep tan skin on her forearm as she bit her bottom lip, each memory layer stripping away until her thoughts were back at the primitive world where she and her fellow pirate shipmates had been stranded. In her mind's eye Angel saw him alone, the brash pirate captain who swept her off her feet and saved her, allowing her to escape from her home world of Tenebrous. She remembered him as she last saw him, standing amongst the Alliance Stellar Naval crew who *finally* arrived to rescue them. He was charming, charismatic, daring, and way too stupid. *No, not stupid,* she silently corrected herself with an inner sigh, *but he had to do it, didn't he?* Maybe it was to prove something to his crew, who blamed him for crashing their ship there in the first place. However, the truth never eluded her. She knew it was merely a feeble attempt to protect his pride. Angel fidgeted nervously as the scene played itself again in her mind, the pirate captain's gun coming up, his target clearly the Alliance ship's captain. She wanted to yell, to warn the only people who could save them from their self-imposed prison, but instead it was not the pirate's weapon which fired, but her own. She recalled, all too easily, the surge of power flowing through her body as the energy bolt struck the first man she ever loved, killing him instantly. Then she internally flinched as she remembered the pain that followed, as the Alliance stun beams enveloped her, sucking her into darkness.

Angel pushed the infuriating memory aside, her palm still tingling from the imprint of the first time she took a life. Glancing around the office again she tried not to laugh. Her actions saved their fleet captain's life, and the reward was twenty Solar years at a rehab colony, branded a pirate and a murderer. *That's the United Star Alliance's brand of justice for you.*

"And…" continued Doctor Reid, in her monotone speech, not even noticing her patient's vacant eyes, "so it is like the *phoenix* which we are named for. We like to cast aside the inmate's old life, burning it away if you will, to replace it with a fresh new outlook. This will lead the rehabilitated inmate to start anew, beginning over as a happy and productive member of the United Star Alliance…"

Angel tuned out the rest, her gaze focused on the shining gold plaque behind the counselor. In proud letters it read:

Phoenix
Deep Space Rehabilitation Station
United Star Alliance
Founded 2310

Doing quick arithmetic, Angel realized she and the station were about the same age. When she first arrived here last week, the doctor who gave her a physical, determined her age to be approximately nineteen. She had always wondered, but coming from a colony where luxuries such as birthdays were nonexistent, had never been sure. *Somehow,* Angel considered absently, *I thought I was older.*

The counselor continued for some time, until the realization finally came that her patient was no longer paying the slightest bit of attention to her, and she stopped for a moment to stare at the inmate sitting across from her. Angelina's face was pretty, but her cheeks still had some baby fat clinging to her perfectly tan skin, which made her seem younger than her records showed. Her long black hair hung in thick waves that washed about her shoulders, and her dark brown eyes still showed a spark of defiance which the counselor knew wouldn't last long in this place. "Angelina?" she said, her voice becoming sickly sweet. "Are we all right? Or are we having one of our daydreams again?"

"No, *we* aren't. And stop calling me Angelina."

Doctor Reid paused, her patronizing smile never wavering despite her patient's indignant tone. "But that's our name, isn't it?" She paused again as her emotionless eyes drifted down to the electronic pad which rested in her long thin fingers, then slowly returned to their mark. "According to the DNA records we *are* Angelina Calida Sierra Pagán, which is quite an impressive name. We should be proud of our name, shouldn't we?"

"I'm Angel," she said with a quake in her voice which was less than angelic. "And seriously…why do you always have to say *we* or *our*, when you are obviously referring to me alone? Do you see *more* people in this room than the two of us? If you do, then maybe you should be the inmate, and I'll counsel *you* for a while."

The counselor's face contorted for the briefest of moments, then her honey-coated smile returned. "Well, I can see we're going to take some time getting used to it here, aren't we? As a new member of our little community, we should try to make life a bit easier." The doctor's smile grew into a taunting grimace. "After all, getting sentenced to a rehabilitation colony is a far cry from hard labor on a penal planet, isn't it?"

"I don't belong here," Angel replied while folding her arms and sinking further into the couch.

"We killed someone."

"I *saved* someone."

"The weapon we had did have a stun setting, didn't it?"

Angel's lips tightened. "No…yes…I didn't have time to think about that; he was going to shoot the Alliance captain."

"So," the counselor said with the same painted smile on her lips, "I suppose we feel wrongly judged?"

Angel's young eyes hardened, suddenly fixing on Dr. Reid's. "Damn right. I should have let him kill her first, then shot…then maybe you idiots would have believed me."

Doctor Reid's smile faded as she suddenly became uncomfortable, her overconfidence shaken slightly by the vehemence displayed in Angel's eyes. The counselor cleared her throat and attempted to regain control. "We're a bit testy today, aren't we? So, why don't we talk about something else? My files say we are from the failed Terran colony world of Tenebrous. I know all forms of law and order broke down in that world leaving it in utter anarchy, and few people survived to escape the disasters there…that must make us very special."

Angel's voice cooled to a dry whisper. "Actually, it makes *me* very special…and makes *you* seem less than ordinary. Let me guess, you grew up somewhere nice and safe, like Earth."

Doctor Reid tried to hold on to all her years of training at one of the Alliance's best universities. She cleared her dry throat and forced herself to get back onto her intended path. "So, Angelina, sometimes even very special people can have problems, like nightmares."

"What does that have to do with anything?"

"According to my records," she continued, with eyes glinting like a cat's who was about to pounce, "we've been having terrible nightmares. Maybe we can talk about them."

"Personally, I don't really care about your nightmares," Angel said with a sneer, apathetically leaning back on the overly soft couch which was obviously designed to rob its user of any sense of relaxation or comfort.

"We're not talking about *my* dreams, Angelina."

"Though I can fully understand why you have them," Angel continued, ignoring the irritating counselor. "You probably feel guilty about trying to screw with people's minds."

Doctor Reid's bottom lip fell slightly open as her composure was momentarily lost, but it was quickly regained. "Perhaps we should conclude our session later this afternoon. After all, we don't want to be late for our mental awareness treatment today, do we?"

"No…*we* don't."

The young woman stiffly rose from the heavily padded couch and left the room, slowly making her way down the antiseptic corridors of the rehabilitation colony toward the mental awareness clinic room. She was happy to be away from the presence of the condescending Doctor Reid but had little desire to go to her next appointment.

Angel walked along, seeing the blank faces of the inmates who passed by in the narrow, brightly lit halls, as she tried not to glance too closely at the vacant looks in their eyes. Although she had been here almost two weeks already, the high-spirited young woman somehow managed to retain most of her individuality, despite the hypnotic counseling sessions, and the mental awareness clinic. The latter of which entailed a dose of the mind-numbing devices used on the more violent criminals, like murderers, like herself.

When her mind was not being tampered with for 'the good of the United Star Alliance', she was allowed to socialize with the other inmates in the common room. However, this wasn't enjoyable unless you didn't mind spending an afternoon chatting with people whose grip on reality had long since left them. Worse yet were those who had been mentally drained to submissiveness by the cruel machines in what Angel nicknamed the 'tomb of horrors'.

Lost in her thoughts, the young woman bumped into an inmate who was traveling in the opposite direction. Angel gazed up to find it was Jenkins, a gentle man who had been here for the last six years.

He glanced down at her with eyes of stone which were hollowed and empty. For a moment, Angel almost thought he was going to say something, however, he simply turned to walk away.

Driven by an impulse, she grabbed his arm and spun him back to face her again, though she avoided meeting his gaze.

"Jenkins," she asked, her voice a whispered plea, "do you know who I am?"

The tall man remained silent for another moment, then slowly nodded. "You are Angelina," he said in a numb voice devoid of emotion. "I am sorry I bumped into you. Have a nice day." He then turned and walked off.

Angel let him go, suddenly drained of any desire to reach someone else. Then she smiled as she thought of Sinclair. He was the first inmate to reach out to her and make her feel she wasn't alone. However, even this thought darkened her mind. Sinclair was the one other inmate here she dared call a real friend. What if it was *his* blank stare which faced her one day?

Taking a deep breath, unable to consider this train of thought, she turned back in her original direction and continued. Finally, arriving at the 'tomb', the young woman signed in at the retina scanner and sat down in the waiting area. She seriously considered leaving before her session could begin, but she knew the punishment would have simply been double sessions to make up for it. Her eyes rolled at the thought. *The colony wouldn't want anyone running around who had a will of their own now, would they?*

The door slid open as the technician who ran the machines in the mental awareness clinic came in, followed by a flock of wide-eyed cadets who were touring the facility. He acknowledged Angel's presence with a casual nod and a wave of his hand, signaling her to wait a few minutes, then returned to the lecture he was giving to the students.

"What does this machine do?" one of the future Alliance Naval officers asked, her eyes sparkling with concentration and curiosity.

"Let's see," technician Boone replied, trying to make something which was complex sound simple, "it emits a soothing wave of energy that subtly alters the thinking patterns of the patient."

"How?" The same inquisitive student continued, her eyes darting to the intricate machinery, her lithe form turning away from the technician. For a moment she locked eyes with Angel, and the two exchanged brief smiles.

Angel's smile faded rapidly as she watched the students with detached apathy. *They're young and energetic now*, she considered, *but one day they'll be another bunch of nameless cogs in the Alliance machine…no different than those who sentenced me to be here.* The inmate suppressed a yawn as the same young student, an alabaster white skinned alien from Proxima, continued to listen to every detail Boone was willing to divulge to her, eating it up.

"By slightly depressing the higher brain functions," Boone continued, "it makes a violent patient more passive and open to…suggestions."

"Sounds a lot like brainwashing," the same student commented.

Wow, a cadet with a brain, Angel sneered to herself.

"So, I see our time is up," technician Boone quickly responded. "Your next stop will be their resting quarters. Thank you for stopping by."

The one student tried to remain longer, to have her question answered, however, she was sturdily ushered out of the clinic. When they were gone, the technician turned back to face Angel. "Ah, Angelina," the torture master of the 'tomb of horrors' said, "good morning. How have we been today?"

His smile formed into the same plastic grin shared by her rehabilitation counselor, and everyone else in the asylum.

"I'm swell, Boone," Angel said, her voice laced with sarcasm.

"Oh, we *are* grouchy today, aren't we?" technician Boone said as his grin turned into a sneer. "But we'll have a smile on that sour puss of yours soon now, won't we?" He led the young woman to the behavior modification chair and gently strapped her in.

"Students getting on your nerves?" Angel asked with an innocent smile.

"None of your business, young lady," he said, never letting his false smile falter. "I see we are being nosey today, aren't we? Not that it matters. You won't remember any of it anyway." A touch of contempt escaped through his molded facade.

"Go to hell."

"Temper now." The torture master grinned while preparing the machine. "We wouldn't want me *slipping* while handling this delicate equipment. I might accidentally set the levels too high. That would depress our higher functions to the point of us becoming a vegetable…and that *would* be sad now, wouldn't it?"

"*Bastard.*" Angel said, her eyes afire with hatred.

She struggled against the restraints as her thoughts focused on ripping the smug grin from Boone's face, but the bonds which held her were much too strong.

"We're violent today also, I see. What a shame…a young, attractive girl like you…we should be more *cooperative.*"

His lips formed into a sneer as he reached out and stroked the stain of red which was rising in her cheek.

Angel forced herself against the restraints one last time, and although they did not give, she did manage to kick the technician in his groin with enough force to make him double over in momentary agony as he stumbled back.

"You little brat!" He said as he braced himself against the control panel and struggled not to collapse, his eyes watering from the pain. "You're going to regret that. Actually…you *won't*, since you'll soon have the thought capacity of a fruit salad."

He turned to the machine's controls and wildly activated them, freezing Angel in throbbing pain as the luminous energy beam lanced out of the firing nozzle on the wall and struck her forehead. She could almost feel her brain unraveling as her cerebral fluid coursed with radiated power, setting fire to each nerve ending in her body. A soft cry barely escaped her lips, a child-like whimper that was swiftly silenced by her quickly drying throat. Her eyes fixed themselves on the bold Alliance insignia on the opposite wall as they glazed over, like ice atop a still pond.

It was then Boone finally allowed himself a genuinely self-satisfied grin and limped over to the room's monitoring devices. One by one he turned them off and erased the last five minutes of events from the computer's memory. Without hesitation, he returned to the controls and set them to maximum upper function depression, bypassing the safeties. "Goodbye, Angelina," he said as he smiled down at the sightless, senseless young woman who sat paralyzed in pain. Her body relentlessly, uncontrollably trembling as the mind ripping waves washed over her. "After all, an accident can't happen if I was in the room to stop it now, could it?" He shut off the main lights as he left, closing the door to the clinic behind him, sealing the room in shadowed darkness.

Minutes, hours, days passed in the tormented dreams and nightmares of Angel's mind, sinking her further into oblivion. She never knew it was barely a few moments after Boone's departure that the door slid open once again.

~ * ~

For a moment the 'inquisitive' student stared at the clinic room with a mixed sense of awe and confusion. She hoped to catch the technician alone to question him further, and was puzzled by his absence, especially when a patient was apparently in a session. She stood silently in the dark doorway, her alien eyes easily adjusting to the dim room. Slowly, her gaze was drawn to the young woman who was strapped in the chair, and a shudder went down her spine. Never had this cadet seen someone in so much mindless agony. It was as if every drop of the young woman's humanity was being drained by the luminous beam which pierced her forehead in pulsating waves. The patient's eyes began to bulge, the pain and horror written clearly within them for any to see. For a moment the Proximan cadet stared dumbly at the horrific sight, indecision freezing her actions. She quickly looked around, finally deciding on two facts. The first was there should always be someone monitoring this activity, and second the device was never intended to be set that high.

Realizing doing nothing would cause more harm than anything she could do, the cadet grabbed the beam control and turned it all the way in the opposite direction, hoping to cancel out its effects on the tortured inmate. There was an instant effect, but not the one the student had expected. The energy beam turned from a bright yellow to a bright sapphire, causing Angel's face to contort as she let out a hideous shriek when the higher function draining beam was reversed. Panic ran through the student as she grabbed the first thing she could find, a photon microscope, and hurled it into the controls, shorting them out violently with a shower of sparks.

Angel's rigid body went limp and fell back onto the chair as the beam was finally cut off. At that moment, technician Boone ran back in. His false mask of guilty concern was quickly replaced by one of condemning accusations when he saw the cadet and realized what happened.

"What's going on?" Boone asked. "What have you done to her?"

"Saved her life, I hope," the young cadet said. "Why was she left unattended? She could have been killed."

Technician Boone's face froze as a flicker of apprehension ran through his body. Judgmental eyes melted to erroneous relief as he studied the naval cadet. "You're right, you did save her," he said with a forced sigh, "…thank heaven. I was called out for an emergency, and I'm guessing the controls must have slipped. I'm glad *you* weren't hurt." He walked over to Angel, a slight shake in his stance as his eyes judged her unconscious form. He glanced up at her bio-reading and studied her brain wave readout and allowed himself the smallest of grins. If he was lucky, enough damage had been done so she wouldn't remember any of this, or anything ever again. He paused for a moment in hesitation, then reluctantly pushed the alert button, calling in the emergency medical team.

Chapter Two
Resurrection

Fire coursed through Angel's blood as she fought the battle between light and darkness, consciousness and senselessness, life and death. However, as soon as her torment seemed to begin, it ended. The blackness which clouded her vision slowly melted from her eyes as the image of her sterile hospital room gradually came into focus. At first, unable to recognize where she was, Angel studied the room in confusion…then the rehabilitation colony, and her incarceration here came rushing back to her thoughts. A sudden stab of mind splitting pain pierced through her head. She let out a groan as she raised her hands to her forehead in a futile effort to ward off the pain.

"Doctor," a nurse called at the sound of Angel's voice.

Angel opened her eyes again as a doctor raced to her side, the hypodermic injector in his hands immediately going to her arm. Within an instant of the hiss of the air needle, her pain subsided to a dull ache but didn't fully vanish.

The doctor let out a sigh of relief as a gentle smile formed on his lips. "I'm glad you're finally out of it. You've been unconscious for the last seven hours."

Angel tried to get up as she blinked, her vision slowly clearing. "The chair…"

The doctor nodded grimly as he sat in a chair next to her and placed a gentle hand on her shoulder. "Yes, you had an accident with the mental awareness chair. You're very lucky to be coherent. How do you feel?"

"My head really hurts," Angel said, despite her parched throat.

"That's quite understandable after what you have been through. However, the good news is your brain scans all came out fine." A thoughtful look crossed his face. "In fact, they came out better than fine." He shook his head and smiled at the young woman. "In other words, you'll be all right." He started to get up, his smile never wavering. "By the way, do you feel up to a visitor?"

"I guess so," she answered slowly, suddenly realizing this doctor was the first at the rehabilitation colony to speak to her like a person.

The doctor waved over to the young cadet by the far wall, who had been anxiously awaiting Angel's recovery. "This is the naval cadet who saved your life." He cast a thoughtful glance between them before walking off to give the two young women their privacy.

Angel glanced up to see a young Proximan in a silvery-grey Alliance naval cadet's uniform approaching. She hadn't noticed her at first, as her ivory white skin blended into the wall behind her, leaving her uniform and hair to stand out. She heard of these people, all born naturally empathic. Until now she never met one, and Angel was intrigued that one would have saved her life.

"You're the curious student," she said to the pale-skinned woman as part of her memory struggled to return.

For a few moments the cadet seemed to study the woman she had saved. "How do you feel?" she finally asked. "I was worried you wouldn't make it."

Angel gazed at her blankly, sizing up the alien's curiosity, wondering what her motivations were, but all that came out was, "Can't you tell how I feel? I thought all Proximans were empathic."

Reaching up and nervously tucking a lock of loose ashen grey hair behind a tall, pointed ear, her rescuer's black eyes, which had no whites, narrowed a bit. "I try not to pry into the emotions of others," she said quietly, "unless I feel it's necessary. In fact, I was taught at a young age to suppress my ability unless I actively needed it. Most of us are trained so we can fit in with the other species."

"Makes sense," Angel said, suddenly a little embarrassed at the rude assumption which slipped out.

"Do you remember what happened?" the young Proximan asked, trying to move the subject away from a question of motives.

The pounding in her head increased as Angel tried to think back to the mental awareness room. However, her memories of that moment were of searing agony, and cruel laughter. "No," she replied, shaking her head, which caused her headache to grow even deeper.

For an instant, the pain was so intense she considered asking the cadet to leave, but something inside her reconsidered. "I'm Angel," she said, hoping to push back the vague images in her mind which were causing her pain. "What's your name?"

"Zakaja, I'm in my senior year at the Alliance Naval Officer's Training Academy. Soon I'll graduate and be assigned to a ship in the space fleet."

"I'm sorry," Angel said sarcastically through a strained grin.

A puzzled look crossed Zakaja's oval face. "I don't understand."

"Nothing, it's my bad sense of humor." Her grin faded as she stared at the cadet intently. "I hear you saved my life, which I can't figure out."

The Proximan cocked her head to the side in confusion. "Why?"

Angel momentarily forgot her pain, her face a mask of stone. "Frankly, why an Alliance cadet would stick her neck out for an inmate here is beyond me."

Zakaja gazed at her sadly. "You don't think much of yourself, do you?"

"Actually," Angel said slowly with a half grin, "I think a great deal of myself. It's just that few others share that opinion."

They stared at each other silently for a moment, then laughed, momentarily forgetting the sterile setting.

Angel finally slowed to a chuckle, sobering down. "Anyway, thank you."

"Not necessary," Zakaja said happily. "Besides, you'll make an excellent thesis paper for my Psychology class."

"Great," Angel said as she continued to chuckle, "definitely one of my life's goals."

The door slid open and technician Boone hesitantly came in, apprehension creasing his brow. He studied the two young women from the door in silence, finally approaching them after a minute.

"Hello, Angelina," he said as sweetly as he could. "How are we feeling? We're quite lucky, I hear."

Angel glared at him. Her eyes narrowed as her thoughts filled with a rush of intense hatred she couldn't explain.

Zakaja's upswept eyebrows rose a bit as she was struck by the sudden overwhelming dark flood of emotions coming from Angel, telling her that something happened in the mental awareness clinic she missed, something more than a simple "accident".

"*Leave,* Boone," Angel said, her voice slightly quivering, not from fear of the technician, but of the violent feelings he caused to rise within her. More than the sudden anger was the hurt of not knowing what triggered it.

"Hey," technician Boone quickly replied, "no need to get riled up. I'm sure we just need our rest."

He stared at her judgmentally in silence, his eyes narrowing skeptically. His lips curled back in a twisted grin of victory. "Rest, little Angelina," he said with a cynical chuckle as he turned back to the door. "I'll look forward to having you back in my treatment room."

Zakaja silently watched Boone leave and shook her head. For the first time in her life, she wished empaths could read thoughts along with emotions. Though, upon remembering Angel's cold eyes as the young woman stared at the technician, she quickly forgot that wish and turned back to face Angel's intent gaze.

"I want to thank you again for what you did for me," Angel whispered with an intensity of feeling she rarely displayed. "I won't forget this. I'll make us even someday, Zakaja."

The Alliance cadet smiled, placing a hand on Angel's shoulder, feeling the sincerity of her emotions. She nodded quietly and rose from the bed.

Chapter Three
Blaze

Angel screamed silently as she struggled against the straps in the chair. Technician Boone was going to kill her, she knew it in her guts.

"I will have you, little Angelina, or you will die."

"No!" she screamed again, suddenly falling through the chair as if it were made of soft cream.

Down she plummeted through an inky blackness until landing on the harsh broken pavement back on Tenebrous, the horrible colony world where she was born and was the closest thing she ever had to a home.

The air was thick and humid, the way the city felt after a heavy storm. She glanced around frantically, to find herself in a dark trash filled alley. The silence was instantly shattered with a steady clanging in the distance as steel rang against steel, which echoed throughout the alleys. She knew this was the way the feral gang packs talked to each other, to close in on and circle their prey.

Suddenly, she felt something warm against her leg. Her hand instantly shot down, smoothing into rich fur which held the scent of her loved comrade and covered the steeled muscles of her protector.

"Reaper," she whispered with relief, realizing her dog was here with her…but the German shepherd died back on Tenebrous, how could he be alive now?

Angel knelt and hugged the large dog. A lot of these guard dogs had been sent from Earth to aid the police of this failed and abandoned colony, not that it helped any. Total anarchy still won in the end, and the dogs outlived their masters. Angel found this one in the sewers when he was still a pup, and they soon became inseparable friends.

The clanging brought her back to awareness again. What was she doing above ground after dark? She never left her home in the sewers, under the crumbled city, after nightfall. During the day it was dangerous enough, with the streets full of starving cutthroats and maggots who wouldn't think twice about eating Reaper for lunch. However, at night the wild packs and destroyer parties stalked, searching for those foolish enough to be out at that hour. If found and caught, Angel knew her fate would be hideous. In fact, she could end up being eaten too, but not before they tormented her.

There was safety in the underground sewers, after all, it was where she grew up. Raised, in the beginning, by an old woman who dwelled in the catacomb tunnels. Angel could barely remember the kindly old hag's death ten years ago.

"We better get out of here, Reaper," she whispered into the grey dog's ear.

Hearing a noise from behind, Angel spun around to face a group of men and boys, at least twelve of them. The bloodstained rags they wore told the stories of their past victims. Before she could stop him, Reaper leapt forward and attacked one of the men, and with his powerful jaw ripped out the man's throat in a spray of scarlet rain. Terror gripped her chest like an iron vice as she desperately called out to her dog, fully realizing what was about to happen…she'd seen it too many times before. Her body felt constricted, as if strapped down and in pain. Blood streamed across the pavement in slow trickles, in mimicry of the tears which flowed down her face, both reflecting the horror as the gang members mercilessly beat her only friend to death.

"*You bastards,*" she screamed at them, suddenly feeling heat running along her skin as if she was in the middle of a raging inferno.

The first of the men turned to her, his lead pipe glistening with Reaper's blood. He started to run toward her but hesitated when he saw the fiery pools within Angel's tear-streaked glare. She felt her blood begin to boil as his body suddenly began to writhe in agony, his flesh erupting into a sea of turbulent flames. Endlessly he screamed as the fire engulfed him.

Two more of the gang members moved in, meeting the same gruesome fate, neither of them making it halfway to the shivering girl. One by one, the members of the gang tried to reach the young woman, and one by one each was consumed by the insatiable flames, until all that was left was Angel. Tears streamed down her dirt-caked face as she collapsed to her knees, surrounded by the stench of roasting corpses.

~ * ~

Angel sat up with a start, breaking suddenly out of the nightmare. Shaking her head in confusion at the realization of being back at the prison hospital, she wiped the sweat from her face. She had been tormented by this dream often, reliving Reaper's death on her last night on Tenebrous, right before she finally managed to escape that hellhole. However, never before had she escaped without being violated and beaten to within an inch of her life. *Where had those flames come from?*

She tried to shake the eerie vision as sweat continued to stream down her face. *I must have a fever*, she thought as she glanced around the dimly lit room for some water, *I feel like I'm burning up.* In a daze, she spotted a plastic bottle of water next to her bed and reached for it. Halfway there she stopped as the water inside the clear container started to bubble violently.

It was boiling.

"Am I still dreaming?" she asked aloud, confused beyond reason.

She pushed her dripping ebony bangs out of her eyes and reached for the pitcher again, but the plastic melted inches away from her touch. "What's going on?" she whispered. "What's happening to me?"

She tried to get up, but found herself strapped to the bed by a restraining bracelet which was connected to the frame.

"*Damn*," she whispered in a harsh tone. Instantaneously the restraining bracelet burst into flames and fell off. She quickly pulled her hand back but realized the flames had not hurt her at all. "What's wrong with me?"

"Pyrokinesis?" came from a calm and cheerful voice to her left.

"Sinclair?" she asked, a smile swiftly washing over her face as she turned around to see her friend in the next bed over. "What are you doing here?"

Angel suddenly felt herself calm down a bit, his presence acting like a sponge, soaking up her anxiety. The sudden appearance of her red-haired fellow inmate was a most welcome thing after her nightmare.

"Oh, nothing," he said with a crooked grin. "They told me I had another psychotic breakdown."

"Another?"

"I bit a nurse," he replied, smiling sheepishly.

"Any particular reason why?"

Sinclair looked puzzled at her question. "How else do you expect us vampires to get our food?"

For a moment she was silent, it was always a few seconds of adjustment to accept any new "personality" that encompassed her schizophrenic friend, but usually his new personalities merely remained for a short while. This was a new one to her, but after what she went through, she found the change amusing. In truth, she found his psychosis to be part of his charming nature, or multiple natures as it were. She wondered if that was how he was able to resist the mental sessions in the 'tomb'.

"And they put you here?" she asked, wondering why they would have placed him in the high security medical wing.

"Not exactly," he admitted with a wry grin. "I heard you were here, so I made a fuss until they transferred me."

Angel sighed and shook her head, as the intense heat she felt was replaced by a much calmer warmth. The two fires quickly went out and all that remained was a few wisps of smoke and the odor of melted plastic.

For a moment she sat in silence, absorbing the past day's occurrences. Her lips tightened in determination as she concluded that if she didn't get out of here, Boone would be the death of her.

"What did you say about that pyro-whatever thing?"

"Pyrokinesis," Sinclair answered smoothly, "the ability to create fire by pure thought."

"But I can't do that," Angel said, suddenly confused again.

"You just did...twice."

She tried to search for a rational answer, then wondered if something happened to her in the mental awareness room that she simply couldn't remember. "I'm getting out of here," she said, surprising herself with the level of determination in her voice, "before every security guard in this place comes down on me. One look at all this mess and it's lobotomy time for sure." She swiftly jumped off her bed and started to walk out.

"I don't suppose..." came an almost desperate voice from the "vampire" on the bed, slowing Angel's hasty escape, "there's any chance you would want some company?"

Angel turned back to Sinclair, a smile growing quickly on her lips. With a sudden urge to channel this newborn power, she reached out toward her friend, a fiery twinkle suddenly lancing from her eyes. Almost uncontrollably, a surge of heat rushed through her body, bubbling up like a geyser of boiling water. Fire appeared next to her friend's wrists, causing the security ID bracelet he wore to burst into flames, breaking instantly.

Angel's eyes fixed on the still smoldering bracelet on the floor. "Wow," she whispered.

The thin man quickly jumped off the bed with the grace of an athlete and ran to her side, just as the smoke finally reached the sensors and set off the fire alarms, blaring throughout the hospital wing.

"How are we going to escape?" Sinclair asked with concern. "If I wasn't drugged, I would simply turn into a bat to flee. Though I'm not sure even *that* would help escape a deep space prison built into an asteroid."

Angel responded with a devilish smile. "If they're looking for a fire, let's give them a fire."

She glanced down the dimly lit hall at the main doors, already she could hear the running footsteps of the oncoming guard. With a concentrated effort, feeling the heat grow inside her once again, she set the carpet in the hall on fire. Flames began licking their way up the walls to the ceiling. Grabbing Sinclair's hand, she yelled, "Let's get out of here. With any luck, by the time these fools figure out what's going on, we'll be long gone."

They fled down the back corridor, toward the hospital's shuttle bay, but they found the passage blocked by a force field. Angel glared at the control box which gave power to the field and concentrated. It was more difficult this time, she felt herself growing tired. Still, the box burst into flames, causing sparks to play in a luminous concert. Instantly, the field dropped, and they were through it.

"How are we going to get off of the station?" Sinclair asked.

"We'll take a ship."

"Of course, how silly of me not to have guessed. How?"

She didn't answer as they entered the Omni-lift which would take them to the shuttle bay. Seconds ticked like minutes as they waited for the door to open again. Soon enough, they were in the small hangar bay where the rehab colony's shuttle craft were stored. They ran across the seemingly deserted floor to the shuttle on the pad but were stopped by the lone security officer on duty.

"Freeze," he yelled from behind, leveling his weapon at them.

Angel turned to face him. Her eyes, no longer dark brown but now black as coal, seemed to light from within again as her gaze centered on the gun with the last of her strength. With a brazen roar, the weapon overloaded and exploded, sending the armored security guard flying back against the far wall, to land in a heap. The flames from the weapon struck the fuel containers that were stored along the wall. Almost instantly, they began to violently erupt, engulfing one side of the hangar bay in a conflagration. Without a word, Angel coolly turned her back on the scene and entered the shuttle, where she wearily slid into the pilot's chair.

Sinclair's visage lost its grin for a moment as he glanced at the charred security guard, then he shook his head silently and followed her. "Do you even know how to fly a shuttle?" he asked as he sealed the shuttle's doors and sat down next to her.

"Sure, piloting is easy," Angel said with confidence as she ignited the engines and hit the launch button. "Navigation is my weak point." She laughed quietly at the sudden irony, *at least those stupid pirates taught me something of value.*

The small craft climbed out of the protective dome which covered the rehabilitation colony's shuttle bay and started to quickly rise into space.

Sinclair turned to Angel, a pensive look on his face. "So, how weak is your navigation?"

"I don't know any," she admitted with a sheepish grin, "but don't worry, I'll wing it. I really hope this crate has one of those Cosmic, whatever they are called, devices." She glanced around until she found the device that would allow them to fly through subspace, at least it looked like the device her Pirate ex-comrades showed her once.

"How long do you think it will be before they start to chase us?" he asked.

"At least a half hour, judging from the state of the shuttle bay after that explosion. We were lucky to have gotten out ourselves."

With a grin on his face which spread from ear to ear, Sinclair looked back at the window and put his feet up on the console. "I can't believe we're free. You did a great job, Angel."

She returned his grin and touched the button, activating the small shuttle's star drive engines, then laughed. "I think I'd like to leave Angel's past behind in that prison. Call me Blaze."

Chapter Four
Adalric

Lord Tanus Adalric was troubled as he stormed along the sterile corridors of the Red Star Imperial Star-Citadel. If the Cosmic Surge weapon wasn't ready as scheduled, the Dire Queen would be displeased. Not that he could remember the last time she *was* pleased.

He turned down the long corridor which led to her throne room, his ebony cloak with the crimson lining billowing majestically behind him. For a moment he paused at the great doors and glanced over the tight-fitting, blood-red uniform he wore with pride. The Dire Queen demanded perfection in all her servants, but none more so than in him, her overlord, chief of the Imperial barons which ran her empire. Each gold button which fastened the double-breasted flap was neatly in place, each gold ellipse on his crimson sleeve neatly sewn, his knee-high black boots were polished to a mirror finish. His eyes spotted a string out of place along the fringe of his ceremonial cloak. With a quick and precise gesture, he snapped it off, balled up the now severed piece of string, and placed it neatly in his pocket. After a moment's pause and a last check over himself, he moved forward again. The grey armored guards did not need orders to step aside. The doors opened automatically for him.

Adalric entered the large deeply shadowed room, which was barely lit by four red flamed torches, two along the walls, and two on either side of her throne. His eyes searched the long room until he spotted his sovereign sitting there.

The Dire Queen was in her usual garb, a long black dress which adhered to her alluring silhouette like an obsidian shroud, revealing no flesh. Despite the great number of times Adalric had been here and looked upon her, he had yet to see her face, if she even had one. She glanced down at him from under a drawn hood which blended down and became one with the weave of her dress. Her one visible feature was her eyes, two eerie luminescent crimson orbs that hung freely within the dark shadow of her hood. Taking in a breath, he proudly strode up to the raised dais of her simple, yet precisely carved throne and knelt. Of all the beings in this galaxy, she was the one person he feared.

The Dire Queen looked down on her overlord with a mixture of satisfaction and suspicion. He was here no doubt to tell her of another delay in the construction of her super weapon, and the dreadnought which would carry it. For a moment she hesitated, as if unsure of whether she wanted to talk to her servant. However, it did amuse her to watch such a proud man squirm. *Not too much, though,* she cautioned herself. His power was growing, as was his influence, and she knew given time and room to spread, he might best her one day. For now, though, she need not fear, for her powers stemmed from an energy she was sure he couldn't begin to comprehend and certainly couldn't defeat…at least not alone. *I need him for now, for he's my voice to the outside galaxy…but he must never forget who the master is.*

"Rise, my servant," she finally said, her voice hissing like air escaping a sealed crypt, "and report to me of yet another delay in our plans."

Lord Adalric raised his head and looked up at his sovereign through the dark lenses which covered the eye ports of his armored half-cowl. "We are still having trouble with funds, my queen," his deeply powerful voice explained. "Our fleet is still growing but requires more money to construct. It is difficult for our pirates to steal everything we need without raising too much suspicion in the Alliance and the surrounding empires."

"I don't want to hear excuses, Adalric," she said, her voice barely an angry whisper, "I want to hear the dreadnought is ready to launch, along with the Cosmic Surge weapon."

"It *will* launch on time, my queen," he boldly promised, "even if I have to get the funds myself."

"Then the ship will be ready in one week?"

"All it needs is for you to give it a name."

"Good," she said as a low eerie laugh built in her throat. "Then you may call it the *Demoness.*"

Her eerie cackle grew and echoed through the large chamber like a banshee's death howl. Given the implied dismissal, Lord Adalric quickly rose and walked out of the throne room. The door sealed behind him with a quiet whisper.

~ * ~

The Demoness, Adalric thought as he strode back up the corridor, *I suppose that's as befitting a name as any, especially considering its owner...however, the Overlord would have been far more appropriate. After all, it is I, the Overlord of the Red Star Imperium, which has made all this possible.*

Adalric proudly marched onto the observation deck to look at the almost completed dreadnought *Demoness,* while his thoughts raged turbulently within him. *Where would the Red Star Imperium be without me? When I joined them six years ago, they were a disorganized army of pirates which were on the verge of falling apart. It was I who became the Dire Queen's eyes and voice. It was I who pulled together the ragged forces and created the Darkkrieg Legion...a military force feared now throughout the sector. Without me she would be nothing. True, it is she who taught me about the Cosmic Aura and instructed me in the art of TelSor...but now, as a TelSor Elder, my skills are invincible. It is I who should be running this Empire...and someday I will...*

His thoughts were interrupted as a black-uniformed officer tentatively approached him and waited to be allowed to speak.

"What is it, Commander?" Adalric asked without turning to face him.

"Lord Adalric," the nervous officer began, "the work on the Cosmic Surge is nearing completion, and the dreadnought is almost ready for a trial run."

The overlord nodded then perceived there was more the officer wasn't telling him. Such insight was a gift of his, one of the many bestowed upon him as someone who could master the Cosmic Aura — the mystical energy of the universe. Sensing the surface thoughts of others, like the commander, came easily.

"What aren't you telling me, Commander?"

"It's the United Star Alliance," the officer replied, his voice quaking, "they've sent a battleship to the free space near our outer markers, they must suspect something."

Adalric's thin lips tightened as he brought up his gloved hand to thoughtfully rub his jaw and left cheek, the only parts of his face not covered by his crimson mask. "It appears our new ship will have its first prey sooner than I thought, Commander. Inform the Darkkrieg Legionnaires' commanders their forces must be battle-ready within forty-eight hours. It's time to break from our chrysalis and spread our wings."

The young officer nodded and left, grateful to leave the presence of the overlord.

So, Adalric thought as he turned back to the large picture window, *our old oppressor, the United Star Alliance, wants to know why we have been quiet for so long. Very well, they will learn...and it will be a lesson learned brutally. Long live the Imperium.*

Chapter Five
...Into the Fire

The bright light of the Beta Hydri star was beginning to slowly sink past the horizon, as the four Collians began loading the small spacecraft onto the back of their hover-lifter. Blaze watched indifferently as the members of the black market quietly and swiftly prepared the stolen rehabilitation center shuttle for transport. She knew it was blind luck that the craft came out of subspace so close to the planet Collia. Considering her lack of navigation skills, anywhere else and United Star Alliance's Galactic Police probably would have pinpointed the sequestered shuttle immediately.

Blaze casually surveyed her surroundings. Collia hadn't seemed to have changed since the last time she was here. Same Earth-style architecture, Earth-style weather, and Earth-style garbage in the streets...another over industrialized planet populated by humans. A light wisp of wind played across the escaped inmate's face and reminded her of the biggest difference between Earth and Collia. *This place smells like money*, she mused, *and there is nothing more that Collians seem to love than money.* She watched the black marketeers finish securing the small spacecraft, as the unkempt man who Blaze had been dealing with sauntered over to her.

"You have yourself a real prize there," he said in a decent rendition of Terran as he stroked the brown stubble on his unshaved chin and chuckled. "Still has the Alliance markings and all."

"You mean *you* have a real prize," Blaze replied. "That is, as soon as you pay me the credits."

The black marketeer's silver flecked eyes glinted with the prospect of making a profit as he eyed her up and down and smiled, knowing he had the upper hand. "That's ten thousand credits," he finally said as he brought out the cash, "paid in full."

"It's worth forty," Blaze said coolly.

"It's also hot as a meteor during atmospheric entry. Look, sweetie, you want the deal or not?"

Blaze glanced over at the stolen shuttle and nodded, grateful to be rid of any reminder of the hellhole it came from. "It's all yours."

"And the cash is all yours," he said as he handed her a small metal case, a thick smile spreading from ear to ear. "And, toots, I would get some new clothes if I were you. That rehab jumpsuit's a dead giveaway."

She glanced back at the black marketeer, her dark eyes lighting like tiny fires. "My name is Blaze, not toots," she said, her voice sending a chill down his back, "don't you *ever* forget that."

The cocky grin faded from the man's face as he began to back away. "Yeah...right. See ya." He quickly turned and slipped off towards the shuttle. "That's definitely one weird gal," he quietly said to his comrades as they started up the hover-lifter, "but what a bod."

"What a jerk," Blaze whispered to herself, then tucked the case full of credits under her arm and headed off into the early night to catch up with Sinclair. A smile came to the young woman's lips as the echo of her new name rang in her ears. She knew she'd made the perfect choice, grateful to be closing an undesired chapter of her life, and purging unwanted memories along with her old name.

Blaze found her new companion in a clothing store one block off the brightly lit main casino strip. He was theatrically trying on a long black cloak while practically entangled with one of the store's employees. The harried saleswoman was desperately attempting to get the garment away from him, but all Sinclair did in return was stare deeply into her eyes and command her to fall asleep, which she obviously ignored.

"What's the problem here?" Blaze asked as she approached the entangled pair.

"Hi, Angel," Sinclair called out to her while waving with his free hand. His bright blue eyes smiled playfully at her. Whatever was going on, he was obviously enjoying it.

Blaze glared sternly at her companion as she did her best not to smile, then turned to the saleswoman. "So?" she asked, this time in a demanding tone. "Could you please tell me why you are locked in this tug of war?

"He's trying to take this without paying for it," the woman replied while pointing an accusing finger at him.

"But I must have my cloak of darkness to conceal my skin from the sunlight," Sinclair said in his best attempt at a sinister vampiric voice. "It is death to us vampires to feel the sun's rays against our skin." He then turned back to the Collian woman and dramatically waved his fingers in front of her eyes. "You will now go to sleep."

The saleswoman swatted his hand out of her face. "Keep your paws to yourself, creep!"

"Paws? Paws?" yelled Sinclair. "Do I look like a werewolf to you? I'm a vampire!"

"You're a lunatic."

"Bitch," he replied with an exaggerated look of disgust on his face.

The woman motioned for two large store guards to come over. "Throw this madman out of here."

"That's not necessary," Blaze said quickly, no longer finding this amusing in the least. "We can pay for—"

"They touch me, and I'll drain every last drop of blood in your body," Sinclair yelled at the saleswoman, cutting Blaze off.

The two muscular guards took hold of Sinclair and started to drag him out. Blaze groaned while she followed closely behind him, watching his arms and legs flail about in what looked like an attempt to fly away.

"You don't have to treat him like that," she said in a firm tone, "he's harmless."

One of the guards cast a glance at her, obviously noticing her pink jumpsuit, and sneered disapprovingly. He then shoved her aside and threw Sinclair out the door, who landed on the street with a thud. Before she could protest or even try to reason, the other guard grabbed her and tossed her out also, plopping her down next to her friend. "You people should be in a cage," she heard one of them comment as the glass doors clanged shut.

For a moment the two outcasts looked at each other in silence, as Blaze's eyes flamed angrily.

"I'm sorry, Angel," Sinclair finally said as his frown turned into a boyish smile.

"I told you to call me Blaze!" she yelled into his face, causing him to shrink back as if hit.

He quickly nodded as the young woman rose and brushed the dirt and muck of the street off her jumpsuit. Then she turned and stormed off without a word.

Sinclair also rose and wrapped his newly acquired garment around himself tightly. "At least I got the cloak."

Blaze ignored him and kept on walking, grumbling to herself but soon realizing she truly wasn't angry with Sinclair at all. After all, he was merely being exactly what endeared him to her. *No*, she decided as she gazed up at twin flags of Collia and the United Star Alliance which fluttered over the shopping mall, what was bothering her was they were still under the watchful eyes of the Alliance and still in a lot of danger.

Sinclair silently watched this micro drama play in Blaze's mind through her subtle body movements as she moved off. He stole a last glance back at the saleswoman, who was still glaring at them through the window, and he grumbled as he hurried to catch up with his partner. "Her blood was probably sour anyway."

Blaze felt her hostility melt away as she smiled and turned to face him as he approached, watching him carry his lean frame with a cavalier stride under the billowing black cloak.

Sinclair was in his late twenties, Blaze recalled, but had been in one rehabilitation colony or another for the last five years, ever since his first real skirmish in the Alliance Marines. He still kept a soldier's walk, she noticed, head up and shoulders square. In the darkness, he seemed to be in his element, moving effortlessly despite the dim lighting. She wished he would tell her more about his past, but that was the one thing he denied her. Not that she blamed him, knowing she kept her secrets too. Her smile turned into a grin as the young woman waited for her own personal vampire to catch up with her, suddenly grateful again for his presence.

Together they rounded the dimly lit alleyway, when ahead in the shadows they saw a terrified, dark furred, rodent-like alien running from three darkly clad humans. Despite the lack of proper streetlights, it was obvious they each carried military issue automatic electro rifles. Fleeing blindly, the creature ran into Blaze as he checked behind for his pursuers.

"Watch where you're going," Blaze shouted, "you oversized rat."

"I'm not a rat," he defiantly yelled back in a high-pitched squeaky voice, "I'm a Jarbban."

"Who's chasing you?" Sinclair asked, as he lifted the small being to his feet by the ragged blue tunic which was the off-worlder's lone garment.

Suddenly the pursuers opened fire with their weapons, sending lethal beams of hot white, electrified energy into the darkened alley. For an instant, Blaze could see the attackers clearly. An instant was all she needed.

Blaze heard the ultrasonic scream of the electric energy bolts missing their targets as she felt that now familiar surge of heat beginning to rush through her. Locking her eyes on the shadowy figures, her body didn't need to think about what to do to survive. She shivered uncontrollably as the energy projected outward toward the three attackers.

An explosion of fire erupted in the middle of the assailants, instantly incinerating two and throwing back the third, his shirt ablaze. The blast of heat reached Sinclair, singeing his hair and causing him to shade his eyes. After several long seconds, the fires began to burn down.

The Jarbban's long snouted jaw dropped open as he watched the two bodies twist in agony, to finally lay motionless. He glanced up to see the figure of the young woman, now standing suddenly so still, mystically outlined in the flames. "How did you do that?" he asked, his voice squeaking in a hushed tone.

Blaze ignored him as she strode over to the fire, disappointed when she saw the third attacker was missing. He'd escaped with his life. On Tenebrous, she'd heard that the consequences of leaving a survivor after a skirmish were grave. As her mind flashed back to her incarceration in the *Phoenix* Rehab Colony, she feared the consequences here might be worse. She glanced up and down the next alley, hoping for a last chance to spot him, but he was nowhere in sight.

Sinclair wrinkled his nose at the smell of burning flesh and the lines around his eyes deepened, as if recalling some unpleasant memory. Then he turned his attention back toward the grey furred rodent as if nothing unusual happened. "You never answered my question. Who are they?"

"You mean who *were* they," the Jarbban said as his hands waved frantically in rhythm to his speech. "They were members of the *dreaded* Red Star pirates, ruthless assassins tracking me down."

"They weren't Alliance Security?" asked a highly disappointed

Blaze as she returned. "They had Alliance style military issue rifles."

"Nope."

"Damn."

"What is it, Angel?" Sinclair asked, a note of concern entering his voice.

"What did I tell you? You flightless bat!"

Her comrade blushed as he grinned and shrugged his shoulders.

"I'm worried because of the Red Star pirates," Blaze finally replied as she regained her composure. "They'll be back."

"So?"

"So, one of them got away, and he saw us help this disease infested rat. They'll probably think we're with him."

The small newcomer stood up as tall as he was able to and stormed over to Blaze, a glint of determination in his beady crimson-black eyes. "I'm *not* disease infested and I'm *not* a rat. I'm a *Jarbban*, and what's so bad about having helped me? Probably the first good thing you've done all day."

"Look, lightweight," Blaze said as her face grew stern, "the last thing I need right now are lessons on morality from a three-foot-tall talking rat."

"I'm three and a *half* feet tall," he replied defiantly. "And I'm not a rat, I'm a—"

"Jarbban," Blaze cut in. "I know."

"I'm called The Count," Sinclair said, returning his voice to his vampiric tone, "the king of the undead, and that's Angel—"

"Blaze," she said, cutting in again as she glared at him in annoyance, then looked back at the Jarbban. "What's your name?"

The small creature's ears drooped down, and his long bald tail lost its sway, as if a subject had been raised which he preferred not to dwell on. "My name is Jal'in, but everyone calls me Rabies."

"You're kidding," Blaze said as she tried to contain a snicker and failed.

"And I suppose your parents named you Blaze?"

"No, but my name is a name of choice."

"As is mine," the Jarbban said defiantly, as he turned his back on them. "Now leave me alone."

"Gladly," she said with a grunt and turned toward Sinclair. "I'll bet there's a good reason for his name. Come on, Count, let's go shopping before the stores close."

Sinclair flashed a glance over his companion's shoulder as he shook his head. "Angel, I think *they* have other plans."

Blaze quickly turned to find that the surviving pirate had been joined by more, perhaps ten, all with electro carbines, coming from down the far alley. "I used to be one of them," she quickly whispered to her friend. "Maybe I can reason with them."

"You're a Red Star pirate scum?" Rabies asked.

"No," she answered stubbornly. "I'm no pirate. I travelled with a few of them a while ago, but I never joined them. And they're not scum, lightweight." *Well, not all of them,* she thought as dark memories surfaced in her mind.

"There he is!" the surviving burned pirate yelled, pointing in their direction. "And the two that aided him are here also. Fry 'em!"

"I don't think they want to listen to reason," Sinclair said as he grabbed Blaze's arm. "Let's get out of here."

"It's not too late to try and talk to—" she started to say, but he cut her off.

"No time, Angel," he said with a seriousness his voice rarely had, as he locked his eyes on hers. For a moment she thought she could see flashes of light in his eyes, like the glimmer of a firefight on a darkened battlefield long forgotten. Suddenly, those images seemed all too real, as they realized they were being shot at again. Sinclair quickly pulled her down and rolled with her, dodging the spears of deadly glowing energy.

"Damn," Blaze said with frustration, while entwined in Sinclair's tightly protective hold, "I didn't want to do this." She shook off his grip and turned to face the pirates, allowing the fire within her to brew, but the last attempt exhausted her. With all her strength she tried to summon the power again. Her head pounded in defiance as she brought her clenched fists to her temples.

"No!" she screamed, "I won't let you hurt us!"

She could feel a thin line of blood begin to trickle from her nose, a release of the internal cerebral pressures she was forcing, when suddenly one of the pirates whelped in pain as flames licked out from his chest. Blaze felt the ground spin out from under her as the world turned upside down. She clutched Sinclair by the front of his jumpsuit and held on to him as she struggled to clear her head.

The dying pirate buckled at the knees as the others hesitated for a moment then charged in. Their carbines sent forth deadly beams which were a combination of high intensity electricity and hot energy plasma, merged into one destructive force. Two of the black garbed men managed to catch up to the rodent quickly and reached to grab him.

"Rabies, look out," Sinclair yelled back to warn him, while supporting a dazed Blaze.

Both men hesitated and pulled back, suddenly unsure if they still wanted to grab the Jarbban.

In that brief moment, Rabies slipped out from under them and ran down the shadowed alley, calling behind him in his high-pitched voice, "This way, this way."

"What do we do?" Sinclair asked Blaze as she tried to straighten up again.

"What choice do we have?" she replied wearily as she started to move after the grey Jarbban. "We go that way."

Sinclair looked at the pirates who were closing in fast and wrapped his cloak around him. *"You'd best stay back,"* he warned with a strong voice, which was suddenly captivating in its newfound charisma, *"or face the children of the night."*

At that moment a gust of wind eerily rushed through the dimly lit alley, causing all the Collian eel birds who were hanging in the trash bins to suddenly awaken and take to the sky. In the flurry of feathers and reptilian wings, the pirates were temporarily confused and blinded.

"See?" Sinclair said with a sinister laugh. "Tempt not the master of the dead."

"Sinclair," Blaze called back from down the alley, "get your ass over here."

With a quick turn and wave of his cloak, he ran off after her, leaving the pirates to contend with the easily annoyed, blood-sucking fowl.

The two prison escapees finally caught up with the small creature in the entrance tunnel to the outlying starport. The tunnel was long and wide, so vehicles could travel through it, but it wasn't brightly lit. In truth, nothing on Collia was brightly lit, except for the casinos and resorts.

"Rabies," Sinclair shouted as he kept an arm around Blaze, who collapsed a few blocks back. "Slow down, she's hurt."

The Jarbban stopped running and anxiously glanced back behind him. Once satisfied that they lost their pursuers, he breathed a sigh of relief and approached the two humans.

"I didn't see her get hit," he said curiously as he checked her for wounds. "Where's she hurt?"

"I'm not hurt," Blaze whispered defiantly, her eyes half closed.

"She's exhausted from saving your life," Sinclair said, supporting her. "Now help us find a place to rest."

Rabies looked over the young woman again and sniffed once or twice. "Well...I guess it's okay to bring you to the *Silhouette*...to rest for a while."

"The *Silhouette?*" Blaze managed. "Is that a ship?"

The Jarbban nodded. "It's close now. In the northern landing field."

Sinclair watched the grey furred form scurry off into the starport, then looked back at Blaze, concern welling in his eyes. "Will you be all right?"

Blaze managed to produce a weak grin and nodded. "I'll be fine. I need a place to sit down for a while, that's all."

"Hang on to me, Angel," he said in a low voice, "and I'll make sure we find you some place to rest."

In response, Blaze slipped her arm firmly around his waist as Sinclair protectively pressed her closer to him.

The two of them continued after the Jarbban until he came to the blacktop-covered landing field. Slinking past the dozen or so other private crafts, he finally stopped in front of a sleek merchant-class vessel. It wasn't a large ship, not much longer than thirty-five yards. But unlike the other bulky industrial ships, the one Rabies approached was designed more like a stealth fighter than a full merchant craft, with a flat triangular body and turned up wingtips. In the starry darkness, the jet-black craft was poised like an ebony panther on a moonlit night.

"I'll bet she's fast," Sinclair whispered under his breath, silently appraising it with a judgmental eye.

"That she is," Rabies agreed. "We've even outrun Alliance Security patrol ships a couple of times."

Sinclair suddenly thought he saw movement at the nose of the ship, behind the dark cockpit window. Almost instantly afterward, he saw a woman appear at the top of the ship's entrance ramp and anxiously wave them to enter.

Blaze wearily gazed up toward the woman at the entranceway, curious but still feeling cautious. The stranger's dark blue jumpsuit was decidedly civilian, and the large electro pistol strapped to her thigh looked like something one would need to acquire on worlds like this, with a decent black market.

"Hi, Sloan," Rabies said as the trio came up the ramp, "I picked up some friends."

"I can see that," the woman said while trying to keep the wind from blowing her long blonde hair into her eyes. "Come aboard, it looks like an electrical storm's brewing."

Blaze and Sinclair entered the trim ship together, following the Jarbban down the narrow steel corridor until they finally arrived at a cozy carpeted common room. Blaze made for the inviting comfort of the couch and sat heavily, letting out a deep breath which disheveled her thick bangs. Sinclair followed and stood over her like a knight protecting his queen, though he did allow himself to lean against the wall. Through the observation dome in the ceiling, they could see flashes of blue and pink light beginning to sear across the sky, as a distant rumble was felt.

After a few moments, the steady beat of light footsteps announced Sloan's entrance. Crossing her arms in front of her, Sloan carefully evaluated the two newcomers. At first glance, the dark-haired woman sitting on her couch seemed young, soft and weak, but her darkened eyes told a harsher tale.

She shifted her gaze toward Sinclair, appraising him from head to toe. A slight smile crept onto her lips as she caught notice of his chiseled features and gentle eyes.

Turning her attention to Rabies, Sloan sternly demanded the truth. "With no offense intended," she said, "who the hell are these people and why are they on my ship?"

"Well..." Rabies said, suddenly at a loss for words. "It's like this..."

"They were going to fry him," Sinclair said matter-of-factly as he gestured toward Rabies, "and we stopped them."

Blaze scoffed. "We?"

"Yeah," Rabies added with a sudden squeal, happy they were going to help explain away his dilemma. "They saved my life."

"Who was after you?" Sloan asked in a strained tone, her quick frown plainly showing this was not the first time this had happened.

"The Red Star pirates," Sinclair said, answering for him.

"The *who?* What did you do to get *them* on your case?"

"That's what we wanted to know," Blaze said, cutting in.

"I...sort of...you know," Rabies said as his voice sank to a mumble.

"Stole something," Sloan said, completing his sentence for him, obviously annoyed.

"That belonged to the pirates," Blaze said, figuring out the puzzle.

"What was it?" Sinclair asked.

Rabies hesitated for a moment before reaching into his soiled tunic and pulling out a small computer data disk.

"What's on it?" Sloan said with a sarcastic groan. "Plans for their vibrators?"

"Sort of," Rabies said with a grin. "It's the technical schematics of their new dreadnought, whatever that is...some big ship I'm guessing."

"How did you get those?" Sinclair asked, suddenly more interested.

"They must have been stolen by the Alliance, and the Red Star pirates were trying to get them back." The Jarbban inhaled sharply before continuing. Outside, the roar of the thunder grew ominously loud. "It's like this...I'm walking along, minding my own business, when this guy runs up to me with this disk in his hand...and about a dozen holes in his body. He grabs me by my tunic and asks if I will take the disk to the Alliance's Stellar Defense Fleet Command for him. I asked him what it was, and he told me, and stated it was worth a fortune. So naturally, I took it."

"Let me guess," Blaze said as she sat up, feeling her strength return. "The Red Star pirates saw you doing this and came after you."

"Yeah," Rabies said as he visibly shuddered. "They shouted

something weird like, "halt in the name of the Imperium" and began shooting at me."

"Why didn't you give it back to them?" Blaze asked while holding her head in one hand. "Why help the Alliance?"

"Yeah, why *didn't* you drop it and run?" Sloan asked, echoing Blaze's sentiment, exasperated at the amount of trouble her small furry friend could get her into.

"Because he said it was valuable," Rabies said, standing firm. "This could answer all our financial troubles."

Sloan rubbed her smooth pale chin as a distant look drifted into her aqua-blue eyes. "Our troubles weren't *that* bad," she said sadly as her thoughts began to tumble. "Certainly not bad enough to anger the Red Star Pirates. Heck, they've been calling themselves an empire more and more lately, I don't need enemies like that."

Sloan shook her head silently and looked up at her friend's rescuers, suddenly sad she gave up her military career for a life of smuggling and exploration. "So, what are your names, anyway?" she asked in a relaxed tone.

An eager boyish grin swept across Sinclair's face as he stood in the small room. "I am the Lord of the Undead," he said with a flurry of his cloak, "and this is my companion—"

"Blaze," she said quickly, cutting him off before he could get on her nerves again.

"Lord of the Undead, huh?" Sloan said, then glanced over the disheveled pink rehabilitation jumpsuits they both wore, her brow creasing in silent consideration.

Her eyes rested heavily on Sinclair, who flashed a grin out of the corner of his mouth as he met her gaze, he then looked down shyly.

"I suppose you need passage, don't you?" she asked. "The rates aren't cheap."

"We kinda wanted to stay on Collia for a while," Blaze replied, but was cut off by an increase in the explosive sounds outside.

"That didn't sound like thunder," Rabies said, his voice squeaking louder with anxiety.

"We're being shot at," Sloan said, as she rose and headed for the cockpit in the nose of the ship, closely followed by the others.

The captain and pilot of the *Silhouette* jumped into the control seat while the Jarbban occupied the gunnery station next to her. Outside, lit by the multicolor flashes of the electrical storm, they could see roughly fifteen men in black battle armor firing electro carbines at the ship.

"They can't hurt us here, right?" Blaze asked, as she realized their chances of staying on Collia had vanished.

"I've put up energy force shields," Sloan replied. "So, it will be quite some time before they get through, but it would be wise to vacate the area, maybe even the star system."

"How much?" Blaze asked, her voice laced with annoyance.

"What?"

"You know what I mean, Sloan. How much to take the two of us out of here?"

"Eight thousand, and we'll take you wherever you want."

"Sloan," Rabies said, "they saved my life."

There was a moment's hesitation as the captain stared at her rodent companion. "All right, five thousand."

"You'll take us anywhere?" Blaze asked, trying to confirm.

"Anywhere."

Blaze glanced over at Sinclair, who silently nodded. "Then get us the hell out of here."

With the flick of a switch, the *Silhouette's* engines roared to life.

Chapter Six
The Jewel

The *Silhouette* spiraled out of subspace, its port engine billowing thick purple smoke. Stars reluctantly swam into view as the wounded craft settled into the calmness of normal space, but it was anything other than calm inside the small merchantman.

"We're going to die!" Rabies screamed as he ducked under the copilot's console.

"We are not going to die!" Sloan screamed back, as she fought to regain control of the crippled spaceship. *"Now get back up here and help me, you filthy rodent."* She glanced down but couldn't spot her companion through the azure coolant steam which filled the small cabin.

"This is just great," Blaze said through frustrated anger, as she fought to make it back to her chair through the steam filled, wildly pitching craft. The *Silhouette* rocked again as it continued to spiral out of control. "Can't you steady this heap?"

"We're out of subspace," Sloan yelled over her shoulder. "How do the engines look?"

"I'm no engineer," Blaze responded harshly, "but in my opinion they're trashed. That last blow-out took out both Cosmic Leap and Cosmic Slip controls."

"Slip too?" Rabies said from under the console. "You mean we lost *all* light speed capability?"

"That's what I said, rat."

"I'm not a rat, I'm a—"

"Do you think we'll make it?" Sinclair asked, cutting off the Jarbban as he made his way to a chair and strapped himself in.

"I'll know in a second," Sloan answered truthfully, as she pulled back hard on the controls, then quickly rotated them the opposite way, trying to take advantage of the crippled port engine. With a violent shudder, the *Silhouette* barrel rolled the opposite way for three turns, then proceeded into a flat spin.

"I guess it didn't work," Blaze said, her voice laced with anger.

"Don't sweat it," Sloan said quickly, as she forced the ship to reverse its new spin, causing it to rock violently again.

However, this time the spin of the stars through the cockpit window began to stabilize, until they finally settled down.

"Are we alive?" came a small voice from under the quickly clearing steam.

"So, there you are," Sloan said with a snarl. She removed one hand from the controls to reach down and yank the small Jarbban back up into his seat. "You ever crap out on me like that again and it's escape pod time for you. Get it?"

Rabies' snout went up and down quickly as he swiftly strapped himself into his copilot's chair. "Sorry, Sloan," he said quietly, his voice giving new meaning to the word meek.

The captain stared at her friend steadily, her face slowly losing its sour glare. Finally, she sighed and shook her head, while wiping her sweat-matted hair out of her face. "Forget it."

"What's our situation?" Sinclair asked as he looked at the star which dominated the view outside the front window.

"We're in a stellar system," Blaze said thoughtfully, as she suddenly realized Sinclair dropped the vampire personality during the crisis. She wasn't too surprised, these moods of his never lasted too long, and it was only a matter of time before the next one came up, whatever form his psychosis would take.

Rabies studied the readings on his scanners. "We're still in the Alliance, in the system of Epsilon Eridani, right next to Perus II."

"We'd better land," Sinclair said.

"On *Perus?*" the Jarbban asked, his thin voice shaking.

"Why not?" Blaze asked.

"Be...be...because..."

"Because the Perusians are felines?"

"Forget it," Rabies whispered under his breath.

"What you need is some big brave canine to protect you," Sloan said with a laugh. "Get off it, Rabies. You know the Perusians are quite friendly, and they have good repair stations."

"A *canine...*" Sinclair muttered thoughtfully under his breath, his eyes growing vacant as he sank deeply into his own bizarre illusions.

"We'd better find somewhere that can fix us," Blaze added, her irritation showing clearly.

Sloan's sour look returned as she tried to deal with the young woman behind her. "Listen, sister, it wasn't *my* fault my partner went and grabbed that computer disk and ticked off the Red Star pirates."

"I suppose it wasn't your fault *either* when this heap of junk's Cosmic Leap engines failed to get us into subspace when the pirate ships caught up with us?"

"Heap of junk?" Sloan yelled. "This 'heap of junk' just saved your miserable lives. *You're* the one that didn't spot those Red Star pirate bounty hunters back when we landed on Onoran. We're lucky that, through my great skill as a pilot, we escaped with our necks intact."

Blaze sank back into her own thoughts as steam rose from the deck around her, her eyes turning into wells of darkness lit by a flame. *Calm down, Blaze,* she warned herself, *or you'll toast this entire ship. Things will turn out all right in the end. After all, they couldn't get much worse...could they?*

Who knows, she silently answered herself. *Things certainly seemed to be sliding on a downslope ever since we escaped from Collia a little over two weeks ago. First the Red Star pirates caught up with us on Onoran...those damn bounty hunters. We barely managed to take off from Onoran with our lives...to find a squadron of Red Star pirate fighters waiting for us in orbit...gods those guys must really want that disk back.*

Blaze recalled a time back on Tenebrous when some scrounger stole a case of canned fruit she found. Stole it right out of her home in the sewers. Fortunately, Reaper...*Reaper,* she moaned to herself. He was able to help her find the brat who did it. *Caught that little mutant red-handed.* She recalled how the thief almost died in the fight over the case of goods. She understood, and in some ways even admired, the perseverance of the Red Star pirates. Not that she particularly enjoyed or appreciated getting chased across the galaxy and shot at simply because of the company she was keeping these days.

You know…you spend your life running and hiding from Alliance Security and the Alliance navy, but when you finally need them…then where the hell are they?

Blaze glanced up from her thoughts to find Sloan and the rat were talking to the Perusian space central control.

"I just told you," Sloan repeated, frustration creeping into her voice, "we have no lateral thruster control, and our engines are overheating, we can't stay up here any longer, we need priority landing now!"

"Listen here, *Silhouette*," the Perusian space traffic controller said through a feline growl, "we have a diplomatic snake by its rattle down here. The president of the Alliance is visiting Perus II now and she has full landing privileges, all other traffic will have to wait."

"The President of the Alliance?" Blaze's eyes narrowed as she rose out of her chair and stood over the communications panel. "Now *you* listen here, furball," the young woman said to the felinoid voice on the other end of the comm unit, "and you listen good. We are already caught in your gravity and I'm not going to fry up here because some stupid president is taking a tour of that sand rock you call a home." She paused as her voice calmed to a chill whisper. "We are landing now. Either you clear us a path or we'll smash right into the president's star yacht on the way down if need be."

"But—"

"Save it, we're coming in." Then her eyes locked on Sloan's. "Take us down."

Sloan's shock gave way to anger. "Now wait one damned minute, girl—"

"No waiting," Blaze's voice commanded in a low hiss, turning colder than the darkest moon, "take us down now."

Sloan's anger sank back into shock, as she suddenly turned and started the landing cycle. Though she couldn't explain exactly why she did it, other than for the fact she was suddenly afraid of her mysterious passenger. The merchant captain fixed her attention on the console in front of her, putting her efforts into a safe atmospheric entry and landing, and tried to ignore her suddenly shaking hands.

Disregarding all demands from the control center ordering them not to come down yet, the *Silhouette* dove toward the arid surface. Slicing through the hot amber sky, the crippled Merchantman barely managed to engage its landing thrusters, preventing it from slamming into the desert floor.

Sloan somehow kept control over the wounded craft as she skimmed the arid surface of Perus II, hunting for a place to set the ship down. Finally, in the distance, they spotted one of the tall landing pads which stretched up from the parched red sands at least one hundred yards into the air, resting on three thick pillars.

Confirming it was empty; Sloan lowered the *Silhouette* down onto the flat oval pad which was large enough to hold two ships of this size. The landing gear groaned as they grudgingly accepted the massive tonnage of the wounded ship, and coolant spewed out from holes in the armor plating as the vessel finally breathed a sigh of relief. They had made it.

"Now what?" Rabies asked as he slumped in his chair.

"Now we fix the ship," Sloan answered curtly.

She still felt a bit shaken, though she couldn't decide if it was from the near fatal landing, or the commands she had obediently accepted.

She silently watched Blaze, who was busy talking to Sinclair. Her eyes narrowed slightly as she intently studied the two of them. He was standing over Blaze, his broad shoulders almost hiding her from view. Her chin was delicately tipped up to his face, listening intently, as he warmly whispered and smiled down at her. Sloan felt an uncomfortable tightening in her throat as she silently observed their intimate actions.

The communication station shattered the moment, demanding their attention with its incessant beeping.

Finally, Rabies turned it on. "What do you want?"

"Are you all in one piece?" questioned the same Perusian whom they had ignored before.

"Barely," answered Sloan with a sigh. "Look, we've been through a lot lately, so please don't come over here and try to arrest us, we're sick of fighting."

"We are not going to arrest you," the feline responded with a growl. "But you are going to have to pay a five hundred-credit fine. Do you need assistance?"

"A repair crew wouldn't hurt," Sloan grudgingly answered, angered at the prospect of the fine, plus the repair charges. With a flick of her finger, she turned off the communications, cutting short the Perusian's response.

"You're not really going to let a bunch of felines crawl over this ship, are you?" Rabies asked.

"Then *you* do the repairs."

The Jarbban sulked quietly, slinking further into his chair. "Fine, they can come on board."

"Why, thank you so much," Sloan said with a sarcastic snip. She leaned back in her chair and stretched, listening to the bones in her joints pop from the released tension. "I need a drink."

"Me too," Rabies added.

"I really need to get off this ship," Blaze said, desperate for fresh air.

"Same here," agreed Sinclair.

"Then let's get out of here for a while," Blaze said as she stood up, moving to get some of the clothes she and Sinclair purchased on Onoran. "There must be a bar somewhere around here."

"Oh, there is," Sloan said as she allowed herself her first smile in days, "there always is."

~ * ~

A half-hour later, the companions found themselves at a small tavern in the local city, sitting around a table, gratefully enjoying their respective drinks and trying not to think of the blistering temperatures outside.

"This is more like it," Sloan said with a smile as she downed half of her Collian beer and judged the bar's crowd with an entrepreneur's eye.

She knew there was always a way to make some money in a place like this, you merely needed to know how to go about it the right way.

Sharing in Sloan's sentiments, Blaze leaned back in her chair, grateful to be out of the ship. Space travel never appealed to her. She felt as if it somehow robbed her of that feeling of control over the life she cherished so much, and this latest incident did little to change that perception.

The young woman gazed down at the lavender liquid in her wide-brimmed glass as she began to smile. She ordered herself a Denebrian brandy, a drink for those with expensive tastes, tastes which still lingered from her exposure to the overly self-confident pirate captain who rescued her from Tenebrous. *Damn him*, she thought with a touch of remorse, *he helped me grow so much…why did he have to turn out to be such an ass?*

The smile faded from Blaze's lips as she swirled the cool, pale liquid around. Despite the heat of this desert world, the Perusians didn't take the time to warm their brandy. Focusing the merest of efforts toward her hand, she started to concentrate on the brandy in the glass, stopping when she was satisfied with its new temperature. She was amazed at how quickly she acclimated to this bizarre new power she had, as if she had been waiting for it all her life. Taking a sip from her freshly warmed drink, she turned her attention to her surroundings in the hope that something around her would prove interesting.

The bar was dimly lit by a glowing fireplace in the center of the room, casting the place in dancing orange shadows. All around were Perusians of all colors and manners. From a glance the Perusians could almost pass for humanoids, if you ignored their catlike head, tails and fur covered bodies, but there were non-felinoids around also. At one table nearby there were a group of humans and blue-skinned Onorans. At the bar, a crustacean from Vega sat alone, his large red claws holding his drink and a sausage of some kind.

Blaze quickly decided to center her attention on the humans and Onorans, as they were the most likely source of excitement in this smaller city. Her eyes lingered on the Onoran man, appreciating his looks, before she silently laughed at her sudden interest. The young woman allowed her thoughts to run free as the dim lights played across his deep blue skin and reflected seductively along his long white hair. However, her smile faded as she remembered her last intimate experience with a man.

Far from his new companion's train of thought, Rabies watched the throng of mingling felines with apprehensive mistrust which bordered on mild paranoia. Despite their humanoid appearance, standing upright and acting civilized, in his mind he knew them for the terror they truly were. Those piercing cat-eyes which could find you in the deepest hiding place, those tall ears that would home in on your slightest movement, those fangs that could rip out your throat with the merest whim…all waiting to be used against some poor unsuspecting Jarbban who was a good two-feet shorter than them.

Rabies was jerked out of his self-created nightmare as he realized one of them was standing over him, glaring down, her whiskers twitching with the anticipation of the kill. He shrank down in his seat as she reached out toward him, her claws ready to deliver lethal blows of death.

"Is there anything else I can get for you?" the waitress asked as she purred pleasantly, while picking up an empty glass from the table. "Some more ale, perhaps?"

On the other side of the table, Sinclair watched the shapely waitress with a different eye. Quickly deciding that despite her catlike face, fur, and tail, she was all woman. He found himself letting his eyes wander over her thin, silken grey fur, to the small teal bikini which barely covered her. The combination was stunning, though he understood such attire was common for the three Perus planets, all scorching desert worlds.

"Perhaps there is something I can get for you?" the young feline asked Sinclair, her jade eyes twinkling playfully.

Sinclair cleared his throat nervously as he managed an embarrassed smile, realizing she had noticed his obvious stares. "Ah…no thank you," he finally said.

"Are you sure?" She purred invitingly, her long tail swaying back and forth.

"I…I'm sure."

"Too bad," she said with a wink, then turned from the table and disappeared back into the crowd.

"She didn't ask me if *I* wanted anything," Sloan said, annoyed at being ignored, though she was amused by her small partner's apparent paranoia.

As for Sinclair, he watched the Perusian disappear back toward the bar as his brow creased in thought once again. "A canine…"

Blaze glanced over at him, also amused by what happened but her attention focused again on eavesdropping on the party of humans and Onorans. She was finding their conversation was growing more and more interesting.

"I really think it could be risky," one of the human males said between gulps of beer.

"That's the trouble with you humans," the Onoran female said with a sardonic chuckle, "you have no backbone for a challenge."

"Listen, Tara," the human replied, "you Onorans don't have the market on illicit procurement."

"No," she agreed as she flashed a wicked grin, "but we do manage to accomplish a great deal more of it *successfully* than you do."

"Look, Tara," another human cut in, "do you want in on the jewel or not?"

"Why don't you broadcast it to the entire bar, Tanner?" Tara said through clenched teeth, her face flushing a deeper blue.

Yes, Blaze thought with amused disgust at their foolishness, *please do.*

"Sorry," Tanner whispered as he raised his hand in an apologetic gesture. "Then is it settled? We leave tonight to go to the dune caverns, the jewel is somewhere in that cave, hidden in a skull."

"Are you sure?" Tara asked, so quietly Blaze could barely hear.

"Positive," Tanner confirmed. "Let's go get some rest. We leave at the fourteenth hour."

The group rose up and walked out of the bar, except for Tara who grabbed the other Onoran's arm, causing him to wait. Once the others were gone, she smiled wickedly at him. "We'll let the humans lead us to this jewel," she whispered in the Onoran tongue, "then we'll kill them and take it for ourselves."

"I like the way you think, Tara," he said with a laugh, then kissed her deeply. "Let's get out of here."

"Agreed...our hotel room awaits."

Blaze watched them leave, suddenly grateful she had picked up enough Onoran while with the pirates to figure out the gist of what they were saying. She glanced over to find Sloan staring at her. "You heard?"

Sloan nodded eagerly. "Every luscious word...I think we should go for it. It'll save them the trouble of having to kill each other over the jewel later. With luck, it will be worth enough to give us all a few extra credits, as well as repair my ship."

"Alright," Blaze agreed as she sipped her still-warm brandy. She didn't relish the thought of giving up part of her share to aid the vessel, but she knew she needed Sloan and Rabies right now. They were all wanted by the Red Star pirates, and the *Silhouette* was still her only means of travel.

~ * ~

An hour later they were far outside the city, near what the Perusian at the tourist information center had assured them was the Dune Caverns.

"They don't look like caverns to me," Rabies grumbled, "they look more like holes in the ground."

"Then you should fit right in," Sloan said with a grin.

Blaze ignored this incessant bantering as she gazed about quickly. Epsilon Eridani had begun to set, already sinking below the endless dune sea, leaving the sky an explosion of scarlet and violet streaks.

She shifted her gaze back toward the distant city. Its glow was beginning to illuminate the ever-darkening sky.

"It will be night soon," Sinclair whispered, almost to himself.

"So?" Blaze asked, her eyes narrowing with suspicion.

"The moons will rise soon," he continued, almost in fear.

"How do you know? Maybe Perus II doesn't have any moons."

"I just know," he whispered, that all-too-familiar glazed look filling his eyes again.

Oh fine, Blaze grumbled silently, *it was nice while it lasted.*

"You know, Blaze," Sloan said as they searched around for a suitable entrance to the underground caverns, "we're trying to look inconspicuous out here."

"So?"

"So," Sloan continued, trying to decide the best way to express what she wanted to say. "The black denim pants are fine, but do you think the bright scarlet shirt was the best idea? You stand out in the desert like a flame in darkness."

Blaze smiled at the comparison as she gazed down at her snap down shirt, feeling complimented more than annoyed. She glanced up at her new companion and shrugged her shoulders. "I like the color red."

"But *all* the shirts you bought were red," the merchant captain said with exasperation. "You should have borrowed one of mine, tried to blend into the desert night here."

Blaze's smile turned into a scowl as she glared at Sloan, her voice growing harder. "I told you, I like red."

Rabies was about to cut in with the opinion that red seemed fine to him, when he heard another sand skimmer coming to a halt next to them. The top quickly opened, revealing a pair of Perusians, one male and one female. "Oh, perfect," he said with a sarcastic grunt.

"Who are you?" Blaze asked sharply.

The male Perusian jumped gracefully out of the sand skimmer, his orange and brown stripes flashing in the starset.

"We're sightseeing," he responded cheerfully.

"Yeah," the female added from the skimmer, "we're sightseeing."

Blaze stared at the female, deciding the best way to describe her was that she was a calico, mostly white, with brown and black spots. "I really think you should both leave now."

"Why should we?" the male asked with a defiant snarl.

"Yeah," the calico in the skimmer added, an adolescent whine in her growl, "why should we?"

"Because I asked you to," Blaze answered flatly.

The two felines stared at each other for a moment, speechless.

"Leave," Blaze repeated, her voice sinking to a frosty whisper. *"Now!"*

At that moment an ominous wisp of smoke rose from under the Perusian's sand craft's hood, suggesting possible engine trouble.

"Mrr al ar irr," the female said to her companion in their native tongue, obviously worried.

"Maa," the male seemed to agree as he turned back to Blaze. "We'll come another night." He quickly retreated to his skimmer and gracefully jumped in.

"Yeah," the young Perusian woman concurred, her ears flattening in a pouting droop, "we'll come another night."

Without another word, the male Perusian ignited the sand skimmer's engines and drove off, leaving Blaze and her group alone in the desert night air again.

"Good riddance," Rabies shouted happily after them, his high voice trembling with relief.

"Calm down," Sloan said to her friend. "We're lucky they left so easily…" Her voice dropped off as she realized that a low menacing growl started to come from behind her. With a flash of her wrist, she drew her electro pistol and whirled around, to find the odd noises were coming from Sinclair. Her mouth dropped open as she realized he was growling and panting as he stared up into the sky. "Blaze," she called quickly, "I think you'd better come over here…*now*."

Hearing the urgency in Sloan's voice, Blaze ran over in time to witness Sinclair start to rip at his clothes, as if desperate to get them off. She quickly glanced into the sky, cursing as she found the moons of Perus had already begun to rise, and one of them indeed was full. She slowly started to walk over to him as he began to howl.

"Not now, Sinclair," Blaze pleaded quietly as she tried to keep him from unclothing himself. Already his new shirt was in tatters, and he was working on his pants.

He struggled violently as the young woman attempted to restrain him, froth coming to his mouth as he snarled and snapped at her, his eyes suddenly aflame with moon-lust.

"Angel," he said with a growl, his attention suddenly drawn to her. "I have risen to protect you, my mistress of the night."

"That's really swell," Blaze said with a sigh as she tried to hold his hands, which suddenly shifted from trying to remove his clothes to trying to remove hers. "*Sinclair,*" she whispered warningly, "*stop it*. This is not the time or place."

"I must serve you, my mistress. I must please you with all my animalistic powers."

Blaze's mouth hung open in surprise as she temporarily forgot to keep a hold on his desperate hands. Her shirt easily came open as he clutched forward and ripped at her. As his hands quickly reached toward her now exposed chest, she gritted her teeth in determination, forcing down the urge to fry his face. Instead, she placed one foot behind his legs and pushed, causing him to topple backward, with her on top of him.

He continued to struggle as she desperately held him there, trying not to hurt him. "Now listen to me, and listen good," Blaze said, her voice a harsh whisper. "Do you want to serve me or not?"

He stopped struggling and gazed deeply into her eyes. "Yes, my mistress," he said as his voice continued its low growl.

"Then stop trying to fondle me."

"But I must please you."

Blaze groaned, unprepared for this new development in his dementia. Then a solution came to her. "Sinclair—"

"I am not Sinclair, my mistress. I am the Wolven, the creature of the moon."

"All right," she said as she let out a slow breath. "Now listen to me, Wolven, I need you to please me by helping me find this jewel in the cave. You can please me the other way *later*…all right?"

There was a moment of silence as she waited nervously while Sinclair considered her request. He nodded sadly, the fight gone out of his eyes.

"I will obey your requests, my mistress Angel," he said with a touch of sadness, "but I will look forward to…later."

Blaze nodded as she stood up, holding her ripped shirt closed with one hand. What she was going to do later, she had no idea, but for now, at least, she felt he would remain manageable. She grabbed his hand and squeezed it tightly as she pulled him in the direction of the dune caverns. "I told you…don't call me Angel."

While this whole incident was occurring, Sloan grabbed Rabies by his ear and pulled him away, which wasn't easy to do since he was staring at Blaze and Sinclair in fascination.

"Is that the way you humans have sex?" he asked in a quiet squeak.

Sloan rolled her eyes to the sky and tugged at him harder, finally managing to pull him away. "Don't be ridiculous. They just need to work out some weirdness in their lives."

"What do you mean?" he asked as they walked towards the sand caves, leaving the two struggling humans behind.

"Hmm," the merchant captain said as she let go of his ear and put away her gun, "in my opinion, Sinclair likes Blaze a lot but doesn't know how to express himself in any other way than his psychotic behavior."

"What about her?" the Jarbban asked, confused by all of this. "Do you think she likes him too?"

"I honestly don't know," she answered thoughtfully, a light smile crossing her lips.

"Humans are bizarre," Rabies said as the two of them entered the cave which slowly sloped down into the sand dune before them.

"Yeah," she said with a quiet laugh, "I guess we are."

Blaze and Sinclair caught up with their companions deep in the cave which was solely lit by a phosphorescent substance on the walls, which bathed the narrow cavern in an eerie lavender glow.

Sloan glanced over at her new companions and flashed a grin. "You two going to be all right?"

Blaze gave Sinclair a sidelong glance and nodded. "We'll be fine...right?"

"Grrr..."

"Good," Sloan said, "because we have to find that jewel and be out of here before the fourteenth hour."

"What time is it now?" Rabies asked.

"The twelfth hour," Sinclair said through a growl.

"How do you know? You don't have a timepiece."

"Believe me, I know."

"Sure."

"Enough of this," Blaze said, cutting in. "We have work to do."

Sick of holding her damaged shirt closed, Blaze undid the last two snaps which weren't ripped and tied the shirt closed in front of her. *Sinclair is going to pay for that one,* she cheerfully promised herself. *I don't know how, or when, but he will.* A smile came to the young woman's lips as her eyes lightly caressed her half-unclothed friend. Through the torn cloth, she could see the lean hard muscles in his arms and chest, and suddenly realized he mattered to her a lot more than she would have thought possible.

As they continued to walk along, the tight cave opened into a huge cavern which was brilliantly lit in lavender, with most of the illumination coming from under a huge pool in the center of the rocky floor. Millions of small luminescent creatures danced back and forth under the water, creating an image of a fantastic lavender and pale blue light show.

"Magnificent," Blaze whispered, amazed at the grandeur of what she saw.

"Yeah, magnificent," Sloan said with obvious disinterest as she started focusing her attention on her real longing. "Let's find the jewel."

What little vision these people have, Blaze thought sadly as she watched Sloan and Rabies scurry across the floor like Antarian musk scavengers.

"What is your bidding, Mistress Angel?" Sinclair asked from her side.

"My bidding is that you stop calling me Angel," she replied sharply. However, when she saw the blank look on his face, she shrugged off her annoyance. "Help me find that rock."

Suddenly feeling a lack of desire to search for the jewel herself, Blaze wandered over to the pool and watched the luminescent creatures move around along the bottom of the small pond. Each was no larger than an Earth fly but looked more like a worm. *That's what they probably are,* she decided with revulsion, recalling some unpleasant memories of hers which concerned the large sewer worms back on Tenebrous.

Sloan, Rabies, and Sinclair continued to burrow through the rock and sand in the cavern, each time coming up empty.

"Maybe it's further down in the caves," the Jarbban commented.

"I don't see any way to go from here," Sloan said, while hunting for an exit other than the way they came.

"Perhaps the next area is hidden from view," Sinclair suggested as he scratched furiously at himself and sniffed at a rock.

"Or maybe it's along the walls under those glowing worm things," Sloan added, trying to keep her distance from her obviously lunatic companion.

Blaze tuned out their bantering as she continued to gaze into the pool. She knew she should have been helping them, because she did want the jewel, but she couldn't pull herself away from the water, it was as if she were drawn to it. Then she noticed what was pulling her attention. Down in the depths, right in front of her, was a mound of the lavender worms, as if a large clump of them were piled on top of each other.

Swallowing down the revulsion she had at touching the creatures, she knelt and slowly put her hand into the liquid. At first, she was surprised when the water was warm to the touch, then she wondered how she thought anything could have been cold on this overheated ball of sand the Perusians called their home. Letting her hand glide through the water, the young woman found she had to kneel over to reach the bottom where the mound was. Slowly she reached out with her fingers, still not sure why she wanted to search through the amassing of luminous worms. *I have to do this,* she pressured herself as she paused, inches from her goal. *Come on Blaze, they're only worms.* She forced down the strong desire to pull back as she felt the first of the slimy creatures but compelled herself to push her fingers deeper into the soft mound. *How can something so sparklingly beautiful be so gross?*

The glowing creatures slithered over Blaze's hand, and suddenly she decided they weren't so bad after all, but their movements tickled…a lot. Then, as she was about to pull back, her fingers hit something hard and round. Finding an orifice in the object to grab onto, she quickly began to pull it out. As her new prize emerged from the lavender invertebrates, a pale azure glow broke through, overcoming the luminescent abilities of the worms. More and more of the glowing creatures fell away, revealing the skull of some large humanoid in her hand, which she was grasping through an eye hole. But Blaze ignored that, enraptured by the now fierce blue light which emanated from inside the skull, seeping through the eyes, nose, and mouth.

Without hesitation, she turned the skull over and shook it, and was quickly rewarded as the glowing jewel fell into her other hand. Blaze's moist lips parted slightly as she licked them in wonder and awe, never had she seen something so magnificent. It was flawless in design, a multifaceted sphere no larger than the palm of her hand. Suddenly, she knew she had to possess this jewel, it was hers, by all rights and woe to anyone who attempted to take it away.

Attracted by the new light in the chamber, the others quickly gathered around her to behold its splendor.

"Amazing," Rabies said with a squeak.

"I've never seen its equal," Sloan whispered, deep in her own world of greed.

"Yet it pales in comparison to you," Sinclair said, "my mistress Angel."

So enraptured by her new prize was Blaze that she even ignored her friend calling her by her former name. They stared in silence at the glowing gem, all deep within their own thoughts.

"See?" came a vaguely familiar voice from behind them, "I *told* you we couldn't trust that other group at the bar."

"You were quite right, Tara," another voice added.

Blaze and the others turned around to find the two Onorans and their three human companions standing behind them, all with electro pistols out and aimed at the group.

"Perhaps we should have placed a guard outside," Sloan whispered.

"It's a little late for that," Rabies said quietly.

"But, Tara," came from the man which Blaze remembered as Tanner, "you thought they would try to *steal* the jewel. And here they have gone and found it for us. How thoughtful of them."

Sinclair let out a frightening snarl which caused a few of their antagonists to take a step back.

"You'll take this jewel over our dead bodies," Rabies said, a defiant tremor in his voice.

"That was kinda the idea," Tara replied, a wicked smile crossing her deep blue lips. "Kill them."

Suddenly Blaze's fist whitened around the jewel as she squeezed it hard, causing the stone's azure light to seem to grow in ferocity, and change to a brilliant violet. "There will be death, Tara," she said, an eerie echo in her voice which resounded in the large cavern, "but it won't be ours."

Tara retreated another step, suddenly unnerved by the violet glow from Blaze's fist, added to by the crimson light which suddenly seeped from her eyes. Hoping it was a reflection from the jewel she held, the Onoran woman yelled to her companions, "Did you hear me? *Kill them now!*"

Shaken out of the ominous daze that seeped over him and his companions, Tanner raised his weapon and pointed it at the strange woman in red, determined to burn her down. However, his finger never tightened on the trigger, nor did anyone else's.

For at that moment, Blaze raised her other hand and spread her fingers wide, her eyes a hellishly fierce glowing red now; and before any of them could react, streams of blue flame lanced out from her fingertips, searing into them, consuming them all in writhing agony.

Sloan and the others watched in transfixed horror as their new enemies were swiftly reduced from living beings to a crumpled mass of smoking bones.

"My God," Sinclair whispered, his growl forgotten.

As quickly as it began, the fires died, leaving the cavern in comparative darkness. The fierce glow in the jewel faded to a mere shimmer, and Blaze slowly sank to her knees, her physical form stressed beyond the realm of normal endurance.

Sinclair quickly rushed to Blaze's falling body to catch her before her head hit the stone floor. Once in his arms, he held her tightly, relieved by the soft sound of her breathing. He wiped her sweat-soaked hair from her face and glared at the jewel, its glow almost gone.

"What in the flame pits of Hellion was that?" Sloan finally managed, breaking out of the shock which had enveloped them all.

"I don't know," Sinclair answered quietly, his voice racked with concern, "but she's cold, deathly cold."

"Maybe we should get her outside," Rabies suggested. "It's much warmer out there."

Sinclair nodded, then scowled as he saw the Jarbban reach to take the now dark jewel from Blaze's still clenched hand. "Leave it be."

The Jarbban's long snout twitched as he contemplated how serious Sinclair was, then he pulled back his small hand. "I thought, perhaps, she shouldn't carry it anymore. What if it hurts her again?"

"You idiot," Sinclair said as he gently lifted her limp form, cradling her in his arms, "*she* was in control of the jewel...*not* the other way around. She saved all our lives."

"But at what cost to herself?" Sloan asked softly as her eyes flicked over the blackened skeletons which were still smoking on the floor of the cave, suddenly not too sure if she even wanted the jewel anymore.

They all looked at their fallen comrade in silence for a moment, then slowly headed back up the dimly lit cavern.

Chapter Seven
Victory

Endless black space stretched out before an infinite mosaic of stars, lit by the billions of stellar bodies that inhabit the galaxy, and the occasional ship which drifted swiftly past.

The mighty United Star Alliance battleship gracefully turned on its axis like a guard walking a post and began its voyage back the way it came, as it had done frequently over the last three months. Its star drive engines flared as it sped along the Alliance's border, ever vigilant for any sign that an annoying adversary would dare show its face again.

On board that fantastic warship, a troubled woman rose from the comfortable bed in her cabin and sat down at her desk. There she did what she always did when she was restless, she made a record of her thoughts by confiding to a computer which would keep her words a secret, unless directly ordered otherwise:

"Captain's personal log, United Star Alliance Spaceship Victory, *stellar date 290826:*

The Victory *is in her third month of deep space border patrol now, as we continue to sweep the area between the Romusian and Camillian neutral zones. There has been little to no activity from either of our neighboring empires, which is quite good…though not the reason we are here. Such normal patrolling can easily be handled by a smaller ship, such as a frigate. The only reason to call out a battleship, like the* Victory, *is to intimidate someone, and that's certainly what we have seemed to have accomplished here.*

Almost half a year ago, the Red Star pirates, known

to themselves as the Red Star Imperium, attacked the neutral system of Arvia in an attempt to forcibly annex the planet. After their defeat, the United Star Alliance's Stellar Defense Fleet Command decided to station a battleship along the section of our border which faced their home system, which is hidden within the neutral zone. I suppose Stellar Defense Fleet Command wanted to let them know we are keeping a watchful eye on them. However, the effort seems to have been wasted, as there hasn't been so much as a peep from them for the last three months. In fact, the captain of the battleship we relieved noted a definite lack of usual pirate activity in this area...maybe the Red Star pirates have finally turned their tail and decided to stay home.

I'm hoping Stellar Defense Fleet Command will recall us soon, as my crew is getting quite restless. I'm sure the Admiralty can find a better use for one of its twelve battleships than playing big shot to an insignificant organization which doesn't have anything larger than a heavy cruiser to put in space."

Sharon Mitchell shook her head in annoyance as she lightly touched the bright blue button on her desk, switching off her personal log recorder. She leaned back in her chair, feeling the muscles in her back stretch, and groaned. "Next thing they'll probably do is call out one of our three dreadnoughts to do this tedious task," she said to her empty room and laughed quietly. "But that's the way the upper echelon works, I guess...they'd use an electro torpedo to unlock a door."

The captain of the *Victory* rose slowly from her chair and left her cabin. She was tired of all this waiting for no reason. It was time to put some spirit back into her crew. Stepping into the omni-lift, she signaled it to take her to the ship's bridge.

She contemplated shore leave for her crew as she wondered how long it had been since she had seen her native city of Philadelphia, or Earth at all for that matter. She straightened up and brushed her chestnut hair into military order as the doors to the bridge slid open.

"Captain on the bridge," the duty officer said as she entered the large nerve center of the space vessel.

"Report," Captain Mitchell said as she walked to the midpoint of the oval bridge, where her command chair patiently waited for her.

"Still nothing," her executive officer answered. "I think they know better than to tangle with one of the Alliance's prime battleships."

"You're probably right, Commander," she answered thoughtfully. "But that doesn't mean we should slack off. Prepare for a battle drill."

"Yes, sir," he responded with a curt nod. Then he turned to the weapons officer. "Sound the alert, Lieutenant."

"Aye, Commander." The young officer touched the alert status control, plunging the ship into deep scarlet battle lights.

"Tactical Alert!" the computer forcefully blared. "This is a battle station drill. Tactical Alert!"

Captain Mitchell watched attentively as her crew raced around her, preparing for the altercation which didn't exist. Although her crew had been inactive for some time, they still had a fire within them, and she felt confident they could handle any adverse situation that could possibly arise.

She glanced up from her thoughts to see her executive officer standing at her side, waiting patiently for her attention.

"Yes, Commander?" she asked, turning her clear green eyes to him.

"Efficiency rating for battle drill was ninety-seven percent," he said proudly.

"I see," Captain Mitchell said while rubbing her lower lip thoughtfully. "Let's see if we can get one hundred."

"Agreed," the commander responded as he signaled for the alert to sound again.

The Tactical Alert drill was in full swing when the science officer quickly turned to the captain.

"Captain Mitchell," she urgently called.

"What is it Sciences?" the captain asked as she swiveled her command chair to face the officer, surprised by the severity in her tone.

"There is something on the screen, Captain," the young officer quickly reported. "It's a ship, but larger than anything I've ever seen."

The ship's navigator was a young Proximan, a race whose natural empathic abilities gave them a unique advantage when dealing with strangers, or strange situations. Normally a bit cocky, he lost his bravado as he stared up at the view screen expectantly, his pale white hands tightened as they clutched the controls.

"What is it?" the ship's helm officer whispered as she reached out to her friend, a man she'd known since the Academy, but her voice went silent as the captain turned back to the front of the bridge.

"Cancel alert drill," the captain ordered as she turned to face the forward viewer. "Put our visitor on the screen."

The forward viewer surged as the magnification increased to show a large ship dominating the previously empty starfield. They all looked in awe at the majesty and grandeur of the vessel before them, never had any of them seen its equal, nor would they ever.

"Who is it?" the captain asked her science officer. "Does it have any markings?"

"Scanning," the young scientist responded as she quickly studied her instruments.

Inch by inch the *Victory's* powerful scanners swept over the mammoth form that was swiftly closing in, until it came across what it was searching for, the crimson starburst insignia they had all come to know.

"It's the Red Star pirates," the science officer quickly informed her captain.

"That's impossible," the executive officer replied. "They have no large warships...and that one must be twice our size."

"Much larger," the scientist continued. "It's over twice the size of *our* dreadnoughts, measuring in at almost a mile in length."

"My God."

"*Battle stations,*" Sharon Mitchell ordered. "Get me a line to that ship."

"Ready," came from her communication's officer.

"This is Sharon Mitchell," she firmly said to the quickly advancing ship, "captain of the U.S.A.S. *Victory*. You are approaching United Star Alliance space with a warship. This is a hostile act, and we must warn you to withdraw immediately."

There was no reply.

Concerned, she glanced over at the man who was her executive officer, and her friend, to find him looking at her with the same expression in his face. They both knew if the pirate vessel's powers were in any proportion to its size, then they didn't stand much of a chance.

"Exec," she said quietly, "what have we stumbled onto?"

"Captain," the helm officer reported. "The Red Star pirate vessel is still closing."

"What is its course?" she asked, realizing her executive officer never answered her.

"Directly for us," the navigator answered anxiously, a look of almost terror on his face, as if he knew or felt something the rest didn't.

"Keep repeating that message," the captain ordered her communications officer, "…and get me a priority line to Stellar Defense Fleet Command…"

~ * ~

Lord Tanus Adalric rose from the bed in his grand cabin and stared silently at his most favored possession, his chess set. This was no ordinary, modern holographic type; this proud set was one which had been hand crafted on Earth, back in the eighteenth century. The majestic marble figurines of the ancient Olympian gods stood diligently as they waited to be moved, a fine layer of dust covering them from recent neglect.

"Too long have I been absent from the game," the overlord said under his breath, "…but that will end today." He turned his back on the white and black pieces and strode over to the full luminescent mirror which covered one wall. Once there, he stared at his reflection for a long time, his thin lips set in determined vigilance.

Now is my chance, he considered adamantly. *Everything rides on what I accomplish next…or fail to.*

His powerful hand reached down to the black table before him and picked up the blood red half mask that sat on its obsidian holder. His cold grey eyes filled like angry thunderclouds as he glared at the hated apparel for what seemed an eternity. He looked back up into the mirror, to bitterly remind himself of why he wore it, his jaw tightening at the memory.

61

"Soon," his deep voice whispered angrily, "I'll have my revenge."

With a swift movement that came from years of repetition, he fitted on the armored cowl which left his jaw and left cheek exposed. His uniform complete, Lord Adalric turned from the mirror with a sharp stride and moved toward his personal communications chamber. Once there, he sat down and programmed in the necessary settings for the top-secret priority message to be sent.

"Imperial message sent to the Dire Queen from Overlord Tanus Adalric aboard the Imperial Flagship Demoness, *stellar date 290826:*

My queen, the Demoness' *trial run is a complete success. This dreadnought handles fine under a variety of adverse situations. However, I have decided more rigorous testing is necessary, so I therefore have decided to engage an Alliance warship along the United Star Alliance borders. What better test of our superiority could there possibly be?*

I would have preferred it if our first target had been a dreadnought, as that would have been a superior test, but the battleship Victory *will have to do. I know you will approve of this change in our original plan as we both know our time of dormancy must end. It is time for us to strike.*

Fear not, my queen, for on this day the Imperium is reborn. Long live the Empire."

Lord Adalric set the message to be sent but placed an hour's delay on it.

We wouldn't want the Dire Queen countermanding my orders before the attack could be accomplished, he thought with slight amusement, *would we?*

The crimson-and-ebony cloaked overlord rose from the chair and left his cabin, intent on being on the bridge before they engaged the *Victory*.

All crew members quickly moved out of his way as he marched through the wide halls of the *Demoness*, his stride full of purpose.

The doors to the *Demoness'* multi-level bridge hissed as they opened, alerting all within that the overlord had arrived.

Captain Elias Braddock turned to face Overlord Adalric, his eyes narrowing in concealed outrage as the chief of the Imperial nobles strode past him without so much as a glance of recognition. Once ignored, he turned his attention back to his duty, looking about his new bridge with a mixture of admiration and frustration. He knew the queen placed him in command of this vessel but often wondered if Overlord Adalric's supervisory position allowed him to ignore the chain of command. His mind clouded while he stared intently at the back of the overlord's hooded cloak.

He nervously scratched at his slightly greying hair as he continued to bore holes in the Dire Queen's right-hand man with his eyes. He knew no order had come in from the Dire Queen to attack the Alliance, and the attack had not been authorized back when the ship was in dry-dock. The captain steeled his resolve as he began to approach the noble. Pausing a few feet away as he recalled Adalric's quick temper. He licked his lips nervously as he finally reached the crimson-uniformed overlord, trying to decide how to approach the queen's right-hand man.

"You have something to say to me?" the overlord asked, his deep voice slicing across the bridge as Adalric turned to face the startled captain.

For a moment the experienced Imperial officer paled, uncertain of what to do, then Braddock straightened himself before the overlord who towered over him ominously.

"Yes, my Lord," he finally replied. "I will not allow the *Demoness* to be taken into Alliance space without direct orders from the Dire Queen." He let out a slight smile as his words finished, as if some internal obstacle had finally been overcome.

The junior officers glanced up in shocked horror as they watched this confrontation between the Dire Queen's grand high baron and their captain, then they all quickly looked back at their consoles as Adalric slowly nodded to their commanding officer.

Suddenly, like a cobra striking to kill, Adalric's crimson-gloved hand shot out and grasped the captain by the throat, lifting him almost a foot off the deck. Captain Braddock struggled for air as his legs flailed about. He tried to free himself as he glanced around at his officers and guards imploringly…horrified at their inaction.

"Do you *question* my orders?"

Braddock barely managed to shake his head, unable to do anything but struggle for short gasps of air.

"Perhaps you question my *authority* to give such orders?"

Again, all Braddock could do was shake his head slightly, his eyes half closed from lack of oxygen. He stopped struggling as the last of his strength ebbed away.

With a slight motion, Lord Adalric released the captain, letting him fall to the deck like a discarded piece of trash, gasping for his life.

"That is very wise, Captain Braddock," the overlord said as he turned his back on the captain. "Now prepare to engage the *Victory*."

The bridge crew bustled back to activity, the humiliated captain forgotten.

Slowly, Braddock rose to his feet, panting and wheezing as the color in his face slowly returned. He hesitated as he watched his crew carrying out the Imperial noble's commands, still angered at their unwillingness to protect him. He knew they feared the overlord and the sovereign, both rumored to be demons. Which was probably why the Dire Queen talked with no one but him, hiding in her throne room, shrouded in perpetual darkness.

The captain shook his head thoughtfully as he rubbed at his badly bruised neck, happy to have been spared from the overlord's wrath.

"Captain Braddock" Adalric said, his voice chastising without even turning to face the officer this time. "You will cease to daydream about your childish fantasies of ghosts and goblins and prepare to engage the *Victory*."

Braddock's mouth hung open in shock, as he stared at the overlord, dumfounded.

"The *Victory* is within striking range, my Lord," Commander Harris, the *Demoness'* executive officer, informed Lord Adalric.

"Good," Adalric said as his lips formed into a cruel grin. "Prepare to attack with plasma torpedoes."

"L...Lord Adalric," the captain said as he humbly staggered over. "If we are going to attack, why not test out the new Cosmic Surge weapon? It could demolish the Alliance battleship with one shot and leave no evidence to incriminate us."

"It is amazing how little foresight you have, Captain," Adalric said flatly as he lost his grin. "I *want* the Alliance to know we defeated the *Victory*, and I want prisoners."

"Prisoners?" Braddock asked, his confidence returning. "Do you think that's wise, my Lord?"

The overlord's gaze turned to ice as his vision pierced into the captain's forehead. Despite the fact Braddock could not see Adalric's eyes through the dark eye covers on his mask, he stepped back sharply, as if hit.

"I will *not* caution you again, Captain." Adalric's voice lowered menacingly as it came out between his clenched teeth.

"Orders, my Lord?" Commander Harris quickly asked, his mind racing with thoughts of elation at the prospect of engaging the Alliance.

Adalric turned to take a closer look at the *Demoness'* executive officer. *Good*, he thought with a surge of approval, *this one here is ambitious and loyal, along with being obedient…I must keep my eye on him.* "Commander," his voice rang out compellingly, "activate battle stations. Prepare for combat."

A grin formed on Harris's lips as he brought his closed fist up to cover the red starburst insignia over his heart, in the Imperial salute. "Yes, Overlord."

The executive officer began to order the bridge into action, when the captain finally managed to regain his wits.

"Commander Harris," Braddock shouted across the bridge. "No one but me can issue an order to place this vessel into combat."

Harris glanced over at Adalric for a moment as he felt his big moment slip away, then he looked back at his captain and nodded. "Understood, Captain Braddock, I was simply getting things ready for you."

Adalric laughed silently. *Ambitious, loyal, obedient,* and *quick on his feet. Harris could have a great future in the Imperium*, the overlord decided, *if he is wise also.*

Captain Braddock walked to the center of the bridge, trying his best to ignore the overlord that scrutinized his every move. "Prepare to engage the *Victory*…defense shields up, engage plasma torpedoes."

"We stand battle ready," Harris replied, assuring his commanding officer.

"Captain," came from a communications officer, "they are trying to warn us off. They also have sent a message to their command base in the area."

"Fire at will, Captain," Adalric said, his voice thundering.

Braddock hesitated for a moment, realizing if the Alliance ship sent a message off to its home base, then reinforcements could be on the way. "My Lord, perhaps we should reconsider..."

His voice died as the overlord whirled to face him.

Adalric's jaw went white as death as he stabbed out with his immense psionic power, using his arcane abilities as a master of the Cosmic Aura.

A scream of agony tried to escape the captain's lips as he fell to his knees, clutching at his head. Swiftly his eyes filled red as the immense cerebral pressures, caused by the sheer force of Adalric's will, began to build up.

"You are pathetic and weak, Captain," the overlord said, his voice barely a hiss, "and are not worthy of commanding the queen's flagship. Consider this your dismissal."

He casually turned away to face the executive officer, as blood began to trickle in scarlet streams from Braddock's eyes, ears and nose. The captain collapsed to the deck and curled in agony as his eyes popped in a tiny eruption of crimson fluid.

Harris watched in shocked silence as his captain's lifeless form lay on the deck. He looked up to see the overlord was staring harshly at him. Quickly Harris forced the ghastly vision out of his head and straightened in salute.

"Order the *Demoness* into action, Captain Harris. You are now in command."

With a swift nod, Harris turned to the command station to begin the battle, but not before stealing one last glimpse at his felled former captain, who was quickly being removed from the bridge. He was proud at the chance to prove himself, but not so proud as to be ignorant of the fact that any day now it could be *his* body the Legionnaires would be dragging off the bridge. He gritted his teeth in determination as he signaled the weapons officer to fire, knowing that now failure would mean death.

~ * ~

The gargantuan Imperial dreadnought arced gracefully as it swiftly closed in on the smaller Alliance battleship. At first, the *Victory* attempted to outmaneuver its larger, clumsier opponent, with its energy beams stabbing out as it sped in evasive circles. But the *Demoness'* fusion tracing plasma energy torpedoes caught up with them eventually, like a heat seeker to a flame. Time after time the luminous scarlet balls of electric plasma energy hammered into the *Victory's* energy shields, slowly battering down the smaller craft's resources. Although the Alliance battleship scored many return hits on the *Demoness*, the larger vessel's protective envelope managed to hold out.

Finally, the *Victory* turned to retreat, realizing a stand out fight against such a mammoth vessel was simply more than it could handle. A battle against a dreadnought was one thing, but continuing to fight this opponent was veritable suicide. The *Victory's* Cosmic Slip star drive engines flared a nova blue as the battleship entered supra-light speeds, but the Imperial flagship had no intention of letting its prey escape so easily. Engaging its own colossal star drive engines, the *Demoness* quickly closed the distance, forcing the *Victory* to accept there was no way it could escape its antagonist.

Trying a desperate move, the captain of the *Victory* ordered a sudden turn and struck back at the dreadnought, its own blue-hot electro-fusion torpedoes launching out with deadly accuracy. However, that was precisely what the *Demoness* anticipated.

Phosphoric lightning and explosions filled the vast emptiness of space as the two titans spewed lethal death. Both players danced, with the smaller *Victory* ever trying to avoid the one devastating blow which would end its gallant effort. Energy shields flashed and faded as energy beams and electro torpedoes, fusion explosions and photon eruptions flared mere yards from the two vessels' hulls...until one large barrage from the *Demoness* finally sliced through its enemy's protection and caused one of the *Victory's* rear star drive engines to erupt. The duel was over.

~ * ~

The flash from the vaporizing star drive engine reflected off Overlord Tanus Adalric's dark eye covers as he stood at the front of his bridge and watched the fatal blow strike the *Victory*.

At first, he enjoyed the display in silence, then he started to turn toward Captain Harris, when an electro torpedo from the crippled Alliance battleship struck the *Demoness'* weakened shields, causing the ship to rock and overload several stations on the bridge.

"Those Alliance fools," he angrily whispered under his breath. "They keep on fighting, even after they have been defeated." He glanced back at Harris. "Prepare to transport over our Darkkrieg Legionnaires to take their ship. Seize the bridge and engineering first, I don't want them to have any chance to self-destruct before we have control…and bring me their captain, I want him alive."

"Yes, my Lord," Harris answered.

Now that the *Victory's* shields were destroyed, he could issue the order to send the Imperium's superior fighting force, the Darkkrieg Legionnaires, down to the subspace Cosmic Rift transportation rooms in order to be moved to the crippled *Victory*.

Tense moments passed as the overlord paced back and forth on the bridge of the *Demoness*, waiting for word from his Legionnaires. The energy shots from the *Victory* slowed more and more until they stopped altogether, then the call came in from the officer in charge of the shipboard assault.

"My Lord," the commanding Legionnaire reported over the communications vid-link, "we have taken the bridge and engineering section, and stopped the crew from setting the self-destruct."

A thin smile returned to Adalric's pale lips as he looked up at the officer on the screen.

"And the Alliance captain?" he asked.

"I have her right here," the Legionnaire responded dutifully. "She is our prisoner."

Adalric's smile turned to a wicked grin. "Excellent, have her brought to me."

"The last pockets of resistance are falling now," the Legionnaire proudly continued, as he watched his prisoners carefully. "We are using their own intruder control system against them. The ship should be under our power within a few moments."

"Good work, Major," Adalric said as he signaled for the transmission to end. So," he proudly stated to the entire bridge, or perhaps merely to himself, "…it would seem quite apparent the 'victory' is mine." His grin over his own pun turned into ominous laughter which echoed in deep reverberations off the bridge walls.

Chapter Eight
The Bounty

The exhausted group re-emerged into the desert night as the moons of Perus II shone overhead, like many eyes that vigilantly watched over them.

However, this time Sinclair found no solace in their haunting beauty, as he laid Blaze's limp cold body onto the hot desert sands. Despite the chilled night air, all was still warm up here, away from the depths of the caves as all the heat absorbed by the sands during the day radiated up.

"How is she?" Sloan asked as she knelt next to the two of them, a look of concern on her face.

"I'm not sure," Sinclair replied, his voice laced with worry.

"I still don't know what happened back there," Sloan said as she shook her head. "By all rights we should be dead now. They certainly got the drop on us."

"Blaze is a pyrokinetic," Sinclair replied, as Rabies came in closer. "The jewel must have some hidden power which somehow greatly affected her abilities. I don't know how. Either way it drained her to the point of exhaustion."

"She can keep the jewel," Sloan said, quickly making the decision. "I don't want it."

"Are you *crazy?*" Rabies asked. "It could be worth tens of thousands."

The merchant captain glared at her partner, suddenly sick of his incessant whimpering. "Shut up, rat."

"I'm not a rat," Rabies replied in a quiet hurt voice, "I'm a..."

At that moment, Blaze moaned slightly, her eyes slowly fluttering open. "Where am I?" she asked, her voice hoarse and low.

"Up on the desert surface," Sinclair answered through the broad grin which quickly formed on his face. "How do you feel? We thought we lost you there."

"Like crap," Blaze replied, feeling every muscle in her body ache, as if she had completed a stellar Olympic decathlon, twice. All that was minor compared to the headache she had, as if a thousand warship engines were roaring in her head. She gazed intently at the cold azure jewel in her hand, still in shock over what she had done. "I killed them all, didn't I?"

"You most certainly did," Sinclair answered. "Though I wouldn't advise trying that one again."

"I agree," Blaze answered earnestly.

She lost herself in the seductive blue of the stone as her thoughts drifted, wondering if her powers empowered the stone, or if the stone amplified her. Finally, she found her voice again as her eyes glanced back up at her companions. "I don't like using a power that's not mine, unless my life depends on it."

"Let's hope it never does," her friend reassured. "Besides, I'm sure…" His voice died off as a sand skimmer quickly approached and came to a skidding halt near them.

"I hope it isn't those Perusians I scared off before," Blaze said with a groan as she tried to move her stiffened limbs.

Without warning, an armored figure, enshrouded by a dark cloak, jumped out of the skimmer and leveled an electro carbine at them before any could react.

"What in the fire pits of Hellion is this?" Sloan cursed, annoyed at being caught off guard twice in one evening.

"The pirates," Blaze whispered.

She wondered how long it would take the Red Star pirates, or one of their bounty hunters, to catch up with them. Though she had hoped it would be later.

"Give me the computer disk," the man in the hooded cloak said, his voice distorted by the built-in speaker in his sand mask, "or die."

Sloan's eyes flicked back and forth from her weapon to the new assailant, gauging the outcome of a forced quick draw.

The cloaked man closed in, never moving his short rifle away from the group. "Which of you has it?"

Blaze tried to force her exhausted mind to project her flames, but simply did not have the strength to harm him, let alone create a simple spark. She looked back at the jewel, but its azure brilliance seemed gone, exhausted.

"Tell me which of you has it, or I will kill you one by one." He moved the weapon to point down at the prone figure of Blaze. "I'll start with her."

Rabies reached for the computer disk, seeing no way around giving it back to the pirates now.

As the assailant turned his attention to the Jarbban, Sinclair quickly shifted to place himself between Blaze and the intruder.

Instinctively, the cloaked man whirled toward the movement and fired the electro carbine, sending a lethal scarlet beam at the pair.

The electrified energy blast caught Sinclair in the chest, sending him tumbling over backward to land in a heap in the sand. That was all the time Sloan needed to draw her own weapon and fire. Three green pulses of heated energy sailed out and found their target, searing through armor, skin and bone, mercilessly leaving the unnamed assailant a smoking corpse on the sand.

Through pain and stiffness, Blaze dragged herself over to the still form of Sinclair. *He's all right*, she assured herself through the waves of panic which were seeping up on her, *he has to be all right.*

She rolled him onto his back and sucked in a sharp breath at the sight of the large area of cauterization over his heart. "Sinclair?" she pleaded. "Sinclair?"

A faint smile came to his sand covered lips as his eyes opened a squint. "I'm fine," he said, coughing weakly.

"Bullshit," Blaze said as she gently put his head in her lap. "You better not be thinking of leaving me here."

He tried to laugh, but the pain in what was left of his chest caused him to wince instead. "I guess the power of the moons wasn't with me on this one," he said as he chuckled hoarsely.

"Hey guys," came from Rabies who had been searching the body of the assailant. "I found this guy's identification."

"So?" Sloan snapped as she stood over Blaze and Sinclair, wondering why her friend would try to bring this up at the most inappropriate of times.

Her eyes studied Sinclair's wound, causing her to internally flinch. Then she turned away, her head lowering to the ground.

"His identification…" the Jarbban insisted. "He isn't with the pirates at all. He's with the Alliance. He's Stellar Defense Fleet Special Intelligence…a secret agent."

"*Damn them*," Blaze whispered, her eyes beginning to water. The Alliance robbed her of everything she cherished in life. First her youth, then her freedom, and now the one person in the galaxy she gave a damn about. "They'll pay," she swore bitterly, her face contorted in rage, "they'll all pay."

"No," Sinclair said, his voice barely audible, as he reached a weakened hand up to gently caress her flushed cheek. "Please let go of the anger."

"But it's all I have now," she whispered back, her voice racked with sorrow. She unsuccessfully fought the lump that rose in her throat as her fingers entwined into Sinclair's cool damp hand.

"Don't let it lead you to revenge," he barely managed. "I've gone down that road and regretted it. Please don't let this new power consume you, it will lead to evil."

"I don't understand," Blaze said quietly, as tears started to run down her face.

"You will someday," he whispered through a crooked half grin. "Take care of yourself, my little Blaze."

Despite her immense sorrow, a forced smile came to her moist lips. "You jerk, now you call me what I want?" She felt his cool hand against her face as his fingers lightly wiped away a warm tear which rolled down her cheek.

His weak smile grew to a broad grin, then he winced again, and his warm blue eyes slowly glazed to a cool grey as the last grains of life slipped through his fingers.

Blaze sat in silence, as she held on to him, her thoughts turning darker and darker. Then her face softened as she gazed down at her friend's lifeless body again. But this time no tears came as she gently closed his eyes and held his still form against her chest, under the brilliantly lit night sky.

Chapter Nine
When You Can't Beat Them…

"Are you sure about this?" Sloan asked as they walked along the city streets of Polis, the proud capitol of planet Nyx.

"Definitely sure," Blaze answered earnestly as her eyes anxiously darted about the energetic city. Then she looked back at the two of them and read the worried expressions on their faces, and smiled. "You guys are great, but this never was supposed to be long term. Look, you still have that computer disk the Red Star Pirates want back, plus the Alliance still wants me for a ton of stuff." She shrugged as she motioned around. "What better place to hide than here, on the Red Star pirates' home world? They'll never look for me here."

"But enlisting as a *Darkkrieg Legionnaire*?" Sloan asked with blatant disgust.

"I need credits," Blaze replied with a shrug. "And I worked for them once…sort of." She glanced over to find Sloan and Rabies still staring at her with concern. "Look, I need some stability in my life right now, and I certainly won't find it flying around with a pair of second-rate smugglers."

"Who's second-rate?" Sloan shot back, a grin forming on her lips.

"Besides," Blaze added, suddenly growing serious, "I certainly wouldn't cry if we ended up going against the United Star Alliance."

Sloan and Rabies looked at each other for a moment in silence, both sharing the same concerns.

"You could always change your mind," the merchant captain tried. "You haven't signed up yet."

"You could sign up too. They wouldn't find you here either."

"No thanks," Sloan said with a laugh. "I have no desire to be a foot soldier after all my experiences in space, and you *know* as well as I they would never accept Rabies. Gods, I barely do and I'm his best friend."

At that moment they all fell silent as a squad of Legionnaires marched past, their black battle armor uniforms glinting in the light of the huge red star which dominated the Nyxian sky. As they passed out of sight and the pulsating clack of their armored boots faded back into the city noises, Sloan turned to Blaze again, to make one last attempt.

"Is that what you want to be?" she asked, pointing after the soldiers. "A nameless, faceless, cog in the Imperial machine?"

Blaze didn't answer right away. Her eyes sparkled in the scarlet sunlight as she watched the Legionnaires disappear around a corner. "Did you see that?" she asked excitedly, forgetting Sloan's question. "*Everyone* on the street gave them room to pass. It grew so silent in this busy city street you could *hear* them marching." She inhaled deeply in eager anticipation. "Now that's what I call respect."

"I call it fear," Sloan said to herself, barely loud enough for Blaze to hear.

Blaze flashed an annoyed look at Sloan, her lips curling in a sneer of disgust. "Would you prefer I wear the white and blue armor of the Alliance Star Marine Corps?" Her voice sank with revulsion.

Sloan shrugged. "Actually…yes. At least then I know you wouldn't be serving some sadistic queen that half the galaxy thinks is a demon."

"She keeps order and structure here," Blaze said sharply. "Unlike the petty planetary governments that hold the Alliance back."

"Give it up, Sloan," Rabies said as he tugged at her hand. "She wants to stay…so let her."

"I guess so," the merchant captain said with a sigh. "Then I suppose this is it."

Blaze nodded silently, then smiled again, her earlier irritation forgotten. "I want to thank you both, for everything…especially when Sinclair…." her voice trailed off as she felt an unpleasant tightening in her throat.

Sloan grinned. "Don't worry about it." She let out a laugh and placed a hand on Rabies' head. "Maybe one day, when you're a big shot in the Imperium, then you can return the favor."

Blaze returned the grin. "You can count on it."

Rabies forced back a sniffle, then ran up and hugged their departing friend, wrapping his small arms around her knees. "I'll miss you," he said with a squeak.

Blaze glanced down at the rodent with a mixed look of fondness and distaste. "I'll miss you too, Rabies." *Though I won't miss the way you smell,* she thought as she gently pushed him away and brushed off her pants. Then she looked up at the merchant captain. "Goodbye Sloan."

"You take care of yourself, Blaze."

"You too."

They both stared at each other in awkward silence for a moment, then Blaze slowly turned her back on the last of her companions and walked off down the street, following in the footsteps of the long absent Legionnaires.

She kept on walking with determination, without looking back, until she spotted a Red Star recruitment center.

Pausing for a moment, she gazed intently at the outside of the busy building. There were enlistment signs everywhere, surrounded by majestic portraits of stellar dreadnoughts destroying smaller Alliance vessels, and triumphant pictures of black-armored Legionnaires firing their electro carbines at enemy troops. And there above, was a sign which plainly, yet patriotically stated:

Be a part of the elite force that is
destined to rule this galaxy.
The Proud
The Strong
The Invincible
DARKKRIEG LEGIONNAIRES
The Backbone of the Imperial Navy and Marine Corps.

Wow, Blaze thought as she smiled, then eagerly stepped into the building.

There were a handful of people in the office, and most of them were in battle armor. She saw there were two people ahead of her, so she decided to look around. There were many more pictures here on the walls of the office. There were pictures of Legionnaires in battle, portraits of officers in their tight-fitting black uniforms, and scenes of ceremonies and parades.

I still can't believe I'm here, Blaze laughed silently. *I certainly never thought I'd ever officially join the Red Star pirates. But they have something here that the Alliance doesn't. Greatness is going to happen here...I can feel it.*

She strode over to an empty suit of battle armor which hung on one of the walls and touched it, allowing her fingers to lightly trace a path over the velvety smooth black surface.

How can you see out of these things? she silently wondered as she looked up at the helmet, then her mind returned to her reasons for why she was here.

I need this now, she declared internally. *This will enable me to be happy and in control, away from the recklessness Sinclair thought would plunge me into some realm of evil, whatever that was supposed to mean.*

Her eyes misted momentarily at the thought of Sinclair, then she laughed quietly to herself. *Gods, what a Legionnaire he would have made.*

I'm not going to be a grunt forever, she finally decided as she folded her arms and grinned, *I'm sure given a few years I'll be the captain of my own ship.* Her quiet chuckles died in her throat as she paused in front of an inspiring portrait of a majestic-looking man who was dressed in a tight fitting, blood-red uniform and was wearing a crimson half mask. Around him flowed a billowing cloak as he handed out medals of honor to some of the Legionnaires. Below, the caption read:

The Imperial Overlord Tanus Adalric
Issuing honors after the battle of Charybdis.

Now this was the kind of power that controlled people, she declared silently. She was so engrossed in her thoughts, she didn't hear the sergeant call her from his desk.

"Hey," the sergeant called again, "you coming over here or what?"

Blaze snapped out of her musing, to find the two of them were alone in the office now.

"Hello?"

"Sorry," Blaze apologized as she hurried over and sat down opposite him.

The sergeant looked over his new candidate with a veteran's eye and sighed, unable to remember exactly how many recruits he already processed today. Scratching his crew-cut with one muscular hand and shaking his head, he tiredly touched an activation button on his logging computer. He then glanced up at her, but with a different look in his eye this time. He slowly appraised her beauty, instantly tossing out the idea of her ever making it as a Legionnaire. "What's your name?"

"Blaze," she answered warily, not oblivious to the lingering stares she was receiving from the sergeant.

"That's it?"

"Yes," she answered proudly. "Blaze is my full name."

"I see," he said with a grunt as he scratched at his thin mustache and mechanically entered the information into his computer. "Date of birth?"

Blaze paused, her stomach quivering. No one had ever asked her that, and she suddenly realized she had no answer. She honestly did not know. "What?"

The sergeant looked up at her, his eyes flashing annoyance at being slowed down. "When were you born?" he said slowly, as if she did not understand the question. "When's your birthday?"

"Oh," she said, while smiling sheepishly and hoping to disarm him, "my *birthday*... March 7th." That was the day the old woman, Mattie, found her in the sewers, and it was that day which Mattie used to celebrate Blaze's birthday. Blaze hadn't thought about birthdays since Mattie died all those years ago. "Yeah, March 7th," she repeated. "Earth Standard Calendar."

"Actually," he said through a yawn, "we refer to it as Imperial Standard here."

"Oh."

"What year?"

"What?"

"What year?" he repeated, allowing his annoyance to creep into his voice. "What year were you born in?"

Blaze quickly calculated and answered the year which would make her twenty now. She had read on one of the wall plaques that twenty was the minimum age for enlistment. After all, she knew she must be close to twenty years old now anyway.

"How tall are you?"

"Five feet, five inches."

A grin came over the sergeant's face as he turned off the computer's screen.

"What's wrong," Blaze asked.

"You're too short to be a Legionnaire," he said as he let out a soft laugh. "You have to be between five feet six and six feet six to qualify. The Dire Queen likes uniformity in her troops. That's why we only take humans and humanoids in service."

"That's ridiculous," she protested, refusing to believe she had come all this way to be stopped because of one lousy inch. "I love the Red Star pirates. I even used to fly on one of their rogue ships."

The sergeant shook his head, his grin turning into a lustful sneer. "You don't even have the right attitude to be a part of us. We're not pirates. That's what the Alliance calls us. We are the Red Star Imperium."

"Sorry," she said, suddenly feeling slapped down.

"Look," he said, trying to sound nonchalant, "*maybe* I can overlook the inch in your case."

"You can?" she asked eagerly, feeling some hope returning. "How?"

"Let's see," he said as he stood and started to walk around the desk to her. "If you are *cooperative*, then maybe I can say you're an inch taller."

Blaze's eyes narrowed with instant suspicion. "What do you mean, *cooperative*?"

"You know what I mean," he said with a grunt, his breath short with growing desire.

He reached out to her and lightly brushed his fingers across one of her breasts.

"You bastard!" she said as she shoved him away from her and stood up. "You are so damned high and mighty here about your order and regulations, but you'll let me slip by for a little sex?"

The sergeant quickly retreated to his side of the desk and sat down, as if nothing happened. "Actually, no," he confessed, "I never was going to let you in."

Blaze fumed, her eyes afire with rage. "You mean you would have done it with me, and *still* not let me in?" The chair she had been sitting in started to smoke.

"Sure," he said with a chuckle, not noticing her eyes, "why not?"

Black fury swarmed over Blaze, and she quickly realized if she didn't leave right away then she would fry this whole place, and that would let every soldier on Nyx know where she was. "One day," she said as she glared at him, studying every line in his face and burning it into her memory. Then she turned and stormed out of the recruitment center as his computer's internal circuits started to melt down.

"Now how the hell did that happen?" the sergeant wondered as he looked down to see his computer screen had also begun to melt.

Outside the center, Blaze turned sharply and stormed down the busy street, swimming in her own dark thoughts. Suddenly it all washed out of her and left her with nothing but a feeling of total loss and despair.

"What am I going to do now," she said as she groaned quietly and plopped down on the curb. "I can't join up, and my ride out of here has left." Blaze shoved her hands into her pockets and remembered she didn't even have any money. Despite Sloan's protests, Blaze insisted she'd give them the money she owed plus all she had left from the sale of the stolen shuttle. She figured once she enlisted, they'd give her everything she needed. *Great*, she thought when her stomach began to rumble, *I can't even buy a sandwich.* She let her face fall into her hands as she tried to forget this day ever started.

"Are you all right?" asked a calming voice from behind.

"Do I *look* all right?" she angrily asked as she turned around, then fell silent as she saw who she was facing.

Before her was an Imperial officer, a handsome man in his early fifties. There were many ceremonial decorations on his broad chest, and Blaze couldn't help but be drawn to the gentle look on his face.

"Oh...um, who are you?"

A warm smile came to the elder man's lips. "I'm Admiral Steward, Joshua Steward."

"An admiral?" Blaze whispered in awe, remembering the proud photos back in the recruitment center.

"What's bothering you?" he asked as he offered her his hand to help her up.

Blaze reached out and felt his strong grip close on her as he lifted her up. She looked at him closely for a moment, centering on his pale green eyes, then she smiled. "I wanted to be a Legionnaire, but I'm one inch too short…one lousy inch." She thought of telling him about the sergeant back in the center but decided it was a personal matter between the two of them.

"Too short, huh?" he asked with a soft laugh as he let go of her hand. He gave her a quick militaristic head-to-toe evaluation. Then he nodded, seemingly in agreement with her deficient height, but also with some sort of approval. "What's your name?"

"Blaze," she replied as innocently as she could, knowing he was probably her last chance on this planet.

"Blaze, huh?" he said thoughtfully. "That's an interesting name. I like it."

"Thank you," she said, shocked but pleased.

"I'll bet it's due to your fiery personality," he said with a laugh.

"Well, you could say that," she agreed, flashing him a wide smile.

"So, Blaze, why do you want to be a Legionnaire?" he asked while scrutinizing her once more, taking note of her thin strong body and the spark of intelligence in her dark eyes. His frame suddenly relaxed as he remembered he was not on duty, and he spoke to her in a casual jesting way. "Pretty girl like you in all that heavy battle armor?"

Unlike her reaction to the sergeant, she found the admiral's words flattering, bringing some red to her cheeks.

"I want to be a part of the pi…Imperium. I believe this galaxy lacks any sort of order and justice." She paused to note his reaction, but saw he was watching her carefully, waiting for her next words. "And although the Red Star Imperium isn't perfect, it's a whole lot better than some place like the United Star Alliance. I want to be a part of this, to have a hand in making it the most powerful of all societies, even if it is a small part…and I don't mind starting at the bottom."

"That's good," he said as he let out a long breath, flabbergasted by the apparent sincerity in her words, "since a Legionnaire is certainly pretty close to the bottom of the Imperial pecking order." He looked at her judgmentally for a few more moments, trying to make up his mind. Finally, he smiled again. "I'll tell you what, Blaze. You really want to be a Legionnaire?"

"Yes," she answered firmly, with hope dancing across her face.

"Then that's what you are going to be. I can pull a few strings to get you in, despite your, ah, modest height."

Suddenly Blaze felt suspicious again, wondering what he thought he was going to get out of this. "What's in it for you?" she asked as her smile sank into a firm line of defiance. "I suppose you want sex or something now?"

Admiral Steward's eyes widened in surprise, making Blaze feel like she rammed her foot in her mouth up to the knee.

"Uh, no," the Imperial officer said, coughing into his loose fist. "Actually, I'm married, and quite happily." He cleared his throat. "I merely felt your desire to enter the Red Star forces seemed genuine, and I wanted to help. That is if it's all right?" His voice was carefully cloaked in neutrality as he faced her.

Never had Blaze felt so ashamed. "Yes, sir," she quickly said as her smile timidly returned. "That's most certainly all right. And I'll make you proud to have let me in," she stated, regaining her enthusiasm. "Never will you find someone who desires to do as much for the Imperium as I do."

"Of that I'm sure." He chuckled as he put a friendly hand on her shoulder. "Now let's get you signed up."

They turned and walked back to the recruitment center, as both breathed a sigh of relief.

I'm going to make it, Blaze thought with determination, *I know I will.* A grin formed on her lips as she thought of her life starting over in the Imperium. *Truly, could there be any place nobler than this?*

Chapter Ten
The Prophecy

"Tactical Alert! Tactical Alert!" the *Victory's* bridge sirens howled, reminding her of so much that went wrong.

"Captain," her executive officer yelled, "we've been boarded."

"Power is failing, sir," added her engineer.

"Damn," the captain swore as she frantically looked around at the burning remains of her bridge. "Prepare the log buoy, ready personal weapons."

At that moment the doors to the control center exploded, killing her communication's officer in the blast.

"They've reached the bridge," her helmsman yelled, seconds before she was fried by electrified energy shots.

The captain lifted her service pistol and set it to kill, determined not to go down without a fight. "Computer," she ordered, "set self-destruct. Command override 0-0-1-0 theta."

"That command has been interrupted in engineering," the computer calmly informed her.

Before she could curse again, she glanced up to see the ebony armored Legionnaires closing in on her. Shot after shot she fired across the flaming bridge at targets she could barely see through the thick smoke.

Suddenly she felt a surge of heat rip through her, and her left arm turned numb. The smell of cauterized flesh invaded her nostrils as the shock of being hit finally caught up with her, and all turned black.

Captain Sharon Mitchell felt her head erupt like an age-old volcano as she fought to regain consciousness. *The* Victory, she desperately thought, *I must awaken to save the* Victory.

She felt a small hand fall lightly on her shoulder, startling her from the dream. As she looked around, it was easy to determine that she wasn't on the *Victory* anymore. She was in a small sterile cell with two beds, one opening with a force field across it, and meager means for modesty.

Standing over her was a young woman, whose haunted face held the shadows of a beauty long since lost.

"Where am I?" the captain asked as she pushed the last of the horrid memory out of her head.

The young woman gazed sadly at her new cell mate, recalling a time when all this was new to her also, but couldn't remember if it were just a few months, or a lifetime ago. "You are on board the Imperial flagship *Demoness*...Overlord Tanus Adalric's ship."

"Tanus who?" Sharon asked as she sat up on the hard bed which consisted of a flat plastic frame and a thin foam mattress. Her head swirled as she tried to remember the familiar significance of that name.

"Tanus Adalric," she responded quietly as she glanced up towards the far corner of the room in fear. "He's the Dire Queen's overlord, the high noble Lord of the Imperial barons, chief of the Imperial forces."

"Imperial, huh?" the captain said to herself. *Ah, yes, Adalric*...she grimly remembered hearing the name, and the reputation, in a Stellar Defense Command briefing. Her eyes flicked about the small cell as she calculated her situation. She knew with the *Victory* lost, the Alliance Counsel had to be warned, at all costs. "What is your name?"

"I'm the Lady—" she stopped and looked down quickly, as if struck, then continued in a hoarse whisper, "Alicia. I'm Alicia."

"Well, Alicia, I'm Captain Sharon Mitchell of the Alliance battleship *Victory*."

"An Alliance warship?" Alicia asked in amazement. "Then the attacks have begun."

"What attacks?" Sharon asked as she checked over her uniform for her weapons and wrist communication device, but found both missing.

"The Imperium has begun its takeover of the sector," Alicia responded strongly, as if remembering a sense of pride, long since stripped from her. "My father would have loved to have seen this."

"Who is your father?"

"You mean, who *was* my father," Alicia replied softly, the pride slipping from her eyes. "My father was once a powerful baron in the Red

Star Imperium."

"A baron?"

"Yes," she answered as she looked up again, a weak smile coming to her lips. "The barons and baronesses are the aristocracy of the Imperium and serve under the Dire Queen, as provincial rulers of the different systems in the Imperium. The highest of these is the overlord, who serves as second to the Dire Queen."

"And this Adalric person is the overlord?" Sharon asked, hungry for any knowledge that would aid her in overcoming this situation.

"Yes," Alicia said, her voice turning bitter. "He and my father, who was the Baron of Nyx, had an argument over something. I was never told the specifics." Her voice lost its anger again as her eyes began to water. "Even though my father had some training as a TelSor, he was no match for the overlord...no one is."

"Nyx," Sharon said quietly as she tried to remember the world. "That's the old Earth colony which was abandoned and taken over by the Red Star pirates long ago."

Despite her state, a glimmer of pride flashed in Alicia's eyes. "Imperium," she corrected the captain quietly.

She knew she had hit a sore spot and decided to get back to the matter at hand and asked, "What happened?"

"My entire family was executed," Alicia whispered as her voice lost all emotion. "My father, mother, and three brothers who were all officers in the Imperial navy."

Sharon's brow wrinkled as she gazed at the disheveled young woman. "What about you? Why weren't you executed also?"

"B–because..." Alicia broke into sobs as tears streamed down from her eyes, and she buried her face in shame. "Overlord Adalric kept me as a reminder to the other nobles. He does things to me..." her voice trailed off.

"Things?" Sharon asked, her eyes narrowing.

"No, not like that," Alicia said quietly, seeing the look in the captain's eyes. "He uses his powers. He rips into your mind to take everything away so there is nothing left, then he lets the others see. Everyone fears him now."

"Why spare you and not your family?"

Alicia looked down again. "I had powers once too…not strong like Adalric's, but I could see things…the future at times. I guess he thinks I still have use."

Sharon clenched her teeth in disgust, which turned to pity as she embraced the sobbing young woman. "Can't you escape? Ask your queen for mercy?"

"There is no escape from Overlord Adalric," she said quietly. "I tried. When he first made me his prisoner, I tried. His will is too strong, he can reach into your thoughts and unravel you." Her tears ceased flowing, as if she had spent all that was inside her, leaving dry sobs of disgrace.

Sharon studied the young noble for a long time, the impact of her frailty stirring up anger almost beyond her comprehension. "He's a barbarian," she finally said, as she reached out and stroked Alicia's hair. "How long have you been a prisoner?"

"Two years," she replied in a horse groan which lacked any strength of resistance.

"My God…"

Many moments passed by slowly as they sat on the cold floor of the cell in silence, with the captain's arms holding the younger woman's small body tightly. Finally, a look of defiant determination crossed Sharon's face.

"We're going to get out of here," the older woman said firmly. "Both of us."

Alicia shook her head fearfully as she pulled away from her cell mate and drew her legs up to her chest like an infant in a dark room. "You can't," she pleaded, trying to spare her new friend the torture of punishment. "He will be here for you at any moment."

"How do you know that?" the proud battleship captain asked, her brow creased.

The heavy tear-stained lashes which shadowed Alicia's cheeks flew up in surprise. "Because I know," she replied flatly, as if that was enough explanation.

Sharon searched Alicia's face and saw the roots of the fragile instability which was growing inside the weakened young woman. "He will get no information from me," she said firmly, a look of defiance in her eyes. Then the captain's anger waned, as she gently smoothed Alicia's fair hair again, hoping to soothe her.

"Don't you understand yet?" Alicia said as she brushed a lock of her disheveled hair out of her red rimmed eyes. "He wants no military information from you...he would have already gotten that from your ship or crew."

"Why would he keep me alive?" Sharon asked, not understanding.

Her eyes widened as she looked at her young cell mate again and suddenly understood her peril. To this Imperial conqueror she wasn't an enemy captain to be traded as a prisoner or bartered with, she was merely another toy to break and display as a symbol of his might.

"He won't get what he wants from me," she finally declared.

"There is no way to resist. If your will is strong enough, he'll just keep at it and at it with his psionic powers until he breaks your spirit." She glanced down between her raised knees. "I know, I tried at first..."

"I see," Sharon said quietly. Then she perked up, determined to make a fight of it, despite Alicia's warnings. "Well, he may indeed have powers...but if he wants to break my spirit he'll have to do it over my dead body."

"No," Alicia whispered, as tears somehow found their way back to her strained eyes again, "...he won't."

~ * ~

Overlord Tanus Adalric stormed down the long hallways of his dreadnought, a great intensity in his stride. Anger fumed through him as he cursed in low tones, causing any who were in the hallway to quickly scurry out of the way. Above all else, he loathed defiance. Anyone who *dared* to defy him would surely feel his wrath, no matter who that person was.

He rounded the corner and walked past the guards who diligently stood at his door. Entering his luxurious cabin, he crossed directly over to the communications panel and activated it. The holographic viewer sputtered for a moment, then settled down into an image of the ship's infirmary.

"Well, Doctor?" the overlord asked, his voice laced with anger.

The *Demoness'* chief medical officer felt beads of perspiration form on his brow and top of head, where there hadn't been hair for almost a quarter of a century. He nervously picked up a medical chart, which wasn't easy with his hands shaking, then placed it back down on his cluttered desk. "I'm afraid she didn't make it, my Lord. The cerebral damage to her brain was too extensive." The doctor let out a slow breath and waited for the axe to fall.

Adalric's vision clouded with fury. *How dare she die.* Then he redirected his anger to another source, one he could still affect. "I blame this incompetence on you, Doctor. You can't even fix some simple neurological damage?"

"The d-damage was quite severe, m-my Lord," the doctor quickly replied, his voice stammering from fear. "You caused her body functions to go into a deep shock, she didn't have a chance."

"No, Doctor," Adalric replied sharply, his face emotionless behind his half mask. "It is *you* who have failed me. I advise you to start packing. Your position and career in the Imperium are over. Consider yourself lucky I'm not coming down there to deal with you myself, but it would be in your best interest if I never saw you again."

Before the doctor could even begin to plead for leniency, he was cut off with a gesture from Adalric's tight crimson glove.

For a moment the Imperial overlord stood in silence, contemplating his next move, searching his mind for a new target to vent his rage upon. His powerfully muscled fingers rapped on his smooth black desk, echoing in the grand room like droplets of rain on a window. Then he left his quarters again, and headed back toward his private prison level, his thoughts swirling like an angry blight.

She somehow warned her, told her how to fight back...fine, then she'll pay for this defiance.

Overlord Adalric's black and crimson cloak flowed behind him as he strode down to the detention levels, his lips a straight line of determination. As he approached the cell door, one of his elite grey armored personal guards approached and waited for permission to speak.

"What is it, Shadowguard?" the overlord asked as he watched Alicia cower from the sight of him, to end up in the far corner of the room.

It was this reaction to his presence which gave him his first smile of pleasure since the death of Captain Sharon Mitchell.

"It's the chief medical officer," the Shadowguard reported. "He seems to have abandoned his post, should we find him?"

Adalric shook his head, his eyes never leaving Alicia's shivering form. "He has resigned with dishonor from the service, make sure the records reflect that appropriately and get me a new CMO immediately." He smiled cruelly at the young woman. "I may need one soon."

"At once, my Lord," the personal guard answered, careful to conceal his surprise.

The energy force field across the door opening faltered, as Adalric walked through to end up standing over the small and frail young woman.

"Why are you back so soon?" Alicia asked, anguished at yet another loss she would have to face. "You killed her, didn't you...*you monster.*"

Feeling her remorse and anger erupt, she lunged at the hateful figure, merely to be knocked back effortlessly with the simplest of gestures. She sat on the floor, dazed, then a long-forgotten sparkle shimmered in her bloodshot eyes, and they flashed a luminous indigo for the briefest of moments.

"Do not destroy yourself also, my young one," Adalric warned her, his powerful voice droning.

"No," Alicia said, a sudden wry smile coming over her tear-stained face, "it's *you* who will destroy yourself. I have seen it in my visions, Overlord Tanus Adalric. The end of your life as you know it, has come knocking at your door, but it will be *you* who lets it in."

She began giggling uncontrollably, which turned into a maniacal cackle, as tears flushed uncontrollably down her cheeks. Sucking in her breath, she tried unsuccessfully to regain her composure. Wildly, boldly, she stood and straightened herself before him, her face streaked with vengeance yet to be tasted. "You will let in your own doom, Adalric. May it take you straight to *hell.*"

The Imperial overlord gracefully unsheathed his favored weapon, his electrosword, and ignited it with his sheer will. Then he ended her taunting laughter with one swift stroke of the sparkling multicolored blade of lethal energy. For a moment, he glared down at her in disgust, his eyes filled with impassioned fury.

"I'm sure she was simply crazy, my Lord," his personal guard tried, hoping to pacify his master's wrath.

"No," Adalric said, his fury melting away, as he deactivated his weapon and sheathed it, speaking more to himself than his guard. "I have foreseen something similar but have dismissed it…until now. This girl was the daughter of an Imperial baron, the child of a TelSor elder and a TelSor hopeful herself, and her words should not be taken lightly." He turned his back on her smoking body and faced his personal guard, his clenched fists betraying his concern. "I too have foreseen the coming of someone with special abilities…someone who will try to take my life from me. She must have seen the same thing, and she has never been wrong before. Her visions were the one reason I let her live this long." Taking a deep breath, he quickly made his decision. "Shadowguard, inform the bridge I wish to send out this decree. From now on, any one with overt mutant or psionic abilities, except for the members of the Baronies and the Dire Queen, are to be declared renegades…and put to death as enemies of the Imperium."

"Mutants and psionics, my Lord?" his personal Shadowguard questioned. "But they are so few and far between, hardly a threat to anyone…" His voice trailed off as he felt the darkness within his master overcoming him. "It will be as you wish, my Lord," he quickly blurted, then pivoted on his heels and left the room.

Adalric watched the young man leave, a look of disgust forming on his lips. *That fool,* he thought as he gazed back down upon Alicia's expired form, *he doesn't believe me. But I will find the source of your prophecy, girl…and whoever it is, will wish he had it as easy as you did.*

Chapter Eleven
Darkkrieg Legionnaire

Blaze's eyes narrowed as she circled her adversary carefully. She knew she could easily use her pyrokinetic powers to fry the bastard, but that would give her away, and she had no desire for her superiors to know of her special ability. Besides, she enjoyed feeling her secret gave her an upper hand.

Suddenly her foe struck out with his weapon, a fiery blue laser-staff. Blaze moved to counter with her own luminescent red one, but didn't make it in time, and was struck on the left leg.

Damn this armor, she cursed silently as she felt the heat of the weapon searing into the protective material around her leg. *It makes you move so damn slow,* she fumed, then calmed as she reminded herself a similar blow to an unarmored person would have left her missing a leg.

Down, but not out, she rolled with the blow which knocked her to her knees and came up again, ready to fight. But her adversary would give her no rest. He tried to take advantage of his last hit and lunged forward again, using his laser-staff as a spear. However, that was precisely what Blaze guessed he would do. She repelled the blow easily, countering with a side swipe that burned through her foe's armor and fried his heart…that is, it would have if this weren't a practice session, and these were real laser-staffs.

"Well done, Legionnaire Blaze," her instructor said.

He clapped his hands together, signaling the trainees should come to attention.

When they were all lined up, row after row of alabaster white armored soldiers, the instructor turned to face them.

"You have all done excellently, recruits," he said to them. "For the last four weeks you have mastered the art of being the perfect soldier. You know discipline, strategy, and weapons skills with both the electro carbine and hand to hand. You are all now ready to replace your recruit armor with the full black battle suit of a *Darkkrieg Legionnaire*. May you all serve the glory of the Imperium to your fullest...*conquest or death.*"

"*Conquest or death,*" they all shouted in unison. "*Conquest or death.*"

The instructor held up his hand for silence, then smiled at them all. "Imperial Darkkrieg Legionnaires...dismissed."

Blaze felt a rush flow through her like none she ever felt before. She succeeded, and it hadn't been easy, especially with the instructor coming down extra hard on her for being too short. It quickly became common knowledge that Blaze was admitted into the service through a technicality called an "Admiral's Appointment", which countermanded the height requirements. The instructor, along with the other recruits, kept calling her "admiral's pet" and other similar, though sometimes less polite names. She forced herself to ignore the taunts, an ability she didn't know she had inside her. Instead, the young woman directed her anger outward by excelling in all the instructor would teach. She became the top of her class, and the only one to graduate as a Legionnaire First Class, a rank that placed her above her fellow recruits in basic training. *Yes*, she thought with a happy sigh, *I've made it.*

"You were quite impressive," said a familiar voice from behind her.

Blaze whirled to find herself facing Admiral Steward, his face alight with pride. "Joshua," she said as she grinned, "I'm so glad you came."

Ever since he found her outside the recruitment center, Joshua, and his family had grown close to her. He was the source of her "Admiral's Appointment", and he had taken her under his wing and watched over her.

"I never miss the recruit's last 'battle' which is staged between the two best Legionnaires right before graduation," he stated firmly, trying to convince her his reasons for being here were purely professional. "This is the time to see if there are any good ones to snatch up before anyone else does."

Her eyes flashed at him. "Did you see anything you liked?"

"Couldn't tell," he said with a laugh, "you all look the same in that armor." His laughter was interrupted by the instructor calling all the recruits back to attention, an occurrence that rarely happened after dismissal.

"Later," Blaze said as she winked quickly at him and ran off, back into formation with the rest of the newly graduated recruits. Joshua watched with admiration as the squad was efficiently brought to attention.

"Legionnaires," the drill instructor called, "I have two things to report. First, a decree has been issued from the high overlord, Tanus Adalric. This decree states that anyone with mutant abilities, or unauthorized psionic powers, is hereby declared renegade and is to be put to death. All of you as Legionnaires should be on the constant lookout for anyone who displays such abilities and report them to your commanding officer immediately."

Damn, Blaze cursed silently, *it's a good thing I kept my flames to myself.*

"On a greater note," the instructor continued, "the Imperial fleet has won its first major battle against the Romusian Empire, resulting in the destruction of the Romusian's flag ship."

A deafening cheer rose up from the Legionnaires and the civilians who came to be at graduation.

"Long live the Imperium," he said, raising his voice above the din. "Dismissed."

Blaze sank into her own thoughts, wondering what Overlord Adalric's problem with mutants was, or those with psionic powers. *Such people could aid the Imperium, not hurt it.* However, it seemed such powers were restricted to the barons. *But then again,* she reconsidered, *if everyone had such powers then chaos would reign, and the order I have grown to love would fall to ruin. I'll simply have to be extra careful from now on.*

"Hey," came from Joshua, "you awake?"

Blaze snapped out of her thoughts to turn and smile at him. "Sure, I'm thrilled about our victory over the Romusians. I'm sure it won't be long before we defeat the Camillians too."

"And finally, the Alliance," the admiral added firmly. "I have some good news for you as well. I have your posting here." He held up a small computer disk tauntingly.

Her eyes widened as she licked her lips in anticipation. "Am I being assigned to the *Sentinel*, the Nyx orbital Star-Citadel? Under your command?"

"No," he said quickly and flatly. He watched with a placid expression as the corners of Blaze's lips began to fall into a pouty frown, then winked at her. "You would honestly be bored to exasperation on my Star-Citadel."

"Then where?"

A broad proud smile grew on Joshua's face, as he slowly dangled the words in front of her. "The *Demoness*."

Blaze's mouth parted in shock. "The *flagship? Are* you sure?"

"Would I kid an armored woman with an electro carbine?"

"*Yeah,*" she yelled with delight. This was beyond any hopes she had. To serve with the overlord himself, what an honor. "You have done so much for me," she said warmly. "Thank you."

"You deserved it, Legionnaire First Class. I knew I wasn't making a mistake when I decided to help you out."

She straightened to attention. "Thank you, Admiral." She paused, widening her eyes gleefully at the man who almost had seemed to have adopted her as a wayward daughter. "Now take me out to dinner," she commanded mockingly.

"Yes, ma'am," he replied with a teasing edge biting into his warm smile.

They both laughed as Joshua put his arm on her shoulder and they left the commencement field.

~ * ~

In orbit above that small field, and several hours later, Overlord Tanus Adalric strode across the grand control center of the Star-Citadel *Sentinel*, high above Nyx. His mind was racing since the moment he arrived at this base for its usual Imperial inspection. *The prophecy*, he thought, *I must prevent this accursed prophecy.* He came up to the commanding admiral of the Star-Citadel and scowled at him from under his crimson hood which overshadowed his mask.

"Any more news, Admiral Steward?"

Joshua Steward looked at the overlord with a mixed sense of confusion and fear, snapping out of his reflections of a fine dinner with his protégée. Something was driving the Dire Queen's right-hand man harder than anything had before, but he wasn't sure what it was. He glanced down at his latest report and nodded. "Yes, my Lord," he quickly responded. "Our Legionnaires have picked up two more mutants on the T-7 colony. They have them in custody now."

"And it has been confirmed they are psionically active?" the overlord asked harshly.

"Yes, my Lord."

"Have them put to death," Adalric ordered flatly, "and keep me apprised of any more news."

Joshua inhaled deeply. "Yes, Overlord." The admiral paused in silence for he loved the Imperium with a passion, but killing loyal citizens for some natural talents they had seemed insane. Not even considering that some entire races had abilities not natural to humans. He wondered if this would lead to total genocide, and how far it would go before the Dire Queen put an end to it.

"Overlord Adalric," called a deck officer, "the Dire Queen demands you report to her chambers immediately."

Adalric nodded, his chin tightening, and left the control center without a word, leaving the room in a much-relieved state.

~ * ~

In the Imperial throne room, the Dire Queen waited for her prize servant to arrive. She stood up and smoothed out the obsidian dress which clung to her figure, then glided over to one of the ghostly, red fire torches that were on either side of the throne dais. She reached up with an ink-black hand that was and wasn't there and passed it through the flames. *Warm as the stars,* she mused, *and cold as space.*

At that moment the large doors parted to reveal the overlord, who strode up to her and went down on one knee, his head lowered.

"Rise," she commanded, her voice barely more than a corpse's whisper. "We need to discuss matters."

"I will find the person of the prophecy, my Queen," he boldly stated, anticipating her concern, "I just need more time and men."

The Dire Queen's fiery red eyes leered from within the complete darkness in her hood as they fixed on the overlord. "You already have more than half of my new fleet out scouring the planets for people with overt powers. And what has it gotten you? Over one hundred dead mutants and psionics, and still you massacre more."

"I will find the right one—"

"*How?*" her voice cut through his, silencing him. "You don't even meet the people you are killing anymore. How will you know when you are successful?"

"I'll know," Adalric said firmly. "There is no other way to explain it. I have the feeling the person is still out there and getting closer. When that feeling is gone, then I will rest."

"You are making yourself *useless* to me, Adalric," she said, her voice hissing with a rampant fury. "I need an overlord who inspires respect and fear, not one people consider to be a maniacal butcher."

"That is not what they think."

"You are obsessed with this, and I am putting a stop to it now. I have a war to wage, a galaxy to conquer. I want you to recall the fleet from your manhunt and send them against our enemies."

"But—"

"That is *my* decree, Adalric." She cut him off again, pointing down at him with a ghostly black finger. "You may keep on searching for this prophecy person of yours if you wish, but you will do it *on* the *Demoness*, while attacking those who stand against us. Do you understand?"

"My Queen—"

"*Do you understand?*"

His head bowed in compliance. "Yes, my Queen."

"Good," she said in a calmer voice. "Then go and conquer for the Imperium, and I'm sure your prophecy person will surface soon enough."

Adalric nodded, then turned from the Queen and left the dark throne room without looking back.

He is getting bolder, the Dire Queen's dark thoughts soured, *too much bolder. I fear the time when he will try to rise above me is coming sooner than I had foreseen.* She glided back to her throne and sat down. *Perhaps this prophecy that has trapped Adalric into obsession can work for me instead. Yes,* her thoughts danced as her guttural laugh filled the room, *I must keep a watchful eye…*

Chapter Twelve
Tenebrous

Blaze gazed absently out the large window of the observation deck on the *Demoness*. It had been over two months since she had been assigned here, and so far, all she had accomplished was getting to hear about the battles which occurred with the flagship. *Being a ground assault Legionnaire in a space battle is like being a hairbrush owned by a Saurian, neither has any use.*

Though I hear we have been doing quite well, she thought with some measure of pride. *This "Cosmic Surge" weapon has been cutting through the Romusian and Camillian forces like a knife through whipped cream. In the last month alone, the Imperium has grown to almost six times its former size. I'm sure it's merely a matter of time before those two former empires surrender, leaving the one real force to contend with in this sector, the United Star Alliance.*

So why am I here brooding, she contemplated silently as she glanced around the darkened, empty deck, then back out the window. *Is it because I'm missing all the action? Is it because I miss Joshua and his family? Or is it because I really hate space travel? No,* she decided, although those things bothered her, none were the immediate source of her unease.

It's the Alliance, she firmly decided, *we're on their borders now, getting ready to make our first ground assault today against the Alliance marine base that was recently set up to ward us off.* She knew that was the crux of her feelings, for the base was on Tenebrous, her hated ex-home. *I can't believe I'm going to set foot on that slime pit again…especially on this of all days.*

Don't worry about it, Blaze, she could almost hear Rabies squeaky voice assuring her, and she smiled. *Gods,* she realized in amazement, *I kinda miss that little rat…oh, sorry, I meant Jarbban.*

Not that she even saw people like Rabies here. In the Imperium, humanoids were scarce, and non-humanoids practically nonexistent. Humans alone were allowed to serve the Dire Queen. Though she heard there was an elite corps of Proximans who served Baron Koroqo, and she heard rumors of a baroness who was a Perusian, but you never knew who to believe here. She even heard the ludicrous rumor that the reason no one saw the Dire Queen, besides Overlord Adalric, was because she was some sort of creature, a demon or something. Now the floating tale was Adalric, and the Dire Queen were lovers.

"Rumors," she said with a short laugh as she shook her head.

She suddenly realized, with some regret, that despite the fact she had been on the flagship *Demoness* for over two months, she had yet to catch a glimpse of the overlord in person. She wrote to Joshua about this, and he wrote back something along the lines of, "You'd be better off if you never met him."

Suddenly, the alert stations sounded, ripping Blaze out of her thoughts and telling her she had to get down to her drop-ship immediately. *So, this is it, I'm going into battle for the first time, and against the Alliance, no less.* The young woman backed up and looked at herself through the darkened eyepieces of her black battle armor. Her reflection in the observation window was distorted and dim, and she had to strain to make out her lines out at all. *That's funny,* she thought with a smile. *You don't look twenty.* She turned and hustled to the omni-lift, readying her electro carbine along the way.

As the wide elevator carried her to her drop-ship, she started to clear her mind, as she had been instructed to do at basic training. *Don't let random thoughts cloud your ability to follow orders cleanly and efficiently,* she could remember her instructor telling her. *When you are in battle, you are the sum of the whole and no longer individual parts.* She shook her head, clearing the last of the visions of basic training, as the omni-lift opened, revealing the hangar bay.

Legionnaires were already lined up, and Blaze had to run to get in place in time as Adalric stepped out of a far door and approached, a ground-assault major at his side.

Blaze was shocked. A few moments ago, she was thinking about him, and now he was here. The young Legionnaire anxiously eyed him as he approached the assembly. Flanked by four of his personal Shadowguards, he marched across the large bay like something more than a soldier. He seemed regal and strong.

How powerful he looks, Blaze thought in awe as the overlord strode in front of them, inspecting each as he moved down the line. *This must be a very important mission if Overlord Adalric is here to inspect us personally.*

For a moment he paused right in front of Blaze, and looked down at her, his firm jaw tight in concentration. His close proximity sent warm nervous rushes throughout her body, and she had to resist the urge to look up at the high noble, who was practically a foot taller than her. He then turned and walked back to the major, a young officer who was obviously anxious to please his master.

"Today is a great day for the Imperium," Adalric addressed the Legionnaires which had been chosen to lead the assault, his deep voice booming through the hangar bay. "It will be remembered as the day of the first major victory against the Alliance marines. They have a base set up on Tenebrous, and you are going to seize it in the name of the Imperium."

Blaze could feel an enormous sense of pride swelling throughout her body as each of his powerful words charismatically flowed through her, caressing her ego. She suddenly knew she would be honored to fight for the Red Star Imperium, to squash its enemies. If that required her to lay down her life…then so be it.

"Do not fail the Imperium," Adalric concluded, "do not fail *me.*"

He turned to the black uniformed officer at his side. "Major, ready your troops for their ground assault. This will be your finest hour."

"Yes, my Lord," he said with a salutary bow of the head, then turned to his soldiers. "All right, Legionnaires, let's show the United Star Alliance what we are made of. Load into the drop-ships."

Blaze quickly turned and followed the Legionnaire in front of her onto the large personnel carriers which would take them down to Tenebrous. Once on board, she went to her drop chair and stowed her weapon safely away, then held on.

"All ready?" came a voice over her helmet's commlink. "Three-two-one-drop."

She felt the world fall out from under her feet as the large ship was dropped from the *Demoness* like a bomb from a fighter. They plunged into the stratosphere as the drop-ship fired its fusion drive and pushed them toward the base.

Why can't they use Cosmic Rift transporters for stuff like this? Blaze wondered as she felt her stomach do flip flops inside her, even though she knew the answer, for it had been taught in basic training. The transportation devices couldn't send more than a few of them at a time, making them sitting ducks. While landing in multiple drop-ships, they sent a ton of them at once and instilled fear in their intended victim. *However*, Blaze wondered, *doesn't it also give the intended target ample time to prepare a suitable defense against the impending assault?*

Before she could answer herself, the major was ordering everyone to get their weapons ready. He started to go over the plans, though it was difficult to hear him over the roar of the ship's engines.

"Alpha and Beta squads will go in first," he informed them, "followed by the last ten squads."

Blaze nodded, honored to be in Beta squadron. She would relish the opportunity to go in first, her carbine avenging all those moments of pain which the Alliance had been responsible for. *This one's for you, Sinclair*, she vowed silently, as she felt the drop-ship land with a bone jarring thud.

"All right, Legionnaires," the major bellowed. "Get up and ready, it's time to destroy!"

The drop-ship's heavy doors clanged open onto the dusky terrain of Tenebrous, the dust clouds that were formed from the landing were still swirling about the large craft, slicing into the warm chamber. The dim orange sun was setting on the bleak horizon with scarlet fingers stretching across the darkening sky. To the left, Blaze could see the crumbled remains of a city much like the one she grew up in, and she briefly wondered if it was the same one. The once great metropolis' half fallen skyscrapers sagged in ruins, like defeated goliaths. Roads which should have been highways, leading to what should have been happy suburbs, lay broken and tattered. Now they only led to a barren desert. To the right, Blaze saw their target. There, amidst the lifeless terrain, was the Alliance base. Modern, clean and sleek, the pearly white walls gleamed in the fading evening light.

"Alpha squad, Beta squad," each of those two squadron sergeants suddenly called, "let's go."

With a shout of battle lust, the fierce Imperial Darkkrieg Legionnaires raced out, their electro carbines roaring as they delivered electric plasma death.

The Alliance wasn't merely ready for the assault, they were *really* ready, with weapons and manpower that the Imperium had not anticipated they could prepare on such short notice.

Blaze glanced around to see the air clouded with multicolored electro-energy bolts, and the sky filled with smoke and flashing lights, as explosion after explosion sounded through the battlefield. The dark sky raged in storm overhead as bodies fell to the right and left of her, bone mixed with melted armor and blood. Ahead, she saw the white and blue armored Alliance marines, letting loose with their semi-automatic electro rifles. Legionnaire after Legionnaire fell before her, their bodies cauterized to a lifeless pulp by the merciless accuracy of those accursed white armored devils. Blaze gritted her teeth in determination. *This* is why she joined in the first place. *This* is why she was here. She pulled her electro carbine up close and began firing as she ran forward, slicing down any Alliance marine who dared to show his face.

Suddenly she felt an intense surge of pain flash through her chest as a spray of red-hot electrified energy bolts fanned across her, burning through her armor and cauterizing her skin. The force of the blow lifted her off her feet, and threw her black to land amongst all the others who had already fallen that day.

For what felt like an eternity, Blaze lay there in stunned pain, waiting to die. However, after what must have been a few moments, she slowly realized her wound was not going to be fatal. In fact, she realized that despite her intense pain, she could get up and continue the fight.

Blaze thought to move to stand up, when suddenly she paused, remaining in the position where the shot threw her. For some reason the shock of her wound drained her of the battle lust Overlord Adalric's words filled her with. Gone was the fury, gone was the feeling of the need for revenge. All that was left was the harsh reality she had almost died, fighting over a planet she cared less for than any other place in the galaxy.

Damn, her thoughts raced as she lay there in what could have hardly been described as a comfortable position. *What would Sinclair say if he saw me like this, cowering on the ground while my squadron fought and died all around me?* Suddenly, she smiled under her helmet, which was half burned from another shot that had almost gone through. *He would tell me to keep down and play dead. He would also probably yell at me for joining up in the first place.*

She paused from her musing and allowed herself to look around the battlefield. The intense center of fighting seemed to have moved further down the base, away from her. Yet she remained in the same position, lest someone from her side notice she was alive also. *Tenebrous hasn't changed all that much,* she decided after trying to see over all the dead bodies without sitting up. *Dreary sky, shouts of pain and anguish in the air, the smell of burning bodies…no, nothing's different at all. Boy, I was lucky to have gotten off…and I actually volunteered to come back down! If I die here, I know I'll end up as a ghost, doomed to haunt Tenebrous for all eternity.* A shudder ran through her as she contemplated that dreadful vision.

Now what was that old Earth saying? She tried to remember what Mattie had taught her as a child. *A coward dies a thousand deaths, a brave man dies but once? Something like that. Well…It isn't cowardice to want to stay alive. I can't believe my one active presence in a battle of this size would make any difference whatsoever. Though I do wonder how we're doing. I hope we win. I can barely hear the shots now, they're so far away.* Her flurry of thoughts drifted off as she decided she had lain still long enough.

Blaze sluggishly sat up and glanced around her, slowly allowing her harsh surroundings to assault her senses. There were bodies all around her, all fellow Legionnaires. She was in a courtyard of some sort, she realized with amazement, shocked she had made it inside the Alliance base. Ten feet to her right she spotted a fallen Imperial officer, but his face was down so she couldn't see who it was. Curiosity getting the better of her, she finally stood and stretched, still feeling a lot of pain from where she had been shot. "It better not leave a scar," she grumbled to herself. She walked over to the officer and knelt over him. "Are you alive?" she asked as she rolled him over. Her words died in her throat as she realized he had no face, nothing but the blackened remains of cauterized flesh from a direct hit to the head.

Something caught her eye on his collar as she glanced down, and she found he was wearing a major's star cluster. *So,* she thought with a sense of irony, *I guess this isn't going to be your finest hour after all.*

She sat down next to her expired ground commander and gazed around her, realizing the sounds of battle were getting closer again. *That isn't good,* she decided. *That means we're getting beaten back. I'll wait…yes wait 'till I see my people again and fall back with them. What a wonderful day this turned out to be,* she thought with a sarcastic laugh. *Well, Blaze…happy birthday to me.*

~ * ~

Although it seemed much longer, it was barely an hour later when Blaze and her five fellow surviving Legionnaires waited under the scrutiny of the Imperial overlord, as they all stood diligently at attention back on the *Demoness.*

"How is it," Adalric asked, his voice full of rage, "that my entire *division* of Legionnaires was destroyed on Tenebrous, but you five survived?"

Who knows? Blaze thought bitterly. *Maybe they played dead, too.*

Adalric whirled on her, as if sparked by her thoughts, and reached out a crimson gloved hand, his finger pointing accusingly. "What is your name, Legionnaire?"

Blaze's mind went blank as she realized the second in command of the entire Imperium was talking directly to her. Finally, she reassembled her thoughts. *I can't sound like a coward to him, of all people.* "My Lord," she said proudly, "I am Legionnaire First Class Blaze,"

"What is your first name?"

"That is my full name."

"I see." He glared intently at her, and decided she wasn't telling him all she could, but dismissed it. Under his cowl, his brow creased in thought, and a grim smile formed on his lips. He turned back to the rest of the survivors and sighed. None of them were above the rank of Legionnaire First Class, and there but one of those. He stared back at Blaze, and realized she would have to be the example.

"Legionnaire First Class," he said, facing Blaze, "as senior ranking survivor, the loss of the battle below is your responsibility. Therefore, you will have to pay the price." He let his words come out slowly to heighten the effect on the other Legionnaires. "And as I'm sure you know…the price for failure in the Imperium is quite high."

Blaze's mouth opened in shock as what he was saying slowly sank in. *He's going to make me the scapegoat for this entire foolhardy mission! If that's the case,* she thought as her level of anger started to rise, *what have I got to lose?* "My Lord," she said as she fought down the desire to let her pyrokinesis flare out, "the mission was idiotic from the start. We should have had intelligence reports to know they outnumbered us three to one." She steadied her breathing, letting her levels of courage rise. "And the slow landing in the drop ships was ridiculous. Why wasn't the base just obliterated from orbit? How can you hold a lowly soldier responsible for *your* mistake?"

Now it was Adalric's turn to feel some shock, as he realized this Legionnaire was telling him how to wage war. "Your job as a Legionnaire," he said, his exposed cheek flushing with anger, "is to follow orders, nothing else." He menacingly drew out his electrosword. "You are hereby charged with cowardice in the face of battle, Legionnaire First Class. You are unfit to wear the uniform of the Imperium and will be summarily executed!" He ignited his weapon and held it high over his head, as the muscles in his arm tensed. He considered using his TelSor powers to eradicate this nuisance but decided it would be more dramatic to the others if he struck her down with his sword *after* he used his other powers to humble her first.

Adalric's free hand formed into a fist which came down hard, as if pulling a great weight.

Blaze suddenly felt an inescapable force pulling her down to her knees, as if some invisible person was there, using all his strength. Once on her knees she looked up at the man she had grown to admire, who represented the Imperium to her. Deep down she understood the need for an example to be made, but she'd be damned if it was going to be her. She had fought to keep her pyrokinesis in check, out of fear of the decree, but now she knew she had no choice. For the first time in what seemed a long while, she let the power build up in her as she began to focus her attention on the overlord.

~ * ~

Adalric's sword hand trembled in rage as he prepared to carry out his sentence, but then he hesitated. From inside the Legionnaire, a massive amount of psionic energy was building up, he could feel it in every fiber of his body. *Could this lowly Legionnaire possibly be a mutant or psionic?* His fury was instantly replaced by curiosity and suspicion. *I must find out before she is killed...for all I know, she could be the one I have been searching for.*

Slowly he lowered his arm and deactivated the sword. "Perhaps, I have been too harsh in my swift condemnation of your actions."

Blaze was about to let it go in a fiery blast, when the overlord's kind words sliced into her, confusing and draining her of her ability to flame out. She gazed up at him and suddenly realized she was trembling. "I...I don't understand."

Adalric reached out a powerful hand and offered it to her, which she slowly accepted. She felt a chill run down her back as he gently but firmly lifted her up to a standing position.

"I simply realized I should be proud of my survivors, not angry," he said, his lips twisting into a half smile. "And your suggestions were quite intelligent, Legionnaire First Class Blaze."

"They were?" she asked, astounded by this change of heart in the overlord.

"Yes," he replied, his deep voice soothing her spirit. "In fact, I am going to promote you. You are now no longer a Legionnaire...you are now one of my personal *Shadowguards.*"

~ * ~

A Shadowguard? Blaze's mind spun. *They were the elite who guarded the barons and baronesses...and he wants me to be one of* his *personal guards.* Suddenly her mind clouded with suspicion and her visions of grandeur dropped out of cloud nine, as a chill ran over her body. *He knows,* she suddenly realized. *Somehow, he sensed my abilities...what I was about to do. But then why not kill me? Perhaps he isn't sure, and that's why he wants me by his side. I'll have to be extra careful from now on, since they say he knows everything that happens around him.* "Thank you, my Lord," she finally said. "I am quite honored."

Adalric nodded thoughtfully as he turned to his guard that waited behind him. "Take this new Shadowguard to the armory and properly outfit her, then bring her to me in my chambers."

His two Shadowguards nodded, then walked over to her and grabbed her arms as the overlord turned from the stunned crowd and strode out, his mind cluttered with what was to come.

Chapter Thirteen
Aftermath

Blaze walked along silently behind the overlord, astonished at still being alive, her thoughts in turmoil. With mixed feelings of apprehension and terror, she contemplated the tenuous hold on life her situation had put her in, as she let herself wonder where she was being led.

Adalric's strides thrummed with sharp clarity, the anger steaming from him like waves of heat off a burning branch.

What's he going to do? she silently debated as she struggled to keep up with his long steps. *We were on our way to the armory, to change my armor, when he suddenly ordered his guards to bring me along with him while he dealt with Tenebrous. Is he going to send down more troops? I hope he doesn't want to send me down again.*

Her thoughts were cut short as they entered the large bridge. She drew in a sharp breath as she gazed at the grand splendor of the multi-level control center of the flagship. In all her time on this ship so far, she had never been here. *But why now?* Blaze knew she was supposed to be trained as a Shadowguard, but for the moment she wasn't one yet. She still wore the black of the Legionnaires, still marred by the searing damage done to her on the planet's surface at the hands of the Alliance, and she was still in pain. Dressed as she was, she wondered if the bridge was the best place for her to be at this time.

As if on cue to her thoughts, Adalric turned to her and gestured toward the large windows and the viewscreen. "I thought you should see this before my Shadowguards have you outfitted and tended to by the medics."

Blaze gazed up at the huge viewer to find they were still in orbit around Tenebrous. The greyish-brown image of her birthplace hung on the screen like a cancerous boil in space.

"What are you going to do about that?" she asked through a voice laced with caution and fear.

She wondered if he brought her here to remind her of her failure on the planet's surface, which resulted in the Imperium's first loss since the new offensive began.

A strange smile came to Adalric's lips as he gestured with his gloved hand toward his main gunners. "I truly despise losing, Shadowguard Blaze. So therefore, I never do." He then turned to his captain. "Are weapons prepared, Captain?"

Blaze glanced up to see a tall, thin man with wavy red hair come forward, his Imperial uniform pressed and shiny. "All ready, my Lord," he dutifully replied.

The smile on Adalric's face seemed to turn into a grimace of malice and revenge as he signaled the main gunner. "Fire the Cosmic Surge weapon, Captain Harris."

Blaze felt a chill run down her spine at his words, as her eyes widened in nervous anticipation. She heard mixed reports on what the Imperial "super weapon" was and wondered if the Cosmic Surge was a space to surface bomb to attack the marine base with.

"Hardly," Adalric said as if in answer to her thoughts. "Prepare to witness the full power of the Imperium."

At first, Blaze thought there was something wrong with the ship, as a slow rumbling started to vibrate the decks. She glanced quickly around to see if anyone else was in a state of alert, but everyone on the bridge was calmly attending their stations. Suddenly, the vibrations turned into an actual shuddering that rocked the ship as waves upon waves of energy were channeled through its superstructure.

Blaze stood in sheer awe as she watched the *Demoness* expel the built-up energy in one charge which caused the mammoth dreadnought to lurch from the kinetic energies that were released.

The screen lit up as a fantastically bright pulse of blue hot energy lanced out toward Tenebrous and disappeared into its clouds. Blaze suddenly felt tightening in her chest that reminded her she had forgotten to breathe.

For an instant all seemed calm on the screen, as it should have been, then a low light began to glow under Tenebrous' thick cloud layer, a glow which slowly flared back up again as the planet she once called home transformed itself into a flaming ball of red-hot destruction.

For a long moment she found she couldn't speak. Slowly, the words came out, almost inaudibly, as if in shock. "What did it do?"

"Destroyed it," the overlord replied simply, obviously proud of himself.

Blaze turned her eyes back up to the screen, to the ball of molten primeval lava that once was her birth planet. And now it was destroyed. *How could one ship possess such destructive energy? It simply isn't possible.* "I don't understand," she managed to whisper, "but I want to."

"The *Cosmic Surge*," Adalric said proudly, "is charged by the very Cosmic Nodules which power our ship's stardrive, but never has such devastating power been put directly into a weapon like this before. The stellar energy sinks into a planet and ignites its core, tuning the world back into the molten ball of magma it was at its birth." He allowed himself a grim laugh. "Perhaps Tenebrous will be habitable again…in a few billion years. No force in the universe will be able to withstand the Imperium now."

Blaze's mind continued to be clouded with shock and numb amazement as she watched the one place she called home melt away into oblivion. She knew of the power of the mysterious Cosmic Nodules as much as anyone did, those mystifying energy deposits in space which had been the only source of power strong enough to breach subspace and allow interstellar engines to work. But as a weapon? Never had such a thing been dared, not enough was known about the Nodules, they were too unstable. Finally, she managed to coalesce her thoughts into a question which suddenly seemed pertinent. "What would happen if you fired that against a ship?"

"You will see," Adalric promised, "you will most certainly see."

~ * ~

Overlord Tanus Adalric was true to his word, relishing in the sights he allowed Blaze to witness as one week melted into the next. What she saw boggled her mind to recall it all. Battle after battle as the Imperial fleet bore its way into the Alliance.

It was two weeks after the destruction of Tenebrous, when she first saw the Cosmic Surge used against a ship. Despite what occurred in the colony world, she once again was in awe of the power the Imperium possessed. It happened when the *Demoness* engaged the *Constellation*, an Alliance dreadnought. For an instant the *Constellation* glowed a fierce blue, and when the glow was gone, so was the ship, leaving nothing but the stars.

It was at that time she learned the weapon's drawback. It required a massive amount of energy to fire, momentarily diverting the power of the Cosmic Nodules to the weapon. This rendered the ship virtually powerless afterward for a few minutes, but as long as the rest of the fleet was there to protect it, it wouldn't matter.

Weeks turned into months as the power of the Imperium continued to spread in all directions, which left Blaze with a feeling of euphoria she never could imagine ending.

There were times late at night, however, when alone in her cabin, it was not so grand. Laying in the darkness, the explosions would play back in her mind, and she felt she could almost hear the anguished cries of the many massacred crews of the ships which were destroyed in similar fashions, without even a chance to fight back. She would find herself wondering if it was right to wield such power, and she even questioned the toll it was taking on her humanity. At times, Sinclair's haunting last words would stay with her as she tried to rest. She'd play them over and over in her head which made her, more than once, question what "evil" truly was. However, she would always answer those sleepless nights with the firm conviction that what was good for the Imperium was good for her also. She had to believe that, or it would all seem too overwhelming to comprehend. Indeed, she even convinced herself that perhaps she wasn't hearing anguished cries at all, but merely her call to glory. Though, if that was true, then why couldn't she get those damn reoccurring visions of a burning Tenebrous out of her head?

Chapter Fourteen
Shadowguard

"Angel? Angel, wake up."

Blaze felt a firm hand gently tug at her shoulder, but it was the rhythmic metallic pounding which shook her into awareness.

"Come on, Angel. Get with it."

Blaze felt the blood in her face drain as she blinked the shadowed image clear. "Sinclair?" she whispered.

Despite the darkness, she could make out his familiar features. He knelt beside her, anxiously crouching near. As the pounding grew louder, he shifted his head from side to side, as if searching through the dark.

"Sinclair?" she asked again, this time reaching her hand to his cheek and gently pushing it, so he faced her. For a moment she shrunk back, his skin was cool and moist under her touch, but then she realized it was raining.

Holding his gaze, she let her eyes caress his features, settling lastly on the vibrant varied hues of his blue eyes, which remained as she remembered them. "You're dead, Sinclair," she said, trying to keep her voice calm.

The boyish playfulness she knew so well jumped onto his face as he flashed a smile. "Didn't anyone ever tell you it takes a silver bullet to kill a werewolf?" He didn't give her time to answer as the joy in his voice faded quickly, replaced by dreadful concern. "We have to get going, we don't have time," he insisted as he slipped his cold hand into hers, and pulled both of them to their feet.

As she rose, Blaze was able to see further into the darkness which surrounded her. *An alley,* she thought as she brushed some wet newspapers off her jeans, *I fell asleep in an alley?* She shook her head, trying to clear the heaviness which weighed down her thoughts. "What am I doing here?" she whispered while squinting to pierce the blackness.

"Angel," Sinclair said as he faced her sternly, his face streaked with fallen rain, "there's no time for questions." He grabbed her by the shoulders, as if to shake her. "Listen…don't you hear that?"

Like a ritual chant, the clanging echo penetrated Blaze's ears with a deeper, frightening meaning. "What are you doing here, Sinclair?"

"I'm here to help you get out, before you're in too deep," he said, while stroking Blaze's damp hair away from her eyes. "The packs are coming."

"I can handle them," she replied confidently.

"Not this time."

Sinclair pulled her by the hand, trying to escape the incessant noise which seemed to surround them. The louder the sound became, the faster they moved through the deadened darkness, turning and twisting down desolate alleys littered with trash. Blaze saw nothing besides a blur of indistinct images and unclear memories. She felt nothing, but Sinclair's cool hand tightly grasped in hers, and the pounding of her feet against the harsh pavement.

The metallic chant penetrated Blaze's skull deeper with each beat. The sound became that of a hammer striking, repeatedly. Each blow felt like it was hitting between Blaze's eyes. At each push of the echoing pain, she squeezed Sinclair's hand tighter as they kept on running. But, at every turn, it seemed inescapable.

"Where is it coming from?" Blaze screamed into the rain. She felt weakened by the pain which drilled its way into her mind, allowing a terrible cold to come over her. Stumbling, she tripped into Sinclair's arms and clung to his chest, as he stopped to support her. Wrapped in his strong embrace, he felt like the Sinclair she always knew, but different somehow. It was then she realized it was his scent, like moldy bread. But she didn't care…it was the pain which mattered.

"Sshh," he whispered into her ear. "I'm trying to find us a way out of here." The clanging echoed teasingly around them from all angles.

"I'll fry them," Blaze managed to say through her tightened lips, trying to fight down the pain, but the agony which coursed through her nerves was worse than anything she'd ever felt. She had heard the term *migraine* before, but never imagined what one felt like, until now.

"No, Angel, that's what *they* want. It's how they'll find you."

Blaze held him tightly with each beat, while trying desperately to regain her strength, and suddenly it abruptly stopped; the clanging, the pain, both gone. She pulled away from Sinclair, feeling lighter and stronger now. No longer did the city echo. The rain dwindled, leaving a misty drizzle. Straining, she listened and heard the rustle of approaching footsteps. The anger in her built as shadows began to take on human form.

Alliance Security in sky blue uniforms, doctors in pastel lab coats, and Alliance soldiers in stark white and blue surrounded them and eyed her hungrily, dangerously. As each face became familiar, a spark of pain returned to Blaze's tormented body until at last, the pain was replaced by rage. Hot blood sped through her veins as the heat within her started to rise.

"No!" Sinclair yelled as he desperately reached for her, the chill of his touch quenching her inner flame. Shaking her violently, his voice pleaded with her. "That's what they *want* you to do." Forcing her back to her feet, he dragged Blaze down an alleyway which was not there before, the crowd dissipating like ghosts in the confusion. "This way, Angel." Again, the rhythm stalked them, first low and distant, then more persistently.

As if to shut out the sound, Blaze clamped her eyes closed and continued to let Sinclair guide her. She heard the hiss of steam from the wet pavement as her body cooled down. Slowly opening her eyes again, she saw the familiar dilapidated coffee house which stood near the sewer entrance to her underground home. "Sinclair, come with me," she said as she desperately tried to tug on his hand, but instead slipped out of his grasp as his fingers became insubstantial. She began running toward the concealed entrance, blindly reaching for something familiar, something safe, barely hearing Sinclair's fading protests. She made for the door but was halted abruptly as she collided with a large, solid force. The bright red of the crimson uniform blinded her momentarily.

High Overlord Tanus Adalric towered over her, the corners of his mouth twisting into a satisfied grin as if a long wait was finally over. Blaze fell back a step, the quick pounding of her heart now filling her ears like the taunting metal chant had before. His powerful fingers dug deeply into her shoulders, communicating tension and urgency which made her quiver in his grasp. She looked up into his face, and saw her own eyes—glowing fiery red—reflected back at her in the darkened eyepieces of his cold mask...she screamed.

~ * ~

Blaze fell off her bed with a hard thud, shattering the dream. Entangled in her white sheets, she had to scramble to regain her composure, finally managing to get off the floor. Nervously, she glanced around the small room with its four grey walls and relaxed when she realized she was still in her cabin. Her desk clock blinked the time at her, revealing she did not have to be on duty for several more hours. Deciding she did not feel like trying to go back to sleep, she opted for a shower instead.

Blaze was decidedly grateful her promotion gave her the privacy of her own cabin. True, it was a small cabin, barely large enough for a single bed, a tiny desk, and a chair. But the room was clean, comfortable, and her own. Since Shadowguards were approximately equivalent in privilege as junior officers, her cabin also contained a private toilet, sink and shower.

She let her sheets fall onto the steel grey carpet and headed straight for the shower, the images of her dream already falling into forgetfulness.

After her quick cleansing, she dressed in her usual uniform of dark grey battle armor, holster and weapon. Before leaving the room, she picked up an electronic letter to Joshua from her desk and scolded herself for not sending it sooner. Pausing to memorize the positions of her few possessions, as she always did before leaving her quarters, she then locked her door behind her and started toward the mess hall.

It amused her the way regular Legionnaires would watch her as she strode down the halls, especially freshly recruited troopers. To them, she was something special and perhaps even mysterious. Being a Shadowguard, she decided, was a lot like being special security in the Alliance navy. Not an officer but not a grunt, Shadowguards walked a line between the two. Plus, there weren't many of them aboard the *Demoness*.

Blaze was famished by the time she arrived at the mess hall. She spied two other Shadowguards, and recognized the names imprinted on their chests. She even called a quick greeting to them as she passed, even though she knew they would ignore her anyway. For some reason, she was having a hard time making friends. She knew the Legionnaires would be wary of her and that the officers looked upon her with disdain, but she did not understand the cold attitude of the other Shadowguards. She tried to convince herself that maybe it was part of some sort of initiation, but something deep in her heart told her they were probably jealous. Adalric practically always requested her as an escort instead of some of the others, a position of honor amongst the Shadowguards. She mused that it was hard always being by his side, but she knew she secretly loved it.

Making her way through the food line, Blaze grabbed a tray-full and had it all put into a paper bag. As a Shadowguard, she was entitled to one meal per day in the officer's dining hall, which she enjoyed for the higher quality, but she also noticed the quantity was far less than in the crew's mess hall.

Living in the ruins of a desolated city makes one appreciate the presence of food, since it was rare to get three balanced meals per week, let alone per day. Blaze spent most of her childhood eating half-rotted vegetables and freshly killed rats, while still being left hungry. So, she had no trouble with the normal Legionnaires' fare, which was gourmet in comparison. As long as she could get plenty of it, she was happy.

However, what she did not enjoy was eating alone in the mess hall, so lately she had been bringing her meals either back to her room or to the observation deck. She did not mind eating alone in the officer's dining hall as much as the crew mess hall, because the tables were arranged more privately, and she usually did not get as many stares. Today she wanted to eat breakfast under a cascade of starlight, so she strode to the observation deck, walking quickly as hunger motivated her.

Once finished with her meal, Blaze stood in front of the huge windows on the *Demoness'* observation deck for a moment, admiring herself in the shimmering reflection. How long ago was it since she traded in her black battle armor for the dark grey of the Shadowguards? Half a year? More? So much happened in such a short amount of time. How wrong she had been about her suspicions of why Adalric chose her. Never had he accused her of anything, and she was with him practically all day long, every day. She got a break when he was asleep, and his other Shadowguards relieved her to guard his door.

Although she found space travel to be boring, seeing it all from the overlord's side was another matter altogether. She was always there when Adalric made important decisions and led the *Demoness* and his fleet into battle. Looking back, she was sure if someone told her a year ago this was where she'd be, she would have laughed.

She had even been there to witness one of the rare occasions when someone dared to defy the overlord. His name was Captain Fallen, former commander of the Imperial battleship *Dragon*. She had stood dutifully by Adalric's side as he crushed the defiant captain with a single thought, and watched in awe as the Legionnaires dragged the captain's lifeless form off the bridge. She had, then and there, quickly decided it would be wise to be even more careful around her master.

Not that she let down her guard around him before. In fact, she was always diligent, watching her thoughts and actions whenever in the overlord's presence. From then on, though, she governed her thoughts like a hawk, coalescing them into a "mental shield" of concentration, concealing her inner abilities.

She realized her feelings about the Imperium, and especially the overlord, at times seemed confused and erratic. She could be frightened at one moment, fearful for her own life and marking time until Adalric discovered her prohibited talents. But she also savored the status of being one of his personal guards. She was like an extension of him, his eyes and ears when he was not available. She even spoke with his voice, carrying his commands to different parts of the ship at times.

All power has its price, she reminded herself. She read that statement somewhere and always liked the sound of it. She even wondered what price Overlord Adalric paid for his much greater power, it had to be steep.

Despite the many exciting times Blaze experienced over the last half year, she valued these times the most when she had a few moments to herself. It was a chance to let her mind wander free, without the worry of him always watching her.

She let her thoughts slip back into the present time as she removed her helmet again and gazed at her face, wondering if she would get some time off, now that the *Demoness* was finally on its way back to Nyx. *After all,* she thought with pride, *we have crippled the Romusian and Camillian*

Empires, and over a quarter of the United Star Alliance is now ours as well. There's no one that can stop our taking this sector of the galaxy. It's only a matter of time before the Alliance falls like the others. Next, we will expand into the outer sectors, to the distant empires which lay there. However, we do deserve a break, and I deserve a vacation. She laughed silently. *It's hard serving the overlord all the time, guarding his back against possible subversion. Not that he can't protect himself, it's almost like we Shadowguards are simply ceremonial. Sometimes I feel more like his personal valet than his personal guard...perhaps in Overlord Adalric's case, they're the same thing.*

Her thoughts were interrupted as a voice came over the loudspeaker. "All hands to duty stations, we have reached the rendezvous point with the *Wraith*."

Blaze felt a surge of excitement running through her body. *The* Wraith, *that's the* Demoness' *new sister ship, which was completed and commissioned a few weeks ago.* It was coming to replace the *Demoness* at the front lines so the flagship could return and report to the Dire Queen of their progress. But that wasn't the source of her excitement, for what she hoped was that the rendezvous of the two super-dreadnoughts would give Blaze her first glimpse of another Imperial baron, as only ships of such colossal size were privileged to carry a person of such importance.

The young Shadowguard gazed at herself in the window's reflection one last time, as brief fleeting visions of a still burning Tenebrous suddenly flashed across the deep recesses of her memory. For a moment she allowed the old shadows to haunt her as she breathed in sharply, forcing the memories down to focus on the stars once again. "This is your home now," she said confidently as she put her grey helmet back on and picked up her electro carbine. Then she rushed out of the observation deck, knowing the overlord would surely expect her to be by his side when the two ships met. As Blaze entered the omni-lift that would take her to the desired deck, she pushed the last of the dark visions out of her head, and silently vowed she would never allow herself to think of Tenebrous ever again.

~ * ~

Lord Tanus Adalric lay on his huge bed, feeling the steady rhythmic pulse of the *Demoness'* engines gently vibrate though his body. *Six months*, he thought with irritation, *six months and I've learned nothing about any abilities she has.* Running a pensive hand across his smooth chin, he angrily sat up and slung his legs over the side of his huge bed, his mind racing with unsolved enigmas. The plush black carpet sank under his weight as he strode out of his bedroom and to his desk in his adjacent office. The computer glared at him with the most recently accessed file still glimmering on the screen. A shadow of annoyance crossed his face as the computer seemed to taunt him with the information that was etched in light on its silver screen. He had called up this particular personnel file many times over the past half year and had never ceased to be appalled by its lack of helpfulness.

In fact, it was probably the sloppiest, most inefficient file he ever saw. Many lines were left blank, and the photo-images were blurred practically beyond recognition. It merely had the name, "Blaze", height, and the date of birth which seemed to be completed. Except for some basic training grades and the bold lettering "ADMIRAL'S APPOINTMENT - Rear Admiral Joshua Steward", it was a worthless source of information. The admiral's appointment did strike his curiosity every time he reread the report. He decided he would have to speak with Admiral Steward and find out his motivations for using a privilege that was usually reserved for appointing cadets into officer's training classes.

Adalric clamped his hands behind his head and leaned back into his leather chair, stretching the vertebrae in his spine with a satisfying pop. His eyes still fixed on the screen, he made a mental note to arrange a time to meet Admiral Steward. He also reminded himself to reprimand the people in personnel, for allowing such an incomplete file into the system. With a casual flick of his finger, the computer died, its light fading into darkness.

Frustrated, the overlord rose from his chair and crossed the room, stopping at his crimson uniform which waited patiently in its rack. He paused for a moment in front of his mirror to examine the deepening lines around his eyes and mouth which, he reminded himself, came from stress and not age. Knowing it would soon be time to start his day's duties, he put on each piece of his uniform with the loving malice which had become habit. Once properly attired, except for his facial mask, Overlord Adalric glanced up at the crimson and ebony figure in the mirror and felt his muscles tighten. Never one to look at his own image for long, he quickly turned from his reflection and sat down in his lounge chair, to resume a game that was already in progress.

Gazing down at his marble chess set, he grimly made his next move, bringing one of the white knights out from behind the pawns' protective wall. *Could I have been wrong?* He suddenly wondered with dread as he absently picked up the white queen and rolled it between his strong fingers. *Perhaps in my moment of anger, I misread her. Not that it has hurt me any,* he rationalized, *she is an adequate Shadowguard and has the qualities I like most in a servant. She is loyal, ambitious, and intelligent. But I must keep alert, she may slip up yet.* He gazed down at the board and suddenly wondered why the white queen was missing, then realized he was holding it in his tightened fist. For a moment his brow etched in perplexity, then he placed the piece back, and waited for his opponent to finish moving.

Instantly his concentration broke as he glanced up at the communications panel. Although it had been silent all morning, he now stood and walked over to it, pausing to put on his half mask, and sat down next to the console. As he finished seating himself, the unit whistled for his attention and he turned it on, illuminating the screen with a holographic image of the bridge, and Captain Harris.

"My Lord," the commander of the flagship reported, "the *Wraith* has arrived. She has pulled out of Cosmic Slip and is closing in on fusion power."

Adalric's thoughts turned dark at the concept of talking to *her* again, but he simply nodded. "Very well, Captain. I am on my way to the main hangar bay. Meet me there."

"Yes, my Lord," Harris quickly replied, then deactivated the screen.

The overlord stared at the darkened panel for a moment, his upper lip curling in annoyance at the prospect of this unfortunately required meeting of cordiality. But then his mind cleared as he turned to his chamber's front door…a presence was approaching, one that he had grown accustomed to over the last half year. With a flick of his finger, the door seemingly opened on its own, to reveal that his main personal Shadowguard was arriving to escort him to the hangar bay, as he knew she would.

~ * ~

Blaze paused when the door opened right before she reached it, she hated it when he did that. She sometimes felt certain he knew she hated it and did it specifically for that reason anyway. Dutifully, she entered the foyer of Lord Adalric's chambers, and as usual he was at his desk, finishing what seemed some sort of important business.

The first time she had been summoned to escort him, she expected his rooms to be as Spartan and sterile as her own cabin was. She was surprised to find such a luxurious suite on a warship, decorated simply in black, red, and white. However, what dominated the grand rooms were the exquisite works of art, mostly from Earth's past, she noted.

She particularly liked the thick, soft carpeting which covered the floor in a sea of black, though she thought that it would look better in red. Although she had never been beyond the entrance room in which she now waited, which contained his office area, she suspected his personal chambers were composed of other smaller rooms in addition to the usual bedroom and living area. In fact, she could almost see down the short corridor which opened to the rest of his chambers. She shifted her position to see if that was the corner of a bookshelf she saw in the room beyond, and decided she was curious about what sort of books Tanus Adalric, Overlord of the Imperium, read.

"Wait there, Shadowguard," Adalric said in his usual deep voice. He barely glanced at her as he rose from the desk panel and walked over to the mirror to fasten his long hooded cloak over his crimson uniform.

Blaze looked at the overlord she served, her thoughts edging on sublime confusion. *Why me?* She wondered, careful to guard her thoughts around him. *I have become his number one guard, but he treats me with no more respect than any of his other servants. Yet there are times on the bridge when he will confide in me or even ask me my opinion of a situation. Stranger and stranger, I wonder if all the members of the Imperial Nobility are like this.*

Adalric finished preparing himself by strapping on his electrosword, then he turned and marched past his guard, leading the way to the hangar bay.

Blaze quickly caught up and stayed two paces behind and to the left of him, as he preferred. It was always difficult to match pace with his powerfully long strides, but it was something she had become accustomed to.

Adalric suddenly turned his head toward her as they walked along, a slight smile ruffling his serious lips. "You are, of course, curious about the baron on the *Wraith*," he stated as though he knew it was fact.

Her mouth opened in surprise, though she didn't know why, nothing the overlord did surprised her these days. "Yes, my Lord," she admitted, lying to him would be a useless gesture, he could always see through a lie.

"I assure you of this," he said with a hollow laugh, "I am quite unique."

Before she could think of the proper response, they arrived at the hangar bay and strode in regally, with Blaze holding her position behind him like a dark grey shadow. The large chamber was filled with row after row of perfectly lined up Legionnaires and officers. As Blaze surveyed the bay, she tried to imagine being one of those Legionnaires, one of the many, and remembered the facelessness of what it was like to be among them. Now she was Overlord Adalric's Shadowguard, and everyone was looking at *her*. Even if they couldn't tell what she looked like through the armor and helmet, it was her they admired. She watched as Captain Harris approached them, marching confidently while trying so hard to impress them with the efficiency of his crew. The captain quickly walked up to the overlord and stood at attention.

"My Lord," Harris reported, "the shuttle from the *Wraith* is coming in now. The air shield is already in place."

"Very good, Captain. Bring her in."

Her? Blaze wondered silently. *Is he referring to the shuttle? I wonder why barons never use the Cosmic transportation rift. I guess they're afraid of putting their fates completely in someone else's hands. Not that I blame them, one slip of that device and who knows what could happen to you.*

Her thoughts sliced off as the *Wraith's* shuttle slowly floated into the hangar bay. For an instant it hovered there, almost as if it were judging the area in which it wanted to land, then it came down softly, letting out a pulse of coolant steam around it.

Blaze waited as her eyes tried to pierce through the quickly dissipating clouds to the opening shuttle doors. She watched for a glimpse of the Imperial noble who governed over the *Wraith*. Finally, she saw two Shadowguards come out and stand to either side of the small ramp, and she could almost make out another silhouette in the haze. She squinted as she cursed the darkened eyepieces on her battle helmet, and vowed if she were ever given the choice, she would never wear one again.

The noble figure penetrated what was left of the steam and walked up to the overlord, as Blaze's eyes opened wide in amazement. *Wow*, she thought, *the rumors were true after all.*

Before her was a female Perusian, with fur as white as Arctic snow. This contrasted strikingly with the one-piece garment she wore. It was a low-cut midnight-blue body suit which left her legs and arms bare, as was typical Perusian style. Despite her tall matching boots, her footsteps whispered her approach. Her long matching cloak, which cascaded behind her, gave her the illusion of gliding across the deck. Even from a distance Blaze could see her luminous blue eyes which sparkled like sapphires in a pearl-handled blade. The simple elegance this noble displayed, as she approached the overlord, caused Blaze to drop into a sense of envious awe. She could feel the power flowing through the feline before her, almost more than she felt in Adalric.

The overlord glanced over at Blaze, his chin setting in tight vexation, then he turned back to greet his guest. "Drusee-la," he said with sweet distaste through a smile which looked as though it had been nailed onto his resistant face.

"Tanus," she replied as her low purr vibrated with her words and her tail twitched back and forth beneath her cloak, revealing that although she seemed at ease, she was not.

Tanus? Blaze recoiled in shock over Baroness Drusee-la's informality and waited as she read the anger in his clenched jaw. Instead of acting on his feelings, as the young Shadowguard might have, he merely smiled again and nodded. Blaze's mouth opened slightly as her thoughts tumbled, she had never seen the overlord behave in such a fashion before. He never tolerated anything he considered an insult from anyone of lesser rank than himself, and Drusee-la was technically below him, since the overlord was the chief of the Imperial barons. *Unless there is more to their relationship than one can see.* She quickly decided she had better watch the Perusian closely.

The exchange of pleasantries finished with what seemed a temporary cease fire. Then the overlord motioned with his gloved hand, and the two of them, overlord and baroness, left the bay together, with their guards following closely behind.

As they walked out, Blaze glanced over, noticing Drusee-la's personal bodyguard for the first time. Her seven-foot-tall protector was a golden furred Narman, a member of the lion-like cousin race of the Perusians. For a moment they glared at each other as they walked on, silently judging to see who the more suited protector was. A menacing grin spread across the Narman's mane framed face as he glared down at her, his pearl white fangs glistening in their silent challenge to his diminutive opponent. For an instant, Blaze felt like stepping back, for there was no mistaking the look in his cold yellow eyes.

Instead, she merely smiled under her helmet and turned back to face her master with a new sense of admiration flowing through her. *That is why he's the overlord,* she realized intently, *he doesn't need to radiate his abilities or have massive bodyguards to show his strengths. Perhaps that's what true power is…not having to flaunt it.* She walked even more proudly realizing she was more than enough for Adalric's needs.

However, despite this conclusion, she still watched the baroness in fixed fascination. *I wonder if she has similar skills to Adalric's. I've heard the overlord referred to as a TelSor mystic or elder. I wonder if she's one also.* Blaze noticed that unlike Adalric, there was a wrist laser attached to the baroness' arm, along with the electrosword on her belt, and decided Drusee-la seemed to prefer to be heavily armed. She wondered why Adalric wore the sword alone and concluded that he didn't need to wear any other weapon any more than he needed large bodyguards. *Not that I'm inferior,* she assured herself while glancing at the Narman again, who was watching his mistress intently, *I'm sure I could fry his face off in a moment…but that would surely give me away.* Blaze sighed as she continued to walk along. *What a burden it is to have a natural ability and not be able to use it…* She stopped herself when she realized what she was thinking. She quickly glanced up to see if he was looking back at her, but no, he was still talking to Lady Drusee-la. *That was lucky, Blaze,* she scolded herself, *very lucky.*

As they continued, Blaze found herself watching the Baroness Drusee-la again, an intense curiosity flowing through her. *Here we are in an Imperium that is human dominated, and this Perusian is a baroness. She even carries herself like nobility,* Blaze realized with disgust as she glanced down at her own clumsy movements. *Of course, Drusee-la is a feline, and isn't wearing a ton of battle armor.*

They finally reached the conference hall, where Adalric led Drusee-la in and gestured to the large table.

"Be seated," he said, with a definite air of commanding authority.

After a few moments of staring in response, Drusee-la sat down. Once comfortable, she slowly slipped off a long fingerless blue glove and placed it on the table before her. Then she gingerly licked the palm of her hand with her small pink tongue, and with a grace which came naturally to her race, smoothed out the fur behind her tall milky ears. Blaze noticed Adalric was watching Drusee-la's movements intently, and wished she could read his mind.

"So, Tanus," Drusee-la said as she purred playfully, "here we are on your ship."

Blaze watched a muscle in his jaw jump at the continued informal use of his first name. She could feel that a part of him wanted to lash out and discipline her attempts at insolence, yet still he maintained control. As far as she understood the Perusian way of naming, *Drusee-la* would be her entire name, but she admitted she didn't know much about those felines.

"Yes," Adalric replied, his eyes fixing on the Perusian, "so we are."

Drusee-la fidgeted uneasily in her chair for a moment under the overlord's glare, then a mischievous grin came to her face as she stroked her long white whiskers. "Not a bad ship you have here, Tanus." She continued to purr as she gazed around thoughtfully. "It's a shame it's not as nice as mine."

"There is no difference between our two ships," Adalric replied curtly, "except in the caliber of its ruling noble."

Ouch, Blaze thought as she winced in sympathetic pain for Drusee-la.

The Perusian's ears flattened a bit, then sprang quickly back up. "I simply meant my ship is so much newer, and more powerful. You should remember that Tanus."

"Perhaps you should be more *respectful*, Drusee-la. You're not thinking of the future."

"You mean when *you're* the sovereign?" the baroness said with a laugh. "The Dire Queen has had enough of you, Tanus, and she's starting to get her other barons ready." She paused, letting every word sink in. "Why else do you think she gave *me* the new ship, and is recalling *you* back to Nyx? Think about it."

Blaze winced again under her helmet, this time awarding Drusee-la the point. Still, she was surprised at Drusee-la's casual innuendo concerning Adalric becoming sovereign ruler of the Imperium. Could he truly be plotting something?

"You are foolish, reckless, and inexperienced. You should learn some manners more befitting a guest when on your overlord's ship."

The baroness' tall ears sank down as she quietly hissed through her needle-sharp fangs, then she stood up abruptly. "So, I think that's enough chatting for one day. After all, I have *your* front lines to take over."

Adalric slowly stood up, hardly sorry to see her leaving. "Yes, and I have urgent business with the Dire Queen which cannot wait."

"I'm sure." The baroness started to walk out, then turned back to the overlord. "But think on this, Tanus. *I've* been home while you were out conquering stellar systems. *I've* been the one talking to the Dire Queen lately, not you. *I've* been—"

"Shadowguard Blaze," Adalric cut into Drusee-la's words, "escort the Baroness back to her shuttle, then see she gets safely off *my* ship."

Blaze looked up in surprise. She was so entwined with what they were saying that she almost didn't realize she was being talked to. "Yes, my Lord," she said, then quickly walked over to the ivory feline and gestured to the door. "This way, my Lady."

"Until we meet again," the baroness said, her tail twitching back and forth rapidly.

"Until then," he responded flatly.

Drusee-la stared at him for an instant, as if their locked eyes were waging a duel of their own, then she nodded to him in a farewell gesture. "Tanus."

"Drusee-la."

The feline noble turned and left the room, her midnight-blue cloak rippling behind her.

Blaze ran to get in front of her, so she could lead her back to the hangar bay. Her mind was jumbled as she tried to review what had transpired. *They hate each other…I think. But there is no doubt she wants to be the overlord.* Blaze glanced back over her shoulder at Drusee-la, to see if she was following her, which she was. *Well,* Blaze thought with a silent laugh, *Drusee-la certainly has the bravado to be the overlord. I've never heard anyone stand up to Adalric like that and live.*

"What's your name again?" Drusee-la asked as she began to walk alongside the Shadowguard.

"Are you talking to me, my Lady?"

"Of course I am," the Perusian said with a grin on her face. "You're one of Adalric's personal guards?"

Blaze nodded, a strong sense of pride flowing through her body. "I am the overlord's number one Shadowguard." She then pointed to the red letters imprinted like a brand on her armor. "My name is Blaze."

"I'm impressed," Drusee-la said through a laugh, "since you are also Adalric's first female guard."

"I am?"

"Of course. Tell me Blaze…it was Blaze, wasn't it?"

"Yes, my Lady." Blaze couldn't believe she was talking to her as if such occurrences were normal, and they were long-time acquaintances. Adalric never spoke with her like that, despite her being in his service for many months.

"Well then, Blaze. Does he bring you with him down to the prison level when he tortures his toys?"

"I don't understand."

"The prisoners that Adalric keeps," the feline continued, amused at Blaze's apparent naiveté on the subject, "so he can break them into submission."

"I've seen no such thing," Blaze quickly replied, suddenly angry at the baroness.

"Perhaps you should check it out, then. Especially since if you ever displease him, I'm sure that's where you'll end up also," she said as they entered the hangar bay and approached her shuttle.

"Fine, I will," Blaze replied, annoyed that this noble seemed to have no issue with insulting Adalric to his face, and behind his back as well. "With all due consideration, Baroness Drusee-la, don't you think you should be more respectful of the overlord? He *is* second under the Dire Queen."

"For now," Drusee-la said with a sneer, then turned to face the Shadowguard, her eyes widening in amusement. "There's something about you I like, Blaze, even though we've barely met. If you should manage to hang on, then I'm sure we'll meet again."

Blaze bit back her surprise, then quickly nodded. "Yes, Baroness Drusee-la…thank you."

The Imperial noble turned and glided up the ramp of her shuttle and entered, closely followed by her Narman, who shot a parting toothy grin at Blaze, then entered the ship also.

So that's a baroness, Blaze considered as she watched the shuttle take off and softly slip out of the *Demoness*, to return to its home. Despite how indignant the Perusian had been to her master, she found herself hoping they *would* meet again. Oddly, there was something she liked about Drusee-la as well, though she couldn't place her finger on what it was. However, there *was* something she was going to place her finger on right away, and that was the truth about Adalric's prisoners on the detention level. She felt her spine chill at the thought of people tortured for someone's enjoyment.

"Look who we have here," her memory taunted as visions of street gangs came to haunt her.

"All alone on the streets at night."

"What should we do with her?" The first one said as he laughed cruelly.

Her heart cried out as she watched Reaper leap forward in her mind. "No!"

"Are you all right?" a Legionnaire asked her as he placed a hand on her quivering shoulder.

Realizing she cried out aloud, she turned to him and tried to shrug his hand off her shoulder. "I'm fine, really."

"Where are you headed?" he asked as he took his hand away from her. Blaze was startled by the concern that seemed to seep out from under his helmet.

At first, she felt like asking him what business of his it was where she went, but there was something in his roguish voice which made her change her mind. "I'm headed down to the detention level."

"I work in detention. Is there something I can get for you?"

At first, she felt like forgetting the whole subject, but she found she couldn't. She pulled the black armored Legionnaire over to the wall, away from everyone else, and removed her helmet, grateful to let her face get some air. "I need to know something."

The Darkkrieg Legionnaire followed suit and removed his helmet, revealing a young man with a straight jaw and neatly cut black hair. He let his soft silver eyes drift across the delicate lines in her face for a moment and offered her a disarming smile. "How can I help you?"

She thought he had to be Collian by his rough features and eye color, but since he refrained from calling her "babe" or "sweetheart", she wasn't certain. She could feel the approving gaze he was giving her, and the tingles that fluttered in her stomach reminded her it had been a long time since a man looked at her like that. With a marked effort, she cleared her mind and returned to the point at hand.

"Look, I'm the overlord's personal Shadowguard," Blaze said, her voice lowering to barely a whisper, "and I need to know if he has any prisoners in the detention level."

"Oh, is that all?" the Legionnaire said easily, relieved it was nothing serious. "Not now, he doesn't."

"What's that supposed to mean?" she asked, her voice rising a bit.

"Just that Overlord Adalric hasn't had anyone down there since that Alliance captain died, a little over half a year ago."

"Alliance captain," she said as she absorbed what he said, then it hit her. "Six months ago? Are you sure?" Anxiously, she bit her bottom lip and waited in cool silence for his answer.

"More like eight." He stepped back, wondering why she was asking about this. "Does it matter?"

"No," Blaze replied with a sigh, the tension in her face visibly draining, "I guess it doesn't." She gazed up at him and flashed an apologetic smile, hoping to erase the confusion in his eyes. "I'm Blaze," she said while putting out her hand. "Thank you."

The Legionnaire accepted the handshake and grinned in response, flashing straight white teeth. "Anytime, Blaze. Oh, and I'm Travis."

"Just Travis?" she asked.

"Just Blaze?" he said back with a laugh.

She laughed as well and shook her head, then turned away and headed back, knowing Adalric would begin to miss her soon.

"Will I see you again?" Travis called after her.

"I'm sure you will," she replied as she put her helmet back on, "and thanks again." She made a note of his rank, Legionnaire First Class, and committed his name to memory.

~ * ~

The whole walk back up to Adalric's cabin, Blaze's mind fought with what she learned. *Why does it bother me so much? So, he kept prisoners to break their spirits in the past, it isn't like he's doing it now...right? Who knows what he really did to them or what they did to deserve imprisonment?* Her memories lashed out at her again, burning into her soul and darkening it, as she fought down her hatred for anyone who misused a person who was trapped. She threaded her way along the grey hallway and entered the omni-lift, her mind trying frantically to put her confused emotions together. Because, despite all her resentment, there was something else, something she couldn't explain. She wasn't merely angry, there was a definite knot in her stomach. She suddenly realized that in some bizarre way she was jealous of the attention he gave to those he imprisoned and that made no sense to her. She wanted to know more about him, to know what made him tick, to truly have *his* attention. Most of all, her insatiable curiosity yelled silently, to see under that blasted cowl. *His face couldn't be so bad,* she quickly decided as she exited the omni-lift and approached his door, *after all, what's exposed is quite handsome.*

The door to his cabin opened with a rush, as his deep voice seeped out. "I appreciate the sentiment, Shadowguard, but we have work to do."

Adalric walked out and strode past her, on his way to the bridge.

Blaze found she had to trot extra fast to keep up with him this time. For a long while she remained silent, her trained willpower suppressing the turmoil of thoughts which besieged her. Finally, she felt she had to speak.

"My Lord," she said, curiosity overcoming her better sense of judgment, "are you worried about Baroness Drusee-la?"

The overlord glanced over at her, then continued to head toward the bridge. "No, I'm not."

"Why not?"

"It's something you wouldn't understand, Shadowguard. There are things about the Imperial nobles you couldn't possibly comprehend."

"Like about all of you being TelSor mystics?"

The overlord stopped and turned to face her, his eyes narrowing behind the dark lenses, then a slight smile came to his lips. "You are full of surprises, aren't you?"

Blaze grinned beneath her helmet, relieved he wasn't angry. "Always, my Lord."

"I see," he replied while studying her. "Do you even know what the TelSor are?"

Blaze heard many stories but wasn't sure what to truly believe so she shrugged. "People who have psionic abilities?"

"It's more than that," he replied, "but that's not important now. The barons aren't all mystics or elders. Only the strongest and most disciplined of the TelSor ever achieved that title."

"But being one," she asked, amazed he was talking to her this much, "that's what makes them barons, right?"

Adalric seemed to think about it for a moment as he started walking again. "Yes, we can't have those with such powers not be part of the barony. The one exception to this is Baron Koroqo, he is not a TelSor, but he has natural skills native to his race."

Adalric reached the door to the bridge, then he stood still for a moment. Slowly, he turned his broad shoulders back to his Shadowguard. "There was something else, wasn't there?"

Blaze's mouth fell open. Could she dare? Should she?

"Speak, Shadowguard," Adalric commanded.

"My Lord...I was wondering...are you planning to overthrow the Dire Queen? Was what Baroness Drusee-la said true?"

The overlord stared at Blaze for a long moment, surprised at her open questions. "You would question my intentions?"

"No, my Lord. It's just that I expected you to be harsher with the baroness. She insulted you to your face and you allowed it."

Adalric read the disillusionment in his guard's mind and for a moment felt his anger wane. "You are quite bold, Blaze," he said, his lips twisting slowly into a smile of slight admiration.

His frown returned as her walls of protection slipped momentarily in her mind. The muscles in his cheek pulsed once then he spoke. "However, that is not all you want to tell me, Blaze. Continue."

She sucked in a deep breath to calm her tense nerves and knew what was still haunting her thoughts. Before she realized it, her thoughts had found a voice. "I think..." Her voice faltered momentarily as she mustered all her strength. "I mean...I've heard about the lower detention level, and I think if it's true, then what you do to your prisoners belittles your nobility," she said with her eyes fixed on his chest instead of his face.

Overlord Adalric allowed her to writhe in his silent glare longer than was necessary, his rigid jaw betraying his anger. For a moment his hand started to move towards the hilt of his electrosword, but then slowly returned to his side, balled in a fist. "You are, of course," he finally spoke, each word slicing like the electrosword he bore, "in no position to judge or understand my actions or motives."

Blaze melted as she realized he was right, and she was *not* in such a position. Although, at that moment, she deeply wished she was, more than anything else. She finally shook her head and looked down.

Seemingly satisfied with her reaction, Adalric turned and entered the bridge, calling out to the captain as he walked towards the center. "Harris, take us to Nyx. We are going home."

Many smiles flashed across the various officers and crew as they worked on their consoles. They had been out a long time and were all anxious to get some rest. The bridge bustled with activity as the *Demoness'* powerful star drive engines flared up again. All except for Adalric, who stood motionless as he gazed out the screen at the sister super-dreadnought that hovered there. "The future will tell all, Drusee-la," he whispered to himself, "and we shall see which of us turns out to be right, and which one turns out dead."

The image of the *Wraith* wavered on the screen, then finally disappeared as the *Demoness* entered Cosmic Slip to head for home, leaving the Imperial battlefields far behind.

Chapter Fifteen
S'teka

Despite how much space Imperial Overlord Adalric had conquered for the Dire Queen, Blaze was astonished that it only took a week to return to the Tartarus system. There, its one planet, Nyx, hovered like a lone warrior under the eerie glow of the red giant.

Home again, Blaze thought with a sigh as she turned and leaned against the cool panoramic window on the observation deck, putting her back to the majestic scene outside. *So why aren't I happy?*

She knew the answer, of course, for it was Adalric. Things had changed since Drusee-la left, and she had been foolish enough to openly question her master's actions. She spent many days wondering about what she asked and learned, but decided that what Adalric did to those prisoners must have been blown out of proportion by rumors and lies.

However, her rationalizations of Adalric's motives hardly changed the present. Ever since her little scene with him, less than a week ago, he started to use another Shadowguard as his main escort. He still called her to go with him to the bridge, but that had been only twice since the change. *He must be furious with me,* she decided, and suddenly felt remorse as if she betrayed a mentor. She considered apologizing to him, but quickly realized such a gesture would seem insignificant, coming from someone like her.

Blaze turned back to the window and put her head against it, pressing her thick dark hair flatly against the cool trans-glass, as she fought down the despair which was rising in her. *Why have I been so stupid?*

"Miss walking on good ol' terra-firma, huh?" asked a cheerful voice from behind.

She glanced over at the tall man who was quickly becoming a much-needed friend and scowled at him. "This isn't Terra, Travis."

The Legionnaire removed his helmet and smiled the wolfish grin that

Blaze was becoming familiar with. "That's an expression for solid ground."

"Oh."

Travis gently reached out a black armored hand and lifted up her chin to face him, his eyes twinkling in the red starlight.

"Yeah," she said through a half sigh, half smile, "I guess I do miss walking on a planet." She gazed up at him for a moment, then pulled away and looked back at Nyx, which was quickly enlarging to dominate the scene as the *Demoness* pulled into orbit. "I hope Overlord Adalric lets us go on down."

"The overlord usually doesn't make such trivial decisions," Travis said as he watched her intently, the glow from Nyx's clouds shimmering in her dark hair. "I'm sure the captain will authorize shore leave, depending on how long we're staying here. It's more than likely the overlord has a lot of people to talk with on the Star-Citadel, especially the Dire Queen."

Blaze's heart sank as she thought about all the exciting people she would miss meeting because of what she said to Adalric, especially the Dire Queen. She wanted to know if the stories of her being something unnatural were true. In her mind she was sure they weren't. *After all, how could such a thing be? The dead couldn't rule the living, or at least they shouldn't.*

Travis read the confusion on her face and sighed. "What's going on in that lovely head of yours?"

Blaze glared at her friend, a look of scorn in her eyes. *Why does he say things like that?* She disregarded it and returned to the vision of Nyx. The Star-Citadel orbital base was now in view, filling the window with its grand splendor. Four or five ships the size of the *Demoness* could fit inside the colossal structure, and it was better armed than a dozen dreadnoughts, with the exception that it had no Cosmic Surge weapon. It was because of that planetary defense base the Red Star Imperium had never been defeated, for any fleet which made it to Nyx would find itself decimated by its sheer force. Despite her poor mood, it filled her with pride to see it up close, to know that she was, even in a small way, responsible for representing what it stood for.

"Why did you join the Imperium?" she asked Travis, suddenly needing to know someone else's motivations besides her own.

"Huh?"

"Why not the Alliance?" Or some other faction?"

"The Alliance?" He let out a short laugh. "I grew up down there," he replied, pointing at Nyx. "There was never any doubt in my mind since I was a child that I would serve as a Legionnaire, even when there weren't any, and this was still referred to as the Red Star pirates."

Blaze grinned. "So, what you're really saying is that you grew up wanting to be a pirate."

"Um…no," Travis said with an embarrassed smile. "Not really."

"Sure," she said with a laugh, feeling her spirits rise.

"Why did you ask?"

"Hmm," she answered, a serious look replacing her smile as she turned back to the window and shrugged, "I guess I really wanted to know if anyone else loved the Imperium as much as I did."

Travis smiled and placed a hand on her shoulder. "We all do, Blaze. That's why we fight so hard to win."

For a moment, she felt her eyes start to sting, as the emptiness in her heart cried out. "I'm going to miss all the great things that will happen on the base, aren't I? All because I couldn't keep my mouth shut."

"Nah," he said with a laugh, trying to cheer her up, "if the overlord won't take you there, then I will. Any military personnel are allowed on the Star-Citadel."

She turned to face him, a smile covering her soft lips. "Thanks, Travis." Although she tried to be happy, she suddenly realized her thoughts were with another man, one who would continue to dominate her life, even if he chose to remove her from his.

~ * ~

Tanus Adalric gazed intently at his chess set, his mind dancing with endless outcomes of different scenarios. Slowly his cold eyes fixed on the object of his obsession, the black queen. "What are you planning?" he whispered through his dimly lit chambers. "Have you put her in a position to replace me? Or is it merely her fanciful delusions of grandeur shining through?" *No,* he thought silently, *there is no other explanation for Drusee-la getting the* Wraith…*none at all. With her out there, at the front, and me back here…that feline is now effectively "acting" overlord. While I'm gone, she'll be building loyalties among the fleet captains, strengthening her position, and the Dire Queen has engineered it all. The Dire Queen has lost faith in me over this prophecy…but if I can find this person soon, and show her I was right, then she will trust me again. I need her trust…for now, I am not yet ready to confront her.*

In the meantime, though, I must do something about Drusee-la.

His swirling thoughts were interrupted by the whistle of his communications unit. Grabbing his armored cowl, he slid it on easily and approached the panel. With the feeling that it was someone he wished to talk with anyway, he sat down expectantly. A mere flinch of his finger made the screen spring to life.

"My Lord, Adalric," said the still flickering image.

"Admiral Joshua Steward," Adalric responded with a smile, as the holographic image of the orbital base's commander came into focus. "What is the status of the *Sentinel*?"

"The Star-Citadel is at maximum efficiency, my Lord," he quickly replied. "I have a message for you from the sovereign."

"Speak," he commanded, anticipating the request. It was customary for the Dire Queen to voice her orders, via the communications links, to the admiral, or some other noble, while the overlord was away from Nyx. But it was he alone who had the privilege to see her in person, at least that's how it had been for years.

"She demands you report to her at once, to brief her on the situation at the front."

"As expected, Admiral," Adalric said, without emotion, as he reached to turn off the image.

"She also wants a full report on your handling of your 'little problem'," Steward added quickly.

"Explain," Adalric replied, knowing full well what he meant, though he wished to see what the Admiral knew.

"I don't know, my Lord. That is simply how she told me to tell you."

"I see," Adalric whispered to himself, satisfied that the admiral was simply carrying out the queen's orders. Sparked by the mentioning of his "little problem", unresolved business surfaced in his mind. "Steward, I want to talk to you about one of my Shadowguards."

"You do?" the *Sentinel's* commander asked, his face plainly displaying his confusion.

"Her name is Blaze, and I know little to nothing about her. Her file is an absent disgrace."

Joshua Steward lost his breath for a moment. Ever since he heard she had been promoted to Shadowguard he dreaded this might happen. "I honestly know little about her past as well, my Lord."

"She got into our Imperial navy through an admiral's appointment," Adalric replied fiercely, "*your* appointment, Steward."

"I know her name, and that she was born on an Alliance colony world and hated it." The admiral felt beads of perspiration forming on his forehead. "The colony did not keep very good records. In fact, it was in ruins by the time she came of age, so even she doesn't know much about herself. No history, no next of kin, but I sensed something in her that told me she would do great things serving the Imperium. She showed great spirit, my Lord, and I believe in her. Call it a gut feeling."

Steward waited tensely for Adalric's reaction, hoping he learned what he needed to know. It was clear the overlord was angry, and despite any rumblings Steward heard about a new overlord possibly being chosen soon, it still was unwise to make Adalric angry.

However, Adalric's wrath seemed to be diminishing, giving way to curiosity about this woman he had allowed into his life. "An Alliance colony? Which one?"

"Tenebrous, my Lord."

"Tenebrous?" Adalric said, surprised for the first time in a long while. He fell silent for a moment, then nodded. "Thank you, Admiral." He turned off the communications unit with a wave of one finger.

"Tenebrous," he repeated to himself. "Then she's a runaway, from an Alliance world which she watched me vaporize." Adalric smiled, suddenly feeling he understood his enigma a bit better. *Perhaps I should give her a second chance,* he silently mused. *After all, I would hate to lose a decent guard.* Yet he was still troubled.

Adalric tried to understand his own visions of Lady Alicia's dreaded precognition. He sensed the instrument of his destined destruction was near.

However, he could not focus the vision on Blaze. He doubted she could be the mutant from the prophecy since she could not possibly have hidden such talents from him for so long. *Although,* he considered, *perhaps she is the key to unlocking the secret.*

What was it about that girl that caused him to spare her, even though she openly questioned his actions? Why was it now that he felt he wanted her by his side again, despite her insolence?

It is because she's a puzzle that I still don't have all the pieces to, he rationalized, *and I never leave a puzzle incomplete.* With his motives safely lined up in his mind, the overlord stood up and fastened on his cloak, preparing himself to go to the *Sentinel*, where the Dire Queen kept her throne.

He lightly touched a button, calling Blaze to him. After a few seconds without the standard acknowledgment, he pressed it again, once again his call went unheard. He hit a different button, causing the screen to illuminate with the bridge duty officer. "Why isn't my Shadowguard responding to my call, Commander?"

The duty officer quickly looked in his logs, to find out who the overlord had recently summoned, then glanced back up at the screen. "My Lord," he said quickly, "we are now in dry-dock at *Sentinel*. Shadowguard Blaze was off duty, so she went on leave with some of the other troops. The captain gave authority at seventeen hundred hours."

Adalric glanced at his time piece, marking her time of departure at a half an hour ago. At first his anger started to build in him…*how dare she leave without asking me.* Then he calmed down, remembering he had dismissed her as his main guard, which did place her in an off-duty mode. "Hellfire," the overlord whispered to himself with disgust, "I *am* growing soft."

"My Lord?" the duty officer questioned, not sure what Adalric asked.

"Disregard, Commander, and send me one of my on-duty Shadowguards, I'm going to the *Sentinel* to speak with the queen." Before the duty officer could respond, he turned off the unit, causing the lights that had been reflecting in his eyepieces to shimmer for a brief instant, then die out.

~ * ~

Blaze gazed curiously around the huge Star-Citadel, as she and Travis wandered through the large plaza that composed the orbital base's reception center and shopping arcade. They were on the lower level of the central chamber, from where one could look up to see up almost forty stories in concentric rings. Below their feet, was a grand shimmering image of the planet below. Many people bustled about like busy ants around a mound. Some were outfitted in uniforms, some not, though all wore an expression of being hurried, worried, or both. Although Blaze and Travis were technically off duty, they still remained in their respective suits of battle armor, as was required by all members of the Imperial navy when in a military place, though neither wore their weapons.

"I can't believe we're here," Blaze said with glee. "It feels so good to get off the *Demoness* for a time."

"Yes," Travis agreed as he watched her intently through his darkened eyepieces, "it does."

"I wish we could take off our helmets," she said with a sigh, feeling a bit claustrophobic.

"We can go to one of the dining centers," suggested Travis, "we can take them off there."

"Great idea. I'm famished."

"You always seem to be famished," he said with a laugh.

"True," she agreed with a smile as they continued to walk along, "when you grow up on a crap pile like I did, then you learn to appreciate food for what it really does."

"And what is that?"

Blaze grabbed his arm and turned him, so he faced her. Then she looked up at him, her dark eyes piercing through both sets of helmets with their intensity. "It keeps you alive, Travis."

"Oh, right."

They stared at each other for a few moments, until Blaze's attention was snapped away by a new presence in the central plaza. Although Blaze had seen some non-human races milling about, they were the definite minority, and none of them wore uniforms of any sort. What she saw now caused her to become riveted to this new arrival, an arrival which almost made her laugh in disbelief.

There, in the distance, was a small group of what Blaze would have almost called Ninjas, elite assassins of Earth's ancient history. Blaze recalled Mattie showing her pictures and telling her grand stories of their mythical expertise, back when she was growing up in the sewers. Now these antiquated warriors were here, in the present, in the most advanced empire in the sector. Perhaps half a dozen of these figures marched neatly and silently into the central plaza. Akin to the Legionnaires, these people were also like identical toy soldiers. They were all dressed in black cloth uniforms which covered their bodies and heads, leaving a wide slit that revealed kindred predatory eyes. Their only visible weapons were the swords on their backs, but Blaze imagined many other mysterious devices tucked into the folds of their black garb. Two things separated these people from the Ninjas she learned about as a little girl. First was the grey stripe which slashed down their legs and arms, and second, they were not humans.

Despite their humanoid appearance, Blaze was quick to recognize that what was revealed was a narrow slit of porcelain-white skin and coal black eyes. She also noticed the slight folds above the eyelid and upward curve of the darkened brows, and the creases in the fabric which gave away their tall, pointed ears, causing her to realize they were Proximans under those ancient uniforms. Blaze certainly held no animosity toward Proximans, as her last meeting with one saved her life, but to find them all in strange uniforms, here in the Imperium.

"Who are they, Travis?" she quickly asked, intrigued by this new development.

"Who?"

"Them," she said with a nod of her head in the right direction, "the Proximans dressed like Ninjas."

"Ninjas?" Travis asked, confusion in his voice. He surveyed the area several times, finally letting his gaze fall to where Blaze gestured. "Oh, you mean the *S'teka*."

"S'teka?" Blaze asked.

"Sure," he answered nonchalantly. "They're Baron Koroqo's elite force of warriors. The S'teka are masters of the martial art of Trimar. It's said they can't be defeated."

"Are they all Proximans?" she asked, her curiosity over this fascinating development growing.

"Yes. I've heard they start training at the age of five, at least I think. Anyway, you must be born into one of the highest caste families in Proxima to become one. They say each would give his or her life gladly for Koroqo."

"Proxima is a planet inside the United Star Alliance. What are they doing here?" Blaze asked Travis, knowing his knowledge of the Imperium was greater than hers.

"I guess Baron Koroqo has a lot of pull on his planet," Travis replied with a shrug. "Besides, although Proxima is located inside the Alliance borders, they aren't a formal member."

"So, who's this Koroqo guy?" she wondered aloud, remembering Adalric had mentioned him once.

"He's one of the Imperial nobles," Travis said as he tried to quiet her down. "He's also in charge of the queen's secret service, so I'd watch what I say around him or his S'teka if I were you."

"Secret service," she said with a sneer, "armed with swords? They must be wonderful in a laser fight."

"Don't laugh. They defeated the Camillian forces in the battle of Denal, and they were outnumbered seven to one."

Blaze tried to imagine one of those Ninjas or S'teka, or whatever they were, fighting against seven-foot-tall reptiles, armed with heavy lasers, and winning. "Those six are the only ones left, right?"

"Heck, no. Koroqo has over a hundred of them. They lost a mere two on Denal, after killing over six hundred Camillians."

"Two?" Blaze scoffed in disbelief.

"I'm serious."

She let out a brief chuckle, then gazed back at the Proximans, who were staying in a tight group. She noticed that even though they were in the safety of the Imperial Star-Citadel, they constantly seemed on guard, moving with grace, agility, and purpose. Suddenly a chill ran up her spine, as she tried to imagine the battle they must have had. "Did they fight anywhere else?" she finally asked, her voice barely a whisper.

"A few other places, all with similar results. The Dire Queen rarely uses them like that. She reserves them for secret service duties…assassinations and the like. Why else do you think the Romusian Empire surrendered right after their Warrior Emperor mysteriously died overnight?"

She breathed out quietly. "Huh…and they're totally loyal to Baron Koroqo? Is he also a Proximan?"

"Of course."

Blaze couldn't understand, she had been taught by the Imperium that humans were superior, but now she knew of two barons which were non-human. "If these S'teka are more loyal to him than to the Imperium, then what's to stop him from taking over as sovereign?"

Travis shrugged. "I don't know for sure, but they say he's totally loyal to the Dire Queen. Some even say they're lovers."

Blaze scowled at Travis. She was getting sick of these unsubstantiated rumors. "They say that about Adalric and the Dire Queen also. For all I know they say that about Drusee-la and the Dire Queen too. I don't believe any of it."

"Believe what you want," he said through a grin, "but I'd stay away from the S'teka if I were you. They have authority to kill on sight, even a Shadowguard."

"You're kidding."

Travis shook his head as he shrugged again. "Let's forget it and get something to eat. I'm starved."

Blaze was about to agree with him when she saw where the S'teka were headed. At the far end of the plaza a regally dressed Proximan emerged, flanked by two more of the elite warriors. He was dressed in a dark blue version of the S'teka uniform, without the headpiece, thereby exposing his intently handsome face, strong jaw line, and gently pointed ears which accented his features. The dark charcoal cloak, which signified his station as an Imperial noble, rippled behind him like a banner, giving him the appearance of a flawless white statue. Baron Koroqo carried himself regally like a warrior prince, or at least like someone who had once been a prince. The six S'teka quickly flanked him as they turned to allow his entrance into the plaza.

"Looks like he's here to meet someone," Blaze whispered, then felt her stomach tie in a knot as she glanced across at the other end of the large room. Sure enough, there was Overlord Adalric, with *another* Shadowguard. She fumed at the sight, then turned to face Travis, betrayal flushing her cheeks beneath her helmet. "Let's get some food."

"Sure," he agreed, wondering at her sudden change of mood. Noticing that the overlord and Baron Koroqo arrived made Travis' decision to leave all the easier. Such meetings held little interest for him anyway. Taking Blaze's armored hand in his, he started to lead her out of the area, even though she was still looking back at the majestic figures in the distance.

~ * ~

Overlord Adalric gazed across the large open plaza which made up the reception area of *Sentinel* and sighed quietly. He had no qualms about meeting with Koroqo, for even though he did not trust the Proximan noble, there was no man in the Imperium he respected more. However, although it was customary for any arriving dignitaries to be first met by Koroqo, Adalric felt it was an intrusion, especially since he was overlord and Koroqo's superior. *What I would give for an army like his,* he thought enviously, *then I could finally claim what is rightfully mine.*

Suddenly his thoughts were disrupted by a familiar presence, one which had been in his mind of late. Guided by his instincts, he scanned the plaza's central chamber until he spotted a Shadowguard holding hands with a Legionnaire and watched as they started to make their way out. "Blaze," he whispered to himself, recognizing her instantly, despite her full armor and the distance that separated them.

It was then that an odd sensation came over him, but not emanating from her. It was the Legionnaire next to her. *He is feeling something for her...for* my *Shadowguard. My Shadowguard, who should be by my side at this moment.* With a harsh gesture he reached out to her with his mind, demanding her to come to him. With the slightest flinch of his hand, he dismissed the guard which he arrived with and waited impatiently for his former personal guard to come as requested.

~ * ~

Blaze finally turned to follow Travis, when she felt it hit her like an electro-shot to the head. Instantly she raised her mental shields as she had become accustomed to doing, to hide her fiery secret. "He's calling for me," she whispered to Travis. "He needs me now."

"What are you talking about?"

"Overlord Adalric," she explained as she quickly dropped his hand, "he wants me by his side again. I have to go."

"But..."

"Thanks for the tour, Travis," she called back to him as she began to walk away.

Blaze turned and started a quick pace across the plaza floor, as a strange sense of elation began to flow through her body, though she could not explain it. All she knew was the overlord needed her, and it was her duty to be there for him. She quickened her pace so as to not keep him waiting, but knew it would be uncouth to run. She wanted to reach him before he reached Baron Koroqo, so she could be by his side for the meeting, where she belonged.

Blaze arrived perfectly in time to fall behind him as Adalric and Koroqo met in the center. Both had been given a wide berth by the populace that milled around them. Although the overlord did not say a word to her when she arrived, he simply nodded his approval, then turned to face the head of the secret service.

"It's been a while, Overlord Adalric," Koroqo said, his Proximan accent thickly coating the Terran language he spoke.

At least this man shows the overlord the respect he deserves, Blaze quickly thought as she gazed at the exotically handsome noble. Blaze decided she liked the way his dark grey hair was trimmed neatly behind his upswept ears but left to slightly trail down the back of his collar in small waves. As a Proximan, his age was indeterminable. He walked with a youthful stride, but the intensity of his black eyes and the lines around them made Blaze believe he was probably a good deal older. He was tall, but not as tall as Adalric. However, his appearance was not what made Blaze like this Proximan from the start. There was plainly no malice in his dark eyes, none of the brazen challenges that was prominent in Drusee-la's. More than that, she felt Koroqo truly respected the overlord, and all he stood for. It was a simple inner feeling, but those had never betrayed her before.

"It has indeed, my friend," Adalric replied, his voice rising above the Proximan's.

"We must discuss many issues," Koroqo continued. "Things have changed since you were last here."

"You mean with Drusee-la?"

"And with the Dire Queen," Koroqo replied quietly. "I would watch both if I were you."

"Your advice is well taken. However, this is nothing I haven't already suspected. We must talk further, but in a more appropriate place."

"Agreed. After you talk with the sovereign."

Blaze was impressed with Koroqo's servility and obvious loyalty toward Adalric, though she once again felt overwhelmed by the number of guards the Proximan had, while Adalric had but one…her. Then she smiled as she recalled her earlier conclusion that one was all he needed.

For a moment Baron Koroqo glanced over at Blaze, his left eyebrow rising in an expression of perplexed curiosity. Over what, she did not know.

"I will talk with you soon," Adalric said, concluding his meeting with the Baron of the Secret Service.

Koroqo nodded, then ventured away quickly, flanked by his elite warriors.

"My Lord," Blaze asked as she watched the baron leave, "does he ever go anywhere without them?"

"I don't think so, Shadowguard," Adalric replied as he turned away. "Come, I must meet with the Dire Queen."

Blaze's mind turned blank as the reality of what he said finally hit her. *Meet with the queen of this great Imperium? What if she could tell the truth about me? What if I do something wrong? What if she really is a demon?*

Adalric was lost in his own thoughts as he tuned out his surroundings to prepare himself for this long-awaited meeting. Soon he would find out if what had been spread around were merely rumors, or if they were indeed fact. Above all, he knew he had to convince his sovereign, she simply wasn't ready to rule the Imperium without his aid.

Blaze's thoughts shadowed her master as she tried to make sure he would be proud of her in front of the Dire Queen. He was so troubled over this meeting, she could almost feel that inside of him. *It must have something to do with Drusee-la*, she decided. *There must be some truth to that feline's threats.* There were times when she almost wished she could reach out to him, to offer her strength to help him, but she knew it was impossible.

Lost in her thoughts, she didn't see the other Shadowguard until he was almost upon them. Not that another Shadowguard was strange to see, but this one instantly struck her as wrong, as if every instinct in her body was yelling out a desperate warning. *What was it?* She quickly decided it was the way he walked. All Shadowguards had to have once been Legionnaires, so they were used to the bulk of the armor, but this Shadowguard was walking along like battle armor was a whole new thing.

She scolded herself for being paranoid. *Why should I worry,* she laughed silently, *no one with malicious thoughts could get near Adalric since he knows what's on everyone's mind around him. But look at him,* she reconsidered as she studied the overlord, *his fists balled so tightly…is he taking notice of anything?*

By that time the awkward Shadowguard reached the two of them. Bowing his head in reverence to the overlord, he continued past.

Relief spread through her body, and for once she was glad her instincts were wrong, yet still she kept him in her peripheral vision. Suddenly her relief turned to near frantic panic as her fears were confirmed. The Shadowguard forcibly shoved Blaze aside as he turned sharply toward Adalric's back, drawing a strange and ugly weapon resembling a hydraulic spear-gun pistol.

For an instant, as she lost her balance and began falling backward, she was sure Adalric would whirl around and turn the attacker's head into neural mush, as she had seen him do before. However, he didn't, he simply kept on walking, his jaw set tight in concentration.

As she landed on her rear, the galaxy suddenly seemed to slow down in her mind, as if the clock went to a crawl. Still, she did not have enough time to think. The assassin was moving in for the kill, two more steps and he would be there…and the overlord was oblivious!

Automatically, she reached for her weapon, but felt her panic grow when her hand met her empty holster. *Of course,* she cursed, *we left our weapons on the ship.*

The assassin's arm lifted, bringing the strange weapon up to Adalric's back, right below his neck, as his finger tensed on the trigger.

"No," Blaze screamed as she reached out with her pyrokinesis, causing Adalric to turn and face his attacker for the first time.

It was too late, the weapon shuddered as the luminous spear lanced out toward Adalric's neck, mere inches away.

Suddenly both the weapon and deadly projectile disintegrated into flames as Blaze desperately ripped off her helmet and stood up, her eyes becoming glowing hellish pools of fire. Without consideration of consequence, her thoughts stabbed out again, causing the attacker to instantly combust, licks of searing fire escaping from inside the grey armor. With a screeching howl of agony, the false Shadowguard fell to the ground, to writhe in a macabre dance of death.

The huge plaza fell into horrified silence as the stench of molten armor and charred flesh wound its way throughout the central chambers. Onlookers gawked at her with dumbfounded shock. From the far side of the chamber, Travis shook his head with amazement and remorse. Baron Koroqo, who was almost out of the chamber, turned and began running over with his guards. However, this all paled in comparison to the overlord, who simply stared at his personal Shadowguard, his lips parted slightly, his thoughts a whirling tempest.

Blaze sank to her knees, her body feeling the tired expulsion of what she had bottled up for so long. Although she felt relieved, her thoughts whitened with fear as she gazed up at her master, unsure of how he would take this unexpected turn in events. She hadn't even realized what she was doing until it was over, instinct replacing reason as she did the one thing she could to save him. Even though that action had preserved his life, it betrayed her.

"It *was* you," Adalric finally whispered as Koroqo arrived to investigate the dead assassin. "The prophecy…she told me I would let in my own doom…."

"My Lord…" Blaze said weakly, her body shaking from both fear and exhaustion.

"You will be silent!" Adalric yelled as he pointed an accusing finger down at her. "Say another word, *mutant*, and I will kill you now."

"She *saved* your life, Adalric," Koroqo said quietly as he removed the dead assassin's helmet to reveal a cindered Proximan underneath. "By the sacred lights."

Adalric looked down at the dead assailant, then up at the Proximan noble, his eyes narrowing behind his darkened eye pieces. Then he glanced back down and knew his path was clear. "What she did does not matter. She's an illegal psionic, and an enemy of the Imperium."

Blaze choked inside, her eyes watering, every word of anger from her mentor piercing into her. She wanted to explain to him, to let him know she revealed herself to *save* him, to make him understand she could not be an enemy of the Imperium. She *loved* the Imperium. Instead, exhaustion overtook her, destroying her resolve.

"She will be taken before the Dire Queen," Adalric continued like a judge delivering his death sentence, "and she will be executed."

Adalric reached down and grabbed the still weakened Blaze by the neck and started to drag her away.

Koroqo sprang up and blocked his path, knowing fully the chances he was taking. "She saved your *life,*" he repeated, realizing it needed to be said again.

"She lied to me by concealing her psionic powers," he replied, his voice caked with the ache of betrayal. With her powers revealed, the prophecy seemed to unwind in his mind. "She knew the law and broke it. She must be destroyed. Now get out of my way."

Koroqo stood aside, for he realized any further resistance could bring about a confrontation between the two of them, and that would be disastrous.

"My Lord," Blaze barely managed to get out, her words scraping through her dried throat, desperately attempting to speak through the iron grip that was still clamped around her neck like a vice. *"Please…"*

Adalric glared down at his favorite guard, suddenly realizing he never saw her without her helmet before. The tears that rimmed her reddened eyes and trailed harshly down her face, were almost indistinguishable from the beads of sweat that streaked her flushed cheeks. Her thick dark hair dangled as he held her there, disheveled and disarrayed. Painfully, her deep red lips contorted as she tried to speak against his grasp again. The overlord watched as the pink spray drained slowly out of her cheeks, giving way to a sickly pallor. However, despite her torment she was magnificent, and for an instant he felt his heart softening towards her again, then his lips tightened.

"You *are* the girl from the prophecy," he said coldly, refilling his heart with dark hatred, the pain of betrayal. "I am taking you before the Dire Queen, and she will see I was right all along."

Without a further word, the overlord turned from the grisly scene and stormed toward the Imperial throne room, dragging a weakly struggling Blaze with him. Behind him remained a stunned crowd, a disappointed Koroqo, a dead Proximan, and a greatly heartbroken Legionnaire, who turned from the forum and silently walked away.

Chapter Sixteen
Queen's Gambit

By the time they reached the throne room, Blaze began to regain her senses and perspective on her situation. Not that she thought any of that would help her, but she had no intention of dying like some weak-willed crying child who was incapable of at least fighting for herself. She tried to shut out the pain in her body and soul, but Adalric's slicing words drove deep, and it was hard to ignore pain when the man to whom she devoted her last half year was dragging her around by her neck.

Blaze barely saw the throne room doors swing out as they approached. It was the smell of the stale air which let her know they were no longer storming through the corridors.

"What is the meaning of this?" came an unearthly voice that whispered harshly.

"My queen," Adalric quickly said as he sank to one knee, bringing Blaze down with him, "this is the person to whom the prophecy refers. I have revealed her treachery and brought her before you, for execution."

"I see," the Dire Queen said, as she glanced down at the armored but disheveled woman who was dangling on the ground, desperately trying to pry off Adalric's grip. The sovereign allowed herself a silent chuckle, as she realized the moment she was waiting for finally arrived. "Release her before she expires," the Dire Queen ordered, her luminous red eyes fixed on the young woman.

Adalric glared in confusion but did as she requested. He released his vice-like grip, causing Blaze to fall away from him, choking and gasping for precious breath.

After a moment, Blaze managed to roll onto her stomach, finally able to understand where she was. Her red-rimmed eyes looked up into the room which was barely lit by a few crimson fires, to settle on the woman she swore loyalty to at her Imperial induction. The Dire Queen was in black, with no apparent body, save for what her clinging dress and hood gave her. Where there should have been skin, there was an inky blackness in the shape of a woman. Blaze glanced up further to meet with the two glowing red eyes which hung, seemingly suspended, inside the queen's hood. She found herself blinking in confusion, her panic giving way to curiosity. She could feel a cold aura emanating from the Dire Queen, a presence of darkness which engulfed the young woman and made her forget the pain. Slowly she rose to her feet, feeling now, of all times, she had to show strength. It was that or die.

For her own part, the Dire Queen watched the young woman rise, feeling an admiration grow within her. She instantly skimmed the Shadowguard's surface thoughts to reveal what happened, and scoffed, her hollow laughter echoing in the throne room.

"I don't understand," Adalric finally said, his jaw tight with confusion. "Why do you laugh?"

"This woman saved your life, Adalric," the Dire Queen said in response, "and you reward her with a death sentence."

"But the prophecy…it is *her*," he replied, angered she would even question his actions. "Surely you cannot ignore the danger she poses to the balance of the Imperium."

"You are mistaken, Adalric," the Dire Queen said, her voice laced with malice. "Your obsession has taken you too far. She is *not* the one." The Dire Queen let her gaze burn into her overlord, long enough to make him retreat a step.

She turned toward his former guard, her harsh voice softening to a chillingly sweet tone. "What is your name, child?"

Blaze was suspended in shock, but only for a moment. The Dire Queen of the Red Star Imperium, whatever she was, seemed to be taking *her* side in all of this. A new confidence warmed Blaze's stiff muscles as she bowed, proud to be counted as a servant of the Imperium. "My queen, I am Shadowguard Blaze."

The Dire Queen nodded as her thoughts waged a miniature war within her darkened soul. *Adalric is a fool,* she laughed silently, *but he* has *found the one the prophecy foretold. Yet, I cannot let him destroy her, for she is precisely the tool I require. I sense an untapped power welled inside her, a glorious fire that could easily be turned to my will. Yes,* she decided, *Blaze will suffice nicely, allowing me to leave such positions to humans as it was meant to be, and not overgrown cats.* "I am impressed with you, Blaze," the Dire Queen said softly. "You have great strength of mind and will. Your loyalty to the Imperium is clear, as you risked your very existence to protect its overlord…and," she paused and seemed to cackle to herself, "anyone who can fool Overlord Tanus Adalric for six months is surely worth an investment."

"What?" Adalric shouted. "I brought her here to *die*, not to be praised."

"I have pardoned her," the Dire Queen decreed.

"You can't," the overlord said, stunned by her words, and the strange emotions they elicited from deep within him. "By Imperial law, which *you* sanctioned, only the noble elite are allowed to have psionic powers, and tap into the Cosmic Aura."

"She is *now* a member of the elite," the Dire Queen said, her voice an angry hiss, enraged at the resistance Adalric was giving her.

"What do you mean?"

"Never again speak to me in that tone, Adalric," the Dire Queen coolly warned. "My meaning is clear. Blaze shall now be a member of the elite, a baroness of the Imperium."

Blaze's mind shrank back as her lips parted in shock.

"Impossible," Adalric said. "The other barons won't allow it. She has no province to rule, no office to fill."

"Won't allow?" the sovereign yelled. "I can do as I see fit, Overlord. As for her position, she is now *my* personal advisor, Baroness to the Dire Queen." The Dire Queen looked over at Blaze, her crimson eyes aflame with determination. "Child, do you accept?"

Blaze quickly realized that once again she had to show strength of will or be ready to accept death. "I do, my queen," she stated proudly, her voice shaking a bit as she went down on one knee and bowed her head in reverence to her new mistress. She looked back up, her eyes fixing on those luminous orbs. "I will make you proud of me, my queen, you won't regret this."

Adalric glared over at his Shadowguard-turned-noble in fuming silence. "Personal advisor to the Dire Queen? That's *my* job. I will *not* stand for this," he declared strongly.

"You will be silent, Adalric!" the Dire Queen yelled, her voice screeching like a banshee's. "Not only is she to be my personal advisor, but *you* will be the one to train her to be a *TelSor*. Shape her so she can control the raging fires within her soul."

"You want her trained?" Adalric asked, in total disbelief of all that was happening. "She's nothing…a guard…*my* guard."

"Not anymore," the Dire Queen said, her voice sinking back to a harsh whisper. "Now she is *my* personal advisor."

"Where does that place me, the overlord?"

"You are as you were. *Your* position as military advisor and overseer of the nobility is intact, as is your place on the *Demoness*," the queen explained, trying to calm her servant. "*Her* position is to further aid me, not depose you."

Adalric glanced down as he tried to coalesce his thoughts into some semblance of order. "Very well, my queen," he finally said. "I will do as you wish."

"A *wise* choice," the Dire Queen replied.

She glanced over at her new advisor and quickly decided new garments were needed, some befitting her new position of authority. "We must have you cleaned up, my child," she directed at Blaze, "you must be ready to face the public with this news."

Blaze glanced down at her armor, its bulk and constriction now seemingly heightened. What had once been a symbol of pride and achievement now felt like some hated shell she was metamorphosing inside of. A caterpillar becoming a butterfly, a soldier becoming a noble.

"Adalric will see to it that you have new quarters here on board the *Sentinel* and are properly clothed and armed for a celebration in your honor tonight."

"Excuse me?" Adalric asked, sure he misunderstood the queen's request.

"I want you to get her more fitting attire, Adalric," the Dire Queen softly repeated, a warning tone in her voice. "Also, get her some suitable chambers on this Star-Citadel, chambers befitting one of her new position." An evil grin formed in her darkened mind. "In fact, give her yours. You can stay on the *Demoness* while here, you don't need two noble staterooms. When you are finished, prepare her for a celebration tonight."

Adalric felt his patience, and his pride, snap like brittle kindling wood. "You are putting me in the position of her servant...I am the overlord, not a *valet*."

The Dire Queen's eyes flared up. "You won't even be *that* if you continue, Adalric. You are *not* her servant, merely her instructor and mentor. Any more defiance and I will have her take your title as well."

Silence reigned in that dark room for what seemed an eternity, then Adalric moistened his lips with his tongue and nodded. "Very well, my queen," he replied curtly, then turned to his former guard. "Baroness Blaze," he said as if he had swallowed bitter fruit, "come with me."

"She will join you shortly," the Dire Queen said, her command clear.

Adalric's lips turned white as his jaw clenched tighter. He nodded and angrily strode away, his crimson and black cloak billowing behind him.

For an instant, Blaze's elation turned sour as she watched Adalric leave. First, he had been angry with her, then he forgave her, then he was furious again. Now she was a baroness, the personal advisor to the Dire Queen, but for some reason the one thing Blaze could think about was that she wished he would forgive her again, and wondered at the pain this whole scene must have caused him.

The Dire Queen scrutinized Adalric's exit, but also carefully studied Blaze watching him as well. *That foolish girl. I see I have much to undo,* she laughed in hollow silence. *She admires him, and all he wants now is to kill her. No matter, he would not dare harm her now that she is my personal servant. Blaze,* she continued to muse while watching her troubled advisor, *you may feel that you are confused now, but soon you will learn to control your abilities, as well as mastering other talents. With proper guidance, you will rise above my other nobles and be more powerful to me than any three combined. As Adalric teaches you his parlor tricks, you will learn from me to be fully loyal, as I mold and shape you in my own image. Yes,* her thoughts rose to near elation, *everything is going perfectly.*

~ * ~

Overlord Adalric's heavy footsteps echoed in Blaze's ears even after his departure. Blaze stood up slowly, squared her shoulders and held her head high with a swan's grace, but there were still many questions lingering in her mind. However, she knew that for now she had to adapt, for adapting was survival, and she was determined to survive.

She turned back to the dais, the firelight playing against her armor. "Your majesty?" she asked.

No one was there, merely an empty throne and a wisp of charcoal smoke.

Chapter Seventeen
Confrontation

Blaze waited patiently in the queen's throne room for Adalric to return with her new attire. She wished the Dire Queen had not left but was also relieved to be out of her presence. *What is she?* Blaze pondered. *She's there, but then she isn't. I saw a body, or was it just a black shadow? I felt so cold when she was looking at me, as if she could see into my very soul. Even so, she saved me from Adalric's wrath...what does she want from me in return?*

Her thoughts closed off as the large doors opened, revealing Adalric as he re-entered the throne room. In his hands he held a crimson bundle of cloth and a pair of tall red boots, which he let fall at her feet as he reached her.

"Here is your raiment," he said, his curt words slicing at her, his powerful voice filled with disgust.

Blaze glanced down at the pile of clothes at her feet, half surprised it was not another suit of battle armor as she had been wearing as a Shadowguard, or an Imperial military uniform variant like Adalric's. She looked back up at him, her eyes trying to see through, into the man she had been serving until now. *What can I say to him?* she wondered. *I can feel the anger pouring from him. I wish I wasn't the object of his hatred.*

"You waste your time with idle thoughts," Adalric commented coolly. "Get dressed, then come out and I will take you to *your* chambers."

"Why is it that you can read me so easily?" Blaze asked, suddenly feeling bold toward her master.

Adalric gazed down at her silently as he pursed his lips, then turned and walked away. Halfway to the door he stopped and glanced over his shoulder at the young woman he left behind, realizing that if her words were true, then he wouldn't be here now. "It is a skill I have." He looked back at the door, as if fighting with his own emotions. "You will learn it in time." He continued out, leaving her in darkened silence.

Time seemed to stand still as Blaze stared at the closed doors. *Am I really going to learn such skills?* She absently wondered. *Do I deserve this?* Once again, she questioned the Dire Queen' motives but could see no reasons behind them.

Finally, the young woman knelt and picked up the clothes the overlord provided for her. Although she had, at first, considered the bundle to be cloth, she now realized it was more. Even though it was light, it felt strange, as if made of some durable, resistant material. Blaze pulled at the fabric, revealing hidden filaments of reflective material, indicating the cloth was energy and electric repellent. Shrugging her shoulders, she carefully shed the armor of the Shadowguard, as if sliding out of her chrysalis. For a moment she stood before the throne, nude, and felt a change coming over her, as if she were stepping out of one life and into another.

Slowly, but intently, she picked up the bright-red bodysuit Adalric provided and slipped into it. She gently put in both legs, then pulled the sleeveless, collared, one-piece jumpsuit over her shoulders and tugged the tiny zipper up the front as high as it could go, which stopped at a point between her full breasts, leaving some cleavage exposed. Blaze paused to examine the matching boots. So light and delicate to the touch, they were a sharp contrast to the clunky combat boots to which she had become accustomed. Pulling the long boots up over the footed pant legs of the bodysuit, she noticed the slight heels which accentuated the strength of her firm legs, and gave her almost two extra inches of height, but wondered about their practicality. Next, Blaze slid the long bright-red gloves gently over her arms, feeling them reach almost up to her shoulders, yet leaving her fingers free as there were no tips to her gloves. She picked up the thick black belt, with attached sheath, and fit it snugly around her waist, though she wondered why the sheath was empty. Wasn't Adalric supposed to arm her also? Last was the long crimson cloak, closer in color to the deep red of Adalric's uniform. This she handled almost with awe, feeling chills tingle down her spine as she pulled it around her shoulders and fastened it to the tiny black studs on the open collar of the body suit. For a long moment, she stood still, feeling the silky fabric caress her skin. *Strange*, she thought, *it* *doesn't feel armored…*but somehow, she knew it was. Blaze gazed around but noticed there were no mirrors in the throne room. *No matter,* she thought as a smile spread across her lips, *I just know everything is perfect…it feels great.* She ran her hands down the length of her new uniform as her smile turned into a wide grin. *I must look fantastic,* she decided as she glanced down at herself again, to the form-fitted bodysuit which hugged every curve with perfect precision. From the length of her legs to the size of the boots, from the fit of the gloves to the snug way it held her curves, it was all flawless.

Perfect, she thought again, suddenly feeling a bit suspicious, *almost too perfect. How does he know my exact measurements?* she wondered, her lips pressing together thoughtfully, *it's not as if they're on file anywhere. Forget it,* she scolded herself, *you have more important things to consider now, Blaze…Lady Blaze…Baroness Blaze, advisor to the Dire Queen.* Her smile turned into a soft laugh as she looked around the throne room in a different way, settling her gaze on the throne itself. She wondered what kind of person you had to be to be the sovereign, to control all the Imperium, and to control men like Adalric.

Suddenly an icy breeze whispered through the room, chilling her down to her bones. She hugged herself as she wrapped her long cloak around her tightly, taking comfort in its satiny embrace.

"You have great ambition," came a solemn hiss from the empty air, "but do not mistake that for power."

Blaze whirled around, to find herself face to face with the Dire Queen. *Damn,* she cursed silently, *I didn't even hear her coming…or had she ever really been absent?*

The Dire Queen's scrutinizing gaze measured her new assistant, her scarlet eyes silently judging the young baroness' attire, as the sovereign speculated as to what Adalric's motives were for so enticing a choice. "It definitely compliments your figure, child," she said in her rasping voice.

"Is it appropriate?" Blaze asked, concerned about its distinct sensuality.

"Yes," the Dire Queen answered after re-appraising the entire outfit. "It gives you an air of nobility." A slow grating laugh escaped the Dire Queen. "Besides, there's no reason you can't be my assistant *and* a woman at the same time."

True, Blaze silently agreed. *After all, my outfit is no more revealing than Baroness Drusee-la's, maybe less since it covers my legs.* "Thank you, Your Majesty."

The young baroness gazed up at her new mistress, fighting the chill that the queen's close presence caused in her. "I truly appreciate all you have done for me, but how can I possibly advise you? I know so little about politics."

"Indeed," the Dire Queen said, then lightly laughed, "but you know much about true human nature, and knowing that gives you an advantage over people like Adalric, who see the galaxy as one large battlefield. The universe is made up of people, some human, many who are not. I wish to establish the human species as the ruling dominance, and to do that I have to understand them better. You will help me to do this."

At last, Blaze thought with a rising confidence, *now this makes some sense. I may not know much about strategies and war, but she's right, I do know people and how to judge them. It's a skill you pick up growing up in a pit like Tenebrous. You either learn it or you die, it's as simple as that.* "My queen, I will not disappoint you."

"I know, child. I know you will serve me excellently, in many ways. More ways than you can possibly imagine."

With the implied dismissal, Blaze turned away, her cloak billowing behind her as she marched out of the throne room, gaining more confidence with each fluid stride.

~ * ~

Tanus Adalric paced back and forth in the long hallway which led to the throne room, firmly convinced this was the worst day of his life. *What's taking her so long,* he silently fumed, *all she had to do was get dressed.*

The four Imperial Shadowguards watched the overlord with worried intensity, each totally aware of his fury, each hoping to avoid being the brunt of his wrath.

How could this have happened? Adalric continued silently as he sank deeper and deeper into the darkened pit that consumed his every thought. *I discovered the truth about Blaze, and what happens? The Dire Queen doesn't execute her at all. She knew how long I searched and yet she let her live.* The anger within the overlord sizzled at the chafing memory, laced with the confusion he had felt when he knew she was not going to die, confusion that he realized was relief she was still alive. He forced his thoughts back to the issue, recalling the Dire Queen's pardon. *Now she's titled...a baroness...her assistant no less. What does that make me?* He boiled silently as his pacing quickened, causing the guards to shudder with each pounding clang of his sharp heeled boots. *I am the overlord, which means the ruler over all the other barons. It is my job to advise the Dire Queen. This can only mean one thing,* he firmly decided, *which is that the Dire Queen is setting up Blaze to take my place. She was probably intending to do that with Drusee-la, but Blaze would be better. Blaze is young, impressionable, and unknowledgeable about the proceedings in the Imperium, therefore the Dire Queen can effortlessly manipulate her. With the Dire Queen guiding her talents, Blaze could easily become powerful enough to hold the position firmly against the other barons. Clever, my queen,* he laughed sarcastically, *very clever. However, it's* not *going to work. I will not stand by and train this woman to assume my position. But,* he thought with remorse, *I can't kill her without cause...at least, not while she's in the queen's favor.*

Adalric looked up, a malicious sneer crossing his lips. *Of course,* he decided, *I don't have to kill her at all. No, it would be far preferable to break her into submission, to crush her spirit right away like I did with Alicia. Then the Dire Queen would lose faith in her and will have to start again, which could give me the time I need to prepare. And the method to proceed with is plainly clear.* As clear as he knew it would be from the first moment he saw her without her helmet on, her stirring visage writhing in silent protest against his grasp.

Nodding to himself with determination, he faced the guards. "Inform Baroness Blaze to meet me at my former quarters here on *Sentinel.* I'll be waiting for her there." *It is there,* he finished silently as he turned and walked down the corridor, each step fueling his growing rage, *I will finish this quickly and neatly...before it gets a chance to go too far. Suddenly,* he thought with a smile, *this day doesn't seem so bad after all.*

~ * ~

Blaze emerged from the throne room to find the hallway devoid of the overlord. "Where could he have gone?" she wondered aloud. "Have you seen him?" she casually asked the Shadowguards, then cringed internally as she realized how common she must have sounded. *I have to start thinking like a noble,* she scolded herself.

"Yes, my Lady," one of the guards reported. "He wants you to meet him in your new quarters, which are his old ones."

"Fine," she answered, then bit her bottom lip. "Where's that?"

The Imperial Shadowguards glanced at each other in confusion for a moment. Then one of them stepped forward.

"I am going off duty, my Lady," he said. "I will escort you there if you wish."

Blaze sighed mentally, *they can feel my confusion, yet they are still willing to help. I won't forget this.* "That would be suitable," she slowly answered, choosing each word carefully. She had to start acting her position or no one would take her seriously, especially herself.

The long walk to her new cabin seemed endless as the two of them marched along, the baroness and the Shadowguard. Blaze could feel the stares of those she passed penetrating deeply into her as they walked through the plaza. Even as they crossed the spot where she had revealed herself not two hours earlier, she kept her chin up and remained firm, no matter how much she was shaking inside.

~ * ~

Across the large central area of the station, Baron Koroqo watched attentively, his conversation with a S'teka guard silenced by the appearance of this new Imperial noble. *Impressive,* he sternly thought as his lips formed into an approving smile, *quite impressive. The girl is taken there to die and comes out as a noble. Look at her,* he continued to himself as he appraised her with his seasoned eyes, *she is terrified, I can feel it in every fiber of my body. Yet despite that, she walks along proudly, her head held high. She has an appealing innocence, and none of Drusee-la's cocky arrogance.*

However, he considered as his smile faded, *her greatest challenge is yet to come. I hope you are ready,* he silently contemplated as he sensed the events which would soon transpire, *for your sake.*

~ * ~

Blaze exited the plaza and felt a great weight lift from her shoulders as she scolded herself for her childish feelings. For a moment she turned back and watched the busy mixture of Legionnaires, Shadowguards, and officers, then continued her trek, following the lead of the Shadowguard ahead of her. *Why are you afraid of them? Do you think they deserve their positions any more than you do? The Dire Queen wants you to be her personal advisor…you. So, stop this cowardice and straighten up.*

Blaze's thoughts jerked to a halt as the Shadowguard stopped in front of a set of double doors. To either side of the doorway stood another two Shadowguards, their weapons set in honored salute. For an instant Blaze wondered if she should still be with them, but cast those thoughts away with the rest of her misgivings. She was a noble now, one of the powerful privileged few. Waiting beyond those sealed doors was the overlord, the man who would be her mentor and teacher, who would educate her in the ways of the TelSor, whatever that meant. *No,* she quickly decided, *I mustn't keep my new instructor waiting.* With a nod of her head, she thanked the Shadowguard for showing her the way.

For a moment he looked like he was leaving, but then he turned back to her. "W-with all due respect, my Lady," he said quietly, "I wouldn't go in there if I were you."

"Oh," Blaze replied, amused by this sudden advice. "And why is that?"

"He's furious," the Shadowguard continued as he kept glancing over her shoulder at the large grey doors. "I think he means to kill you."

Blaze's eyes narrowed as she evaluated the guard's words. *What could he possibly gain by lying?* she pondered silently. *No,* she decided, remembering all she had been through, *he is telling the truth, but that doesn't mean he's right. Many were the times I mistook the overlord's contemplative moods for anger. Surely these* Sentinel *Shadowguards don't know him nearly as well as I do.* "Thank you," she finally replied. "I'm sure I'll be fine."

The guard nodded, then quickly walked away.

Blaze glanced back at the doors, and taking a deep breath, opened them.

Her new suite was somewhat like she expected it to be, in other words, like Adalric's chambers on the *Demoness.* She felt her boots sink into the thick black carpeting as the double doors slid closed behind her, sealing her in her new sanctuary. It was dark inside, but she could make out a short corridor which led to her new office and bedroom. Dim light flickered into the hallway, as if a window were letting in starlight, casting fanciful shadows on the far wall. Blaze suddenly wished she had taken the time to notice where the lighting controls were in Adalric's chambers on the *Demoness,* for now she could not find them at all. She also could not make out any sign of the overlord, yet she knew he was there, somewhere.

"Overlord Adalric?" she called out into the darkness, yet there was no response.

For the first time Blaze felt the absence of her yet-to-be-acquired sword, or the electro carbine that she rarely used. She slowly continued, edging down the hallway of her new home, her new resting place.

You're being a fool again, she scolded herself. *Adalric is simply not calling out to you, he expects you to find him yourself.* Reaching out with her feelings, and calming down her paranoia-laced thoughts, she realized he was in the bedroom. *Of course,* she instantly realized, *he's probably removing his old personal effects, like the art collections and books he has on the* Demoness. Blaze squared her shoulders and walked proudly into her new bedroom, to find Adalric standing on the far side, waiting silently in the shadows.

"I'm here," she said, spewing the first thing that came to mind.

The overlord stared at her for a long hard moment, then nodded thoughtfully. "So, you are." He moved from the wall, advancing toward her like a cat stalking prey.

Blaze felt her skin tingle as she watched him circle her slowly. *Why was he acting like this? He didn't seem angry, like the Shadowguard warned.* "So," she finally said as she glanced around, trying to crack his chilling mood, "these are my new chambers."

Adalric stopped circling for a moment. Then he nodded again. "Yes...they are."

"I want to thank you," she said, hoping to get back on his good side, hoping he had one. "I appreciate you teaching me to learn the ways of the TelSor. I don't deserve it."

Adalric continued to stare at her, his face frozen like a cool statue, his lips a thin grey line.

Unnerved at the overlord's silence, she cleared her throat as she tried again, desperate to quell his obvious displeasure with her. "I know this must feel wrong to you. I mean, me going from being your guard to the Dire Queen's advisor. Don't misjudge the situation, I consider us to be equals." Blaze internally flinched when she realized what she said.

Adalric's lips parted a fraction of an inch, the lone betrayal to the concealed furious embers within being stoked by her every word. His eyes narrowed behind the dark lenses on his mask, as he let his gaze slowly scrape across her body. He continued circling her, only stopping when he put himself between her and the hallway back to the office and door. His gloved hands curled into tightened fists as his vision rested heavily on her face. Somewhere in his mind he registered that she was strikingly beautiful but knew this wasn't about any newfound desire...he knew he had to break her, destroy her spirit. "I appreciate your sentiment," his powerful voice whispered, as if each syllable was causing him pain. "I'm sure our times together will be quite...stimulating."

Blaze froze as the pit of her stomach began to knot up, there was something in his voice that was different, something that set off alarms inside her and yelled one thing, *get out of here.* He had no intention of training her, she now clearly understood that. He agreed so the Dire Queen wouldn't kill him. *That Shadowguard was right, he still wants me dead. I have to get out of here, and now!* She paused for a moment, then began walking purposefully toward him, intent on leaving the bedroom.

Without a moment's warning, Adalric's hand shot out as she tried to pass, and landed squarely on Blaze's chest. For a split second it rested there, then swiftly pushed out, tossing her effortlessly back across the room to land in a heap on her grand new bed.

Rolling frantically to free herself from the black velvet sheets, she regained her balance on her hands and knees. With sudden rage, she glared up at the overlord, her lips forming into an angry snarl.

"Leaving so soon?" Adalric asked, his sudden smile becoming a sneer as his voice dropped to a low menacing rumble. "There's so much you still have to learn."

The force of her landing knocked all ideas of compromise and reconciliation out of her mind, but she had no intention of letting him kill her now. Blaze felt her temper flaring as she crouched on the firm mattress, grasping the black sheets in her tightened fists as she felt her muscles constrict in readiness. It had required great restraint to quell her fiery instincts throughout the day's bizarre happenings, but now she felt the need to live. Now nothing was going to keep them in check as they begged, ached to be released in a growing pyre of fury. "Perhaps there's a lesson *you* need to learn as well, Adalric," she whispered in return, her voice as low and menacing as his.

Her thoughts stung with the memory of his attempt to have her executed, accentuated by this new attack. She was devoted to him, and he cared nothing for her in return.

The overlord's lips tightened firmly in shock, then twisted into a grin, as if he were pleased that she was going to fight back.

Blaze saw his patronizing smile and decided, *enough.* She moved to get off the bed as Adalric made a slicing gesture in the air with his hand. Without warning, her legs swept out from under her as if an unseen wave of considerable force came along, pulling her onto her back amidst the flowing black sheets. It was then the attack began, as she felt a stab in her mind as he forced his will into hers, threatening to overpower and unravel her psyche.

She could barely concentrate as she felt him jump onto the bed and physically pin her there, his darkened eyepieces staring down at her. His will pushed deeper and deeper, hoping to break hers.

"Now, Blaze," he said as he held her down, his face close to hers, "we will see if we are truly equals, or if I am still your master, and you, my slave."

His words fell on deaf ears, for suddenly all she could feel was the memory of the searing pain of the mind-numbing device in the rehabilitation colony, all she could see were the gangs of Tenebrous closing in, their hands covered with Reaper's crimson blood. This all added to the already mounting furnace she began building up internally, like a volcano about to erupt. She cast away the ghosts of her past as her eyes opened slowly, funeral pyres dancing in each darkened orb which now glowed fiercely, and she focused her years of pain on one man, the one man who would pay for it all. *Damn him*, she silently cursed as the fire within her built to a peak that grew higher and higher, *let him burn!* With an explosive outpour, she released her fiery demons as never before, determined to leave nothing but ashes for a tiny urn.

However, Adalric felt the change in her, and read it in her suddenly glowing cold eyes as he straddled her. It was barely a second of warning, but it had been enough. His mental barriers were instantly erected, and he summoned all of his mastery of the Cosmic Aura into a protective energy shield, as his body was engulfed in the tremendous inferno that she suddenly released. Like a discarded rag, the eruption tossed the overlord across the room, slamming him into the far wall, to finally land in a pile of burning sheets and smoking carpet.

Blaze felt her anger drain away as she fell back onto the singed mattress, both physically and mentally crippled from fatigue, tiny flames dancing along what was left of the sheets. She lay there in shock for a moment, still in disbelief over what she had done. *I've killed the overlord*, her numbed mind concluded. At first relief swept over her, which slowly was replaced with a sudden sense of sorrow. But both emotions drained away with the last of her strength, as she saw movement out of the corner of her eye, then despair flowed over her as she heard his hollow laughter.

"Good, Blaze," he barely was able to say through his scorched larynx, "very good…but not good enough."

She opened her eyes again to see that Adalric had gotten back up, his cloak gone, wisps of smoke spiraling off his charred uniform. *How can that be?* her mind screamed weakly, *I gave it everything.* Blaze tried to summon the fire again, but there was no use, her last expulsion had wiped her out. Suddenly, her eyes began to sting as she felt the last of her will ebb away. She was finished, and she knew it. Without her pyrokinesis, she was defenseless against his might. Hypnotized by his power, all she could do was shrink from him, like a dying flower.

Adalric watched her eyes water as a single glistening tear flowed gracefully down the round hollow of her cheek and breathed a gratifying sigh of victory. But then the sigh died in his throat. He suddenly felt exhausted, defeated...broken? He felt his own eyes sting and his lips fell open as the realization that somehow the struggle of their wills and explosion of mental powers had not truly broken either of them, but instead locked their minds momentarily together.

He felt her repressed desires for him and total feeling of betrayal.

She felt his repressed desires for her and total feeling of betrayal.

She wasn't even fully aware of sliding to the edge of the bed as he stumbled over to meet her. It wasn't like two people coming together, but two minds that were unsure of where one ended and the other began. For a moment they stared at each other, wisps of smoke all around the bedroom. Suddenly their lips met as they embraced, and she pivoted pulling him down onto the bed, this time it was she who straddled him.

Her lips found his again, and for a moment he tried to push her back up and away.

"Stop," he finally managed to say as he tried to separate his psyche from hers, but it was no use.

"Why?" she asked, suddenly smiling through her confused feelings. "What are you afraid of?"

"There is nothing I fear," he said, suddenly unsure of his own words.

"Let's find out," she said as their mutual resolve melted away allowing them to truly fall into what was about to happen.

~ * ~

The Dire Queen leaned back on her throne, restless in her ashen thoughts. *Something is wrong,* she decided, *very wrong.* She reached out again, tugging at the dark psychic vibrations in the Cosmic Aura that flowed around her. "He has attacked her," she whispered quietly to herself. "Devil spawn, I hope she hasn't been killed." The Dire Queen rose up and glided around her throne, to stop at a large ruby sphere that was securely mounted atop a pedestal behind her dais. She gingerly, almost lovingly, reached out a shadowed hand to caress its scarlet warmth. This gesture activated the secret fire within its multifaceted surface, causing it to light up, spilling soft crimson light across her form. "No," she whispered with relief as she soaked in its power, "they both still live."

She withdrew her hand and moved back to her throne, like a spider returning to its web. *I will have to be watchful in the future,* she quickly decided. *His animosity toward her is stronger than I predicted. If she cannot survive his wrath, then she is of no use to me anyway. Still, I must be more careful with her…she is young and has no idea of how to handle him yet.*

"Time," she said as she cackled quietly, "that's what I need. Just a little more time."

Chapter Eighteen
Celebration

Tanus Adalric lay on his back in bed for what seemed to him an eternity as his thoughts twisted, rose, and fell, fighting the inner turmoil that raged within his mind. *How could my resolve have failed me so?*

He moved his left hand slightly, still feeling Blaze's supple warmth against his skin. Her soft hair was right under his chin as she rested her head against his broad chest, still sound asleep. It was there that she collapsed after their "confrontation", falling into a deep slumber. Adalric had been sorely tempted to follow her example, for he too felt exhausted by the ordeal. Yet he would not, could not, allow himself that luxury. *She is still my enemy,* he reminded himself as he absently traced the tender curve of her hip with the tips of his fingers, *and I must always remain on my guard.*

How did this happen? He angrily wondered as he continued to gently caress her. *How did our minds fuse? Is her will stronger than mine?* Yet still he held her against his body, as if afraid to move away, to break a delicate moment that could easily be shattered.

With her asleep, he wasn't sure if he was still connected to her.

What weakness is this? This hold she has on you must be broken…now, before it is too late. With determined resolve, he compelled his hand to slide back up her body, until it rested firmly around her silken neck, still bruised from before. For an instant he let himself enjoy the feel of her skin beneath his palm, then he slowly applied hardened pressure, intending to snuff out her young life. *Yes,* he thought with determination, *do it now, while she is sleeping.* His grip tightened as his powerful fingers contracted, applying compression to her carotid arteries. He could feel the gentle pulse of her blood flowing beneath his grip, a little more pressure and it would all be over.

Blaze moved slightly, nuzzling her face deeper into the corded muscles of his chest, seemingly oblivious to her impending fate.

Adalric felt her hand move along his chest, as her fingers dug snugly into his skin, and he froze. He tried to continue the deadly pressure, but his hand remained motionless, as if made of rock. He inhaled her sweet fragrances deeply, and felt his powerful grip melt, until his hand fell away from her.

With a gentle movement, he quickly slid out from beneath her and sat up in the grand bed. Even though it had been over a half hour since their confrontation, scattered tendrils of smoke still rose from the mattress and around the room. Timeless moments passed as Adalric tried to stand up and leave, to vacate as quickly as possible. Instead, he gazed back down at her, exposed on the bare mattress. Unblinking, he simply watched her, her chest rising and falling with each smooth breath, his fingers aching to touch her again, to feel her electric warmth. He let his gaze drift lazily over her gentle curves, yet it was not enough. The room's darkness, once an ally, now seemed a bothersome impediment accentuated by the tinted lenses of his cowl.

A growing desire suddenly filled him, one that could not be quelled, and his hand slowly rose up to the armored mask that encased his face and most of his head. With firm resolution, he carefully started to slide off the one last piece of clothing he still had on, the piece that he hated the most. For an instant he hesitated...*what if she awakens and sees me? She would be repulsed.* He had to see her without the mask, to view her with naked eyes.

Adalric quickly finished removing the cowl and placed it on the mattress, next to her thigh. He let his eyes return to the treasure before him, to truly see her for the first time.

"So beautiful," he whispered, almost inaudibly, shocked by the change without the mask. In that instant, he loathed the need to wear that thing more than ever before, and briefly considered destroying it. No, it was a fantasy to think such thoughts and allow himself to stay here with her, when he should be off plotting her "accidental" demise.

He suddenly thought of how tired he was, realizing that between both of their psionic attacks, plus the bizarre bond it formed, it nearly drained him. Deep down he knew that he had barely stopped her pyrokinetic retaliation. *That is now*, he reasoned as he tried to regain his anger but found it so difficult, *when she is undisciplined and unfocused. After I have trained her to control the Cosmic Aura, or the Dire Queen has, then I might not be able to withstand her flames. No, she must be destroyed now, before it is too late.*

Adalric turned to telekinetically call for his sword, when she moaned slightly and rolled completely onto her back. All thoughts of his weapon died as he gazed at her body, every delicious curve, each exquisite hollow. As carefully as possible, he allowed himself to reach out and gently lay his fingers on her delicately tanned stomach. *How perfect she is*, he thought as his hand traced an amorous path across her skin...*almost angelic.* As his fingers lightly ran along her curves, she let out a soft moan, her body surging slightly to his firm touch. Adalric withdrew quickly, as if burnt, suddenly realizing how careless he had been.

You weak-minded fool, he cursed himself, *how can you let this woman influence you so? You let this situation get out of control, and it could have cost you your life. You must put an end to this, you simply must. This young woman cannot become a TelSor.*

Determination returning to his body, he quickly rose off the bed and put on his uniform, ignoring the sting the clothes brought to the light burns on his skin. Gathering up his charred cloak and discarded electrosword, he prepared to make a hasty exit. Locating his old electronic timekeeper in a dresser drawer, he activated it and placed it on the table next to her sleeping form, then turned and walked to the bedroom door.

Adalric almost left the room when he froze, then gazed back one last time, as if pulled by sudden gravity. He knew he didn't want to leave her and that made him angrier. For an instant he considered giving in and going back to her, to take her into his arms again, to feel her gentle caress. However, he did none of these things, he merely glanced down for a moment, then placed his cowl back on, and was quickly gone.

~ * ~

"Wake up, Blaze," the harsh voice sliced into her blissful slumber, "you must wake up now."

"Mmmmmm?" She made some complaining noises, trying to

awaken.

"You have to be at your celebration in thirty minutes. Wake up, Blaze."

"Mmmmmm?" she tried again as she forced open one eye.

"You have to be at your celebration in twenty-nine minutes."

Blaze let out another groan as she lashed out with her arm, knocking the timekeeper off the table. It landed on the soft carpeting and rolled to a stop at the foot of the bed.

"Wake up, Blaze," the diligent voice continued, "you must wake up now."

Blaze's eyes focused in annoyance as the small black timepiece began to smoke, its internals melting away.

"You have to bee aattt yyyyooooouuuurrrrr ccc—"

Flames licked out from the hole in its side as it went silent forever. A satisfied smile crept across her lips as she sat up in her new bed. She stretched out her arms and leaned back, attempting to crack her stiffened spine. Despite the lingering comfortable warmth that filled her, she hadn't felt more exhausted in a long while. Exhausted, yet invigorated.

Slowly blinking the remnants of sleep out of her eyes, Blaze's attention was then drawn to the huge mirror which covered the opposite wall, and found herself staring at a disheveled nude woman sitting amidst a singed mattress with a few scraps of sheets left. Momentarily confused, all she concluded was she was alone in the vast chambers. *What did I do?* Blaze wondered apprehensively, as she fought the haze that covered the confrontation's events and clouded her memory. *He tried to kill me...I tried to kill him,* she realized slowly as she rubbed her bruised wrists. *What happened afterward, was it all reality or a dream?* Although she wasn't sure of the answer, she realized what happened in those faded moments would never, should never, occur again.

Was I feeling his thoughts? Her mind wondered. *Did he feel mine too? What the hell happened to us, between us?* She laughed quietly, trying to forget the tingles that still ebbed in her wearied muscles. *He knows I'm not an easy target now, that's for sure. Will he train me as the Dire Queen ordered him? I'll have to see how he reacts to me at the celebration.*

The celebration! she frantically remembered as she picked up her deep red bodysuit from the floor where Adalric tossed it. This time she dressed faster, afraid of insulting the queen by being late for a party in her own honor.

As she finished attaching her flowing cloak, she turned to face the mirror again, grateful her long gloves and high collar covered her dark bruises. Suddenly, she started to smile, realizing she had discovered the answer to an enigma which plagued many about whether Adalric was a man, some machine, or even a foul demon. *No,* she decided firmly, *he is very much a man.*

Blaze momentarily dwelled on the encounter, feeling that all her senses, except one, had been satisfied. She had certainly seen him, but not truly. All she knew for certain was the muscular outlines she saw in his uniform were totally deserved, yet still she knew there was one thing left. *One day,* she firmly decided, *I will see under that mask of his, no matter what the consequence.*

Perhaps worse than her unquenched thirst for answers was the disturbing feeling that something was left undone. Maybe it was something that should have been said, words that needed to have been spoken. Uncertain about what nagged her, Blaze decided again it would probably be best to forget what happened. *After all, what else could I do? Tell the Dire Queen?* Blaze shook her head and chuckled quietly. *I can see it now,* she laughed, "My Queen, your overlord tried to destroy my will, and I fought back and somehow, we ended up in bed together."

Blaze's laughter died as she looked at herself in the mirror again. *So different,* she thought as she walked close enough to touch the reflection. She let her eyes stroll down the figure before her. No longer a dirty forgotten sewer child or an anonymous bulky soldier, she gazed at a graceful Imperial noble. *Perhaps Travis was right,* she thought while looking deeply into her own eyes. *Perhaps there is something genuinely lovely about me.* The young baroness nodded to herself with a smile, then turned away from the mirror, her body straightening with a new sense of pride. With determination, she left her new quarters and headed to the ceremony which waited in her honor.

As she walked out her door into the dimly lit corridor, set for the night mode, she abruptly halted. The Dire Queen was calling for her. It was nothing she could actually hear, but she knew it all the same, she felt it inside, like round worms pulling under her skin.

Blaze nervously bit her bottom lip as she tried to shake the feeling which was almost making her nauseous. Realizing there was only one way for it to stop, she changed her direction and headed toward the Dire Queen's throne room. *What could she want? Does the Dire Queen already know what happened?*

Putting her thoughts safely to rest behind her mental barriers, as she had done so many times around Adalric, she strode directly toward the Imperial Chambers. As she came into the grand hallway that led to the huge double doors, the Royal Shadowguards stepped to the side, opening the pathway. Blaze barely noticed their existence, or that of the Shadowguard who followed her to that point, as she entered the darkened room which was lit in scarlet shadows. Slowly she approached the tall throne, the crawling sensation under her skin thankfully fading away, but was quickly replaced by the chill that seemed to accompany her new mistress. She knelt at the base of the dais and waited to be recognized.

~ * ~

The Dire Queen glanced down at her newest servant with a resurrected sense of pride. *How quickly she came,* she thought with satisfaction, *it took Adalric much longer to realize I was calling him the first time. How much more acute her attunement to the Cosmic Aura must be. Perhaps any damage he did to her can be quickly repaired with a few words.* "Rise, my child," she said, her stale voice scratched as soothingly as it could. "Rise and talk with me."

Blaze tentatively gazed up into the darkness within the sovereign's hood, centering on the fiery eyes which floated within. The young woman wondered what it was about the queen that so terrified her, unaware she was allowing her thoughts to roam. Slowly she stood up and waited for the Dire Queen to speak again.

Yes, the Dire Queen's thoughts drifted, *open your mind to me, my child, let me see into your soul. Let me know what it is that will help me to mold you. Ah,* she recoiled slightly, *so Adalric did attack her. But what happened? She is obviously intact.*

Blaze felt the Dire Queen's penetrating stare bore deeply inside her. Defensively, Blaze closed off her mind again, realizing this mental tactic was becoming easier each time she used it.

The Dire Queen's glare snapped back as her luminous eyes brightened with anger, *how dare she shut me out of her thoughts.* She then forced herself to calm down. *Blaze is still young, and unsure of my motives. In time she will open herself up, and when she does, she will be truly mine.* "My child," she said as her eyes grew in intensity, "I called you here to discuss the celebration."

"The celebration?" Blaze asked, her voice a bit shaky.

"Yes," the Dire Queen replied, letting her voice soften again. "You must understand what they will expect of you, and what I expect also."

Blaze glanced down at her feet with uncertainty, then she looked back up at the Dire Queen, her eyes searching for advice in the sovereign's steely glare. "What must I do?"

The Dire Queen gazed back into Blaze's dark eyes and read the resolution within them. Once again, she realized how perfectly she chose. *I can do much with this one…but first we must establish a common ground, she must trust me fully…as Adalric once did.* "Sit," she said as she gestured to the base of the platform below her.

Blaze nodded and sat on the edge of the dais, and looked up at her mistress expectantly, anxious to learn what to do, and how to behave.

"I was not always as you see me now," the sovereign's thin voice continued, a slight trace of remorse hidden within. "Before the time of the Red Star Imperium, or even the United Star Alliance, over a century ago, there was the Terran Imperial Dominion." Her voice swelled with pride, rising eerily to a macabre fullness. "The Terran Imperial Dominion was the greatest single force this area of the galaxy ever knew. For over one hundred years it had ruled with a mighty fist, controlling all we now view as separate governments. At first it was small, but it grew as I did, a Terran child of that great era."

The knowledge that the sovereign had once been human sent a shiver of surprise through Blaze. The young baroness leaned forward with renewed intent as her insatiable curiosity won over, demanding to know the whole story.

"I loved the Imperial Dominion with all my heart," the Dire Queen continued, an almost tender quake in her firm voice. "As I grew, I vowed to become a part of its workings, to rise as far as I could."

"Were you born of a high family?" Blaze asked, eyes wide as she listened.

"No, my child," she said with a chuckle and gazed down at Blaze, "I was an orphan like yourself. Though I had certain advantages, for I was a mutant, a natural-born psionic. Attuning myself to the Cosmic Aura came naturally for me."

Blaze's lips fell open in wonder as she felt a sudden common thread wind between them. She wanted to ask more, especially about the Cosmic Aura, but forced herself to be patient.

"Like you," the Dire Queen went on, "I kept it hidden out of fear of retribution, for the emperor had declared psionics were outlaws, and were to be put to death. You see, he, and many others, had harsh memories of the Psi-Genetic war which plagued Earth many years before. Despite his efforts, that bloody conflict left the seeds of its memory even to this day. The hatred continues, but so do the occasional mutants." She faltered for a moment, as if needing to take a long breath. "It was easy at first, spotting and destroying those with obvious vile deformities. The rest went into hiding, hoping to quietly breed out the mutations, not realizing their future generations would still carry the same gift. Blaze," the Dire Queen whispered quietly, "you and I are the children they feared."

The Dire Queen smiled internally as she read the sense of wonder in her assistant's eyes, then she continued, her voice winding its way through the darkened room. Gazing down at Blaze, she resumed. "Always feeling like an outlaw, I grew up drifting from one place to another until, by chance, I met the captain of the Imperial guard. I was barely eighteen then, but he was taken with me instantly…as I was with him." She paused and shook her head, almost sadly. "He was handsome, tall and proud. Within two months we were married, and I assumed a position in the royal guard under him. However, it was not only the captain's fancy that I captured, for the emperor himself noticed me whenever I was stationed to guard him. The emperor's desires knew no bounds. He had my husband put to death on my twentieth birthday and took me for his bride that very same day."

The Dire Queen' voice washed over Blaze, but the torment that laced her words lingered. Perhaps the sovereign's words merely reminded the young baroness of her own grief, her own losses. Blaze was stunned as she continued to devour the tale, admitting there was so much more to the Dire Queen than she could have possibly thought.

"Yes," the queen said, her voice slicing through Blaze's thoughts, feeling their bond grow, "I'll never forget that day, when the emperor held a celebration to present me to his officers and nobles. How beautiful I was then, with delicate pale skin, and long black hair that gently flowed down past my shoulders." She paused for a moment, as if collecting her thoughts, remembering a past almost forgotten. "My frame was not unlike yours, not too tall, and nicely proportioned," casting her gaze across Blaze's body, she almost seemed to laugh girlishly, "…though perhaps a trifle less developed."

Blaze's lips pursed as she glanced down at her figure.

"Do not worry, child," the Dire Queen soothed, "you are more than perfect."

A smile came to Blaze's face as she gazed back up, hoping the Dire Queen would continue her story.

"As I was saying," the sovereign said, "back then I was exquisite. Yes, I was young, ravishing and doomed…doomed to marry that wretched hideous old man. Still, it was wondrous…when I entered the ballroom for the celebration all fell silent, allowing me to be properly announced. I was dressed in a midnight blue gown that was so dark you could barely distinguish it from black. They watched me in awed silence, from the lowest officer to the highest lord. All loved me and anguished in their desires over me.

"It was during these years I started learning the dark arts of sorcery, to enhance my powers, similar to the ways of the TelSor, but so much more. My powers and my connection to the Cosmic Aura grew with my popularity. Soon it was I who made all the public appearances, and the emperor hid in his throne room, despising the loyalty that was building around me. I continued to grow strong, while he withered into weakness and old age. Intent on destroying me and ending my threat, he attacked me one night as we slept together…but he was no longer a match for me, and I ended his foul life with one fell thought.

"After that, things went quickly, my power grew and so did the Terran Imperial Dominion. However, a cancer started to develop within its skin, one I didn't notice before it was too late."

"A revolt?" Blaze asked, anticipating the next part from pre-United Star Alliance history lessons Mattie had given her.

"Yes," the Dire Queen replied, her voice hissing with malice, "the *revolutionaries*. They grew to quite some force, made up of many humanoids and non-humanoids that resented Terran rule, and led by a few dissident humans who wanted the republic back. They attacked one day and caught my fleet around Earth by surprise." She paused for a moment, unsure if she wanted to go on, to relive the bitter horror. "I was in my orbital base at the time, like this one, but much less powerful. My fleet was scattered, and the base destroyed."

"With you in it," Blaze whispered in awe, suddenly starting to comprehend.

"Yes," she replied, "but as all vaporized around me, I called out to the source of my dark powers to save me, to not let my existence be snuffed out by this petty insurgence. My prayer was answered, and I was spared.

"For a long time, I drifted through space, powerless, until I was able to become more...to become this," she said as she gestured to herself. "I gathered up the few remnants of the Dominion and brought them here, to a place where we could rebuild, and this time not make the same mistakes."

"So, you are a...a..." Blaze half whispered, trying to speak the word rumored about the Dire Queen, and feeling the chill within her grow, as images of wraiths and demons filled her mind.

"No, my child," the Dire Queen said, her voice softening again, as she sensed the sudden fear. "I am merely the embodiment of the spirit of the Imperium. All of my hopes and wishes...trapped in this saddened form."

Blaze was awed by the Dire Queen's devotion, and by her need to live, a need which was so great she had made priceless sacrifices. Blaze understood that desire and doubted she would have done any differently, as she felt her heart suddenly go out to the Dire Queen.

"Do not mourn for me, my child. Instead, I want you to represent me here, to be my flesh and blood. I want you to go to that celebration for me, and make them all respect the power I have, to respect *you* and your desire to serve *me* and the Imperium. Together we will crush the United Star Alliance and put the Imperial throne back where it belongs, on Earth."

Blaze stood up solidly and faced the Dire Queen, a determined smile on her face. "I will make you proud, my queen."

"I know you will."

The baroness pulled in a deep breath, then turned toward the door and started to leave, anxious to arrive at the celebration.

"Blaze," the Dire Queen called after her, "remember that it is me you are representing, it is me who is walking into that ballroom with you."

Blaze turned back to the shadowed figure on the throne. "I won't forget it."

The Dire Queen smiled to herself. "I know. I have full confidence in you."

Blaze felt her spirit elated by this honor, an honor she intended not to disappoint. "Thank you, my queen." Then she turned and left.

The Dire Queen watched the tall doors slowly close, then allowed herself to relax. *Perfect*, she thought, *absolutely perfect…*

~ * ~

Tanus Adalric stalked the grand ballroom on the *Sentinel*, weaving through the heavy crowd like a wolf following a scent. He was determined to find the one man who could help him now, knowing he should be easy to spot among the human officers, ambassadors and governors.

The overlord grew annoyed at the sheer number of people present, some dancing, some at the buffet table, most milling about in groups as they gossiped about the reason for this celebration. Knowing the explanation for this ceremony, it irked him to find so many Imperial officers wasting an evening in idle activity. Adalric scanned the room, his stomach churning at every elaborate decoration, every exotic plate of food. The pomp and circumstance of this event appalled him. There were easily two full squadrons of Legionnaires lining the walls, and six Shadowguards protecting the double-doored entrance which loomed ominously on a far wall. He could effortlessly think of better uses for all of them than standing about unproductively at a wasteful party.

Finally spotting his quarry, the overlord quickly moved in, sliding past the S'teka guards.

"Koroqo," he said, his deep voice rising above the crowded din.

The Proximan baron looked up as the overlord approached and raised an amused eyebrow. Instantly sensing something unique had happened, Koroqo was always grateful for his race's natural empathic abilities. The fiery emotions that emitted from Adalric were astounding, causing him to wonder what had transpired. "Overlord Adalric," the S'teka master replied, "how did things go with your *situation*?"

"Not well," Adalric admitted, then moved in closer, knowing there were over-attentive ears all around them, "we must talk."

At that moment, the celebration announcer, one of the few junior officers present, stepped onto the raised platform next to the great double doors. Clearing her throat, she then unraveled a scroll and eyed the spectators tentatively. "Imperial officials, lords and ladies, barons and baronesses," she boomed to the attentive crowd. "By the decree of the Dire Queen, supreme ruling monarch and absolute sovereign of the glorious Imperium. I give you the newest addition to the Imperial nobility, and the Dire Queen's new personal advisor...the Baroness Blaze."

Slowly, the large doors parted, sliding silently into the surrounding walls. Obligatory applause sounded through the large hall as the new baroness emerged.

Blaze stood motionless in the doorway, as she slowly absorbed the sheen and glitter of the ballroom. Nameless faces peered inquisitively at her, while the ringing of the half-hearted applause stung her ears. Her fists clenched tightly in her bright-red gloves, and she knew even the darkest night on Tenebrous would be easier to face than this gathering of people. Squaring her shoulders bravely, she felt her heart quickening and wondered if anyone could see the way her lower lip trembled. A wrenching in her gut reminded her she could not run, could not turn away from this. So, she did the next best thing, she smiled at them. At first, merely a demure grin, slowly her lips curled into a wide disarming smile. Meeting the eyes of as many people as she could, she then straightened and glided to the raised platform and waited patiently for the rote applause to silence. Feeling all eyes upon her, she cleared her mind for a moment and drew strength from the depths of her soul. Faintly, she licked her upper lip and swallowed hard, forcing down her own tension.

Her voice rang out strongly, like a sweet bell, cutting through the expectant silence. "Thank you for honoring me in this fashion." She paused as she gazed at her captive audience, her eyes softening each speculative, and sometimes accusing, glare. She inhaled slowly and continued. "Because you, fellow citizens of the Imperium, have been so gracious to me. I think that I should, in turn, be honest with you. I have not always cared very much for this Imperium." Quickly, low murmurs and gasps spread throughout the ballroom.

In a far corner, one such silent gasp escaped the lips of Adalric, as his eyes widened in shock. He waited tensely for the crowd to storm the platform and rip her into scarlet ribbons, unsure about what he would do when it happened. It never did, she simply began speaking again, her soothingly sultry voice lulling the assemblage into quiet observation.

"No," Blaze said, "I came from a despicable United Star Alliance colony, from which I barely survived. Because of this I grew up hating the Alliance with all my heart. Back then, I knew nothing about the Red Star Imperium, or Pirates as you were referred to then. That is, aside from the lies and propaganda which the Alliance fed me.

"Fleeing from the injustice and grief I came to know there, I ended up here...thankfully," she added slowly with a warm smile. "I joined the Imperial military and was educated, fed and clothed. All the things the Alliance claims they do for its people, for its children." Blaze's mind sank deep into her own memory. She no longer saw the din of people before her, for she could only see the Alliance seal burning painfully into the recesses of her mind. "I never saw the so-called *graces* of the United Star Alliance, because those privileges are a myth. In the Imperium they are reality. Like a child again I was reborn here, and you all gave me the nurturing I needed to thrive and ascend. I have come to love this Imperium as much as I love life, and I swear I will serve its best interests, as long as I live.

"I know that the Dire Queen would have wished to be here herself, but I am honored to represent her at this commencement. She wants you all to know how proud she is of our conquests, and of all of you...from the lowest Legionnaire to the highest baron. And," Blaze's voice rose fiercely, "she wants *us* to continue on strongly until all of our enemies are utterly *destroyed*." There was a brief moment of silence as the Dire Queen's new advisor seemed to hesitate, as if unsure of what to say next, then she let a shy smile cross her scarlet lips. "Thank you all."

The applause started up again, scattered at first, then rising to an appreciable level as the members of the celebration allowed her powerful words and charisma to seep into them. Blaze felt the rumbling ovation wash over her. No longer a dull stinging in her ears, the hard rhythm was a vibrant massage against her tightened muscles. As the applause finally lowered, she bowed her head to them and turned back toward the small stairs, her crimson cloak rippling around her. She then descended into the crowd to meet with those she had now risen above.

Back across the ballroom, Koroqo touched the overlord's arm, and they both stepped away from their guards and moved to a private section along the wall farthest from the stage.

"I see your problem," Koroqo whispered.

"Now she *dares* to speak for the sovereign? She must be stopped," Adalric said, his voice a low growl, "before she undermines all of our authorities."

"Is it truly *all* of us you are worried about, or just yourself?"

"What are you implying?"

Koroqo stared long and hard at the man who was his superior, and his friend, or at least as close to a friend as the Proximan allowed himself. He shook his head, letting out his breath at the same time. "Listen to yourself, Adalric," he tried to comfort. "She hasn't even been in power for more than a day yet, and already you have her sitting on the Imperial throne."

Adalric stepped back, realizing this particular image was one he had *not* yet considered, but now he wasn't sure.

"Give her time," Koroqo continued, "and I'm sure she'll hang herself. You above all others know how difficult it is to please the Dire Queen. Within a day or so, Blaze will make an error that will upset Her Majesty, and that will end it."

The overlord contemplated the Proximan's words for a moment, then nodded. "True. She *is* bound to make a mistake, and the Dire Queen is *not* an easy one to please."

"There you have it," the S'teka master said with a grin, "your simple solution…a solution which doesn't endanger you at all."

Adalric flashed a look of anger at the Proximan noble, suddenly irked by his words. "You are insinuating she could possibly best me?"

"No," Koroqo replied as he let out a long breath, annoyed at how all the non-empaths here had to have the simplest feelings spelled out for them. "I simply meant Blaze is obviously in the Dire Queen's favor now, or else she wouldn't be alive. You did take her to the sovereign to be executed, didn't you? She came out as an Imperial noble instead. If you kill her now, the Dire Queen might have you executed as well."

"You could kill her for me," Adalric suddenly said with a smile, realizing the perfect solution. "You are a master S'teka, the perfect assassin. You could eliminate her and make it appear to be an accident."

Koroqo's sharp eyebrows knotted thoughtfully as he considered the overlord's words. Then he shook his head. "No, I can't do that."

"Are *you* afraid of her?"

A spark lit in the Proximan's dark eyes as his voice lowered to a quiet whisper. "Which *her* are you referring to…the Dire Queen or Blaze?"

"Either."

"Neither, then. However, that changes nothing. I still refuse."

Adalric stared at his subordinate for a moment, then let his voice fill with the anger that was brewing inside him. "You refuse, yet the assassin that tried to kill *me* was a *Proximan*, like yourself."

At the harsh insinuation, Koroqo's eyes narrowed into obsidian slits, his anger reflecting the overlord's. "Tanus," he replied in a cool, even tone, "if that Proximan had been one of my S'teka that I felt worthy to accomplish such a task, you wouldn't be here now."

Retreating inwardly, Adalric instantly regretted his words that sliced into a long-founded trust. Thoughts of vengeance against the true perpetrator fueled his anger, but he chose instead to direct it back outward.

"You *will* do it, Baron Koroqo, that is a direct command from your overlord. It is your duty, as chief of the Imperial Secret Service, to see to the stability of the Imperium."

The S'teka master's jaw tightened for an instant, then he shook his head again. "You and I both know, *Overlord* Adalric, that the sovereign *alone* can order me to assassinate another baron. As for the stability of the Imperium…as I stated before, the one person that I think is in any threat of de-stabilization is you."

The overlord's lips tightened in contained fury as his gloved hands formed into iron fists.

"Now if you'll excuse me," Koroqo said, glancing over at the front of the ballroom, "I think I'll introduce myself to the new baroness and ask her if she wants to dance." He allowed himself a devilish smile, and added, "Adalric, there are *other* ways to deal with beautiful women aside from killing them." With a swift turn which snapped his cloak out in a flurry, the Proximan strode away from the overlord, and disappeared into the crowd, closely followed by his loyal S'teka.

~ * ~

Adalric's thoughts darkened into murky blackness as he watched Koroqo leave, but he regained control and forced rationality to show its head once again. *He's right,* the overlord consented with disgust, *Blaze is my problem, and my problem alone. The Dire Queen would know if Koroqo assassinated her new assistant, and he would most likely be executed for the deed. However, I am much stronger psionically than he is, and could hide my intentions from the Dire Queen. Yes,* he realized as a grin slowly formed on his lips, *I must handle this myself, and quickly. The way to do it is clear. I can't break her, that much is apparent, but the training of a TelSor is a dangerous task, not without many risks to the student. The Dire Queen knows this completely, as my own training almost finished me more than once.*

For an instant he felt his resolve waver as he watched her cross the ballroom floor, carrying herself like a noble, not a woman who was a guard mere hours ago. The smile returned to his lips as his deadly plans materialized in his mind. *Yes,* he silently decided as a quiet chuckle formed inside his throat, *perhaps the training of Blaze will be a bit more intense than she is ready for, and it would be a shame if an accident occurred which sorrowfully proved to be fatal.* Adalric let his smile broaden as he watched his new student.

~ * ~

Of all the Legionnaires who stood along the walls of the ballroom, diligently standing guard, there was one who could not take his eyes off the new Imperial noble. From the moment she entered the large celebration, he simply could not recover from the shock at seeing her alive again, and in this of all forms. Travis shook his head to see if he was imagining things. But no, the Baroness Blaze *had* to be the same Shadowguard Blaze, his friend he had watched carried off by Overlord Adalric to be executed by the Dire Queen. He wanted to run over to her, to see her up close, to be sure. Of course, he could not. As a Legionnaire representative of the *Demoness*, his place was at attention against the wall. Even letting his head follow her as she moved could be considered a breach of etiquette and protocol. No, he simply would have to wait until she was closer to be sure. Her face and hair looked so similar, but he had never seen her without the battle armor. He silently watched her graceful figure from behind his tinted eyepieces, straining to keep her within his gaze, as she continually kept disappearing then reappearing among the crowd. Every time she grew closer, a tingling sensation would grow within his body, to fade again as she moved further away. He watched each person she spoke with, envying their chance to look directly into her face, to walk with her, to sink into her warm eyes. He tried to return to his duty, to simply put her out of his mind, but all he could do was watch her and wonder what miraculous occurrence must have taken place in the Dire Queen's chambers earlier that day.

~ * ~

Blaze wandered about the large ballroom with her head held high, a graceful poise in her stride, never having felt more terrified in her life. She watched the people staring at her as she tried to read their faces for any hint of their disposition toward her, but all she could read was a reflection of her own confusion as they tried to understand her as much as she tried to understand them.

I move about them, and I am now their superior, all except for the other barons. What is my relation to them, she wondered, *am I their superior as well? As personal advisor to the Dire Queen, does that put me above them? I'll have to ask her later. Gods, I'm going to be talking to her again, on a regular basis.* Her head spun with the concept of it all, and the enchantment of her new situation. Before, when the Dire Queen proclaimed her a baroness, it seemed like a dream. Later on, that dream turned into a nightmare when Adalric attacked her, changing again into unexpected passion when things turned around. Now it came crashing down as it all started to hit her. These people expected her to be a baroness around them, to act as one of the elites. Not that Blaze felt this task was beyond her capabilities, but it was all so sudden. She immediately realized she wanted some stability in her life now, a familiar voice that would give her the edge of sanity she so desperately needed. Quickly scanning the large room, she searched for the one man who *had* to be here, as this was his orbital base, but she still could see no sign of Joshua. *Damn,* she silently cursed, *where is he?*

"Excuse me, Baroness Blaze?"

She quickly whirled around to find herself looking into Baron Koroqo's dark exotic eyes, which, without whites, strikingly stood out from his pale skin. For a moment she was speechless, her tongue feeling as dry as bleached sand. Then she managed to nod to him, to at least recognize his presence.

The Proximan noble smiled. "I didn't mean to startle you," he said casually, the silky tone of his accent making it sound like something deeply intimate.

Blaze felt his cool voice drift over her like a calm summer breeze and suddenly felt at ease again. *Strange,* she thought, wondering what could have brought the immediate change upon her. "It's quite all right," she quickly answered, feeling her confidence rise. "I'm not used to all of this yet."

"Quite understandable," he said with a grin, his alabaster white teeth blending into his alabaster white skin. "I must tell you, Baroness, I am most impressed with your achievements so far."

She nodded, realizing he was referring to the fact she managed to make it through this day without dying, an accomplishment which she was now beginning to feel proud of. She felt herself stand taller as she faced her fellow baron, suddenly understanding the pride and trust the Dire Queen placed within her. She gazed at the Proximan noble again, quickly deciding that despite his alien features, he was handsome. No, it was more than that, there was a definite charisma which flowed about this man, like an aura of some sort. She decided that where Adalric was forceful and commanding, Koroqo was sensuous and charming. Two different forms of power, often equally effective. *Of course, he's an empath, like all other Proximans,* she realized. *That could easily explain my change in mood, he could be projecting his own confidence.* Allowing herself to swell with the festivity of the occasion, she permitted a slow smile to escape her lips. "Why thank you, Baron Koroqo. Please call me Blaze. All these titles are beginning to get to me."

A low chuckle came from Koroqo as he nodded in agreement. "You are right, of course. You must call me Troivaka, it's my first name."

Blaze scrunched her eyebrows as she decided it was too formal a name to use in person. "Troivaka, eh? May I call you Troy?"

Koroqo's breath caught in surprise. "Yes," he finally replied, then made a mock serious face at her. "It will have to remain between the two of us. I want you to know such informality is something I rarely allow."

Blaze nodded, realizing how rash she had been, and how nobly Koroqo was handling it.

"So, is Blaze your full name?" he asked. "It doesn't strike me as a name parents would give out."

"I had no parents," she admitted, feeling a little of her ego deflate. "I was raised by an old woman in the Alliance colony of Tenebrous, an orphan."

She felt her pride fill again as she realized she had nothing to be ashamed of, for not one in a thousand other women could have survived where she had. "I named myself Blaze when I discovered my…talents."

"Regardless," he said with a laugh, "the name fits your personality." Koroqo found himself re-appraising the young human, and felt his admiration grow. "I was wondering," he asked, his smooth voice gently sifting through her, "if you would do me the honor of letting me dance with you?"

Blaze had drifted into her own thoughts, of celebrations and the gallantry of this all, and was taken aback by his request. "You want to dance with me?" She quickly scanned for Adalric and saw him across the room, wondering what he would think.

Koroqo watched her gaze and saw where it landed, then he raised his eyebrow again in consideration as he read the emotions flowing off of her, and he smiled. His dark eyes probed past the soft curves of her face and into her raging spirit, a garden of vibrant emotions growing in beautiful arrangement.

She thought she saw the overlord for a moment, then lost him in the crowd, so she turned back to Koroqo and gave him a smile. She learned, many years ago from Mattie, some of the more formal dance steps, but had honestly never thought she would ever need them. Suddenly anxious to experience this new thing, she nodded eagerly. "Why thank you, Troy, it's I who would be honored."

Koroqo offered to take her hand, to which she gladly assented. Allowing her fingers to cradle in his palm, she suddenly pulled back. His touch was hot, feverish.

He simply grinned at her and gently recaptured her delicate hand. "You've never touched a Proximan?" he asked.

"No," she admitted, smiling innocently.

"Our body temperature is a bit higher than humans, that's all."

Waiting for her consent to continue, he then led her out onto the dance floor. Blaze felt clumsy in his heated proximity, but his steady leading soon made them a graceful duet, unaware of the hundreds of curious eyes which hungrily followed them.

~ * ~

Two of those eyes watched in smoldering flame, through darkened lenses, as the Proximan baron swept the beautiful baroness across the shiny dance floor. *How dare Koroqo*, Adalric silently cursed as his soul filled with a new form of rage which he had never before experienced. Suddenly, the S'teka master's words about "other ways to tame beautiful women" made their full impact on him. The overlord knew of Koroqo's reputation for charming women, and his intentions now seemed perfectly clear as Adalric watched him slip a roaming hand down to the base of her back. *It is I who should be dancing with her,* Adalric angrily thought as he started to march ferociously forward, then stopped himself short. *What am I thinking? ...is this jealousy I'm feeling?* With great strength of will, he forced himself to turn away, pushing his anger down. He then reminded himself of the self-edict he had proclaimed to the Proximan many times, *overlords do not dance!*

~ * ~

Travis watched her dancing with Koroqo and felt his jaw clench. What he once thought might have been growing between them now felt unobtainable, out of reach.

"Princesses don't fall for paupers," he whispered so quietly he doubted even the Legionnaires next to him could have heard.

~ * ~

Blaze had not felt happiness like this in a long while, though she was growing more than aware of the many deep stares she was continually receiving. Suddenly feeling self-conscious she began to wonder if people would associate her meteoric climb to the man sweeping her across the dance floor. With a sudden but gentle motion, she delicately broke away from Koroqo and stepped back.

Sensing her change in mood, the Proximan noble nodded to her, absorbing the concerns within her. "It's quite all right, Blaze. Perhaps another time."

Blaze felt her anger lessen as she realized Koroqo understood, and she instantly decided she liked him. "Thank you for the dance, Troy. Unfortunately, I must mingle."

"True," he said with a laugh, his good nature shining through, "I mustn't keep the main attraction all to myself. I'm sure there are many others who wish to talk with you also."

She started to blush then had to hold back a laugh. "I doubt that," she finally said, then gave him a nod of her head and moved back from him, as she tried again to locate Joshua.

Koroqo watched Blaze drift away, disappearing into the crowd. Smiling in amusement, he speculated about the coming events that would be unfolding. He turned, and walked toward the buffet table, acutely aware of the slicing feelings that were still emanating from the overlord.

~ * ~

Blaze finally spotted the *Sentinel's* commander across the grand room, and she grinned. This was the first time she saw him on his own base, and in a dress uniform no less. He made a dashing figure in the snug, jet-black jacket which wrapped closely around the ebony undertunic, topping tight black pants and shiny black boots. Except for the scarlet Red Star insignia and red sash which held up his ceremonial sword, he looked like a shadow in this brightly lit room. *I still don't have my own sword*, Blaze realized in disgust as she thought of her empty sheath she chose to leave in her room.

Insecurely tugging one of her gloves back into place, she headed toward Joshua then stopped, suddenly realizing what an awkward situation she could be approaching. How long had it been since he plucked her off a street curb and placed her into the Imperial Armada? Her thick brows wrinkled in admission that it had not been very long. *Well*, she decided as she continued to make her way through the throng of people, *he's become family. That hasn't changed.*

Finally reaching the far wall, where Joshua was talking with a number of other officers, she walked up behind him and waited, wondering how long it would take him to notice her presence.

It was Captain Brook, who was talking at the time, who first noticed the stunning Imperial noble approach. When she stood right behind the admiral, he fell speechless, wondering what they did to deserve such attention.

Joshua Steward observed his underling's conversation die, and watched as the captain's lips parted slightly in awe. Sharply turning his head, he found himself face to face with the Dire Queen's new personal advisor, the striking young woman whom he had practically adopted into his family. "Why, it's the Baroness Blaze," he said, as he bowed curtly in polite respect.

"To what do I owe this honor?"

Blaze was visibly taken aback by the admiral's sudden formality, for his voice held none of the familiar recognition and warmth she expected. Her eyes widened, and her chest wrenched, as she hoped he was merely worried about the same things she was, people getting the wrong impression over what they saw, or what they thought they saw. "Good evening, Admiral Steward," she said as regally as she could. "May I speak with you privately, about my quarters on the *Sentinel*?"

"Why, of course," he quickly responded.

Blaze faced the two Shadowguards who were still following her.

"Wait for me here," she instructed, the beginnings of imperiousness lacing her words.

"But, my Lady," one of them said in protest.

"That's an order," she firmly replied. She made a quick mental note that sometime soon she would have to choose her own guards. Ones she knew she could trust, and not ones appointed by the overlord. Her fierce stare bored into the Shadowguard as she desperately tried to read the face behind the helmet. Visually drilling him, she waited for a few moments to see if he would challenge her further. He did not. Relieved, she walked into the corner with Joshua, leaving her Shadowguards to wait with the officers. Once they were in reasonable solitude, she turned to him cautiously, her face apologetic like a naughty child confronting her father.

"It's been awhile, Blaze," Joshua said with a grin, putting his broad hand firmly on her soft shoulder. "I've missed you, kid."

Blaze felt a weight lift, and a smile crept across her lips, wordlessly whispering her pleasure at being in his company again. *He isn't mad*, she quickly decided, *he seems as happy to see me as ever.* "You don't mind?"

"About what?"

She sighed, then shook her head at him. "You know, about me rising to the rank of baroness."

"Oh, that," he said with a grin as he shrugged. "Certainly was a shock, but I always guessed you'd come to greatness. I knew I was right when I gave you that admiral's appointment."

"I owe you so much," she said, realizing he had become like the father she never had.

"You owe me nothing, my Lady," Joshua responded to her firmly, suddenly taking on a serious air. "If you feel the need to pay off anyway, do it by serving the Imperium faithfully, for the greater good of the *Imperium,* not yourself."

"Are you implying some of the barons don't?"

"I wouldn't want to get into any trouble, but some of the barons are more concerned with their own ends and not the Imperium's, like the overlord, for one."

"Oh, but you're wrong," she quickly said, her voice taking on a defensive tone. "He may seem manipulative, but he's doing it for the good of the Imperium. He has to keep us all together under his strong hand, to prevent us from falling into smaller factions and weakening. Look what we've accomplished under his command."

"But it's the Dire Queen, our sovereign who rules, not him."

"She speaks the words," Blaze replied, desperate for Joshua to understand her feelings, "but Overlord Adalric has to interpret them and act on them."

I'm defending him? She suddenly realized, shocking herself.

"Perhaps. Sometimes it feels like the actions Overlord Adalric takes are intended to usurp the Dire Queen. Not support her."

"Such as?" Blaze asked, expecting some proof to support his allegations, and also hoping he couldn't produce any.

"Many things…like his initial attack on the United Star Alliance battleship *Victory,* an act which wasn't sanctioned or authorized by the Dire Queen."

"But that attack initiated all we have now accomplished. Joshua, the Dire Queen wanted war, but didn't have time to get the orders to Adalric, so he had to act quickly, as was his obligation as overlord. Without that attack we would still be a small pirate force, and not the advancing Imperium we are now. Why, a year ago we ruled this star system alone, with less than a dozen ships. Now we control over forty percent of this sector, which is *more* space than the United Star Alliance has. Besides that, our fleet is growing into one of the most powerful armadas the stars have ever seen."

"I see," Joshua said, astounded by the fervor in her voice. "What about his wanton destruction of that Alliance colony world…what was its name?"

"Tenebrous," Blaze said under her breath, momentarily fighting her own mixed feelings on the subject. "Don't you see, Joshua? It had to be done. I was *there,* as a grunt, a foot-soldier. I saw how badly we were defeated by the Alliance marines on that dingy planet. We lost our first major confrontation. If we didn't come back strong, then they would have come at us like sharks in blood-infested water. By showing them our ability to destroy a planet…and believe me when I say *no one* will miss that small, pitiful world, we demonstrated to the entire sector that the Imperium is not to be taken lightly.

"It's that fear and respect that gave us the necessary time to launch our crushing campaigns against the Romusians and Camillians, without the Alliance breathing down our necks. It's that extra time Overlord Adalric bought for us with that simple act, which allowed us to come back and wage a successful campaign against the United Star Alliance itself." Blaze let out a deep breath, astonished at the convictions inside her. "I would think, as an admiral, you would admire the overlord's military genius," she added, her voice suddenly low and cold, "not accuse him of disloyalty."

Admiral Steward stood silently for a moment, as he felt her words sink into his soul. Gazing into her hardened face, he considered what she said, then smiled like a proud father. "Thank you, Blaze," he said as he filled his chest with a deep breath, "I now understand a little better. I think I understand *you* a little better as well."

"Me?"

"Yes, you. You have shown this old admiral there are still people that care for this Imperium as much as he does, and are willing to do more than talk about it. I'm very pleased that you are the Dire Queen's new advisor, my Lady, and I shall be quite honored to serve under you."

Blaze felt her heart swell with pride again, as a wide grin came to her lips. *He has no idea how much that meant to me,* she silently glowed, as she fought the desire to give him a great hug. Then she nodded to him, determined to keep up the air of professionalism he always carried with him. "Why thank you, Admiral. May I say I too am honored to have such a fine commander serving under me in the Imperial Navy, as the Dire Queen is also."

Suddenly Blaze recoiled as if shocked. *How did I know the Dire Queen felt that way about Joshua? Maybe she's feeding me her thoughts. What a strange idea...does that mean she can read my mind also? I must ask Adalric.* At that moment an officer came up and stood at attention, diligently waiting to be recognized.

"Yes, Lieutenant?" Joshua asked, looking over at the junior officer.

"Message for you, Admiral," the young woman reported as she stole a curious glance at the new baroness.

"What is it?" Joshua asked, noticing the lieutenant's sidelong looks at Blaze.

"The *Sentinel's* duty officer needs you in command central, to accept a personal message from the *Wraith*."

Drusee-la, Blaze thought, *I wonder what she wants...or has to report.*

"Very well," the admiral replied as he turned back to Blaze. "If you will excuse me, my Lady, duty calls."

"I understand, Admiral, we'll talk more later."

With a sharp nod, Admiral Steward and his lieutenant walked off, quickly leaving the grand ballroom.

~ * ~

Within a moment's pace, Blaze's Shadowguards were back at her side, awaiting orders.

"Don't you two ever get bored of following me around?" she asked, her voice edging with annoyance.

"Problem, Baroness Blaze?" a deeply familiar voice rang out from behind her.

Blaze did not need to turn to see who addressed her. Unconsciously she paused in silence, not answering the inquiry but instead letting Adalric's compelling presence cradle her tense body. Slowly she turned on her heels and faced him, the certainty that he was not there a moment ago nagging in her tightened jaw. "Please don't sneak up on me like that," she said while lifting her chin up to meet his great height.

A thin smile came to the overlord's lips and quickly faded again as he read the startled worry in her mind. He had considered ignoring her for the rest of the night, memories of the earlier evening warding him away. However, he *felt* her impassioned speech to the admiral from across the room, and suddenly needed to talk with her again. He had to know why she defended him and his actions against the Alliance. After his attack on her, Adalric had to assume she now knew he intended her harm. But as he gazed down into her fresh spirited face, harming her was the furthest thing from his mind. Feeling his stance soften, he shook all distracting thoughts out of his mind and faced her coldly. "You must always be on the alert," he finally said, as his eyes stabbed down at her. "You will need all your senses kept sharp if you wish to be a TelSor."

Blaze squirmed under his penetrating glance as she absently ran a hand along the side of her body suit, smoothing out imaginary wrinkles. Realizing this was the first time they spoke since the encounter in her new room, she felt her tongue wrestling with awkwardness, leaving all the words she wanted to speak in strangled silence. Mutely, she stared at his huge frame, encased in his tight-fitting uniform, and clung to the vague shadows that were almost faded from memory. Finally, she collected some of her thoughts and looked up to meet his glare. "About my training," she asked strongly, determined to show this man no weaknesses. "When will it start? Also, where is a sword for me to use?"

Adalric's jaw tensed as he felt her mind resist his curious probes. There seemed to be no trace left of the mental bond that fused them in her room. "Tomorrow at dawn," he stated without emotion, "you will have both then." The overlord turned to leave, when she suddenly reached out and lightly grabbed his arm, causing him to stop and look back. "What is it?" he asked, as he quickly shrugged off her touch, annoyed at the feelings it stirred in him.

"I can choose my own personal bodyguard, can't I?" she asked. "A person to be my chief Shadowguard."

"Like *you* were to me," he replied, watching for any betrayal of emotion in her eyes at the reminder but finding none.

"Yes, and I have someone already in mind."

Suddenly Adalric's thoughts turned the same shade of darkness he felt as he watched her dance. "Not the one you were with earlier on the base, that Legionnaire."

"Why, yes," she said while trying to contain her surprise that he knew of him. "His name is Legionnaire First Class Travis. I want to promote him and make him my number one."

"You can't."

"Why?"

"Because…he's not even a Shadowguard yet."

"I went from being a Legionnaire to becoming *your* personal guard," she reminded him, a note of irritation in her voice.

"That was different."

"Once again, why?"

"Because I'm the overlord—"

"I'm the sovereign's personal advisor," she said sharply, cutting him off, astonished at the new source of courage within herself.

Adalric felt his anger mount, as he internally readied to permanently silence her for her brashness. But even as he mentally prepared the imaginary death blow, he paused, suddenly remembering her as she had been in her room, her body entwined in his arms. Like water in a sink, he felt his anger drain away, replaced by renewed resolve to end this as soon as possible. "Alright," he finally said, shattering the momentary silence, "do as you wish. Do not be late tomorrow morning." Without waiting for a response, he turned away and moved back into the crowd, his crimson and black cloak rippling behind him.

~ * ~

Blaze watched the overlord leave, suddenly feeling more at ease with him gone, though it was then she realized she couldn't feel his mind anymore, and suddenly she missed it. Shaking such thoughts out of her head, she scanned the rows of Legionnaires along the wall, wondering if her friend was numbered among them. Oddly, as she thought of Travis, she felt a pull toward one of the statuesque soldiers on the far wall, one who was obviously watching her from behind his stodgy black helm. *That's Travis, all right,* she laughed quietly, then started to where he diligently stood.

Travis watched silently as the young baroness came closer and closer, gliding across the polished floor with grace, until she stood directly in front of him. Beads of perspiration appeared under his armor as he realized finally it was indeed her.

Blaze gazed up at Travis, feeling the stunned shock which was cavorting through his stiff form. *Maybe I have one or two empathic bones in my body also,* she silently wondered, then smiled at the expectant soldier. "Legionnaire First Class Travis," she said as officially as she could.

The Imperial warrior felt his mouth suddenly dry up, and no matter how hard he tried, he could not utter a sound.

"I would like to appoint you as a personal bodyguard," she continued, noticing the stares she was now receiving from the other Legionnaires in the nearby ranks. "Starting tomorrow, you will be a Shadowguard, my personal Shadowguard."

Still no response from Travis, as he tried to fully comprehend her meaning. All he understood was he would once again have the opportunity to be by her side.

"Is that understood?" Blaze asked, confused by his silence.

"Y-yes, my Lady," Travis said, forcing himself to return to reality. "It's an honor."

Blaze mentally grinned, suddenly realizing how awkward this must make him feel, in front of all his peers. However, she was not oblivious to the penetrating stares she was receiving from behind her, from her two Shadowguards that waited, who had recently been supplanted by a mere Legionnaire. *That is their concern,* she quickly dismissed, *Adalric's guards had to deal with it when I came along, and now my guards will have to follow suit.* She turned on her guards and glared intently at them, hoping they would realize that if they didn't like the situation then they had better keep it to themselves. Under the intensity of her stares, her guards stepped back and nodded in acceptance. The conversation that issued no words had been clearly understood by all.

"That was most wise," she whispered sternly at them under her breath, then turned and walked away, suddenly surprised at her own feelings. *I was actually threatening them,* she realized as she returned to the thick of the crowd. She wondered what she would have done had they disobeyed her. Her silent query went unanswered as all attention was drawn to Admiral

Steward, who reentered the ballroom and walked up on the platform, raising his hand for attention and silence. After a few moments, he received both, allowing him to proceed with his announcement.

It was at this instant, as all gathered close to the podium, that Blaze first noticed the soldiers holding the holo-receivers. *Must be a part of the military press*, she decided, realizing her entrance and speech must have been recorded also, for a later showing throughout the Imperium.

"Attention all, please," the admiral said into the microphone, causing the last few stragglers to go silent, "attention. Moments ago, we received a message from the front lines."

Drusee-la! Blaze thought as she hastily searched for Overlord Adalric, finally locating him near one of the exits at the far side of the grand room. *What is she up to now?* Her thoughts went silent as she heard Joshua begin to speak again.

"There has been a major space battle inside the United Star Alliance borders, near the system of Wolf. The conflict ended in our favor, adding that system to our glorious Imperium. Word has come from Baroness Drusee-la that they have begun the invasion of Wolf itself and expect a quick victory. Thank you." He turned and walked off of the stage.

A great cheer went up in the room as all rejoiced in the news of this victory. Wolf was a major world which marked the edge of the Alliance's inner systems. All knew that this meant there was a real chance now that the United Star Alliance could truly be defeated.

Blaze felt a smile come to her lips as she realized the end of the Alliance might actually come about, but felt it die as she glanced back at the overlord, who simply turned and left the room, unseen by any save her. *Adalric should have been out there to lead that battle, but instead he is here. Why?* she wondered. *Certainly, the Dire Queen isn't detaining him solely to train me, is she?* Her thoughts came to a crashing halt as she overheard two officers quietly talking behind her. She suppressed her desire to turn and face them but listened to their words attentively.

"So," the first officer asked, his hushed voice thick with a husky accent, "do you think this really will spell the end for Lord Adalric?"

"I don't know," the second answered, her smooth voice barely a whisper. "But this does bear favorably for Lady Drusee-la. Her influence is growing rapidly, despite the fact she isn't human."

They continued, speculating about the politics of the Imperial nobility until their voices were lost in the crowd as they moved away.

Damn, Blaze's mind raced as she turned and hoped for a glance of the two of them. However, all she could see were the hundreds of officers and dignitaries. *That does it,* she decided, *I've had enough for one day.* With determination she turned toward the nearest door and made a hasty exit.

As she entered the dimly lit hallway, she was quickly reminded as to how late it had become. Letting out a deep breath, she slowed down her pace and began to walk away, happy to leave the exuberance of her first celebration far behind.

"Leaving so soon, my Lady?" a pleasant voice addressed her.

Blaze turned and peered into the shadows, finally making out the Proximan noble, and his three S'teka guards. "Yes, Troy," she answered calmly, impressed by the suave manner he always seemed to carry with him, "it's been quite a long day for me."

"I'm sure it has, Blaze," he answered with a smile as he stepped more into what little light glowed in the corridor. "I'm sure it's a day which will live in your memories for the rest of your life."

"However long that is," she said with a laugh.

"True," he answered, suddenly growing more serious. "That is why I wished to talk with you again."

Blaze glanced back at her two Shadowguards, then at his S'teka. "Should we move from the guards?"

"The first thing you must realize as an Imperial Noble is to ignore your guards. They are an extension of yourself that you must learn to live with, and trust. They are sworn to live and die at your command."

Blaze looked back at her Shadowguards, then back at the Proximan again. "So, I could order one of them to kill himself, and he would?" Her two guards began to fidget nervously as they glanced at each other.

"By law, yes," Koroqo acknowledged.

Blaze remembered back to her own Shadowguard training, how her instructor told her she was expected to give her life for Adalric at a moment's notice, but the reality of that never truly sank in until now.

"However," Koroqo continued, "a baron must weigh that power with his or her responsibility to those who are sworn to protect your life. That is why you choose them carefully."

"Overlord Adalric gave these two to me," she said thoughtfully, "but I have chosen my own personal guard to start tomorrow."

"That's good," Koroqo said with a grim smile, "you'll need someone on your side tomorrow."

"What do you mean?"

"Tomorrow, you start your training as a TelSor, correct?"

"Look, Troy," Blaze said, hoping not to offend the Proximan's feelings, "I really need to get some sleep."

"Just answer me."

Blaze let out a sigh, wondering why he was so interested in her training schedule. "As a matter of fact, yes, it does start tomorrow."

"I see," the S'teka master said thoughtfully. He wrestled with the right words to continue with, but came up short, and settled on the simple ones. "Please be careful."

"Why?" Blaze asked, her infamous curiosity aroused.

"Because you should."

"I'm always careful," she defended with a weak smile which was heavily laced with exhaustion.

"We shall see."

"And how shall we do that?" Blaze asked sarcastically, a little annoyed at this game Troy seemed to be playing.

"By seeing if you come back alive," he firmly replied.

He turned and walked away, disappearing down the corridor.

Blaze stood, dumbfounded for a moment, her wearied thoughts trying to make some sense out of what Koroqo had said. Then she slowly shook her head and began to return to her new chambers.

~ * ~

Adalric's mind whirled with a turmoil of darkened images as he put more distance between himself and the celebration. Images of her lying next to him were clashing with scenes of her and that Legionnaire together. So intent was he in his inner world he passed right by the junior officer, who was quietly trying to gain his attention.

"My Lord," the lieutenant said again, as he ran to catch up with the Overlord.

Adalric stopped in his tracks, causing the junior officer to pass by him, almost falling over himself in the attempt to stay with the overlord.

"What do you want, Lieutenant?"

"Captain Jerrel sent me up from detention on the *Demoness*, my Lord," the junior officer quickly reported, anxious to get his message out and leave the overlord behind. "He wants you to know that three more provincial lords tried to dissent and were arrested. They were executed but they had family."

Adalric stared at him blankly, his impatience growing.

"As per your standing instructions, they were held so you could personally interrogate them," the lieutenant continued, "would you like to inspect them now?"

The overlord's mind cleared for an instant as the junior officer's words sank in. He half turned his head back toward the celebration as a sneer of delight formed on his thin lips. However, as quickly as it formed, the grimace faded away. His teeth pressed against each other, the result of the inner conflict which waged a silent war in his soul.

"Let them go," he finally said, before he even realized it was what he was going to say.

The junior officer stared at the overlord in frank disbelief. "My Lord, these are enemies of the Imperium. Their fathers—"

"Have paid the price for their disloyalty," Adalric's deep voice sliced in, causing the lieutenant to retreat a step. The overlord glanced back toward the celebration, half ready to return there, but instead he turned back toward the officer. "Release them immediately and have them returned to their home worlds." He dismissed the lieutenant with a wave of his hand and continued on toward the shuttle bay.

Chapter Nineteen
TelSor

Taking a deep breath to steady her shaking nerves, Blaze finally opened the door which led into the overlord's chambers on the *Demoness*. "What the hell am I doing here?" she whispered, while steadily creeping toward the bedroom, the one place where she knew he would be.

She gingerly reached out and pressed the fiery red button which would activate the small door and was instantly rewarded with the portal sliding open. Pausing for a moment on the threshold, she allowed her eyes to adjust to the absence of light in the large bedroom. However, although she couldn't see, she could hear the steady breathing of the overlord coming from the center of the room, where the grand bed lay.

Slowly, ominously, a low red light filled the room as one of smaller "night effects" lamps began to illuminate. Her eyes adjusted to this new light as she carefully watched the prone figure lying still on the bed. Despite the fact he seemed as if he was sleeping, he was still wearing his crimson uniform, and the ever concealing half mask cowl which covered both face and hair.

Blaze watched him carefully for what seemed an eternity as she tried to gauge his sleep. Was he truly slumbering, or awake? She finally moved a few hesitant steps forward, bringing her within arm's reach of the bed, and him. She froze, wondering again as to why she was here. Was it to be with him, to hope for another moment to occur like the last, or was it to end his life?

Hesitantly, she allowed herself to sit on the bed, painstakingly careful so as not to disturb his sleep. She reached out and lightly caressed his exposed cheek.

It was this touch, more than anything, which broke the overlord's slumber, causing him to quickly sit up.

"Why are you here?" he asked quietly, shocked she could gain access to his room without his sensing it.

"I don't know," she admitted while glancing down, a brief flicker of girlish youth dancing across her eyes. "I needed to see you again, after what happened between us."

Adalric felt his thoughts muddle as the memory of what occurred earlier that day drifted back into his mind. "What happened shouldn't have," he finally said, his powerful voice barely a whisper.

"But it did," she said, looking back up, her eyes firmly meeting his darkened eyepieces. "It happened, and it was real. You felt it, and so did I."

Adalric's eyes squeezed shut as his internal war waged more fiercely. He struggled to fill his mind with darkness, but all he could feel was the urge to touch her again, to feel her delicate warmth against his skin.

Blaze's eyes softened as she gazed at the mask, the barrier that still separated the two of them. Slowly, she reached out and grabbed the edges of the form-fitted cowl and began to pull up.

Adalric's lips parted in shock, at the realization of her intentions. *How am I allowing this,* he demanded of himself, *how can I let this happen? But it* is *going to happen.*

Blaze finished taking off the hated apparel, and slowly allowed herself to look back up, to view his repulsive deformity for the first time.

Her endless scream broke the peaceful silence, and she fell back in horror, as Adalric quickly tried to cover up his terrible imperfection, sorrow wracking his ears more painfully than any scream that could ever have been issued.

~ * ~

Tanus Adalric sat upright in bed, the soundless scream in his dream still reverberating in his wounded ears. Beads of perspiration drifted down his face, caressing the one part of his visage he allowed no one to see. As if stung by acid, he reached up and lightly touched his right cheek and forehead, his anger melding with the sorrow that wanted to tear apart his soul.

"This nightmare must end," he said with a groan as he let himself fall back to the dampened sheets. "I must end it soon, before it is *I* who is destroyed."

~ * ~

The loud buzzing at the door brought Blaze awake with a start as she reoriented herself, suddenly unsure as to where she was.

I'm on the Sentinel, she quickly remembered, *I'm a baroness…I think.*

The buzzing sounded again as she forced herself to look for her timekeeper, and grumbled when she remembered toasting it yesterday. Slowly she forced herself out of the luscious bed which silently demanded her return. Wrapping her nude body in one of the new crimson satin sheets she appropriated before going to sleep, she wandered out of her bedroom and stumbled to her front door. Taking a deep breath to force some consciousness into her weary brain, she pushed the button to open the door, caring little about how she must appear.

"This had better be important," she said, before even looking to see who it was at her front door.

"It is, my Lady," replied the Shadowguard at her door. "Good morning."

"Travis?" she asked, unable to get her mind working enough to recognize his presence.

"Yes, my Lady," he proudly replied as he let his eyes caringly roam over her barely covered form that still sagged from exhaustion. "Overlord Adalric instructed me to get you up so you can begin your training."

"My training?" she asked, suddenly realizing the outside corridors were still dimmed in their "night mode" setting. "What time is it?"

"Zero-four hundred hours."

Blaze forced her mind to struggle for a moment, remembering Imperial time was the same as Earth time, since it dated back to the time of the Terran Imperial Dominion, and Nyx had a very similar rotation to Earth. She shook her head in annoyance. "Four in the morning? Why can't we start at ten?"

Travis stifled a laugh. "The overlord's orders."

"I thought you just obeyed me now?" she asked, suddenly growing suspicious of her friend.

"Of course, I do," he quickly replied, realizing what her tone change inferred. "My loyalty starts and ends with you. However, I must also show respect to the other barons and convey their messages to you."

"Oh."

"So, my Lady, unless you intend to go to your training like this, you may want to get dressed, then I can escort you to him."

Despite her exhaustion, she found it hard not to smile. "Fine, on one condition."

"What is that, my Lady?"

"That you call me Blaze when we're alone, Travis. Save the *my Lady's* for when we're around other people."

"With pleasure," he said, the helmet concealing his broad smile, "Blaze."

~ * ~

A half hour later, the two of them, Imperial noble and Shadowguard, walked along the still dim corridors of the orbital base *Sentinel*. Their one encounter was with the few guards who were active at this wee hour of the morning.

"Where are you taking me?" Blaze asked as she made sure her long cloak was firmly attached by the small studs on her collar.

"The hangar bay, to your personal shuttle."

"My shuttle?" she asked as she fastened her ebony sword belt which carried her still empty sheath. She figured Adalric had to arm her today, if she was to train.

"Yes, Blaze," he replied as they walked through the doorway into the *Sentinel's* main hangar bay. "I am taking you down to Nyx."

Blaze smiled, it had been some time since she was on the surface of a planet, breathing real air. "You know what, Travis? I think this is going to be a great day."

Her Shadowguard nodded as he led her to the long and sleek grey shuttle that had two more of her Shadowguards waiting outside.

Blaze let herself take in the shuttle's simple grace and beauty. It was not large, being only designed to carry a dozen or so, but it was heavily armed. She walked around it once, admiring her personal shuttle, then glanced back at Travis, who was waiting by the entrance to the craft.

"It needs to be painted red," she said as she walked on board, finding a small waiting cabin with her name on the doorway.

Inside was a comfortable lounge chair and view screen, so the travelling dignitary could watch what was occurring without having to be up front with the pilots. Blaze made herself comfortable and strapped in, anxious to arrive on Nyx to begin her training as a TelSor.

Travis assumed his place at her door and grabbed the hand hold, as he signaled up front to start the engines and depart.

With a dignified roar, the shuttle's fusion engines flared to life, lifting the small craft up and out of the orbital Star-Citadel as it turned toward the Kelly-green planet known as Nyx.

How similar it looks to pictures of Earth I've seen, Blaze absently thought as she watched their approach on her tiny viewer. *Someday I hope to visit there, the planet of my ancestry,* she decided, *but as its conqueror, not its servant.*

~ * ~

The trip down was faster than she thought it would be. Of course, it would have even been simpler to use the Cosmic energy rifts which could transport a person through space in seconds, but since Adalric never did it, she wasn't surprised to find he didn't want her to do it either. However, it did surprise her when the shuttle glided over the capital of Nyx and headed out toward some old ruins, many miles away from any sign of civilization.

"Are you sure this is right?" she asked Travis, suddenly unnerved as to how far away from the city they were flying.

"Yes, my Lady," he quickly replied as he looked up toward the front to see their direction. "Overlord Adalric directed us to the old suburb ruins, abandoned since the last uprising."

"Uprising? What do you mean?"

"I'm not sure. Perhaps it was nothing. Probably some Alliance troops that slipped in a few years ago and had to be destroyed."

"Hmm…how much longer?"

"We're here now," he replied, as the shuttle's engines slowed down and they began to descend.

Blaze felt the ship gently touch down, and quickly unstrapped herself from her seat, excitement beginning to build inside her. She checked herself over one last time as she heard the engines begin to cool. Her bright-red bodysuit was snugly in place, her gloves and boots were securely on, and her cloak added the fine touch of class which framed her outfit.

She briefly considered bringing along her special crystal, sure she would need all the help she could get. In the end though, she disregarded the idea as foolish, and left it in its hiding place under her mattress in her new chambers. Blaze was still convinced the blue crystal she found in that cave merely acted as a mental focus back on Perus II. It had been *her,* not the stone, which saved her life by toasting those people. Satisfied she was now ready for anything, she strode to the open shuttle door and descended the ramp.

It was not until she reached the grassy floor that she realized she was alone. Glancing back up at her Shadowguard, who was at the top of the ramp, she motioned for him to follow.

"I'm sorry, my Lady," he sadly explained to her, not liking the situation one bit, "but the overlord instructed you to go on alone. No guards are permitted to witness the training."

At first Blaze grew angry but quickly realized the rationale of the situation. Of course they had to be alone, or else her guards would learn to become TelSor also, at least she assumed that was the reasoning. "Where do I go?"

Travis pointed at a small desolate town in the distance. "Go to those ruins, my Lady."

Blaze looked over at the buildings and decided they had to be at least half a mile away from the shuttle. "Can't we fly closer?"

"No, my Lady. The Overlord said we must land here."

"Alright," she said with a shrug, then let out a light chuckle. *You're growing soft, Blaze. You used to walk ten times that amount to find food back on Tenebrous. Not to mention all the marching as a Legionnaire.* Taking a deep breath, she began the trek across the weed-infested field, which led to what once had been a prosperous small town.

As she walked along, she suddenly realized how beautiful it was outside. Dawn's light was filtering in, and the air was alive with the music of various birds. It had been a bit chilly when she first left the shuttle, but now she was warming up as the large red sun rose over the ruins. *How different it would have been to grow up in a place like this*, she sadly thought as she pushed out visions of her sewer home. Off in the distance, she saw a small rodent-like creature hopping about in the brush. At first, she thought it was a rat, the only rodent life form she had ever seen. However, this one was different, it had long tall ears and a short fluffy tail, and besides all that, it was cute. *How strange and lovely it is here,* she decided as she finally reached the edge of the old town.

Although it was desolate, Blaze had not expected it to be abandoned. Not a soul was in sight as she walked down the cracked pavement street which was covered in dirt and had weeds forcing their way up through the cracks. Many buildings were in sight, banks, bakeries, and short office buildings. All were burnt out and hollowed, with broken glass and fallen timber. Life had been here once, she could easily see that, but it had ended brutally. *Now this*, she decided, *was more like home.*

"Why here," she whispered, almost inaudibly, "in this of all places?"

"Because it is the most fitting for what we have to accomplish," came the familiar voice from behind.

Blaze turned and saw the overlord before her, a long-wrapped bundle in his arms. The still rising red giant cast eerie reflections off his crimson uniform, giving it the impression of being stained with blood. She felt herself instinctually take a step back, then forward, as his presence struck her like a strong undertow, pushing her then pulling her back in.

~ * ~

"Welcome, Blaze," Adalric said in a firm voice, "to your first day of training, your first day of many."

"How many?" she asked, steeling herself by allowing her own presence to fill the deserted street.

Adalric felt her projected psyche and smiled, knowing she was still a fighter and almost regretted the course he had to take. "That depends on you."

"What do you mean?"

Adalric shook his head, annoyed by the questions. *There's work to be done,* he thought as he let his mind darken, *she must be prepared a bit before I can destroy her. It must look like an accident…a normal occurrence in the training of a TelSor warrior.* "No more questions for now," he said as he walked over to a large pair of rocks in the street.

Sitting on the taller one, he curtly gestured for her to take the other.

Blaze walked over and sat down next to him and looked up expectantly.

Glancing down at her and taking in her open face that seemed so eager to learn, Adalric once again felt a moment of indecision. *What if she was trained and chose to stand by my side? She has so much potential. No,* he chastised himself, *you weak fool. Do what you must and end this destructive situation. Teach her…but not enough to save herself.*

"Let me begin by explaining what I am," he said, "and what you are to become."

Blaze's ears perked up as her inquisitiveness overrode any doubts about Adalric which still lingered in her mind. For this information she would put up with anything, even sitting on an uncomfortable rock in the middle of a burnt-out town.

"I'm a TelSor," he said slowly, as if choosing each word carefully. "Only a dozen or so people in the galaxy, who are currently alive, can make that claim…and almost all of them are in the Imperium."

A smile of superiority curled on Blaze's lips as she considered this with pride.

"We date back quite far," he continued, "before the rise of the Terran Imperial Dominion." He paused for a moment. "Do you know what the Cosmic Aura is?"

She shook her head. She'd heard too many stories to know which was the truth and would prefer to let him tell it in his own fashion regardless.

"The Cosmic Aura is the life blood of the universe," he continued slowly, almost as if trying to explain this to a child. "All life comes from the stars, and it is there the energy of the Cosmic Aura is born. Since everything is born from this energy, all creations radiate the Cosmic Aura as well…people, rocks, comets…everything. It's a lot of raw energy and sometimes you can see its true power…in a nebula as it forms new stars…in a supernova as old stars die out. You probably know it best in the form most have seen it in, when the energy of the Cosmic Aura forms into hard glowing points called Cosmic Nodules."

She beamed, at last a name she'd heard. "Sure, the things that power the Cosmic Slip and Cosmic Leap star drive engines."

He nodded. "Yes, it is the massive power of the Cosmic Nodules which allows ships to either fully enter subspace in a *Cosmic Leap*, or to create a bubble of subspace around the ship for *Cosmic Slip*. Both methods allow the vessel to travel faster than light. It's the same power which allows for small, contained rifts in subspace, which lets people transport from a ship to a planet's surface in an instant using the *Cosmic Rift* transporter. I'm sure you know how rare and beautiful, not to mention expensive, these Nodules are."

She nodded again. Every ship that had star drive engines had to have at least one of the Nodules to power those engines, big ships like the *Demoness* needed four or five of them at a time. She saw them plenty of times and knew the fist sized balls of energy came in various colors. "Sure, I think the Cosmic Nodule on the *Silhouette* was blue," she half whispered to herself as she began to fall into memory.

He could see she was drifting off and wanted to get past this basic nonsense as quickly as possible. "That is the science side of the Cosmic Aura, which most people know. But there is much, much more. For the power of the Cosmic Aura can do more than let a ship break the light speed barrier by entering into subspace. It can, in the right person, unleash untapped powers. The first to discover this were priests on the planet Ellera, around a millennium ago. They are a race of natural telepaths and thus were more open to discovering just what the Cosmic Aura was, and how it could enhance someone. They were also the ones who found that there were rare individuals who were so attuned to the Aura, they could harness the energy within themselves, unlocking vast psionic powers…Telepathy, Telekinesis, Chronos Thought, etcetera."

"Chronos thought?"

"Visions. Seeing glimpses of the future, the past. That's far more advanced than you need to worry about for now, and not all TelSor can even do it."

Blaze nodded, then did a double take. "Wait…what? Ellerans? They're all pacifist…and they are members of the Alliance."

"As I said, this was a millennium ago, and though they are the ones who discovered the Cosmic Aura, they are not the ones who refined what a person could do with it, that was us, Terrans. Ellerans are predominantly a peaceful people, but power can do strange things to even peaceful people, and those that harnessed the power of the Cosmic Aura began to fight amongst themselves…an Elleran civil war. For, you see, when you train to harness the power of the Cosmic Aura, you have to tap into one side of the energy…positive…or negative, and despite what you may think, it's the negative energy that opens more powers within. However, these two sides tend to oppose each other, and that caused the war that devastated Ellera. When that war was over there were only a handful left who knew how to harness the Cosmic Aura, and they were banished. With the knowledge of the Cosmic Aura and Nodules, they were one of the first races to master lightspeed travel, and those early mystics left in their primitive vessels, and ended up finding Earth. But this was an Earth of almost a millennium ago, an earth in the fourteenth century. The Elleran mystics disguised themselves as humans and blended in to try to survive. They used their powers to aid humans where they could, often being called wizards or sorcerers…or witches. More than that, they found rare humans who were also attuned to the Cosmic Aura, and they passed on their knowledge to them. It was a small group of such humans who coined the name *TelSor*…telekinetic sorcerers, and the name stayed with us."

Adalric paused as he looked to see what effect his words were having. Seemingly satisfied by the attentive glaze in Blaze's soft eyes, he allowed himself a small grin. "The name truly fits, for by tapping into the Cosmic Aura, we unlocked our full potential, allowing ourselves to enforce our will over the matter and people around us. We also disciplined our bodies, to raise them to their fullest abilities."

"Wait…I'm confused," Blaze said. "You talk about the Cosmic Aura and how the TelSor disciplined themselves to use that energy, and that those attuned could master it, but something doesn't make sense. What about the mutants, like me?"

Adalric's smile turned into a hoarse laugh which quickly died out in the silence of the dusty street. "And now the science side of this must come back into play. You remember the Psi-Genetic war that Earth fought in the twenty-first century?"

She nodded.

"That was when scientists tried to duplicate the power of the TelSor with genetic engineering, to unlock the mind so anyone could master the Cosmic Aura. They were partially successful, creating a band of mutants who had some powers, but they couldn't control them, and it took a bloody war to finally round them all up and eradicate them."

"But..."

"It's hard to 'close Pandora's box' once it's open," Adalric continued. "Yes, they tracked down and caught all those who had been given the psionic enhancement serum, but *not* before many had already mixed with other humans. Most of the offspring were fine, but a few displayed powers, sometimes the powers would only manifest after puberty or a traumatic experience."

Blaze's mind drifted back to Boone and the "Tomb of Horrors" at the Rehabilitation Center.

Adalric watched her reaction. "To this day, mutants still pop up, though they are much rarer now. We TelSor still try to track those we can, to see if they also have the attunement and could be trained...like you do."

"You weren't training mutants when you found me, you were *executing* them."

"That was a special situation...and that is all behind us now. Besides, most mutants don't have the potential to become a TelSor, they just suck up the precious Cosmic Aura around them and waste it needlessly." Adalric paused, to let his next words sink in. "As *you* were doing with your pyrokinesis."

Blaze glanced up sharply, but the overlord continued before she could get out a word in her defense.

"So now, I need to know which path *you* are going to follow, Blaze."

He laid a firm hand on her smooth shoulder, shuddering ever so slightly as his fingers made contact with her bare skin. "Will you continue to follow the chaos of your flames; your wasteful use of the very energy you and the people you care for emit? Or will you accept control...my control...so you can truly master the Cosmic Aura and become a full-fledged TelSor, taking your place of honor among us?"

The young baroness' face held a pensive look, as if waging an internal conflict. "Can't I learn to better control my pyrokinesis," she finally asked, her eyes shimmering with hope, "incorporate it into my other abilities?"

Adalric felt a cold knot pull in his stomach, for this was the one question he knew she would ask. How could he tell her that it had taken all his discipline and energy to defend against her attack in the bedroom? He knew that with proper control, she would truly be his equal, and that was one thing he couldn't afford. "No," he finally said as he shook his head. "Your pyrokinesis is too undisciplined, too chaotic. It would interfere with your ability to develop your new skills. I felt its raw power yesterday...in your bedroom. It is too far out of control. Perhaps in the future, when you are a full TelSor...then we will discuss it again."

Despite her obvious disappointment, she nodded, filling with elation as she gingerly placed her hand over his on her shoulder and smiled at him. "I will do as you wish, Overlord Adalric."

The overlord felt his mouth dry up as he experienced her warmth through his glove. For a long instant he paused there, then pulled his hand away, and opened the wrapped bundle on his lap.

Blaze's hand lingered on her shoulder for a moment as some of her elation drained away, then she glanced down at what he was exposing.

From out of the cloth bundle, Adalric revealed an exquisite sword. Its hilt was a glimmering silver in color. Outshining that was the long, crystal-clear blade that made the weapon appear more like a conversation piece than an instrument of death. For an instant he held on to the weapon, as if unsure what to do, then slowly he handed it to her, allowing her to feel its weight for the first time. He let her soak in its sheer elegance, her eyes sparkling as her gaze caressed its entire length. *How like me she is,* he laughed silently, *when I first held my sword.* Then he mentally scowled and pushed the memory out of his mind.

"This is an electrosword," he informed her, though he knew she saw his more than once. "It's one of the finer weapons known to us at this time, and it's one of the TelSor's most preferred."

Blaze shivered with excitement and anticipation as she carefully gripped the hilt in her right hand and looked for a switch but found none. Suddenly, she was instantly rewarded with a crackle of energy, as multicolored flashes of light raced up and down the inside of the blade, causing the sword to radiate with energy. "How *magnificent*," she whispered, her skin basking in its luminous glow. Yet something was off, though she couldn't feel what it was. She turned back toward the overlord, more questions in her mind. "Why not just use guns?" she asked, suddenly wishing she had not by the sour look which crossed his lips.

"Any fool can fire a gun at a target and kill it," he replied in a scolding tone, "but a sword is finer and more dignified, a weapon for the hands of a noble."

"I've heard of other people besides TelSors using electroswords and other bladed weapons," she pointed out.

"True…but in the hands of a TelSor it's different. Our blades have something the others don't. Also, we are the only ones who can do what you just did…will the weapon to ignite. To anyone else, a TelSor's weapon is merely a crystal bladed sword. There is no switch."

"How did I turn it on?"

To respond he pulled his own electrosword out and she saw it looked the same as hers, but the hilt was black instead of silver. He pointed the pommel toward her and unscrewed the base. Once the end came off, a soft red glow emanated from inside the otherwise seemingly empty hilt."

"What…" she started to ask but then lost her words as she felt the raw power coming from the glow, that same rush whenever she was near the star drive engines of a spaceship, it felt like it was calling her.

"Let me back-track for a moment," he said calmly as he gazed into the red glow himself. "As you know, the Cosmic Aura has so much excess energy it sometimes condenses into the Cosmic Nodules that we use to power the star drive engines. These Nodules have been found in all seven colors of the spectrum: Red, Orange, Yellow, Green, Blue, Indigo, and

Violet."

"Right," she said, having heard this from Rabies more than once when he was teaching her about the engines on the *Silhouette*. "The color makes no difference, they all power engines the same."

"They make no difference to a *non* TelSor," he said, correcting her. "To those of us whose very life, very religion is devoted to the Cosmic Aura, we know better. Each of us is born with a natural affinity to but one of those colors. When we harness a Nodule of *that* color, special things can be done, like powering our electroswords. My affinity is red, and thus I have placed a small part of a red Cosmic Nodule in my sword, and that's its power source. Only another TelSor with such an affinity could activate my sword, and I know of none other alive now."

"What color am I drawn to?" she asked the obvious question.

"Orange," he answered without hesitation or doubt.

"How can you tell?"

"Your eyes," he replied while tapping the tinted lenses of his cowl. "When someone like us taps into the Cosmic Aura to do amazing things, our affinity is revealed by an iridescent glow in our pupils. If I were not wearing this mask, you'd have seen my eyes glow red more than once when using my powers. Yours were revealed to me when you used your pyrokinesis to kill the assassin back on the *Sentinel*, and again when you…used your flames during our…encounter. I saw the orange glow in your eyes both times. However, the final test was now, open your hilt."

Without deactivating the sword, since she wasn't sure how, she unscrewed the base of the hilt and removed the end cap. Suddenly a soft orange glow emanated from inside the hilt. It was beautiful…but didn't call to her like his did.

"Only someone tuned to the orange nodules could have started up your sword easily…It would have been very hard for me. Thus, I guessed correctly for you."

She shook her head in wonder. "So, any old person with this natural affinity could suddenly activate my sword?"

"No. First, they must be on the path of knowledge that each TelSor travels, as you have begun. Before you ask, no, none of the other TelSor use orange either, which is good for you."

"How do I turn it off?"

"The same way you turned it on, by thinking about it."

"So, I have a glowing sword, how does that make it special?"

His strong lips tensed for a moment, but he remained patient. "It's not merely some sword, Blaze, by using a Nodule we are attuned to, it becomes an extension of our powers and connection to the Aura. With this weapon you will be able to accomplish things no mortal man should."

"Oh." Blaze glanced down, realizing that in some way she had insulted him. But she tried to forget it, as she glanced back up at her shimmering blade with pride. "I think I will call it *Vindicator*."

"You are naming your weapon?" Adalric asked with surprise, seeing no sense in this.

"Of course," she said with a grin. "Why not? The ancient kings on Earth named their weapons...such as King Arthur and his sword, *Excalibur*." She smiled at him, then glanced at her sword and wondered if it would ever feel as powerful to her as his did.

Suddenly Adalric's sword flared to life in his hands, and he dropped it, his lips open in obvious shock.

"I'm sorry," she quickly said, somehow knowing she was responsible.

As fast as the sword ignited, it turned back off, laying in the smoldering dust, then hers turned off as well.

His lips tightened for a moment, then he shook his head. "It's these damned lenses and those fires which seem to flicker in your eyes along with the glow. I was sure I saw orange, but it must have been red. Let's be sure. Ignite your sword again."

She looked at her weapon and concentrated on it, this time it was harder and still made her feel slightly off. "Light, damn you!"

The overlord's sword lit up again.

"Well..." He removed her sword from her hand and tilted it, letting the luminous orange nodule slip into his hand. Then he pulled out a small case, no bigger than two inches square, and opened it, revealing another red Cosmic nodule piece inside. "My spare," he said as he removed it and put the orange one inside instead. He placed the other small red ball of energy into her sword's hilt, then closed it and handed it back to her. "We will have to be careful, having the same cosmic affinity, but as you get attuned to your weapon, it should eventually respond to you alone, and you'll stop accidentally igniting mine."

She glanced down at his still lit weapon, laying in the dust.

She hadn't asked, and he was glad about that, because he didn't know the answer himself. He picked up his sword and willed it back off and closed up the hilt, his thoughts a dark turmoil.

Hoping to change the subject, Blaze asked something that bothered her since his lesson began. "So, you explained all about how humans became TelSor…but what about Drusee-la?"

"Mutants are a human thing…and now some humanoid hybrid aliens as well since humans have a tendency to…be prolific. As for the very rare natural affinity to the Cosmic Aura, any race can have those, even a Perusian like Drusee-la."

"Oh, okay. So, what happens now?"

Adalric hesitated, realizing suddenly how much he was enjoying talking and spending time with her. It felt natural, and that bothered him, so he forced himself back to his agenda. *Now we get to the part that matters,* he thought grimly, *now we will see what she is truly made of.* "Now? Now you begin your training as a TelSor."

"Is it long?" she asked, wondering how you taught the Cosmic Aura to help you.

"Once again, that is up to you," he replied curtly. "The training is quite simple."

This made no sense to Blaze. How could it be simple to become a TelSor? "If it is so simple, why doesn't everyone do it?"

"Haven't you been listening, girl? You must be born with the attunement, the special ability to tap into the Cosmic Aura to become one. Without that you can't even start. Moreover, not *all* TelSor can train another, you have to have mastered its powers and understanding…to become an Elite…a Mystic."

Blaze nodded, suddenly understanding. "So, the same inner connections I have to the Cosmic Aura that made me a pyrokinetic, will allow me to become a TelSor because I also have the attunement."

"Yes. As I said, only a few of us are born with such inner strength, and among those few, even less would survive the training."

Blaze's eyes opened wider. "I thought you said the training was simple."

"It is…for the trainer, not the trainee. As my connection to the Cosmic Aura is to its negative energy, that's how I'll train you as well. However, there is no real way to teach the ability to tap into the Aura that surrounds us. All I do is put you through a series of special 'trials' which will force you to open your mind and draw in the Cosmic Aura around you. At the same time as you try to draw in the power, I'll use my gifts as a Mystic to unlock the mental blocks within you that would keep most from accomplishing this. At night, I will instruct you on what you did wrong, and how you can fix it."

"That's it?" she asked, unbelieving.

"That's it," he said with a grim smile. "You either have a TelSor inside of you, or you don't."

Blaze swallowed hard, suddenly feeling cold all over. "If I don't have a TelSor inside of me?"

His response sliced through the air with bitter finality. "Then you will die."

There was another long moment of silence as Adalric watched her every expression. *This is it,* he realized, *her last chance to back out. If she does, then the Dire Queen will abandon her, and she will have to be executed as a mutant.*

Blaze spiraled down into her own thoughts as she absently drew circles in the dirt with *Vindicator.* Suddenly Troy's words came back to her, and she remembered his warning, but knew there was no turning back now.

The young baroness gazed back up at her teacher, her eyes flashing with determination. "I'm ready to start, Lord Adalric. Let's get on with it."

The overlord nodded silently as he accepted the finality of what she said. *The play is in action,* he grimly thought, *we have our stage, our characters, and even our plot…though we must give her some time. After all, the Dire Queen would never accept her dying on the first day. No, then she would know I did it on purpose. So, Blaze, you will get some training. However, don't be fool enough to think the Dire Queen doesn't know how deadly training can be…your expiration is closer than you may think.* "Very well," he said as he stood up, "let's begin."

Blaze slowly stood up also and wondered what he would teach her first. "What do I do?"

A grin formed on his face, as he gestured out into the ruins. "You go for a walk."

Her eyes narrowed with suspicion. The last thing she wanted to do was stroll about *this* place. "Alone?"

"Of course."

"For how long?"

He chuckled for a moment as he stared directly down at her, his firm gaze piercing into her soul. "Until you make it back to the shuttle, hopefully alive."

"That's it?"

He nodded. "Again, that's it."

Blaze felt her nerves tingle with a mixture of mistrust and excitement and bit her bottom lip. "So, it's like a game, a hunting game," she said half to herself. "I can do this."

Taking another deep breath, she stood and walked away from the overlord, heading for a group of buildings in the distance.

"Remember, Blaze," he called after her, when she had cleared some distance. "Any simple psionic or mutant can use the power clumsily, but only a full TelSor can master it. Allow yourself to open up, absorb the Cosmic Aura around you. Above all else, *you must maintain control over your feelings.* When you lose control of those, then the ability to use the Aura will slip from your grasp...and that can cost you your life."

~ * ~

Blaze turned to ask him a question, but he was gone, leaving her deserted in the heat-baked street. The morning chill was completely gone, and she felt the hot rays of the red giant, Tartarus, burning fiercely overhead. A few drops of perspiration began to bead on her forehead under her loose bangs. *Now where could he have gone so quickly?* she wondered as she held up her hand to ward off the brilliant glare and scanned the surrounding rooftops.

Realizing she was truly alone, she tried to reevaluate her immediate goal. *He said I only had to make it back to the shuttle alive…but do I merely have to leave the town?* Either way, it seemed simple enough to her, as the edge of the ghost town lay less than four blocks away. Straightening her shoulders with firm resolve, she put her sword away in her previously vacant sheath, and began to determinately walk toward her shuttle. As the seconds passed, and nothing happened, her strides quickened, causing her crimson cloak to billow behind her in ripples.

The weight of the sword on her hip felt uncomfortable as she continued along, and she finally decided to keep one hand on the silver hilt; partly to keep the weapon from bumping her leg, but mostly for the feeling of security its cool touch gave her. First one block went swiftly past, then another. The edge of the destroyed town was now plainly in sight, giving way to the suddenly luscious fields of weeds to the side of the road that led to the safety of her shuttle. As she felt the tension building within her, she silently cursed this bizarre method of training a TelSor. Glancing back over her shoulder at the empty streets behind, she wondered why she felt as if he was still next to her, watching her every move. She wondered if perhaps he was bluffing, and her lesson was already over for the day.

Above all else, it was the silence that finally broke into her concentration and started to unravel her alertness. Back on Tenebrous, when the gangs were closing in, they always made a lot of noise. They gained great satisfaction in knowing the distress their banging and hollering caused in their intended victims. The noise they made gave you time to run and hide, though usually not enough time. However, she learned to use that time to her advantage, moving in directions they couldn't guess or anticipate. This felt completely different. Despite the similar surroundings, this place seemed rotten, like a corpse which had long been dead and buried and was now being exhumed for some ungodly reason.

"Where is he?" she half said to herself as she reached the edge of the town, her heels sinking into the moist mud as the broken road turned to dirt and disintegrated into the tall grass.

Blaze allowed herself a moment to peer across the field, to let her eyes rest on her grey ship in the distance. It seemed so far away. Looking back to the town one last time, she let a smile cross her lips as she realized she had already passed the first test. Not so hard after all…

The blow that struck her from the front was completely unexpected.

She didn't see what exactly hit her, other than it was large and oval, like a clump of sod which lifted off the ground and slammed into her with enough force to throw her back into the town a dozen or so yards.

Blaze tumbled backward through the air, her arms and legs flailing wildly as she tried to stop herself. However, the hard brick wall of the nearest building did that service for her, as she struck it and slowly slid to the warm broken pavement below. For a few moments she lay there, senseless in a half shock. She felt a gritty taste in her mouth and decided it was dirt.

No, Blaze forced into her half-dazed mind, *mustn't lay still…keep moving. If I want to stay alive, I have to keep moving.* Her survival instincts of her childhood finally kicked in, rising to dominate over the dull pain which wracked her numbing body. *How could I have let that happen?* she wondered as she forced herself to stand. As she gained her feet, she staggered for a moment and fell back against the wall. Finally, she managed to push herself off, looking around to regain her bearings. She was covered in wet dirt and grass, confirming her suspicions as to what struck her. *Nothing broken,* she decided as she felt her darkening bruises. There were a few scratches on her exposed skin, but most of her body had been protected by the resilient suit, confirming her suspicion it was an armored fabric.

"Concentrate, Blaze," Adalric said, his commanding, disembodied voice seeming to come from everywhere, and right beside her. "If you don't concentrate, you lose control…and if you lose control then you will die."

"Why don't you come out here and face me?" she yelled as she circled around, attempting to gain the location of her antagonist.

"If you want to find me, you must use your mind." His powerful voice drifted around the buildings of stone and wood, denying her a direction. "Use what is within you to satiate the fury that is growing inside. Use it if you dare."

Blaze's lips curled in an angry sneer, as she drew *Vindicator* out of his sheath for the first time and turned to face the town. Thoughts of the safety of her shuttle were forgotten, as she began to head back in again. She realized there was no leaving these ruins, at least not until what she had to do was done…whatever that was.

With a resolve which surprised her, she strode down the main avenue, realizing it was probably best to avoid the buildings and keep to the open streets. That way she would have plenty of time to see another attack coming and react to it. She slowly circled the rocks where they had talked, her clear blade out. *He said I could do amazing things with this sword,* her thoughts echoed, *so let's keep it ready and see.*

She barely had time to react as a shadow crossed her peripheral vision, giving her all of one second to dive for cover. The rusty steel-tipped lance, which had once been a part of some form of transportation, grazed through her hair on its near lethal journey, and embedded itself into the wall of the broken-down store ten yards behind her. Blaze came up from the dive and looked at the pole, still vibrating in the far wall. Her lips parted slightly as she observed how deeply the shaft had penetrated the hard wood, the realization sinking in.

That was no clump of dirt, she thought bitterly, *that could have killed me…easily. Well,* she quickly decided, *if that's the way you want it, then fine. Use my mind, huh,* her thoughts angrily raged within. *Let my feelings find you?* Suddenly she glanced up as it struck her, something drawing her like a mental magnet. He was out there…she could *sense* him as though she could see him. A smile crossed her lips, just as a strong internal warning lit within her, making the fine hairs on the nape of her neck stand on end. *What is this sensation?* she gasped as she felt a pulling behind her, as if psychic strings were demanding she turn around, leading her like a marionette. For a moment she almost felt like she was in a sea of multicolor light, and she had to follow the current. Willing *Vindicator* to obey, her electrosword lit with lightning fury as she turned to face whatever was demanding her immediate attention. At first, she thought it had been her imagination, as she observed the silently empty street, but the feeling simply would not subside, growing more intense instead.

Finally, Blaze saw it, lazily floating as it flew toward her, almost as if she were directed to it by the now fading colors of light. It must have been a beam of wood, sharpened by blasts to form a deadly spear. She watched it for a second, feeling as if she was in some slow motion holo. *It's merely an illusion,* she suddenly realized as she watched the spear bear down on her, skimming across a river of air on its graceful path of death. *This feeling of having lots of time…all an illusion. Act, idiot,* she demanded of herself, trying to force action into her suddenly limp limbs, *act now!* With a sudden rush of energy, she brought her ignited sword up in front of her in a protective arc, to have it suddenly intercept the spear, mere inches from her chest. There was a cloudburst of sparks as *Vindicator* destroyed her would-be assassin, sending it into a downpour of splinters to rest behind her.

As the tightening sensation was released, she felt as if her world returned to normal. She slipped to one knee, suddenly fatigued. Despite her growing exhaustion, elation filled her every pore. She did it, anticipated an attack and defended herself against it. Exhilaration flowed within her, revitalizing her wearied limbs.

"Better," came his voice from behind her. "You've taken the first step, but you still have much to learn, and the day's barely begun."

Blaze whirled to face her teacher, only to find the streets behind her devoid of life. That mattered little to her. For despite his seeming firmness, she felt the pride within him. He was impressed by what she did today. That's when it hit her that their psychic link wasn't truly gone, at least not fully.

Not knowing how long the power would last within her sword, she turned it off and she sheathed it, confident that her newfound "sixth sense" warning system would give her plenty of time to ward off any future attacks. She would have thought that what she just learned would have been enough for the day, but obviously he still wasn't satisfied. What would come next?

Her answer came in the form of a sliding sound which suddenly began to emanate from behind one of the buildings to her left. She wanted to go and investigate but stopped herself after two steps. *Maintain control,* she echoed his command internally, *it will come to you, out here where you have plenty of space to deal with it…whatever it is.*

Her thoughts calmed to the low idle of a fine-tuned racing skimmer, ready at the starting gate. *Is he dragging something here…or readying another telekinetic missile for its run? Either way,* she decided firmly, as she pulled her sword back out of its sheath and re-ignited it in one flowing movement, *I'm prepared.*

However, she had not been prepared for what slithered around the corner ahead of her. To describe it as disgusting would have been giving it unnecessary flattery. Resembling a gigantic fat orange worm which was covered in some yellow ooze, it began to slowly come at her, its huge bulk heaving from behind the building…and heaving…and heaving.

Damn, she thought quickly as she fell into what she considered to be a warrior's stance of readiness, *what the hell is that thing?* She continued to stare at it with a mixture of disgust and amazement as it finally cleared the ruins, measuring over thirty feet in length from "head" to "tail". It had no eyes she could see, but its tremendous maw was split in three directions, opening to form a huge triangle. As she stared at its toothless mouth, opening and closing as it crawled toward her, she realized it was large enough to easily swallow her whole.

Could Adalric have sent this against me, she wondered in disbelief, *or was this some freak coincidence?* She doubted even *he* could direct this seemingly mindless atrocity. Reaching out from within, she suddenly realized with conviction that this whole grueling scene was indeed orchestrated by the overlord.

She allowed herself to laugh. Despite its mammoth size, the creature was as slow as sap dripping down a tree. How could this possibly be a challenge to her? She would simply wait for it to get close enough, which could take forever at that speed, and once it was close she would destroy it with her new weapon.

At least that's how she would have liked it to have gone, before the brick struck her from behind, knocking her to her knees as she fought to regain her senses.

"Do not let yourself lose concentration, Blaze," came the damning disembodied voice. "If you allow yourself to fixate on one obstacle, then others can easily slip past. Keep your weapon ready, it's your amplifier to the Cosmic Aura. Without it, you won't have the time to protect yourself from such projectiles."

"You bastard!" she yelled as she rubbed the back of her head, already feeling the large swell rising and the wetness of some blood. She fought to see clearly through what she was sure was a concussion, but the pain and nausea begged for the sweet blackness of unconsciousness to take her. "At least fight fairly."

There was a brief hesitation, then the voice calmly returned. "Why should I do for you what the rest of the galaxy never will? This is not some fantasy, Blaze. This is reality."

"Screw your reality," she yelled as she turned the anger inward, letting it build inside of her like a capped volcano. She knew he forbade her from using her pyrokinesis, but she was tired of playing by his rules, on his turf, against his obstacles. The fury raged within, engulfing her in the purity of her raw emotions.

"No, Blaze," the voice returned, suddenly concerned, "you mustn't."

"Yes," she said in return, as her vision cleared, turning the world into a red haze, "I must."

Wisps of steam rose from the suddenly scorching pavement around her, as the creature closed in, its three jaws opening to engulf the seemingly defenseless girl in front of it.

As its maw closed down, Blaze's eyes flared a scarlet red as she released her hidden flames, sending its searing shafts of fiery death down its gaping throat. For an instant its bloated body expanded widely, as its internal gases superheated, then exploded in a torrential conflagration of flesh and fire.

Unscathed by it all, Blaze shook back her hair and reveled in the glory of the destruction around her. She watched, and smiled, until all that remained were tiny pieces of burning worm, scattered on the still steaming street. The scalding stench finally assaulted her as she wrinkled her nose in distaste. *Small price to pay, though,* she decided with smug satisfaction. She slowly turned as she saw Adalric approaching in the distance, the rubber soles of his black boots sizzling as they touched the pavement. Even though she had disobeyed him, she knew he would be proud. He told her that her pyrokinesis couldn't work with her other powers, but they had, beautifully. Never had she felt so focused with her flames, and she knew it was her growing control of the Cosmic Aura that was the cause. A wide grin came over her lips as she watched him approach, to finally stand over her kneeling form, towering over her.

Blaze gazed up at her teacher expectantly, her eyes shining with self-pride, and a "look what I've done" expression refusing to leave her face. The feeling was clearly not shared by the overlord, that much was obvious the minute she saw his jaw clamped tightly in silent fury.

Suddenly, his mind lashed out and grabbed her tightly as if to squeeze, but as quickly as it began, it faded again. He stared down at her through his darkened lenses, and even though she couldn't see his eyes, she knew they were lit with anger.

"I told you *not* to use your pyrokinesis," he yelled, his deep voice slicing into her. But more than that, she could feel his profound disappointment through the remnants of the link, and that was more painful than any physical attack would have been. "I *will not* stand for this disobedience again." He stood still for a moment, trembling with rage, then swiftly turned and stormed away, leaving her with his final damning words. "I will teach you nothing more today."

For a long time, Blaze remained kneeling on the ground, tasting the warm sting of blood in her mouth from the earlier attacks as she reeled from his angry emotions. Had she so disappointed him by protecting herself with her flames?

"What was I supposed to have done," she yelled at the empty street, *"let the beast eat me?"*

As she sat in the dirt and muck, stewing in her own simmering resentment, she slowly came to the realization that she had caved to her desires, just as he warned her not to do.

Slowly, she dragged her weary body back to its feet as she began to search for the sword she dropped when the brick hit. *Perhaps I could have battled it another way…fought fire without fire, so to speak. If he can throw things with his mind, then perhaps I can too.*

Looking up, Blaze saw her sword laying on the pavement some six feet from where she stood, half covered in oozing worm guts. She resisted the urge to go pick it up, and instead she stretched out her hand and reached out with her mind, letting the anger over his disappointment fuel her resolve. She watched as *Vindicator* lifted into the air and sailed effortlessly into her waiting hand. This surprised her so much she almost dropped her prized weapon as it settled into her grip. She shook the sword out, letting the blood fall from it, before placing it back in its sheath. *He was right,* she finally relented, *there were other ways to deal with the situation. I may still be learning, but that's what Adalric is here for, to help me learn to end my old life and start anew.* She felt ashamed having let him down, as a stronger devotion stirred within her.

Taking a deep breath, she looked one last time at the gory remains surrounding her, then she turned and started back to the shuttle, oblivious to the fact she was limping on her left foot. She knew, with full conviction, the day's lessons had indeed come to an end, but what she was to learn was merely beginning.

Chapter Twenty
Hubris

"What progress have you to report?" the Dire Queen asked, as she watched Adalric pace back and forth before her throne. Never had she seen her overlord more agitated than he had been over the last three weeks of Blaze's training, and she was reveling in every moment of his suffering. Her fierce eyes focused on a part of his long cloak, which was torn and softly smoldering. *Excellent*, she thought with glee, *my little cub has fangs.* "Certainly, you have *something* to tell me."

Adalric halted his pacing and slowly turned to face his mistress, each stiff movement a traitor to the raging torrent in his soul. "She is progressing along adequately," he said through grit teeth, as if each word burned a sore in his tongue. "She is surprisingly talented...and resourceful."

A cruel laugh hissed from the Dire Queen as she slowly shook her head, her luminous eyes floating back and forth across the empty void which made up her visage. "Why, Tanus, my friend," she said as she cackled, "you seem jealous. I hope she's not more than you can handle."

The overlord's chin and exposed cheek flushed red with the anger that coursed through his veins, revealing his frustrations. "Her skills are impressive," he finally managed, as if fighting some hidden impulse that wished to escape. "Already she has more power and control than most of the *other* barons...but she's *not* ready yet."

Temper, temper, the sovereign commanded silently, reading into her loyal servant's feelings. *So, Tanus, all your attempts to dispose of her have so far met with an obvious lack of success. Perfect, she will suffice nicely.* "Blaze has indeed grown quickly. How much longer until she *is* ready?"

"Another week at the most," he informed her stiffly as he silently continued to formulate plans.

The sovereign's glowing orbs brightened as she glared down at her overlord. Her shadowed fingers scratched against the onyx which made up the arms of her throne, leaving deep welts in the precious stone. "Is there something else on your mind...my *friend*?"

Caught off guard by her attempted intrusion into his thoughts, Adalric's lips tightened as his other concerns surfaced. "As a matter of fact, my queen, there is."

A low hiss-like sigh escaped her darkened hood as she leaned forward, her poise challenging his predicted defiance. "And that is?"

Adalric felt the change in her mood and stiffened his own stance against it. He had no desire to show weakness now, especially since he was convinced the Dire Queen desired to replace him with Blaze. "My fleet...Drusee-la is still commanding my fleet."

The Dire Queen sat back, relaxing her composure. *Is that all?* "Your duty now is to fully train the Baroness Blaze. When you finish your assignment, you can return to the war."

"An overlord's place is with his fleet," he firmly insisted, "not baby-sitting the queen's new protégée."

The sovereign stood up from her throne, rising to her full height. Her eyes flared like miniature supernovas as she lifted her hand to point a shadowed finger at her servant. "Your place is anywhere I wish it to be, Adalric. Unless...have you finally gained the courage to challenge me?"

~ * ~

For a long moment, Overlord Tanus Adalric decided he had, indeed, gained enough courage to do that. This was the moment he'd been preparing for. His hand went down to the cool hilt of his electrosword as he stepped forward — one step — then reconsidered, his thoughts a whirling mosaic. He knew with the loyalty of the Imperium divided among the Imperial Nobility, the death of the Dire Queen could plunge the Imperium into civil war. He knew he could count on Koroqo, but would that be enough against the loyalty to the queen and her new protégée, and the wildcard of Drusee-la? He let out the breath he had been holding and slowly moved his hand away from the hilt as he forced himself to retreat a step. His chaos-filled thoughts formed the necessary rationalization as he decided he simply wasn't ready...yet.

~ * ~

The Dire Queen had stood in amazement as her cryptic senses told her that her overlord was *actually* preparing to attack her. She readied the dark powers that flowed through her body to make a death strike to end his life, but hesitated. A moment of doubt crossed the cold recesses of her mind. Adalric's powers had grown much since she recruited and trained him, and she realized she no longer knew his full potential. She let herself relax as he stepped away, the battle would not occur this night. *But why?* She quickly understood it was not fear which caused him to back down this time, it was military strategy, and that bothered her even more. Nevertheless, she knew she must maintain her power.

"That was most wise," she said slowly, her words dripping with venom. "You are not that powerful, Adalric. Not yet."

"My apologies, my queen," he replied as he bowed again to her and spread his hands in a show of acceptance. "I will complete Blaze's training," he continued, trying not to choke on the bitter words which stuck in his throat, "then I will go to my fleet…with *your* permission, of course."

"Of course," she acknowledged, then dismissed him with a curt wave of her hand.

Her burning gaze followed him out of the large chambers, as silent thoughts of absolute damnation flowed through her charcoaled mind. Finally, she closed out her visions and called for the one person who could help her now.

~ * ~

Overlord Adalric stormed down the wide hallways as he searched for a place to gather his thoughts. Having no desire to return to his ship, he instead chose a spot frequented by his bright pupil, the observation deck.

As he entered, he let the natural darkness of the room, which was illuminated solely by the planetary reflection from outside, cover him like a blanket of security. There were three other officers in the large recreation hall when he entered, but they all quickly abandoned the deck when they saw the stony look on the lower half of his face.

After they left, the overlord allowed himself to relax a bit, as he leaned on the hard banister which faced the huge picture windows. For a long moment of silence, he stared intently at Nyx below, the large planet's nighttime reaching its crescendo. Reflections of the dreadnought *Demoness*, drifting in a synchronous orbit with the *Sentinel*, danced teasingly across his darkened eyepieces.

The other shadow in the darkness moved out from where it was in silent observation, finally registering on Adalric's defensive psychic screens.

The overlord turned but was relieved to see it was a welcome form of company, one he could trust. He turned back to the window, this time settling his gaze on his warship. "I should be out there, Troivaka," he said, his deep voice laced with frustration, "not waltzing political circles with the Dire Queen."

The Proximan baron moved next to him, finally becoming visible as his porcelain-white skin caught some of the pale light reflected up from Nyx. His black eyes twinkled as they gazed out at the grand ship, the heart of their discussion. "The overlord has many duties," he finally responded, a light tone to his voice.

"None more important than the expansion of the Imperium," was Adalric's quick response, as his fists clenched tightly around the banister in front of him. "Right now, as we speak, Drusee-la is leading my fleet against the United Star Alliance. She gains political power and backing while I slip into obscurity on this accursed base. The eyes of the Imperium are on what is happening out *there,* not here."

He released one hand from the banister to gesture out the window at the stars, his tight fist scraping the edges of the cool transglass.

"You defeated both the Romusian and Camillian Empires," Koroqo reminded him, trying to invoke some comfort. "Besides that, you won the first major victories against the Alliance as well. All Drusee-la is doing now is continuing in your footsteps. You have nothing to fear from her."

Adalric's tone deepened as the muscles in his face tightened. "Are you so sure? You still haven't reported to me on that attempt on my life, three weeks ago."

"It is difficult," the S'teka master reluctantly admitted, agitated by any covert action that eluded his knowledge, especially one that involved a fellow Proximan. "Whoever set up the attack covered his or her trail with great precision."

"I still feel it was Drusee-la."

"But you must be sure," Koroqo reminded him sternly, "I'm not."

Adalric's voice dropped to a guttural growl. "That *feline* has every reason to keep me away from the front, while she continues to pile her victories on top of mine. She needs time, which is the one thing I can't allow her to have."

The starlight caught in Koroqo's eyes as he studied his fellow noble, and superior. "You're forgetting what I told you a moment ago, of your prior conquests against the other empires."

"They were nothing," Adalric said, spitting the words harshly, "and you know it. The United Star Alliance was always the enemy to defeat, and the person who does it will one day *rule* this galaxy."

"You think the Dire Queen is deliberately detaining you, to let Drusee-la gain favor?"

"I believe those were her initial plans. Now things have changed, and we both know why."

The Proximan noble nodded, seeing where this was leading. "Blaze is merely a pawn in all of this," he finally said. "You must realize this."

"I can't allow her to become a full TelSor, Troivaka," was Adalric's quiet response. "She has too much potential, and she's practically ready. An alliance between her and the Dire Queen would spell my death."

"Blaze knows nothing of any such plans our sovereign may have. My empathy confirms that. You don't even appreciate what you've been handed...she could be your best ally yet."

Adalric's eyes shimmered in doubt behind his mask as he turned to face the Proximan. "Where do *your* loyalties lie, Troivaka? Where will you stand when this all comes to a head...and you *know* it will."

Koroqo studied the overlord for a long time. Reading his emotions had always been a challenge that often gave him conflicting results. "My loyalties lie with the best interests of the Imperium. As head of the Imperial Secret Service, I can do nothing less."

"You didn't answer my question."

The Proximan baron reached out and placed his hand gently on the overlord's shoulder, pushing past the psychic shields. "Yes, I did, my friend."

The overlord nodded gratefully as he turned back to the window, his gaze never leaving the *Demoness*, his thoughts falling into darkness once again.

Koroqo studied Adalric intently, recoiling from the ferocity of the emotions he read in his friend. "Perhaps," he said, his voice growing soft in hopes of producing a calming effect, "your obsession over her has nothing to do with the Dire Queen. Maybe it's your own emotions you are afraid of confronting."

Adalric cocked his head to the side as he turned back to his companion. "Why?" he questioned, his voice laden with sarcasm. "Because she shows such raw talent that even I lack? That once fully trained as a TelSor *and* a pyrokinetic, she might best even me?"

"You're the one who can answer that. Remember, I'm an empath, and even a TelSor can't truly hide their emotions from me. There's no doubt that your feelings for Blaze are intense, but maybe you are denying their true meaning."

"And what meaning is that?"

The S'teka master let out a long sigh. "That is something you must ask yourself. What are your intense feelings if not hatred or fear?"

Adalric's eyes narrowed, his glare piercing through his darkened eyepieces at the Proximan. *If not hatred or fear*, his thoughts echoed Koroqo's taunting words, as his mind began to fill with the supple curves of the one woman he had sworn to destroy…yet could not. The image of Blaze, sleeping on his smoldering bed coalesced in his visions. How he wanted…needed to touch her again…if he only allowed himself the weakness. His thoughts snapped back like a rubber band breaking, as he finally realized what his friend brazenly implied. "You're a fool, Troivaka."

A sly grin formed on Koroqo's lips. "Perhaps. But I trust my instincts. Maybe it's time for you to trust yours."

Any response Adalric might have had died a quick death when the doors to the observation deck opened, admitting the subject of their immediate concerns, the Baroness Blaze.

She came here, hoping to find some tranquility after Adalric's last "lesson" — a lesson which nearly cost her right arm. It had been caught between the wreck of some old vehicle and one of her teacher's paid thug's swords. It was a good thing the medical facilities on the base were excellent, as she had lost a decent amount of blood. Though she had, of course, emerged victorious.

Now, all she wanted was to rest in her favorite spot, only to find it had been claimed by someone she had no desire to see at the moment.

Sensing the situation that threatened to erupt, Koroqo began to exit out the far door, deciding he didn't wish to be around when it did.

"Where are you going?" Adalric asked as his friend neared the door.

Glancing over his shoulder at the two of them, he let a slick smile flash across his lips. "To quote one of your ancestors," he said, "I'm letting discretion be the better part of valor. *Tes arveroir, ni se traino.*" He disappeared through the door, leaving them in silent darkness.

"What did he say there?" she asked, momentarily forgetting her anger.

"He…wished us a good evening in Proximan," Adalric quietly responded, as he contemplated his friend's true words.

Guessing there was more to it than that, but remembering her anger, she decided to let it drop. Although she learned a lot from the overlord over the last three weeks, more than she ever thought she could learn, his actions this morning went too far. "Why are you trying to *kill* me?"

Shaken from his thoughts by the accusatory tone in her voice, he turned to face her, suddenly understanding Koroqo's words much better. "It is simply your training as a TelSor. If you can't take it, then quit." He began to walk out, finding he still had much to consider, and many other barons to talk with.

Her anger drained to despair as she watched his strong form turn away from her, his broad shoulders pivoting with the precision of a soldier. She bitterly berated herself, angered at the way her emotions were shifting, and wondering why he seemed oblivious to how she felt.

Blaze watched the overlord begin to move away, then something snapped inside, as she boldly stepped in his path. "No, there is more to it than that. As I struck out at you in the end, and your cloak caught on fire…our minds linked again for a moment, and I felt…"

The pain caught up in her voice, cutting her off mid-sentence. She wanted to believe in this man, even though she knew she shouldn't…couldn't…but had anyway. He showed her so much, opened her connection to the Cosmic Aura beyond her simple pyrokinesis. Still…all that did was make this feeling of betrayal horribly painful, for more reasons than she cared to admit.

Silently cursing his own carelessness in allowing her to sense some of his motives, Adalric gazed back at her, preparing some great excuse…but the words died in his throat as his eyes met hers. Suddenly he was looking at Blaze the woman, and not the threat the Dire Queen was dangling before his eyes. *Koroqo was right,* he firmly decided, remembering his friend's parting words, *we are combatants, locked in struggle. But why the word traino?* he wondered. *That's a Proximan term usually reserved for quarreling mates…not enemies.*

Finally, he forced these thoughts out of his mind, and cupped her chin in his firm hand. "These lessons are for your own good, Blaze. Soon your training will be complete, and the Dire Queen will wish to send you out to convey her words to the provincial governors and Imperial forces. They will not respect weakness, so I will allow none in you." He paused as he studied her reaction, then continued, his powerful voice gently quelling her inner anger, drowning it from a raging fire to a whispering spark. "What you sensed was merely a reflection of your own self-doubts, not *my* feelings. Believe me…you are still not powerful enough to read *those.*"

Blaze wondered if she had been mistaken, had not truly felt their minds touch. She wanted so much to believe in him, and she had been so certain about his desires to kill her. Still, there had been more than that, she was sure of it. For under that desire to kill, she sensed a deeper yearning, one for her. However, if Adalric was right, and his sequestered thoughts had merely been a false reflection of her own, then it was her *own* desires for him she had felt.

She shook her head quickly, snapping herself out of her train of thought and away from his touch. She started to step back but was caught by his firm grip on her arm.

"No," he said, "it is I who will leave. This is *your* place. I have other duties to attend to. Tomorrow you have another lesson early in the morning, so enjoy some peace and quiet."

With no further words, he turned and left the room, disappearing into the inky blackness that permeated the large chamber.

She stared after him for a long moment, her eyes reflecting the waning light which was beginning to appear around the edges of the planet below. She turned and absently chewed on her bottom lip, then cursed as she saw her reflection in the tall windows, and decided she didn't like what she saw. However, as she stared at the image in the window she started to feel a pulling sensation in her gut. It was a feeling that had become more than familiar over the last three weeks, one there was no way to ignore…the call of her mistress.

Chapter Twenty-one
Confession

Blaze realized she was becoming accustomed to the throne room, as she leisurely reclined on the crimson satin pillow the Dire Queen provided for these long sessions. In some ways they were even more grueling than the TelSor training. Nevertheless, these times with the sovereign became special to her. Blaze had never had another woman take interest in her welfare past her early childhood. No sister or mother to guide her, and despite the Dire Queen's macabre essence, she was still a woman. This much was obvious to Blaze, as she had listened to the Dire Queen regale her with countless hours of her life's stories, over the many occasions they spent with each other. Though this time Blaze felt a difference. Usually, the queen would simply summon her, and they would discuss the Imperium and the old days of the Terran Imperial Dominion. However, this time there had been urgency in her call, almost desperation. Blaze responded with her immediate presence, fueled by her concern, hoping the Dire Queen would share the reasons for those feelings. All she could do was hope and listen. It was most certainly not *her* place to ask. Patiently she waited, while the Dire Queen began with idle chatter.

"...Yes," the Dire Queen continued, her low voice hissing with an almost reflective tone to it. "That was the first time a baron asked me to dance. So, I can imagine what it must have been like for you, at your reception." The sovereign paused in her anecdote, analyzing the effect it was having. She could read the glaze in her young baroness' eyes and realized her thoughts were far from this throne room, from where they should be.

"So, who is he?" the Dire Queen suddenly whispered, her low voice laced with girlish curiosity.

Pulled out of her own deep recesses, Blaze looked up at her mistress with wide, startled eyes. "H-he who?" she finally asked, wondering how the

Dire Queen was able to penetrate the mental psi-shields that kept even Adalric blind about her.

A soft but eerie laugh sounded from the dark emptiness within the Dire Queen's hood, as she reached out with her obsidian hand and lightly drew elaborate designs on the arm of her throne. "I am still a woman, Blaze, and I can tell when another woman is thinking of a man."

Despite herself, Blaze began to blush, feeling the warmth flushing through her cheeks. Perhaps this is what she needed, another person to talk to, one who would understand the inner battle she was so afraid of losing.

"So," the Dire Queen asked, "who is he?"

Suddenly fear sprung up in Blaze's mind, something which warned her to keep silent. Despite how close her mistress had grown, this was a problem she would have to deal with on her own. "Was I thinking of a man?" she tried, reinforcing her psi-shields as strongly as she could. "I've met so many lately."

The shadowed figure on the throne held back some anger, suddenly feeling betrayed at her servant's obstinacy. It quickly faded though, as she remembered the echoes of such feelings she once held. *Even now she struggles to hide his identity from me,* she laughed silently, her bright eyes softening again. *It's probably Koroqo, I heard how closely they danced at the celebration, and he has talked privately with her since then.*

For a long moment the Dire Queen continued to study her servant, with a mixture of envy and admiration, then decided it was time to close the web. The bait had been taken.

Sensing a sudden change in mood that accompanied the grim silence, Blaze shuffled uneasily on the soft cushion, then gently cleared her throat, hoping to get the subject off men. This was a game they were playing, and one which was no less deadly than the one Adalric played with her. "My queen, may I ask something?"

"Certainly, my child."

"What is the prophecy Overlord Adalric mentioned the day he brought me here to be executed?"

The Dire Queen shrank back a bit, truthfully surprised by someone for the first time in longer than she cared to admit. *My young servant has grown, in more ways than one. She has sensed my mood and acted upon it…yes, it is time.*

A whispered cough sounded from the Dire Queen, as if she was clearing her throat, then she reached out and touched Blaze's shoulder, sending chills through her servant's body. "Indeed, we should talk." She paused again and tried to come up with the proper wording, failed, and tried again, still failing. In the end, she resorted to the one thing she could. "Blaze, it is time to tell you the truth…the *full* truth."

The young noble's lips parted slightly as calmness came over her, and she realized at last someone here had said to her the one word she had been waiting for…truth.

"You know I chose you for my servant because I sensed a greatness in you, one that could truly flourish in the Imperium…if given the proper chance, and guidance."

Blaze nodded silently.

"But also, there was the prophecy. It foretold the coming of a person with special powers, one who would destroy Adalric and end his life as he knows it."

The baroness' eyes widened in wonder. "Where did this vision come from?"

"A former baron's daughter," the Dire Queen answered, carefully gauging her every word. "She had the gift of…sight."

"The edict outlawing psionically gifted people…mutants…" Blaze said, her face projecting the sudden realization which came to it, "it all makes sense now. Why did you save me that day? Why make me a baroness if I was the one the prophecy meant?"

The sovereign relaxed, pleased beyond words with the fire within her servant. A fire she could now harness to serve her alone, a fire to incinerate the threat of the overlord. "Because Overlord Adalric had grown unstable, as could be seen with his obsession with the prophecy, one that may not have even been true. As for making you a noble, that was the one way I could legally spare you. I sensed a kindred spirit in you that day, something that told me you would be a great ally, and a close friend."

Blaze felt herself reaching out psychically, as Adalric taught her to. Instead of the cold darkness she expected to encounter, she touched cool nervousness and worry. The Dire Queen was *afraid* of losing her, she could definitely feel it. For the first time since meeting her, Blaze felt herself relaxing around her mistress. All this made perfect sense. "You think I could provide a balance against Adalric's decline."

What delicately proper words, the Dire Queen thought with a smile. "Yes, my child. I foresaw Adalric's irrationalities would one day undo him. I need you by my side when that day comes."

An eerily warm sensation swept over Blaze, slicing through the barriers between them like a bright light on a cold misty eve. It faded quickly, leaving her with the knowledge this was the sovereign's offer of friendship. She suddenly found herself speechless, unable to think of what to say next.

Sensing Blaze's questions reached their conclusion, the Dire Queen relaxed and sat back on her throne, knowing she no longer had to hide the truth from her servant. Her words had not been brazenly plain, but she was confident Blaze understood and would one day fulfill her destiny.

An unpleasant rush swept through the sovereign's shadowed form with the words she had been forced to use, words of tenderness and connection which felt alien to her since her change. She realized, though, that to control this flaming weapon, she would have to play with its emotions even more. Her luminous eyes softened as she gazed down at the young human, then she let out a gentle laugh. "I have regaled you with too much of my past, Blaze. Why don't you tell me how the training is proceeding? What I know of it is what little my overlord tells me."

Blaze recovered from her realizations, and let a smile cross her lips. She wondered if the queen could truly become a friend, beyond her role as a mentor and ruler, and she found herself wishing it could be so.

"Of course. Well, after the initial training session, things went smoothly for the first week. Overlord Adalric would mostly hurl things at me, and yell that I wasn't concentrating enough."

The Dire Queen's eyes brightened with amusement, how this reminded her of a time so long ago. "Please. Continue."

"The second week, things intensified as he started to send more creatures against me, and convicts armed with about anything they could get their hands on."

"Ah, yes," the Dire Queen said with a sigh.

She had heard Adalric was giving condemned prisoners the choice of fighting for their life on Nyx or suffering execution. Given the option, all but the most foolish chose to fight. "Obviously you emerged victorious."

"Yes," Blaze said with pride. "It's strange…people who would have intimidated me a month ago suddenly seem, well, almost insignificant. It was as though they moved in slow motion…even the one with the ancient projectile weapon. I found it almost *easy* to dodge or deflect the bullets while *Vindicator* was in my hands." She smiled, recalling her past successes, then her eyes narrowed, and her voice turned bitter. "However, this last week was different. Along with his usual barrage of hurling objects, and the creatures, and the convicts…he sometimes attacks me himself. He knows I'm no match for him, yet he attacks anyway. I almost lost my arm this morning because of him."

Concern sifted through the Dire Queen as she absorbed this information. *He is combating her himself. But in only the third week? Of course,* she realized *he was hoping for a training accident. I could interfere…but no, Blaze must deal with this herself, or else she will be useless to me.*

"You must be careful, Blaze," her cryptic voice finally warned. "Never lower your guard near Adalric."

"Believe me, my queen," Blaze replied wholeheartedly, "that's the furthest thing from my mind."

The Dire Queen's eyes softened again, *how like him she is…so certain of herself, and her ability to overcome her adversaries.* Her mind traveled to Blaze's future and recoiled in fearful premonition of the power Blaze could someday master. *No,* she realized, *I must seize control now, before it is too late.* The Dire Queen forced her voice to cool to a gentle whisper, as she reached out to her servant again. "Blaze, I want you to call me by my name…call me Regine." She paused for a moment, pleased by the sharp reaction in her servant's eyes. "Now, tell me something of your past, I know so little about you."

"Alright…Regine," Blaze answered as a wide grin spread across her lips, her eyes sparkling a deep red from the flickering lights around her. "I was born in the United Star Alliance, on a small, hateful colony world called Tenebrous…"

~ * ~

"That human…furless…*bitch!*" Baroness Drusee-la screeched as she stormed across the steely grey decks of the *Wraith's* main bridge. Her long ivory tail twitched slowly back and forth, reflecting her levels of fury in smooth metronomic tones. She instantly turned and pounced back to the communications station, to re-read the current update from the heart of the Imperium again. *How could this possibly be right?*

"Who is this person?" she angrily asked her ship's captain, as her cold sapphire eyes bore tiny holes in his mind. "And why is this communiqué three weeks old?"

The captain of the *Wraith* cleared his throat as he stepped back. He saw Drusee-la angered before, but never with this much raw fury. Perhaps he should have waited to give her the Imperial bulletin until after the upcoming battle. "She's the Dire Queen's new personal advisor…and we are quite far from the home star now."

"I know that, you fool," she said, letting her words hiss through her needle-sharp fangs. "Where did she come from? How did she rise so *mmrallkin* quickly? Is she some noble's daughter?"

"No, my Lady. Rumor has it she rose through the ranks, serving the overlord himself."

"A soldier…becoming a noble? Don't be a fool, Captain. She must have had some connections. Perhaps she's Overlord Adalric's concubine."

A look of utter shock covered the captain's face like a shroud as he stepped closer and lowered his voice. "My Lady," he whispered, while glancing around at his bridge crew, most of whom were trying hard to appear as if they were not listening to the conversation, "you *must* watch what you say in public. This baroness may be new, but as the sovereign's personal advisor, she is technically your superior."

"What?" Drusee-la shrieked as her hand lanced out, locking her razor-sharp claws on his unprotected neck. "How dare you speak to me in such a manner. This is all obviously a ploy of Overlord Adalric's to keep him in power longer, while I waste away out here. The turning point is back at Nyx, and I *have* to stay with the fleet?"

The captain barely managed to nod as he desperately scratched at her iron grip. Despite her modest five-foot frame, and her apparently feminine softness, her raw feline strength dwarfed his as she firmly held onto him.

"How *dare* she undermine all I've worked for," the Perusian continued as the crew suddenly became meticulously obsessed with their duties. "All the *years* of planning, the scratching and clawing to make it to the top in an organization that subjugates non-humans. All the time I've wasted out here trying to gain favor with the sovereign, so I'd be named overlord after Adalric's demise. Countless weeks of being imprisoned in this ship while I waste away in empty space." She paused to readjust her grip, allowing him a much-needed breath. "Now this *human garbage* comes along and undoes what I accomplished over the last half decade? *Personal Advisor to the Dire Queen?* She's probably with the Dire Queen right now, licking up to her and trying to gain favor…it is *I* who should be there, not her! Now this *advisor* is the one in the Imperial spotlight, gaining the power to move up…and with Adalric still alive, who knows how more damage she can do." She paused from her rantings and looked up at her captain, whose eyes had begun to water with fear. "I thought I could trust your men, Captain. What happened?"

He tried to gulp again but found it nearly impossible with her grip still constricting his windpipe. "They…erred…in…their…judgment," he barely managed to get out, his vision beginning to blur.

"Erred?" she said, her eyes aflame with anger. "You have utterly failed me, Captain."

With no further words, her other hand dug into his groin, claws extended as she brought him up over her head. He felt nausea mixed with dizziness as the pain from his genitals compounded with the tingling asphyxiation. Then, taking a deep breath, Drusee-la heaved his flailing form over the bridge's center rail, leaving the bridge in deadened silence. Down he plummeted, three stories, to the base floor below. The metal shook as he hit with a thud and a crunch.

"Baroness Drusee-la," came from the *Wraith's* first officer, who had stood ready, waiting for his moment.

He knew serving under this Perusian was difficult and deadly, as opposed to serving the overlord, who, at least, seemed to kill out of necessity alone.

She spun from the rail in a fluid wave and centered her eyes on the new fool who dared to speak. "What do you want, *human*?"

"The battle is ready to commence."

"*So?*" her voice flashed its simple warning.

"So, we mustn't allow this moment to pass," he insisted. "We must act now."

A snarl came to her lips as she sank further into the oblivion of her dark fury. "Are you giving *me* an order?" she asked, her voice laced with poison.

Without warning, her claws lashed out, returning with warm crimson fluid dripping from them.

~ * ~

Lieutenant Sandra Pierce watched the white Perusian noble with a quiet air of detached fear and admiration. It was obvious the appearance of this new baroness destroyed Baroness Drusee-la's immediate plans, and her fury over this setback was intense, almost too intense, as it had cost the lives of more than one officer. However, she was smart enough not to judge the actions of an Imperial noble. With an indifferent gesture, she ordered the cleaning crew to the bridge to remove the carnage that covered its floors, both on the main and sub decks of the command center.

Drusee-la stalked back and forth, her thoughts wrapped around her like a thundercloud, ready to burst again. As quickly as it started though, it vanished with a flash. Her cool feline nerves tensed up again, and she scanned the command central with a quick glance, as she realized what turmoil her outburst had caused. "Who's in charge of this drifting monstrosity now?" she asked quietly, her voice barely over a low growl. "Who's left?"

One young, dark brunette officer with deep brown skin stepped forward, coming to attention. "My Lady," she reported, "I'm Lieutenant Sandra Pierce, fourth officer."

The Perusian baroness gazed at the human, her ice-cold eyes harshly calculating the young woman's worth. "Very well, Captain Pierce, prepare for ground assault on the Alliance target." Sandra nodded nervously as she turned to issue the appropriate orders.

Drusee-la watched Captain Pierce set up for the attack, then turned to leave the bridge, anxious for a chance to wash the blood off her hands, and the anger from her mind.

How unwise of my bridge officers to defy me, she restlessly thought as she glided down the sterile Imperial corridors which led to her personal chambers. *They deserved to die, the fools…is there anyone fit to serve me?*

As if sensing her mute question, her Narman personal guard moved closer to her, reminding her of his presence. She allowed a smile to come to her face as she entered her private rooms. Of course, she always had him. Once safely inside, she turned and stretched her arms upward, issuing the implied request.

With a smooth virile stride, he closed the distance between them and gazed down at her intently. He then carefully pulled down the silver zipper which ran along the front of her furtight, blue bodysuit, and peeled the thin garment off. With one massive arm, he gently lifted her, while slipping her long boots off with the other and laid her down on her bed. Last came her tight, fingerless gloves, leaving her in the nude…a snowflake amidst the deep violet decor. She gazed up at him, her eyes issuing all the commands that needed to be said, as a soft sensual purr rumbled throughout the chamber. As her body became lost to physical pleasures, her mind cleared for deeper, more personal thoughts.

So, she realized, *I now have a rival for the position of overlord. Alright…I like a challenge. It's about time there was a noble that was worthy of my level of powers. Perhaps she will be more fun than the last one who confronted my rising position. Koroqo isn't the only one who can make people "disappear". I shall enjoy disposing of this human bitch in my own, special ways.*

Satisfied that the contest was merely beginning, instead of ending as she had feared, she allowed her thoughts to rejoin her body. Enjoying a much-needed departure from the rigid protocol of life on the front lines.

Chapter Twenty-two
'Till Death Do Us Part

Another dawn streamed its narrow rays of light across the training grounds as Blaze exited her personal shuttle. Although Overlord Adalric was nowhere in sight, it hardly bothered her, as he was rarely there to greet her formally. She was sure he had a greeting of *some* sort prepared for her, of that there could be no doubt.

Her thoughts turned sour, as she closed the shuttle doors behind her and started across the lush green field toward the ruins. *So,* she silently mused as the cool morning breeze lazily blew through her long black hair, *what fun does he have in store for me today? Monsters? More desperate prisoners? Deadly flying debris? Whatever it will be, this can't go on forever…it's going to eventually end in my death…or his.* Blaze shook her head in dismay. She had no desire to be responsible for the overlord's death, and she certainly didn't want her own existence to end either, but every time she thought through these scenarios, those were the only two end results that seemed possible.

She hoped that the brief conversation they had last night had accomplished something, yet she strongly doubted it. The only thing it accomplished was to prove to herself that she could no longer ignore her feelings for him, which made his anger toward her all the worse.

As she reached the edges of the burnt-out town, a place which was becoming all too familiar lately, she reluctantly considered that perhaps he never intended to train her fully. Regine's warning sounded in her mind. *Though we could both be wrong,* she realized as her fingers tightened on the hilt of her electrosword, *maybe today will be the first day of my more serious training.*

Or perhaps not, she thought as danger alerts went off in her mind, causing her to turn scarcely in time to draw and ignite *Vindicator,* to barely deflect a sharp rock which had been on a collision course with her head.

"Better," came the hauntingly familiar voice from above, "but you still have much to learn."

Blaze glared up with flaring eyes, searching for the overlord and finding him standing on a slanted roof, on top of the building across the street from her. The burning red giant of Tartarus outlined his crimson form with scarlet flames, making him seem like a fiery angel of death. She grimaced as she let the anger build in her again, for she needed that fury if she expected to survive the day. Despite how easy she made these sessions sound to her queen, the reality always struck when the next day's session would begin. Yet something seemed different, that rock had come at her with a deadly speed which she had never before seen or expected. "I thought we decided I was to proceed on to the next phase of my training," she said, yelling up at the iridescent image above.

Tanus Adalric gazed down at his student, small and fragile within his great shadow, and his lips tightened, part of him feeling a moment of remorse. His stomach churned with anxiety and tension. He knew today he would end this, but he still could not help but admire her. For an instant, Koroqo's words haunted him, but he shut them harshly out of his thoughts.

"So, you want your training to be more intense?" his voice sizzled with malicious venom. "You want to learn more? Then learn you shall…learn how to *face death,* Blaze."

The young woman quickly raised *Vindicator* as she prepared for the worst. He sounded mad in the past, but today his voice rang with determination, a determination to end her life.

Blaze quickly bolted, and ran down the street, leaving the overlord behind. She knew the one chance she had was to keep moving, giving herself time and distance to prepare for all he could throw at her. However, despite the danger at hand, her confidence spiraled upward. She would see her way through it, as she had many times over the last few weeks.

"Run, Blaze," Adalric whispered quietly, his thoughts a countering black shadow to the brilliant sun overhead, "run all you want…my fury can find you anywhere." Slowly he let his anger take over, as his precisely controlled psionics searched for the proper weaponry to use for their onslaught.

Blaze ran down the first side street she came to and descended into the wreckage of one of the decimated buildings. This was a tactic she had not tried before, for she always tried to stay out in the open, where she could see his attacks coming a long distance away. However, this time the level of danger seemed much higher and that triggered old instincts. *Perhaps he won't find me here, or at least he might have to come in himself to get me.* This thought lent her some comfort, as she doubted he could telekinetically hurl deadly objects at her when he couldn't see her. Her eyes moved quickly around the disheveled room she suddenly found herself in and tried to take it all in. *It must have been a basement at one time,* she decided as she viewed the collection of junk which was cluttered under the thick layers of dust and cobwebs. Her thoughts soared with unwanted memories which called her back to Tenebrous, a place she survived by hiding in places like this.

"No, Blaze," Adalric's voice came from behind her, "there is nowhere you can hide from me."

The young woman spun about, bringing her sword up in an electrical arc that showered an array of sparks as it collided with Adalric's weapon, intersecting its direct path for her neck. Before taking another breath, she did a backflip, attempting to put some space between herself and the overlord who appeared out of nowhere. But this was a defensive tactic Adalric had grown accustomed to her using, and waiting for her landing was a group of disembodied weapons of sorts — iron bars and broken glass, which silently sliced down upon the young student.

Blaze felt the first shard strike her upper arm and was once again grateful for the armor her long gloves, like the rest of her tight-fitting body suit, afforded her. The razor-sharp piece of glass deflected harmlessly off, but the iron pan behind it did not, as it came crashing down on her right wrist, shattering the bone beneath it with a grisly crunch, and sending her weapon sliding across the floor just as something struck her left ankle.

She felt a wave of confused fear wash away her confidence, as she cradled her broken wrist in her left arm, and shifted her weight to her right leg. Adalric hurt her before, but never this viciously. She had no time to linger, that much she could read clearly in his short even breaths. This was no longer a game.

Dodging under the next piece of glass which swung in and curved behind her, she rolled across the floor and came up on one knee, reaching out with her mind to pull her weapon back to her grasp. *Control*, she silently screamed at herself, using Adalric's words to save her own life, *you must maintain control.* Focusing sharply, her thoughts coaxed the power of the Cosmic Aura to fold around the sword, lifting it into the air and returning it swiftly to her good hand. The weapon settled as Adalric caused a solid wooden beam above her to break and come crashing down. With wild desperation, she swung the sword over her head as she dove forward, feeling the splintered wood and metal grind beneath her bright-red body suit.

She suddenly felt like a caged animal, and realized it had been foolish to have confined herself in this small room. Ignoring the pain in her ankle, she leapt straight up through a new hole in the quickly crumbling ceiling, landing safely on the ground level. Intent on leaving the overlord behind, she darted out of the now collapsing house, diving to safety back onto the dirt covered street.

For a moment she lay there in the dust, letting her lungs fill with sweet air, reaffirming the fact she was still alive. It was the sound of the building collapsing that got her to roll over and quickly scooch back from the debris. As she watched the building fold in on itself, she briefly wondered if he had gotten out like she did. Had he even realized the beam he tried to kill her with was a crucial load-bearing support to the dilapidated house? She sat slumped over, worriedly scanning the rubble. Blaze stiffly rose and limped over to the hole of destruction which had recently been their battle ground, and searched for some sign of her trainer. She felt a tightness constricting her chest as she realized there was no movement within, and quickly decided she *had* to find him. Taking another step forward, a short cry escaped her lips as she felt the sharp pain in her ankle which she had tried to ignore. Looking down over her dirty clothes, she was once again reminded that her armor wasn't perfect. A dozen or so small cuts were evident in her tattered bodysuit, and blood flowed freely from half a dozen wounds. The worst of which was the five-inch-long shard of shimmering glass which was still embedded in her left ankle. Wincing from the pain, she knelt and tried to grip the glass with both hands, quickly reminding herself of the pain in her broken right wrist.

"Damn," she cursed as she settled for putting down her weapon and pulling out the glass with her left hand alone. Then she quickly gathered up a filthy rag she spotted on the street nearby and used it for a bandage, to soak up the gush of blood which quickly poured from the now open wound. While slowly standing again, she began to worry. Minutes passed with no movement from the rubble. She had to look for him. *What if he's hurt and unable to call for help?* Not that she could imagine him doing so, no matter how hurt he was.

~ * ~

Tanus Adalric cursed his own foolishness as he pulled himself up onto the rooftop which overlooked the rubble, where he had narrowly escaped his own trap. He had been lucky to get out in time, and he knew that. Once settled in his new vantage point, his eyes targeted the young woman who was sifting through the debris below. *What's she doing? Probably looking for evidence of my demise. Well,* he silently resolved, *she will soon be quite disappointed.* He raised his hand to start the onslaught again, but hesitated as he watched the scarlet rays of the sun reflect in her dark hair. Despite his earlier convictions to the contrary, he somehow knew she was worried for him, and was hoping he was still alive. *How lovely she manages to remain,* his thoughts strayed, *despite the wounds, the dirt, her blood.* He shook his head, driving out the weakness which threatened to overcome him again. *Her sympathy is her frailty, not mine,* he quickly decided as he forced the darkness to fill his mind one last time. *This time, it will cost her everything.*

~ * ~

Blaze froze as she spotted something in the rubble — a piece of the overlord's cloak. She quickly leaned down and picked up the tattered black and crimson cloth. For an instant she clutched it with steadfast strength, then began digging frantically in the spot where she found the remnant of her teacher.

Out of Blaze's vision, a piece of broken wood slowly floated up into the air an inch or so, then swung out, striking her in the left ankle, doubling the pain of the previous laceration.

With a muffled cry of agony, Blaze fell to the ground and clutched her wound, wrapping her fingers around the blood-soaked cloth. She realized through the tears of pain, that she had no time to waste, as she floundered for her sword. Her anguish almost overcame her control when she discovered it far out of her reach, now lying across the street, even though she left it by her side an instant before. Struggling to get back up to her feet, she tried to limp over to her weapon, leaving bloody footprints in the dirt behind.

However, Adalric was far from finished with his lessons for the day. His granite stance never flinched as object after object of debris began to hurl themselves at her with tremendous force. The first was a rock the size of a grenade, which struck her square in the small of the back, forcing her down to her knees in the middle of the street.

Blaze's eyes lit with flames of anger as instinct overwhelmed her to use the last of her strength to form a flaming heat shield around her crippled body. She knew her long unused natural gift would quickly drain her, but now she saw no choice. She had to protect herself long enough to regain her weapon. She tried to call the weapon to her, but it didn't move, as if anchored where it lay. Slowly she crawled across the street, leaving a scarlet trail in her wake, as she desperately concentrated on keeping her heat shield up against the continuing volley of debris. Beads of sweat on her body mingled with the blood of her cuts and abrasions. Even as she managed to finally regain *Vindicator*, she knew she was finished…exhausted, a raging inferno reduced to a smoldering cinder. A raw and primitive grief overwhelmed her at the realization, as the flames protecting her died out. With what strength she could muster, she slowly stood and raised her trembling sword one last time, determined to die as she had lived, facing her fears.

~ * ~

Adalric watched her struggle with each movement, feeling her pain and agony as she forced herself to hold on to life. "Not this time," he whispered, pushing out the remorse which threatened to destroy his resolve. He watched her stand and ready her weapon, but her heat shield finally collapsed under the constant barrage of whirling debris. For a moment he held back his onslaught, as he observed her strength give out. She sank back to one knee, her electrosword dangling limply in her left hand. A smile crept to his lips as he savored this long-awaited moment. *At last,* he thought with sudden satisfaction, *this is it. No more games, no more waiting, and no more weakness.* Yet after all the anticipation, he realized his victory did not taste as good as he had hoped it would. It should have at least outweighed the memory of his defeat during their first confrontation. Instead, it paled by comparison…or was it that what he had faced before was not truly a defeat, but something else.

Clearing his mind, he issued the mental command which would end her weakened life.

From behind Blaze, a long iron rod with a jagged spear point lanced out on its death course, targeted at the base of her neck. With grace and ease it silently sliced through the air, coming in to finish what was left of her. Suddenly, the shaft halted, mere inches from her supple skin, frozen in a mocking poise of death by the steel thoughts of the same man who issued its fierce orders.

Adalric's jaw tightened, and his muscles strained as he struggled to release his hold on the spear, to let it complete its path of destruction. He tried to close his eyes, to concentrate, to regain control. All he could do instead was gaze down on her weary form, let his eyes slowly savor her every inch, contemplate the emptiness he would soon face when she was gone. Seconds seemed like an eternity as he felt an ache grow inside his heart, a pain he never before felt…*or is this her pain? The link?* His emptiness and her anguish, his longing and her exhaustion. It was all there. He didn't want to lose this, lose her, and he felt her thoughts echoing his own. The link between them *was* still there…weak, but there. He felt frozen in a limbo where all thoughts and actions seemed impossible. Finally, his eyes shut, and he bowed his head in concession — as the jagged shaft fell silently to the dirt, its quarry unscathed.

~ * ~

Blaze felt the spear hit the ground behind her and wearily turned around, letting her eyes fall on the object which could have easily ended her life. She looked up again, suddenly feeling the torment above her, as she watched the overlord slowly turn away, and disappear into the glow of the still rising sun. Finally, she felt the last of her resolve give way to exhaustion, as she collapsed on the street. Her mind drifted into comfortable darkness, but one thought refused to easily die. *It's over,* she realized as all faded around her, *it's finally over.*

~ * ~

Hours later, Overlord Adalric sat in front of his elaborate chess set, eyeing the white queen intently, his thoughts drifting aimlessly in the wake of the emotional hurricane he barely survived.

"How could I have allowed this to happen?" he quietly demanded of himself.

Slowly he reached forward and grasped the ivory toned chess piece in the form of Hera, Queen of the gods, and resigned himself to a fate which he no longer felt the will to resist, to a downfall he had allowed himself to augment. "No," he said, his voice regaining some strength, "I *must* maintain control."

Without knowing, his powerful hand tightened on the marble chess piece as he fought his inner turmoil. He didn't even notice when he snapped the queen's head off with a sharp crack, just as he didn't hear the main door to his chambers open silently as the lithe figure slipped in.

Blaze hesitated in the main foyer of Adalric's chambers, a similar conflict raging in her mind. How she ended up here, of all places, she could barely recall. But then again, where else could she possibly have gone? Hunter and hunted, they were one and the same.

She knew she returned to consciousness in the medical wing of the *Sentinel*, but not even the doctors or staff could tell her how she arrived there. After some quick laser surgery on her shattered wrist, and a swift graft on her ankle and other lacerations, she had felt as good as new. Except for the simple fact that her universe now seemed turned around. All she could realize was he could have killed her in her moment of weakness, easily, yet he hadn't.

Taking a deep breath, she affirmed the real reason she came to the *Demoness*, the reason she could no longer deny. She had to know the truth. It was now or never. Slowly she walked down the short hallway, knowing instantly where he was, feeling his reflections of her own emotions. Passing a mirrored wall, she caught a glimpse of herself. Despite her healing, she was a mess. She was still in her tattered bodysuit, stained with her blood, and still slightly favored her good leg with a limp. She was also without her long cloak which she loved to wear publicly, something she had not done since her coronation. Blaze vaguely felt Travis' confused stares back in the medical section where she left him, and now understood why he looked at her in that way. She ignored her reflection, more concerned about what she would say when she faced her mentor again. With a sudden sickening feeling of panic, she realized she *didn't* know what she would say to him. For an instant she considered turning back, but no, she had to go on. Prophecy or no, *she* was the one in control of her life, not fate. She was tired of being manipulated to other people's ends. It was time to take charge of her destiny, for better or worse. She cast her doubts aside, knowing that what to say would come to her when she needed it, she had to believe that. Summoning more courage than she ever realized she had, she forced herself to enter his bedroom, her eyes falling on his stern visage.

Adalric heavily turned his head up toward Blaze, his long gaze penetrating through his half mask and drilling into her soul, but this time she felt no fear, and he knew it. As angry as he was at being disturbed, a great relief spread through him to see her up and walking, healthy again, at least mostly. Attempting to regain some of his earlier animosity toward her, he finally spoke, his deep voice haltingly issuing his quiet words. "What do you want?"

This was the moment, Blaze thought desperately, *this is when those words were supposed to come, when it was supposed to get easy.* A thousand different questions came and left her mind, leaving but one. "Why?" she asked softly, her stiff voice barely more than a hoarse whisper.

A muscle jumped in the overlord's cheek, as he could not find a simple answer to that question. Instead, he chose to look down at his hand, suddenly realizing he had broken his white queen. "My queen," he said absently, disturbed that he could have done this to his favorite possession.

"What?" Blaze asked, unsure of whether he was addressing her or not.

Adalric's sole answer was a shake of his head, as he knelt over to retrieve the miniature marble head.

"I woke up in the *Sentinel's* medical bay," Blaze tried again, desperate to establish some form of communication between them. There were things that had to be said, somehow. "Did you bring me there?"

Adalric continued to stare down at his ungloved hand that cradled the broken piece almost lovingly, then nodded. "You were wounded."

Blaze shrank internally as she still tried to make some sense out of all of this. *He finally had me where he wanted. I was as good as dead. Instead, he spared me and brought me back to safety…across that long field.* "Did you use the Cosmic Rift transportation devices?"

"Of course not," Adalric replied, his deep voice remaining quiet, unemotional.

"It was over a half mile back to the shuttle," she whispered, a warm chill shivering up her body.

Adalric nodded silently then a thin smile came to his firm lips. "You're not heavy."

For a long moment neither of them spoke, each mute with their own thoughts, their own battles, and their own conclusions. Sadly, realizing the conversation had reached an end, Blaze faced the harshness of the reality that she would not know the truth, if there was some truth to discover. Slowly she turned away and headed out of the bedroom, her spirits lower than when she faced her last moments on Nyx.

Then she stopped. She would not give up so easily, not when they came this far.

"Why didn't you kill me?" she finally asked, her back to him, her thin voice barely audible above the room's recirculators.

However, Adalric heard her perfectly, and knew he couldn't pretend otherwise, not this time. "I don't know," he finally managed, facing the terrible truth of his own words.

Blaze nodded, suddenly looking past his words, tasting the emotions which lurked behind, trapped behind their own armored mask. It was then the smoldering fires in her eyes subsided, and she understood. Slowly, but with determination, she turned to face him, her subtle movements finally drawing up his gaze to meet with hers. Clearing the distance between them with a few strides, she knelt next to where he was seated, bringing her eyes level to his.

"Perhaps," she answered for him, an ever-so-slight quiver in her voice, "…it is because of this." Then she leaned over, and with a passion which demanded to be released, tenderly placed her lips against his.

For a long moment, they remained like that, neither one wishing to break the connection. He carefully raised his mouth from hers and gazed into her eyes, no longer wishing to deny his feelings. Letting the broken figurine fall from his hand, he reached around her small waist and pulled her to him, ardently kissing her.

The taste of his lips warmed Blaze and made her hungry for more. A new fire grew between them, but one thing still remained. With slow sensuality, she pulled off her long gloves and let them fall to the ebony carpet. Then she tenderly touched her hands to his cheeks and meticulously outlined the edge of his mask.

Suddenly, understanding her intent, he grabbed her wrists and firmly, yet gently pushed her away. "No," he pleaded, his deep voice trembling, "you mustn't."

"Why?" Blaze whispered, gazing up into his darkened eyepieces, feeling his hurt, his dilemma, "what is it you are afraid of?"

Adalric wanted to resort to his usual stance, that he feared nothing, but it wouldn't come out this time, allowing nothing more than the bitter truth. "That you will turn away from me."

Blaze's eyes misted as a smile came to her lips, then she gently pulled out of his grip, her hands returning to his armored mask. Without waiting for uncertainty to set in, she lifted it off his face, as he allowed her eyes to fall on his visage for the first time. A single tear tenderly caressed her cheek as she looked at him, *truly* looking for the first time. Deep scars covered his face like some exotic alien roadway, each line telling the story of his bitter past. All she could see was the proud man beneath it all, the handsome man he had once been, and still was in her eyes.

Adalric felt her tears touch his hand and mentally cried out. His eyes clenched closed as if trying to wipe away the moment, as his soul prepared for the revulsion he was sure would come from her, but then realized he wasn't feeling that at all.

Blaze placed her hand firmly against his scarred cheek, allowing herself to touch him, then she leaned forward and brushed her lips against his, permitting his presence to engulf her. Again, she tasted the strength of his kiss. *Never again,* she silently vowed, *would she allow him to hide behind his mask when they were alone together.* Suddenly she smiled, then laughed, quietly, happily, as she gazed into his deep grey eyes, the color of a stormy sky.

"Why do you laugh?" he asked, suddenly unsure if he was reading her correctly.

"I never imagined you were blonde," she said with a smile, as she traced her fingers through his dark golden hair.

Her laugh infected him as a weight was lifted from his heart. No, he was not reading her incorrectly at all. Suddenly he felt surer of his own convictions than he had in a long time. Slowly he raised her chin to bring her to him again, and smiled at what he finally allowed himself to truly understand. "I've fallen in love with you, Blaze," he confessed with a tender murmur.

Enveloped by his strong arms, she buried herself in the muscles of his chest, feeling his immense power wash over her like the calm after a storm. This was right, she could feel it in every vein which ran through her hot body…finally, it was right. "I've fallen in love with you too, Tanus."

No further words were spoken as he lifted her up and carried her to his bed, then came down beside her. This time there was no struggle, no duel to be won as they joined, body and mind.

Chapter Twenty-three
Burning at both ends

Overlord Tanus Adalric lay quietly, gently entwined in his black velvet sheets. Somewhere within the deeper recesses of his mind, he felt he should have been angry, as if a valiant battle had been fought, and lost. However, there was no anger marring his stormy soul, merely contentment which he thought was never possible. He moved his left hand slightly, once more feeling Blaze's luxuriant warmth against his skin. He inhaled the gentle fragrance of her dark hair as she rested her head against his chest, fast asleep. *How like the last time,* he thought with a smile, while aimlessly tracing a finger down along the hollow of her back, no longer afraid of touching her. He tried to turn his thoughts to plans for the future — conquest, subterfuge, political coups. In the end, he closed his eyes, pulled her in closer with his strong arms, and fell asleep.

~ * ~

Blaze slept soundly, without harsh dreams, for what seemed like an eternity to her. Then a worm entered her soul, twisted and crawled under her skin, bringing her awake with a start. Her eyes sought out Adalric, and a smile danced across her lips as she saw him sleeping peacefully. She felt it again, a sharp foul sensation which brought bile to her lips. With a start she sat up and realized her mistress was calling for her...but there was a difference. Anger harshly laced the usual subliminal summons. Blaze stood up quickly, her face blanching with a harsh realization. Last night, as she and Adalric mentally and physically joined, it was the first time she allowed her psi-shields to be fully lowered...*the Dire Queen knew.*

~ * ~

The sovereign stood before her treasured crimson sphere, gently cradling its inner fires. *How could I not have seen this happening?* she beseeched herself, her thoughts searing across the darkened hollows of her mind. *Now, if I don't act fast, I will lose her to him.*

The Dire Queen reached out an obsidian hand and lightly touched the glowing sphere, drawing strength from its great power. She let out a low hiss, as her crimson eyes flared a brighter hue. *I must first find out what truly occurred,* she silently decided, *I cannot trust raw feelings alone in this matter.*

Her thoughts were interrupted as she sensed the grand doors behind her open, as her young servant entered. The sovereign breathed in the tingling emotions she felt behind her, the stark open feminism which emanated from the baroness, who even now was kneeling at the foot of the throne. *Total submission?* the Dire Queen wondered, *or is it total deception? Could it be this young woman, whom I have trusted with my future, is playing this Imperial power struggle even better than Adalric?*

Slowly the queen turned to face Blaze, then the black figure sat back onto her throne and gestured toward her servant. "Rise, Blaze, and talk with me for a while." She watched her servant stand slowly and suddenly realized her clothes were torn and cauterized, with patches of dried blood on them. She sensed Blaze struggling to hold up her mental psi-shields stronger than she ever had before, and felt a quiver flush through her darkened form. "What has happened between you and Adalric?" she asked, allowing her tone to soften somewhat. "I heard you were in the medical section, badly hurt."

Blaze was silent for a moment as she gazed straight into the queen's luminous eyes. "Overlord Adalric almost killed me during training this morning," she reported flatly, with no trace of emotion on her slightly cut and bruised face. Their eyes continued to search each other's, as each tried to guess at the other's thoughts.

"I see," the Dire Queen said. "Perhaps the time of Adalric's instability has arrived…the time I warned that you had to be prepared for."

Blaze's lips parted slightly, the one outward trace of the surprise which hit her like a hammer as she tried to gauge what the sovereign did, or didn't, know.

"Regine," she finally said, "Overlord Adalric is a proud and honorable man. His intense training with me is so I can serve you better." She swallowed a deep breath and let it out slowly. "Do not think badly of him for that. He is the right hand which keeps this great Imperium strong."

The Dire Queen's hand curled into a clawed fist, as her mind shrank back deeper into the fiery pit which gave it birth. *She is defending him!* she silently screeched, as a new feeling grew and festered inside of her mind, one she dared not allow.

Blaze flinched, as if hit, her eyes widening at the feelings she suddenly sensed within her mistress. Then she reached out a hand to the Dire Queen. "Regine, are you all right?"

The Dire Queen broke herself out of her mental crypt and stared at the hand offered to her in pity. "I *saved* your life so you could protect me from Adalric when the time came…and now you strive to protect *him*?"

"I am loyal to you," Blaze assured her mistress. "I owe everything I am to you."

"So, we shall see," the Dire Queen said, her voice lowering to a grating hiss, as she realized the course of action which was needed. To save her young servant from the twisted control of her overlord, she must separate them. "I am sending you away, Blaze, to spend some time at the front."

"Away?" the young woman asked, confusion lacing her suddenly soft tone. "I still have yet to become a TelSor. How can I be your advisor if I am at the front?"

"You will better advise me after you have learned, first-hand, what is going on at the United Star Alliance borders." The Dire Queen stood up and retreated to her crimson sphere again, relaxing as she caressed its radiant curves. "After you have gained the knowledge I seek, and some practical military experience, then you can return here, to fulfill your obligations to me." The Dire Queen turned her back on her servant, gazing deeply into her luminous orb. "In one hour, you will take command of the *Demoness* from Overlord Adalric and go to the front lines. There you will relieve Baroness Drusee-la and allow the *Wraith* to return here."

Blaze stared at the sovereign's back, a numb feeling washing over her. "How long will I have to stay there?"

"Until I tell you to return," the Dire Queen replied, her voice scratching like claws against a slate. "Now go."

Blaze stepped closer. "Regine…" But there was no answer, and the Dire Queen continued to hold her sphere, her back to the young baroness. Slowly Blaze turned away and left the sovereign alone in the flickering darkness.

~ * ~

Adalric listened carefully as Blaze explained what had happened between her and the Dire Queen, confessing for the first time the real reasons the sovereign saved her life that day. As he sat there, he realized how much Blaze was like him. Their shared love for the Imperium, their confusion over the actions of the Dire Queen, their strong ambitions, their feelings for each other. He did not relish the idea of turning over command of the *Demoness*, his prize ship. Though he suddenly realized there was no other person he trusted more to take his ship, and reveled in the fact he finally *could* trust someone.

"You must do as the sovereign commands, Blaze," he explained. "Neither of us is ready to defy her yet."

"I don't want to defy her," Blaze replied, placing her hands on his broad shoulders. "I don't want to leave here now either…not after what has happened between us."

"Perhaps that *is* the best reason for you to leave now," Adalric said, voicing a deep concern. "A lot *has* transpired between us, and it could hurt our position if the wrong people found out and exploited that information."

Blaze nodded, realizing the truth in his words, and hating it at the same time. For all her life she had fought and struggled in one long battle to survive; a battle which she had always fought alone. The one other man that she had ever given a damn about lay cold, under the red sands of the Perusian desert. Now that she finally allowed herself to love, she had to leave that man also.

"What about my training? I can't abandon it now."

She watched Adalric study her, grateful he still had his mask off. She could read the intense feelings in his eyes and realized he was gauging her abilities.

"There comes a time," he finally said, "in every young TelSor's training when he or she outgrows the trainer. Like a bird learning to fly, she must be pushed out of the nest…to either fly, or fall."

"A bird?" she asked with an amused smile, seeing a different side of Adalric emerging.

"There are similarities," he continued, returning her smile. "You cannot stay under my protection forever. The final test of a TelSor lies within yourself, and nothing that I can teach you will make you take that last final step."

She glanced over her torn uniform and laughed. "You have a strange definition of 'protection', Tanus, but I guess you're right. I need to find out what I have learned, and see if I can put it to use. Watch out, you may find that when this bird starts flying you have a fiery phoenix on your hands."

Adalric placed her soft hands in his, his smile slowly fading away. "Be careful out there," he warned, his tone full of tender concern, "the Dire Queen does nothing lightly. She has her reasons for sending you to the front."

Blaze recalled the sovereign's cold projections and shivered inside. "I think she's afraid of me," the young woman whispered, giving Adalric's hand a light squeeze. "I felt her fear when she confronted me."

"You *sensed* this in the Dire Queen?" Adalric's lips tightened. "That's amazing." For a moment his thoughts darkened, as he viewed her rising powers in comparison to his…for even *he* could not sense what the sovereign was thinking or feeling. Then he smiled again as he drifted back to the events of the evening. There was no competition here any longer, no malice, only love. He pulled her in closely and held her against his chest, never wanting to let her go. "Blaze, perhaps we should join together."

"What do you mean?" she asked, confused by the conflicting emotions she sensed within him. "I thought we kind of already did that."

"We have an accidental psychic bond which formed during our…confrontation. TelSors can form a deeper psionic bond, you felt it a bit as we joined earlier tonight, but it can be so much more. It can form a connection between us through the Cosmic Aura, joining us together in a way stronger than is physically possible."

"No," Blaze blurted, as her eyes narrowed, and she stepped back. She suddenly felt inexplicably scared of losing the one thing that kept her strong, her individuality, even if it was for a man she loved.

Adalric's jaw clenched, unused to the blatant defiance in her voice. But his need was great…*their* need was great…so he pushed on. "Listen to me, Blaze," he continued as he recaptured their embrace, "this is a delicate time."

"For whom?"

"For all of us — you, me, the sovereign, the Imperium itself. A wrong move by any of us could spell disaster. This is a power play, a war that only a few can survive…and I want *us* to survive. I can't help you if I don't know when you're in danger. The link we have now is not strong enough to span distances, a TelSor bond links us though the Cosmic Aura." His grip on her loosened as he reached out and gently lifted her chin, so her eyes faced his. "I don't want to lose what has taken me so very long to find."

Blaze softly pulled in her bottom lip, moistening its dryness with her tongue. For a moment she feared she was, once again, merely a pawn in the struggle between Adalric and the Dire Queen. However, that would have to make Adalric's love false, and every essence of her mind told her that wasn't true. Then her heart warmed as she recalled the close feeling which they shared, the gentle probes of his mind as he explored hers. Suddenly the idea of spending the next few months without that feeling seemed detestable. He had always been there, first in combat, then in love, or were they both one and the same? She placed her hands around his neck, the delicate line of her chin arching as she gazed into his eyes. Then a smile crested her glistening lips. "I do love you," she said, her voice full of the passion she felt. She wanted to ask how this bonding was done, but then realized she already knew, as she placed her moistened palms on his golden temples and lowered her mental psi-shields once again.

Instantly she felt her thoughts reverberate against his psi-shields, as his eyes widened in surprise, then he let her through. She was inside of him, searching through the inner recesses of his soul which whirled like a tempest. Like a kitten she danced about in his mind, jubilant in the warm embrace which gripped her essence, as the first tendrils of his own essence entered her mind. She was completely open to him, allowing him to feel her, from her anguished youth on Tenebrous, to the torturous birth of her flames and her elation at her escape from the rehabilitation colony. To the death of Sinclair, ending in the excitement of her first love…and this joining now.

She saw him, the young cadet at the United Star Alliance Naval Academy, highest in his class, to his first command of an Alliance battleship, from the great stellar battles he fought and won, to the death of his first officer — the first woman he ever loved — in the same battle which left him a scarred and broken man. The blackness of the Dire Queen, which easily filled that detested void in his life, who with domineering presence shaped and molded him into the greatest military leader the Imperium ever had. His numerous attempts at reconstructive surgery, that for some unknown reason defied success, until he had no choice but to hide his affliction. His devotion to an Imperium that gave him so much, when the Alliance had cost him so dearly. From the growing darkness in his soul as the threat of the prophecy seemed to come true, a prophecy which could undo all he fought for years to achieve. To his mixed desires to kill and cherish the one woman who meant anything to him, ending in his final admission of his burning love for her…and this joining now.

Together they explored each other, their life-forces merging and swirling about the other as the Cosmic Aura formed a mental cocoon around them, to finally separate back to the bodies from whence they came. But they had touched and had been one.

For a moment they stared at each other, neither daring to speak. He pulled her into his embrace once again, allowing her to mold to the warm contours of his body. Blaze wondered how she was ever going to remain loyal to both people, who were so integral to her life and were locked in a death struggle. She knew that Adalric could feel her inner turmoil, for their psi-shields would no longer protect them against each other. She let out a long breath, and embraced him tighter as she gazed out the window at the countless stars that witnessed the ending of their separate lives. His last thoughts danced in her mind.

You are your flames, Blaze…never deny them, for they are you.

Chapter Twenty-four
Personal Advisor to the Dire Queen

Blaze stared out the front window of the bridge of the *Demoness* as she absently chewed on her bottom lip. She always thought space travel was uninteresting while she was a Shadowguard, but the last three weeks had taught her that space travel as a baroness made the trip seem even duller. At least as a soldier she had her peers to talk to and eat meals with. As an elite member of the Imperial aristocracy, no one spoke with her except the ship's captain, and he did that only when he had to deliver a report. If it were not for the warmth she still felt within, emanating from Adalric, she knew the journey would have been miserable. Their bond served as a mental chain-link. So, despite the many light years between them, it held fast, always giving her the feeling he was near. She didn't know his thoughts, but could sense his stronger emotions, like his fear-laced anger when confronting the Dire Queen, and his comfort when sensing her presence within him.

She let out a smile as her thoughts drifted from him back to her duties at hand. Striding over to the captain's position, she stood patiently by his side for a moment, unnoticed, then cleared her throat. "Are we within visual communications of the *Wraith* yet?" she asked, never taking her eyes off the window.

"We're coming into that now, my Lady," Captain Harris informed her.

She was amazed at how easily she took to command. Even though the captain handled the technicalities, she was the representative of the sovereign. Ultimately, this ship and what happened to it was her responsibility alone. Although she missed Adalric fiercely, she reveled in her newfound position. When she first stepped back onto the bridge of the *Demoness*, three weeks ago, it almost felt as if she was a Shadowguard again. However, any trepidation she felt was instantly dispelled when Captain

Harris approached her with a courteous bow and welcomed her aboard the Dire Queen's flagship. Sometimes, it was hard to remember being a Legionnaire on this very ship, and almost impossible to remember before then.

"We are picking up a distress call from the *April* colony," the captain informed her, gently pulling her from her thoughts. "It seems they are having some trouble there."

"What kind of trouble?" the young baroness asked, her attention finally drawn to the tall commanding officer.

"They aren't specific," he answered with a shrug. "They heard an Imperial noble was passing through the system and requested you come down."

Blaze raised a curious eyebrow in hesitation, but was also anxious for any excuse to walk on solid ground again. She gazed intently at the captain for a moment, then turned her back on him and returned to where she had been standing, intent on conferring with the one person on this ship whose opinion she fully trusted. "What do you think?" she whispered.

"It seems like a good idea to check out the situation, my Lady," Travis responded in a quiet voice. "But I'd be careful. You have a lot of enemies now."

A slight widening of her eyes was all the evidence of Blaze's surprise, but then she reconsidered his words and knew them to be true. One did not gain power and status quickly without upsetting more than one person. For a brief instant she almost wished she was back on the *Silhouette*, arguing some insipid point with Sinclair, Sloan, and the rat. Then she straightened up and pivoted back towards the captain, causing her cloak to swirl around her supple form. "Captain," her strong voice commanded, "let's see what the problem is. Enter into orbit and prepare my personal shuttle for landing on the *April* colony." She glanced back at Travis and smiled, then let her stony visage return as she turned back to the *Demoness'* captain. "I also want a dozen fighters flying escort."

"As you command, my Lady," Captain Harris said, then began to issue the proper orders.

"Assemble my Shadowguards," she said to Travis as she strode past him, on the way out. "We have no idea what's going on down there."

~ * ~

An hour later found Blaze waving her hand in front of her face as the dust from the landing shuttle finally began to settle, giving the young woman her first view of the *April* colony.

The small colony developed quickly over the last few years, metamorphosing from a small military camp to a thriving metropolis. Its tall skyscrapers were already beginning to dominate the city commons, as markets and general stores gave way to malls and commerce centers. Blaze couldn't help but be impressed by what the Imperium accomplished in a few years. She suddenly found herself thinking of Tenebrous, a colony not unlike this one, except that one was under the protection of the United Star Alliance, and not the Red Star Imperium. She felt contempt for the Alliance rising in her throat as she proudly watched Travis and the other three Shadowguards form a protective circle around her. Blaze glanced up, as the dozen Imperial fighters raced overhead. The obsidian needle-sleek StarCraft flew in perfect formation, dazzling the spectators with their impressive barrel rolls and synchronized maneuvers. It was a demonstration she came up with, to let the colonists know the Imperium arrived, and their troubles were over...

The sudden explosion which decimated the six-story building, one block over, shocked them all.

"Where did that come from?" Travis asked in his raised voice, as he pulled Blaze behind him, to protect her from falling debris and dust clouds.

"Unknown, sir," one of the other Shadowguards reported as they all readied their weapons.

Blaze's eyes narrowed as she studied the suddenly silent city. The streets became instantly empty as people ran for cover in nearby buildings. Her thoughts swirled into turbulent blackness as she considered this wonderful colony, obviously under some inept governor's control. As the last of the burning wreckage fell to the ground, the baroness straightened up and started toward the capitol building, determined to find out whose skin was on the line for this apparent lack of proper military safety.

Travis ordered the other guards to form a tighter circle around Blaze, knowing that trying to tell her to take cover was useless. "Please be careful, my Lady," he warned while walking close by her side. "I'm sure that explosion was meant for you."

"Unlikely," Blaze replied absently while studying the wreckage all around them. "If I was truly the target, they could have gotten me while landing." She turned to her chief Shadowguard and shook her head as they walked on. "This was meant as a demonstration for me to see, Travis, and I want to know why."

The Imperial procession cleared the last of the rubble, to climb the sharp steps which lead to the capitol building. Once inside, Legionnaires gave way to the grey armored Shadowguards, and the Imperial noble they protected. The inside was barricaded, with overturned tables and reflective mats, as the colony's Imperial forces prepared to defend themselves.

"This is how it begins," Blaze commented with remorseful disgust, as she gazed around her. "With the last representatives of the government holed up in their buildings like cornered rats. Then comes the anarchy...the looting...the gang rule..." Her voice trailed off as her hands curled into tiny bright-red fists.

"Blaze?" Travis whispered questioningly by her side.

"No," she declared, her voice suddenly strong, "it won't happen here because this time *I* can make a difference." She glared at the huddled officers, who were beginning to realize who had come to visit. "Who is in charge here?"

"The governor," one of the sergeants spoke up. "The next office down the hall."

"This is the welcome that a member of the Imperial aristocracy receives in one of its colony's capitol buildings? Especially when you called for me?"

"He didn't think you'd come," the sergeant responded quickly, while trying to look humble.

"Then why ask?"

"He didn't know what else to do."

"Show me this man," Blaze demanded, her annoyance growing. "Show me this governor who has no faith in the queen's representative."

The sergeant quickly rose off the ground and approached the baroness. "Forgive him, my Lady," he said, "we have suffered many casualties here."

He led the Imperial Emissary down the hallway to the governor's office. He tried the door and found it locked, then knocked and received no answer. Glancing over at Blaze apologetically, he prepared to knock on the large steel doors again.

"Stand back," Blaze said, her annoyance finally giving way to anger. She raised her fist toward the door and summoned the powers which she felt emanating from Adalric so many times. Slowly the giant doors began to rattle, first gently then with a great fury, as her eyes became a crimson, fiery glow. Finally, the doors gave way with a crack of the triple-reinforced lock and swung back on their hinges.

At first Blaze thought the grand office was abandoned, then she spotted him behind the desk, his face in his hands. The tall windows which dominated the plush room were boarded up from within, and shattered glass sprinkled the grey carpet like diamonds on a jeweler's mat. For a moment she felt her anger soften to pity, but quickly remembered the explosion outside, and the fear of the soldiers in the foyer who lacked any leadership.

"Governor," she said, her voice steady but low, "I am Baroness Blaze, Personal Advisor to the Dire Queen. You requested my assistance?"

Slowly he looked up, gazing at her through bloodshot eyes which hadn't known the comfort of sleep in many days. He vigorously rubbed his stubble covered face a few times and sat up straight, finally absorbing the fact an Imperial noble came to visit him in his little corner of hell.

He cleared his throat three times, then stood up, the crack in his knees audible to all in the room. "My Lady," he began, his voice laden with the weight of command. "I'm so very pleased to have you here." He stumbled around the ancient mahogany desk and walked over to the party from the *Demoness*.

Blaze felt her spine stiffen up at his words, and her insides twisted painfully as he stood and approached her. For under that unshaven face, and beneath the worry lines which crisscrossed his brow, was the recruitment sergeant who had turned her down over ten months ago...after sexually harassing her. He had been gone when she had returned with Admiral Steward, and she hoped never to see that sergeant again. Now, here he was...military governor of the *April* colony. A sharp piercing in her hands broke the black cloud in her mind, as she realized she had dug her long nails into her palms.

"Governor…" she said slowly, trying to keep her voice calm.

"Mitchell," Travis whispered into her ear.

"Mitchell," Blaze finished, flashing a sidelong glance at her personal bodyguard. Suddenly her desire to rip out the governor's lungs faded, as the responsibility of her position sank home. Something was dreadfully wrong here, and she had to know what. "Could you please explain what is happening?"

Governor Mitchell stopped short of the young baroness and fell to his knees. He gazed up at her with fear clouded eyes which held no trace of recognition in them. "My Lady," he blurted out, "I don't know what to do here. The renegades grow stronger every day, killing my Legionnaires, destroying my supplies. I asked the sovereign for help, but she never responded." He rose up, and went back to his desk, stumbling twice along the way. "What's happened here is of no fault of mine," he said through his shaky voice. "I asked for troops which never came. I requested supplies which I still haven't seen. I begged for—"

"Enough," Blaze shouted, fed up with the governor's whining. She realized her anger for him had always been based on his overconfidence as a recruiter, as he sat in pious judgment of those who came before him, a god to choose people's destinies. However, this deity had fallen, faced with odds he had no control over. "You are a disgrace to the Imperium in which you serve," she reprimanded softly, allowing each word to burn fully in before firing the next. "Mitchell, you have lost control here, and your ineptitude is costing Legionnaires their lives…and the Imperium this colony."

Slowly her fury at him faded into pity, but not for him, for the countless thousands of people who relied, in vain, on him for protection and upholding of the Imperial laws. She found herself wondering if it could have been something simple like this that had destroyed her home world of Tenebrous. The incompetence of one instead of a nation. This time, though, she was here and could set things right…something the Alliance *never* did for her or the thousands who died on Tenebrous each year. Blaze let out a deep breath, finally grateful for the mercy killing which Adalric dealt to that sorry colony, back on that fateful day when she became a Shadowguard. Her gaze sourly fixed on the failed man who was the *April* colony governor, and burned in fiery disgust. "Assemble your troops, Governor. We are going to take back this colony and make it safe."

Governor Mitchell shook his head wearily, all traces of the overconfident man he had once been gone. "I have but a few squads left," he tried to explain. "Forty Legionnaires will never be enough to defeat the renegades here. They number in the hundreds."

Blaze turned from the wreck of a man in disgust and gazed at Travis, who nodded his head in understanding. "We will need our best troops from the *Demoness*," she commanded. "I want four hundred Legionnaires ready to transport down within the hour."

"Consider it done, Baroness Blaze," Travis assured her, as he tapped the communication device in his helmet to transmit the order to the ship.

"Now, Governor Mitchell," Blaze said, her voice laced with contempt as she turned to face him again, "we will show you what you *should* have done with the *five hundred* Legionnaires that you had to start with."

She pivoted away from him and stormed out of the large office, leaving the governor to wallow in his state of despair.

Once back in the hallway, she could hear the random electro-energy fire that indicated the Legionnaires in the foyer were defending themselves against another attack, and it hit home. The one other battle she had ever been in was the one on Tenebrous, where she almost died.

The last months had taught her a new way to survive, with faith in the Imperium, and a command of its massive forces. She now realized she was not the same weak woman who laid there wounded, playing dead. She was a baroness, who had been given great responsibility, and now it was time to prove her worth. To fail here, on the *April* colony, would show once and for all that she was still nothing but the sewer child who barely managed to escape with her life, and that was something she knew wasn't true.

~ * ~

One hour later she stood proudly on the top of the capitol building's steps, as she gazed over the four hundred Legionnaires who bore the insignia of the flagship.

"Tell me of these renegades," she asked Travis while watching her officers gather the troops into attack squads. "Who are they, and why haven't I heard of them before? Why would they rebel? After all, the Imperium feeds, clothes, and educates all of its citizens."

Her personal Shadowguard stepped up next to her and considered his answer carefully. "My Lady, any empire will have its rebellion. The Red Star Imperium isn't any different than the Romusians or Camillian Empires…or even the Terran Dominion which once existed."

"The rebellions in the Romusian and Camillian empires were supported by the United Star Alliance," Blaze interjected. "Do you think the Alliance has anything to do with the *April* colony renegades?"

"The *April* colony isn't the sole target of these Renegade attacks, Blaze," Travis informed her solemnly. "Though it does seem to be worse here than any other place. So far, the renegades have been responsible for minor raids on our freight ships, and small terrorist tactics up until now. This is the first time they have amassed a fighting force."

"How is it I haven't heard of this?"

"You've been quite busy with Overlord Adalric," the Shadowguard explained, then winced at the fiery glare she gave him. "I, of course, mean your TelSor training."

"Of course."

"Perhaps if we defeat their forces here, that will be demoralizing enough to stop the other raids."

Blaze nodded thoughtfully, greatly disturbed by the news of the raids and terrorist attacks. Deep down she was certain the Alliance had to be the cause of it, since the Imperium treated its subjects so much better. It was inconceivable to her that any Imperial subject would want to rebel in that way. "Let's stop it here," she said, her voice proud and sure, "before it goes too far." She lifted her hands, indicating to her officers the attack could begin.

Swiftly the group of soldiers broke up, as the individual Legionnaire squads infiltrated the city streets, overpowering and eradicating any resistance they came across. Pockets of renegades confronted the trained Imperial forces, but these Legionnaires were not misled like the last, and didn't falter at the first sign of opposition. The battle raged across the city for hours, as the renegades tried tactic after tactic. However, Blaze used her newfound mastery of the Cosmic Aura to sense them moving, like watching the whitecaps which indicated a coming wave, and sent her guards to warn the officers. This gave the Imperium the advantage before each sortie. As dusk finally settled in, the Legionnaires were mopping up the last of the resistance. Blaze watched her troops moving about the darkening city from her higher vantage point, tiny flashes of light as the midnight black electro-carbines ripped into the unarmored bodies of those who would defy the Imperium.

"It's all but over," she whispered to herself, almost absently, as she pulled her cloak around her lightly clad body to ward off the chill of the settling night. She could still feel it inside, the despair of the few remaining renegades, who had planned a desperate last act instead of being captured. She quickly scanned the dimly lit streets for any sign of the attack, and spotted the large, armored vehicle skimming across the broken streets toward the capitol building; straight at her. The half destroyed military truck was on fire, swaying wildly from side to side, as its anti-gravity plates struggled to keep it off the ground, and on course. Even from this long distance, their speed and course made their intent clear to Blaze.

"They're making a suicide run on the capitol building," she declared quickly. "I think they plan to detonate once they force themselves inside."

"Our soldiers are spread out," Travis said as he leveled his carbine at the burning suicide vehicle that was bearing straight towards them. "We can't destroy it before it gets to us and detonates."

"Evacuate the last of the colonial Legionnaires from the building," she ordered. "Go quickly."

Travis ran into the building, yelling orders as he sped along. The few remaining *April* colony Legionnaires swiftly began to pour out of the building, as Blaze stood fast, calculating how much longer she could wait for Travis before the armored vehicle hit. Already the flaming skimmer was crossing the capitol building's huge parking lot, smashing smaller vehicles which were in its path into churning debris.

Blaze glanced nervously back into the building, feeling relief flush through her as Travis' grey armored figure appeared through the door.

"That's all of them," he yelled, "but Governor Mitchell has barricaded himself in his office again. I'll need help getting him out."

Blaze looked at the speeding armored vehicle, now less than fifty yards away, then turned back to Travis. "Mitchell has sealed his own fate," she stated without pity.

She grabbed Travis' hand and ran down the steps, the two of them barely able to dive for cover as the vehicle began to swiftly ascend the crumbled steps of the capitol building.

For an instant, Blaze wondered if she could use her new command of the Cosmic Aura to deflect the vehicle, to save the building, then her thoughts settled on Governor Mitchell, cowering behind his mahogany desk. Her eyes narrowed as she watched the vehicle crash through the glass doors of the building and plummet through the floor into the sublevels. All was silent for an instant, then the capitol building erupted into a fiery torrent, sending small bits of concrete and glass for blocks.

Blaze and Travis weren't far from the blast, but she easily used her pyrokinesis to form a flaming heat shield around the two of them, which protected them both from the debris. The baroness stood, for a moment, among the flaming wreckage about her. A tiny smile curled the ends of her lips as she silently turned and strode back to her shuttle, her cloak flowing behind her like a crimson banner of victory in the fire-lit streets.

~ * ~

Overlord Tanus Adalric sat before his prized chess set, now moved back to his reclaimed quarters on the *Sentinel* space station. He gazed at the elaborate pieces in silence, his thoughts light years from the game.

"Have you heard a word that I've said?" Koroqo asked, a look of concern crossing his ivory brow.

Adalric glanced over at his friend and shook his head. "Forgive me Troivaka, my mind is elsewhere."

Troivaka Koroqo watched his overlord stare at the ornate chess set and shook his head, wishing his empathic abilities could reveal more about his silent comrade. "I've always wondered," he voiced his internal question aloud, "who it is you play with? I've often seen the set, at various stages of the game, but I've never seen you move a piece, or have an opponent to challenge you."

"Actually, I haven't played in quite some time," he admitted. "That is because it's her move, and she hasn't made it yet." He gazed back at the set, his thoughts calculating attacks and counterattacks. "I wonder what her next move will be?"

The Proximan baron nodded silently, suddenly understanding. "You've never completed a game yet, have you?"

Adalric slowly shook his head. "When this game is finally over, there will most likely not be another."

Baron Koroqo stood and walked over behind the overlord and placed a hand on his uniformed shoulder. "Tanus," he said quietly, "I'm worried about you. It's been weeks since Blaze left, and you haven't been the same since. There are dark whispers in the halls of the Imperium these days, my friend, and you can't afford to be anything but your best."

The overlord stood up and faced the one man he trusted in the Red Star Imperium and walked to the cathedral window which dominated the lounge in his private chambers. "I am the same man I was a year ago, Koroqo. Nothing has changed."

"Are you so sure?"

"Positive," Adalric assured him as he turned and faced the head of the Imperial Secret Service.

Although he trusted his friend, he knew Koroqo's loyalty would always be for the Imperium, and he must never seem incapable of commanding it as overlord. Suddenly he felt a tightening in his heart and knew the woman he loved was facing possible death. He clutched a hand to his chest and stumbled to his chair. A moment later it relaxed, and he felt the danger had passed.

Koroqo's eyes widened as the raw emotion in the air crashed into him in empathic tidal waves. "You're psionically bonded to Blaze," he exclaimed, suddenly realizing how far their relationship had progressed. Instantly he understood the mixed feelings he had picked up from the two of them, and the new feelings in his friend now that she was gone. "Have you lost your senses? If anything happens to her out there you could be mentally crippled." The Proximan studied his companion, awaiting a response but getting nothing but obstinate silence. "The Dire Queen isn't exactly fond of you now, Adalric. If she found out about this, she would tear you apart...not to mention what she might do to Blaze."

Adalric looked up at Koroqo, suddenly wondering if he, himself, was endangering his love. He shook his head, certain they had to wait it out and be careful. When Blaze was ready to return, she might be powerful enough to help finally put an end to his struggle. "It only took me off guard for a second, that won't happen again. Please don't worry," he assured his friend, "I know exactly what I'm doing."

Koroqo let out a slow sigh of concern, and he placed a hand on Adalric's shoulder again. "I hope so, my friend...for both of your sakes."

~ * ~

Blaze watched out the front window on the bridge of the *Demoness*, feeling better about herself than she had in some time. It had been three days since the end of the uprising on the *April* colony, and no sign of renegade activity had been found. She had searched through her top officers, and chose a new military governor for the colony, with the aid of Captain Harris. She had almost felt like calling home, asking Joshua his opinion, but the supra-light communication would take days to reach Nyx at this distance. Still, she felt a good choice had been made, and that former commander Johansson would make a far better colonial leader than Mitchell ever had. Already the colonists seemed totally relieved at the absence of terrorism in the city. Along with that, the many new jobs created by the rebuilding of *April* colony's capitol, and other buildings, was boosting the economy greatly. It was already increasing the revenue this colony could send to the Imperial core. It amazed Blaze to think about how one facet of the Imperium, like this colony, could have repercussions throughout the Red Star Imperium. She hoped this one-sided victory would have the desired effect with other dissidents on other Imperial worlds.

"Baroness Blaze," came the captain's voice from behind her. "We are receiving an emergency distress signal from the *Wraith*...they are under attack and need help."

Blaze turned to face the commanding officer and read the worry in his face. "Of course, they are under attack...they are at the front lines, expanding the borders of the Imperium. The Alliance has nothing they can put in space which can harm a super-dreadnought like the *Wraith*."

"Normally yes, my Lady," he tried to explain. "However, they are reporting massive casualties. Something has gone dreadfully wrong there and they are in danger of destruction." He paused for a moment to be certain his composure had not been lost. "Baroness Drusee-la herself sent the call to you."

Blaze felt her mind instantly clouded with suspicion. Although she admired the Perusian baroness the last time she saw her, there was no reason not to wonder if this was some sort of trick. Adalric warned her to stay alert and watchful for unusual events, and this distress call was anything but usual. "How far away are they from us?"

"Four light years away," the captain reported. "We can be there in twelve hours if we maintain maximum Cosmic Slip speed. Less if we really push the engines."

Trap or not, Blaze realized she had little choice but to respond. "Prepare to leave orbit, Captain, set course for the *Wraith*."

She turned to the communications station and ordered the lieutenant to raise the new governor for her.

Governor Johansson's silhouette appeared in the holo-viewer, standing at attention. "Yes, Baroness Blaze?"

"We are leaving now," the young noble informed her. "Is there anything you need?"

The new governor shook her head. "The two hundred troops you left will be more than enough, combined with the forces which are still here." She allowed herself a confident smile. "Don't worry, my Lady, the *April* colony is in good hands."

Despite herself, Blaze felt her smile mirroring the *April* colony leader. "I'm sure it is, Governor. *Demoness* out." She cut the communications and ordered the captain to leave orbit.

As the giant warship sped out of the stellar system and smoothly accelerated to its top speed, Blaze silently watched the stars waiver. Her thoughts danced through darkened clouds as she wondered about the truth behind the *Wraith's* distress call, and hoped that if it was true, they wouldn't arrive too late.

Chapter Twenty-five
The Hourglass

The Dire Queen sat nervously curled on her throne, waves of anger searing through her obsidian form. "I send her halfway across the sector," she quietly stated, her dank voice grating against the smooth stone around her throne, "and still he reaches out to her. What hold has he entwined her with? How can I snap her free?" She let out a grunt, knowing that there was only one way to ensure Blaze's total loyalty.

She glanced up quickly as she sensed someone enter the throne room, a pale shadow amidst the crimson ones caused by the dancing torches. This was no surprise, since this shade had been duly summoned. *Strange is he,* the sovereign thought as she contemplated deadly calculations, *not as powerful as the others…and yet far stronger than any of them.*

"Baron Koroqo," she whispered, "I have been expecting you."

The Proximan noble steadily approached the Dire Queen and slowly lowered himself to one knee, then he confidently lifted his head, no trace of fear in his eyes. "You sent for me, my queen?"

"Indeed, I did, my ally," she said while standing up from the throne.

Slowly she slid over to her crimson orb, to lovingly stroke its inner fires. "There is a cancer eating away at the heart of the Imperium…and that cancer is ambition."

Koroqo nodded slowly, never taking his eyes from the Dire Queen.

"Ambition can be a good thing," she continued in her hushed tones, "but it can also be quite terrible." She moved her shadowy palms over the surface of the luminous stone, sending fiery scarlet arcs between the two surfaces. "It can be made to serve the Imperium, or it can be made to serve the individual." She whirled on the Proximan, causing him to stand up straight. "One must never place the individual before the Imperium…don't you agree?"

"Of course, my queen," he quickly agreed with a nod. "I have always strived to place the Imperium first above all things."

An inner smile curled within the empty darkness between the glowing orbs which made up her eyes. "I never had any doubt, Baron Koroqo. As the head of the Imperial Secret Service, you must eliminate this cancerous growth, before it can harm the Imperium."

The sovereign watched as he nodded again, then paused, studying him closely. Despite the fact her empathic baron wasn't even a TelSor, she felt it was hardest to read his thoughts and emotions. There was no psionic shield which barred her way, but when she reached out, she encountered nothing…and that disturbed her all the more. She wondered if she could rely on him, but already knew the answer, which was why she had asked him here in the first place. Koroqo and his S'teka never failed, that was a known fact. "It must be done soon," she commanded, "no later than the falling of the moon…"

~ * ~

"That's barely two weeks from now," Adalric said quietly, while leaning against the huge window in his private chambers.

"Nevertheless," Koroqo continued, "those are her orders."

Overlord Tanus Adalric paced around the small lounge, the clack of his heel dulled by the scarlet carpeting. He came to his beloved chess set and studied it silently, finally moving the black queen to its new position — directly before the white marble statuette of Zeus. "Check," he whispered, barely audible.

"And mate," Koroqo added as he stepped up to the board, lightly knocking over the white king with his hand for emphasis.

"No," Adalric countered, his deep voice reverberating in the small room.

He slammed his fist against the board, cracking the ornate marble and sending the pieces scattering. "It's not over yet." He pulled on his cloak and moved past the Proximan but was stopped by Koroqo's strong hand on his arm.

"This is no game, my friend," the noble warned. "I will give you every last minute that I can, but I *will* carry out her orders by the fall of the moon."

The overlord stopped in his tracks, his face turning to face the man who had stood by his side for many long years. An eternity of silence hung between them as Adalric's glare pierced through his eyepieces.

"I tell you about this because *I am* your friend. I'm breaching a faith of contract by doing this."

"Don't carry out the order," Adalric countered. "If you are truly my friend, then stand by me at this harsh moment."

Once again, no words were spoken, until the overlord turned away, his mind in chaos. For years he played this power struggle with the Dire Queen, always wanting more but knowing of his limitations before his mistress. And now, when it seemed a solution was at hand, she was going to force a confrontation…a confrontation which she was sure to win. "If I had more time," he whispered half to himself.

"But you don't," Koroqo said. "In less than thirteen days I will have to carry out my orders and have you killed."

Adalric whirled back toward the Proximan, fury burning in his eyes. "Are you so sure I would be easy prey, Koroqo?" his strong voice flashed. "You forget who you are talking to."

"I do not," the Proximan replied solemnly. "Even if I fail, there are over two hundred S'teka who will not…one of them *will* succeed."

"I could muster my fleet and my Shadowguards—"

"And start a civil war?" Koroqo said, cutting him off. "If that happens all we have fought for will crumble around our feet."

"What will you have me do then?" Adalric asked. "Why warn me at all?"

"Because I have always placed the Imperium first," Koroqo explained. "That is where my loyalty lies. I feel the sovereign's so-called 'cancerous growth' is in its heart, not within you." He paused to allow his words to sink in as he inhaled sharply. "If a *new* sovereign were to be crowned *before* the fall of the moon…then *that* sovereign could stay the assassination order."

This is what it truly comes down to, Adalric admitted sternly to himself. *Perhaps it is good she is gone, so I have to face this peril alone.*

"Thank you for your council, my friend," he voiced quietly. "I will consider your words strongly."

Troivaka Koroqo studied his companion for a long moment, judging the results his words had on the overlord. He nodded silently and left the room without looking back.

For a moment Adalric gazed at the closed door the Proximan left through, then glanced at the scattered chess pieces, focusing on the discarded white queen.

Chapter Twenty-six
Consequences

Blaze waited in anticipation as they swiftly closed in on the *Wraith*. An uneasy feeling had been building up in her all day, and she could not shake it no matter how hard she tried. It was a mixture of sensations that was culminating in an almost overwhelming anxiety. Even the captain stayed clear of her as she paced back and forth on the long bridge, awaiting news of their arrival.

"Any word yet?" she asked Harris again, as she walked up to his position.

"Still no answer to our calls," the captain admitted as a sour look covered his veneer. "My Lady, it's possible the *Wraith* was destroyed."

Several of the bridge personnel glanced over in surprise, all with looks of disbelief on their faces.

"I thought these two super-dreadnoughts were invincible," Blaze commented thoughtfully, suddenly realizing the fate of the *Wraith* could become theirs also.

"Nothing is invincible," Harris admitted solemnly. "If enough Alliance ships were to gang up, *and* manage to avoid the Cosmic Surge weapon…then maybe—"

"There she is," the first officer proclaimed, cutting the conversation short as all stared at the front screen, awaiting some indication of their sister ship.

Slowly a dot clarified in the starfield ahead, growing to a needle shape, to finally expand to the *Wraith* as they closed in. The dreadnought had not been destroyed but might as well have been. Large carbon scores scarred the length of the vessel, while huge chunks of armor plating were gone, ripped from the hull. Debris filled the space around the *Wraith*, as parts of internal decks, wiring, equipment, and bodies bled out the many gaping holes in the once proud warship. But worse yet was the crumpled and twisted metal where the bridge had been. Many of the *Demoness'* bridge crew shifted uneasily in their seats, realizing the gruesome fate their counterparts on their sister ship had faced. As for the fleet the *Wraith* had been in charge of, debris was all that remained to tell their fate.

Blaze felt numb at first as she gazed at the *Wraith*. She had never seen mass destruction like this, not since the Alliance vessels she watched Adalric destroy were all vaporized with the Cosmic Surge cannon, leaving no trace.

Suddenly she felt a cry of desperation building in her and instantly realized it wasn't her own. Someone was letting out psionic waves of pain, and fear which rang against the Cosmic Aura as clearly as if they were in the same room as her.

"Drusee-la," she whispered. She turned to face the captain. "Harris, are there any enemy ships nearby?"

The captain glanced at his science officer, who shook her head. "No, my Lady."

"Is the *Wraith* likely to explode?"

Once again, he gained the necessary information from his crew. "She seems stable."

"Pull us alongside of her and prepare my personal shuttle," Blaze ordered. "I'm going aboard. Follow me with damage control parties and medical teams."

Blaze started to leave the bridge as she heard the captain issuing orders for the medical bay to prepare to take on survivors, and for the fighters to fly protective sweeps of the area in case any enemies were close by. She glanced one last time at the shattered *Wraith*, an internal shudder vibrating within, then nodded to Travis and left the command center, flanked by her Shadowguards.

~ * ~

Finding an operable shuttle bay on the damaged dreadnought was not easy, but Blaze's personal shuttle and the following medical ships finally made it inside the *Wraith* and were sealed in tightly.

The deck was littered with bodies of Legionnaires and fighter pilots, as the harsh results of internal explosions told their sad tale. The rescue teams maneuvered through the ship, following a maze of decks which had not fallen to decompression, as they started their search for survivors of this disaster.

"I want to know exactly what happened here," Blaze instructed Travis as they walked down one of the few intact hallways. "Captain's logs, visual playbacks, anything you can find."

"Most of the records would have been on the bridge," Travis informed her. "However, I'll make sure nothing was missed."

They continued to walk in silence, as Blaze let herself home in on the quickly fading psionic waves of pain. Somewhere in the back of her mind, she knew Drusee-la was a threat to her, but all she could think about was the pain and remorse which echoed through the empty corridors.

She finally reached the Imperial quarters, the counterpart to her suite on the *Demoness*. The doors were crumpled in by a metal girder which crashed down from the ceiling. Blaze drew in a sharp breath through her teeth as she instantly spotted the dried blood and matted fur on the protruding metal beam.

Stepping into the room she saw one huge, clawed hand, sticking out from under the large debris, its fingers curled in mockery of its last agonistic spasm. Her brow creased as she scanned the room, finally spotting Drusee-la on the floor on the far side, dried blood caked on the side of her head where another piece of exploding metal had struck her.

Blaze quickly ran to her side and touched her arm, breathing a sigh of relief when she heard the Perusian let out a light groan. "Bring a doctor," she commanded one of her Shadowguards, then glanced over the wounded feline for any other wounds. "Can you hear me, Drusee-la?" she asked quietly.

She was rewarded by the wounded feline opening the eye that wasn't crusted over with blood. For a moment the Perusian tried to focus on her savior, then drew in a few quick breaths through her small pink nose.

"You're Adalric's personal guard," Drusee-la said as she coughed in surprise, "I think…"

Blaze let out a smile, pleased the Perusian remembered who she was, a hopeful sign of her recovery. "I'm Blaze," she told her. "I used to be a Shadowguard."

Drusee-la finally focused on whom she was talking to and painfully tried to draw herself up to a seated position. "So, *you're* the soldier who became a noble."

Blaze nodded as she glanced around the destroyed room. "What happened here?"

The Perusian baroness touched a hand to her wounded head and winced from the pain. She looked around, searching, and finally settled her gaze on the body of her beloved guard. Her ears flattened as a tear formed in her open eye, then she gazed back at Blaze. "It was a trap—"

"Explain."

"We were confronted by two Alliance battleships, it should have been an easy kill." Drusee-la finished pushing herself up to a seated position and sadly glanced at the state of her room, her thoughts drifting away with the pain.

Blaze clenched her teeth in annoyance and grabbed the Perusian's jaw, gently but firmly turning her head to face her own. "Baroness Drusee-la, I need you to tell me what happened here. The *Demoness* could be in trouble. Two Alliance battleships didn't do all this, did they?"

"We were powering up the Cosmic Surge cannon as they approached, planning on vaporizing one before they even entered their weapons range. Most of our advance fleet was along our other borders, but I didn't think we needed more than two escorts." Drusee-la touched her hand to her wounded face again. "Is it bad?"

Blaze let out a breath and shook her head, suddenly reminded of the first time she had been shot. "You'll be fine. The doctor is on his way now. Now back to the battle, what happened next?"

"Suddenly our computer went crazy," Drusee-la explained. "Our shields lowered themselves and all weapons powered down. Then the Slip drive deactivated. We were helpless as they smashed us into pieces. Our escorts tried to help, but they were no match for two battleships."

Rubbing her face in her hands, Blaze tried to fathom all she had been told. *The computer losing control...but how?* "Did you find out what happened?"

Drusee-la nodded, glancing up as the doctor approached. "Right before the bridge was smashed, my captain called and told me a scrambled signal came from a private merchant vessel. The small Merchantman was hiding behind the two battleships. It was *that* signal which crippled the computers. I think the Alliance left us alive as a warning to the Imperium."

"A small private Merchantman?" Blaze asked in disbelief. "How could such a puny spaceship have access to our computer's security codes?" her voice died off as the blood drained from her face. "Gods," she whispered, suddenly understanding the source of the anxiety that had been building up in her lately. "Did you see where the Merchantman went?"

"My first officer tried to track the ship from the emergency bridge, to find out if it was acting on its own. I think it went to the nearby system. The neutral world of Ross."

Blaze stood up, feeling every fiber of her body flush with internal fires. "See to the care of Baroness Drusee-la here, and prepare my shuttle again," she instructed her closest Shadowguard. "I'm going to the Ross system."

"Without the *Demoness*?" the guard asked in confusion.

"The ship stays here," she instructed. "What I need to do I must do alone."

~ * ~

The system of Ross was a thriving community which despised large political organizations. Since they had nothing of any real value to take by force, this made them ideal for a neutral world. They remained impartial to the ongoing war, seated in neutral space. There were many inhabitable planets in the system, but the center of it all was its capital world, Ross V.

It had been a simple task for Blaze to find what she was looking for. After piloting her shuttle to Ross V, right under an Alliance battleship's nose. She landed in the local starport and headed for the largest bar in the city. Instinct alone could have sufficed to lead her here, but it was her new abilities that pulled her this time, taking her to her quarry through simple Cosmic Aura vibrations of familiarity.

The bar was dimly lit and filled with smoke from half a dozen types of incense. Blaze paused at the doorway, instructing her Shadowguards to remain outside until summoned. She swept the crowded bar, certain of *her* location.

Slowly she entered the bar, taking long deliberate steps as she approached the threesome at a corner booth. Several people moved out of her way as she strode along, perhaps because of her lavish deep red apparel, perhaps because of the hot coals which burned in her glowing red eyes. More likely it was perhaps because in the wake of her every step, she left a smoldering footprint of flame.

She arrived at the booth and studied the three seated there, as two of them looked back at her, their faces painted with shock.

"Blaze," Rabies squealed with delight, "is that you?"

Sloan's initial smile died quickly, as she studied her old companion closely, from the long crimson cloak to the silver-trimmed electrosword at her side. She glanced back at the doorway, catching sight of the slightly obscured, grey-armored guards and instantly realized her peril.

Blaze watched this reaction with pleasure and let a smile cross her lips, as the fires behind her quickly died out. She realized that despite her anger, it was good to see these two again. "Sloan, Rabies," she said with a smile, "how have you been?"

The third member of the party, a casually dressed man with a pistol at his side, looked at the two merchants with surprise. "What's going on here? We have business to conclude. One test does not clinch the deal."

Blaze's eyes illuminated once more, glowing into hellish pits as she focused her gaze on the man at the booth. Like dry kindling, flames instantly erupted from his clothes, turning him into a screaming pyre.

Sloan tore the covering off the table and threw it over the writhing man, the reek of burned flesh telling her it was already too late. When Blaze motioned for her Shadowguards to enter, many of the bar's patrons began to draw weapons, disliking the disturbance to their peace. However, they hesitated as the six armored warriors assumed flanking positions around the crimson-clad woman, their electro-carbines ready. Calculating the odds, the customers slowly returned to their drinks, suddenly caring little about the goings-on at the booth in the corner.

"*By the fire pits of Hellion*, Blaze," Sloan exclaimed as she stared at the smoldering remains, "why did you do that?"

"Sit down," the Imperial noble commanded, her voice a whispering chill.

For the second time in her life, Sloan found herself compelled to do something against her will, as she slid back to her seat and pulled Rabies out from under the table.

Blaze studied her former companions for a few moments, as she sat opposite them, where the now deceased man recently occupied. "Sloan…Rabies," she said, her smile returning. "Let's talk."

The two smugglers stared at their former companion in shocked silence for a few seconds, as Blaze indicated to her guards to stand back, but stay nearby and watch out for any Alliance soldiers coming down from the battleship above. One of the bartenders came over and dragged the corpse off, never looking up to face the Imperial noble at the booth.

Finally, Sloan cleared her throat and nodded her reassurance to Rabies. "All right, Blaze," the *Silhouette*'s captain began, "what's going on? What's happened to you? We left you to become a Legionnaire…you're definitely not that. Why did you kill that guy? He was a *vital* business contact who meant a lot of money to Rabies and me."

Blaze studied her friends long and hard, suddenly understanding how much she changed since they were last together, and how little they had. *But most people do not become a completely new person within a year.*

Standing next to the seated noble, Travis knew he should remain silent but wholly resented the attitudes of these obvious renegades towards his mistress. "You are in the presence of the Baroness Blaze, personal advisor to the Dire Queen," he insisted.

Blaze held up her hand to her guard, a light smile crossing her lips. "That's all right, Travis," she quieted him, "these two are my friends."

"Friends?" questioned Sloan, a well-hidden nervous shudder in her voice. "Friends don't come over and kill their friends' business partners. What is this nonsense about your getup?" She gestured at what Blaze was wearing.

"Your business partner," Blaze cut her off, "is responsible for the near destruction of one of the Imperium's super-dreadnoughts, and the deaths of over one thousand Imperial troops."

"This is war," Sloan stated. "He was an agent for the United Star Alliance trying to buy something from us."

"Yes," the baroness agreed, "this *is* war, a war in which you have aligned yourselves on the wrong side." She stared at them sternly, as the flame in the kerosene lamp on the table grew in intensity. "That man was my enemy, and I *know* what you were going to sell to him. It's what you just tested out, disabling the computers on the *Wraith* and crippling her so the Alliance warships could pulverize her." She watched them shrink before her verbal attack, her growing anger fed by their apparent fear. Blaze observed Sloan's eyes flicking from Shadowguard to Shadowguard, then back to her. "I know you still have the computer disk...the blueprints of the super-dreadnought and access to all its codes. Give it to me now...because you *don't* want me to have to take it by force."

Sloan's hand flashed to her side, pulling out her electro-gun with a smooth motion which was hard for the eye to follow. In Blaze's mind's eye, she saw the move before it ever happened. Instantly the pistol's hand grip burst into flame, causing Sloan to yelp in pain as the inner mechanisms of the weapon fused together. Rabies began to scramble over the seat to the next booth, terrified and desperate to escape, but Blaze raised a hand and telekinetically pulled at him, causing the Jarbban to tumble backward into his seat, where he remained frozen in panicked fear.

Before the two smugglers could take further action, Travis and his second leveled their weapons on the crew of the *Silhouette*, and the brief incident was over.

The three of them sat in deathly silence for what seemed an eternity. It was Rabies who finally found his voice. "You attacked us, Blaze. I thought you were our friend."

"Friends don't pull guns on friends," was her simple response.

Sloan swallowed hard and rubbed at the blisters forming on her right hand. "I don't know what's happened to you, Blaze, but you're not the same. I don't give a damn about the war, but I do care about the Alliance—"

"The Alliance killed Sinclair," Blaze cut in, her eyes narrowing with the anger she was using to mask her feelings of hurt and betrayal. "Or had you forgotten that?"

"The Imperium has killed many more than that," Sloan shot back.

"And you should know what we do, we do for a profit…if a few Imperials get killed, then so much the better."

"What if I had been on that ship?" Blaze asked.

"You weren't," Rabies replied meekly.

"But what if?"

Sloan's face creased in inner confusion. She hated emotional conflicts, and the pain they caused. "We never meant *you* any harm. You knew we had the disk, why didn't you ask for it before?"

"I suppose I forgot you had it," Blaze admitted.

"And we forgot you could have been on that ship," Sloan explained.

"So where does that leave us?" Rabies asked nervously, finally relaxing a bit. "Are you going to kill us?"

"No," Blaze told them. "You both saved my life once and were there for me when Sinclair died. I promised you I owed you one, and this is it." She extended her hand, palm up…and waited.

Rabies thought for a moment, then glanced at the Shadowguards again and removed the computer disk from his pocket. He hesitated for a fraction of a second, then gazed into Blaze's cold dark eyes and handed it to her.

"Thank you, Rabies," she said with a relieved smile as she stood up. Her face then hardened into a granite mask, her beauty cast in stone. "This is your favor returned…I promise you that if you ever cross the Red Star Imperium again, friendship or no…I will not be so forgiving."

"I wonder what Sinclair would say if he saw you now," Sloan said under her breath as she nursed her burned hand.

Inside, Blaze's heart was a knot which yearned to be released as she paused and stared at the two of them, knowing her past with these two was now history. A line had been crossed here, and things could never be the same as they were. She easily read the controlled anger in Sloan's eyes, and the confused hurt in Rabies'. She wanted to share with them the truths she'd learned, the complexities to the galaxy which she now understood, but knew these simple people could never understand.

Without saying another word, she left the table and headed for the entrance, feeling their strong sorrows follow her out of the bar. For a moment she stood on the city sidewalk, releasing all connections to what was inside the bar, and allowed her mind to clear. Then it struck her without warning, like a psychic stab through the heart. It was far away. It was desperate. It was *him*.

~ * ~

"I have to return to Nyx," Blaze explained to Drusee-la, as she stood over the wounded feline who was still on a medical diagnostic bed on the *Demoness*. "I can't explain it, but I'm needed there as soon as possible." She reflected on her psychic feelings, her brow creasing in thought. "It may already be too late."

Drusee-la watched the young human with curious contemplation, then slowly sat up, trying to ignore the pain which still lanced through her head. "From the moment I met you, I knew there was something special about you." She licked the back of her hand and smoothed out a lock of fur which had become misplaced on her arm, then studied Blaze again. "When I heard of the new baroness, the advisor to the queen, I frankly assumed you were someone's whore, probably Adalric's."

Blaze glanced up sharply at her words.

"I was certain I was going to have to kill you," Drusee-la continued carefully. "Yet our first meeting as baronesses is after you have saved my life." The Perusian tried to stand up, but the pain forced her to ease back to the bed. "I also heard how you handled yourself on the *April* colony, and you alone recovered that lost set of blueprints which disappeared nearly a year ago. I find that instead of hating you, I admire you." Her feline eyes widened softly, as she read the subtle signs most would miss. "But are you sure of what you are doing now? Overlord Adalric is an enigma which I have often tried to solve, to no avail. Only a fool would be deaf to the currents which are sweeping through the Imperium now. Adalric and the Dire Queen will fight, and I don't think he has much of a chance. If you run to help him, then you could end up dead too."

Blaze turned from her, trying to conceal the confusion and anger that flooded her veins. The Dire Queen had saved her life and reshaped it to what it was now, but it always came back to *him*...she loved him and couldn't deny it. "I can stop the fight. They just need someone there to mediate for them."

Drusee-la grabbed Blaze's arm and held fast. "Don't delude yourself kitten, no one has ever bested the Dire Queen. She *is* the Imperium, every fiber of her darkened essence is the fabric that binds us fast. Destroy that, and nothing can hold the Imperium together."

The young woman turned back to the Perusian and shook her arm free. "You don't understand. I can't hurt *either* of them, I owe them both so much…but they both need me now."

The feline let out a painful sigh then lay back on the bed. "What of your mission here? You can't abandon the Dire Queen's orders to race back home."

Blaze straightened up, regaining her posture. "I've been told the *Wraith* is still in bad shape, but her stardrive has been fully repaired. You will remain here, on the *Demoness*. You will regroup with the fleet and continue to hold the front lines against the United Star Alliance. I'll take the damaged *Wraith* back to Nyx for repairs."

Drusee-la's ears perked with attention at Blaze's words. "You would give me command of the flagship?" The Perusian somehow found the strength to sit up again, despite the screaming pain behind her eyes. "Do you know how long I have waited to stand on the bridge of this ship?"

Blaze allowed herself a brief smile. "Then make sure I'm happy that I made this decision." Then without another word, she turned from the feline noble and left the medical bay, intent on starting her return trip as soon as possible.

Drusee-la watched the queen's new advisor leave, as she shook her head in wonder. Pondering whether she would ever see Blaze alive again, a small laugh twitched her whiskers, for somehow, she knew she would.

"Prepare the *Demoness* for combat," Drusee-la ordered her new Shadowguard who stood dutifully by her side, then her eyes danced with a resurgence of pride, "and tell the bridge to track down the Alliance battleships that attacked the *Wraith*…I have a little favor to return."

Chapter Twenty-seven
The Fall of the Moon

Tanus Adalric watched the passing of the moon for many nights as he ran scenario after scenario in his mind. He understood Blaze might be feeling his distress, but even if she could have made a difference, he knew she was too far away to arrive before it was over. The mere thought he might truly need someone, made him shudder with consternation, but he realized a part of him had left on the *Demoness*, and now he wondered if he could face the queen without it.

Nyx's blue moon hung low over the crest of the planet's horizon, creating a dazzling spectrum of lights when observed from the orbiting station. The many colors danced across the blackened eyepieces which dominated the overlord's crimson half mask.

Adalric felt his concentration stiffen as he sensed a presence entering his private observation lounge. The emotions behind him were cool and controlled, marking who they belonged to with clarity that even a face could not match. For a few moments he allowed his visitor to wait, then finally spoke, breaking through the silence.

"An excellent night to die, my friend," Adalric whispered stoically.

"Are you giving up so soon?" Koroqo asked his companion, while walking further into the darkened room, lit solely by the light of Nyx and its moon through the large picture window. "I've never seen you defeated so easily."

Adalric turned to face the Proximan baron and studied him thoughtfully. There he lingered for a few seconds, then looked back at the window, towards the luminous moon. "What time is it now?"

The S'teka master's eyes narrowed, disturbed by this abstract mood his friend was in. "The fall of the moon will be complete in less than three hours."

"At which time you will kill me?"

"Won't you reconsider the alternatives?" Koroqo asked, scant hope in his voice. "The Dire Queen is as worried about this deadline as you are...she remains huddled in her throne room like a cornered arachnid, waiting for the hour to arrive."

"Arachnids are capable of setting some elaborate traps," Adalric said as he laughed hollowly. "So, what are you, Troivaka Koroqo...the bait in the web?"

"I'll be anything necessary to get you to fight for your life."

"Even though you won't help?"

The Proximan shook his head sadly. "I must stay true to the Imperium, and the person who commands it. I wish you understood."

A light smile played across Adalric's thin lips. "I understand much more than you realize, Troivaka." He pulled in a deep breath and patted his friend on the shoulder. "There are things you are unaware of, shifts and eddies in the current of the Imperium. Every day that passes poses a new challenge to this budding galactic force. We have all come so far. The Romusian and Camillian Empires are under our thumb, and the United Star Alliance is buckling under our constant barrage. But we are not strong internally. A great upset, occurring at the wrong time, could shatter this Imperium and destroy the foundation it is built on. One must calculate all actions carefully and orchestrate them to the proper conclusions."

"So, you're waiting," Koroqo elaborated, "but for how long? The fall of the moon is coming swiftly, why hesitate?" Suddenly the Proximan's eyes widened, as the scant emotions the overlord allowed to escape past his walls came through. "You're waiting for her to come back," he stated, finally understanding.

No answer came from Adalric, as he pulled his hand away from his friend's shoulder. The visible lines of his face surrendered no emotions as he gazed steadily at the Proximan.

"She's weeks away from here, and you know it," Koroqo tried to reason. "Reports tell me that the *Demoness* is still at the front lines. It would have had to have left from there weeks ago to be here now." The Proximan rubbed his face with his hands, trying to rub the frustration out. "Adalric, you can't rely on her. Even if she was here with you now, she has strong loyalties toward the Dire Queen…"

Adalric glared sharply at Koroqo, his frame stiffening into a statue version of himself as he tried to suppress the turmoiled feelings within.

"I felt those emotions in her," the Proximan explained. "I'm fond of her also, but I'm not making her into something she simply isn't."

"You could be wrong about her."

"I'm not…" Koroqo shifted his stance, unsure of the base feelings emanating from the overlord. "Your time is disappearing quickly," he tried once more, "will you do nothing to prevent your death?"

"You are my friend, Troivaka," Adalric explained quietly, "and you are an admirable combatant…but even you are too easily deceived by actions and words." He glanced back at the falling moon, its dazzling lights barely visible now beyond the crest of the planet. He walked past the S'teka master towards the door, where he paused for the briefest instant, and glanced back at his friend. "I told you it was an excellent night to die, I never elaborated on whose death I meant." An instant later he was gone from the observation room, leaving the Proximan alone.

Minutes passed as the S'teka master stared at the empty door, then at the moon as it went through its last death throes, finally beginning to fall beyond Nyx's horizon. He pulled his razor sharp K'tanna blade from its sheath and moved toward the doorway.

~ * ~

The Dire Queen paced her throne room for almost six hours, each few minutes stopping back at her luminous crimson sphere to calm her blackened soul. Something was wrong, she realized with growing anxiety, the moon must have fallen by now and no reports had come in yet.

For almost two weeks she watched her overlord's every movement, almost to the point of neglecting the rest of the Imperium. She felt certain he realized what was happening, but he made no move against her or called for any aid.

Slowly a bitter laugh escaped her inky blackness. *He thinks he has a chance against me*, she concluded. *He doesn't realize half of my powers, and when he is gone, I can mold my new protégé into whatever I want.*

"You have grown complacent and weak, my weary servant," she whispered harshly to the empty air, her voice laced with laughter, "the time of your usefulness has passed."

"Do not judge what you do not fully comprehend," Adalric's deep voice sliced through the dancing crimson shadows which gave the room its meager light.

The Dire Queen's eyes flashed a brilliant scarlet as she turned to face her unannounced intruder. *"How dare you enter unsummoned!"*

Adalric stepped closer to his mistress, for the first time approaching without kneeling. He glanced slowly around the darkened throne room, a cocky smile crossing his lips. "When I rule here," he began slowly, allowing each word to sink fully in, "I will definitely have more light in this room."

Never since her day of reckoning had the sovereign felt a greater surge of rage. So intense was her blinding fury that the sharp psionic waves it generated caused Overlord Adalric to fall back a few steps. Her fiery eyes shimmered like hot lava coals as she stood to face her servant, her darkly supple form silhouetted by the dancing torches and the crimson sphere. In her black heart, she knew the day would come when Adalric would oppose her, but this open defiance was more than she expected. Slowly and deliberately, she turned back to her throne, to reach toward the summoner which would call her personal guards.

"After all this time, Your Highness, are you afraid of facing me alone?" the overlord jibed, his voice taking on an almost cavalier tone.

She pivoted back to him as her eyes flashed nova white. The energy burst which hurled out of her obsidian body caught the overlord by surprise, lifting him off the ground and slamming him against the back wall of the throne room with a grinding crunch. He crumpled to the base of the wall, one arm clutching his sizzling midriff to cradle the ribs he was sure had been broken by the severity of the attack.

As Adalric shook his head clear, he realized if his uniform had not been slightly armored, the blow might have easily killed him. He struggled quickly back to his feet but had to labor to keep his knees from buckling.

"Impudent fool," she said, her voice quivering with rage. "Do not assume your powers are any match for mine. I was a mere TelSor Mystic *before* I was even killed, and now my powers are fully aligned with darkness.

You *serve* the Cosmic Aura...but I *am* the Cosmic Aura...a literal embodiment of the negative energy the Aura can produce. You cannot stand against me alone." She paused, allowing her anger to fuel her contempt. "...and you are truly *alone* now, Adalric. No one will come to your side here, because they know that to defy me is suicide. So alone you stand, and alone you shall perish."

Adalric's thoughts raced through his mind as his disciplined training forced away all concepts of pain. There was merely anger. He knew the Dire Queen was right. He was going to stand alone here. He also knew she didn't lie. Now that she was unmasked, he could see the darkened colors of the Cosmic Aura emanating from and around her, revealing her unique connection to that mystical energy. It was indeed almost like looking at a part of the Aura itself. If he hoped to survive, he could not let her words poison his concentration. Slowly he moved across the throne room, as he ignored the harsh odor of melted plastic and charred cloth which assaulted his nostrils. His psionic concentration focused on the Dire Queen, coalescing into an attack which would have dispatched a dozen of his best Shadowguards.

She watched him carefully, her eyes cooling to a deep red, as her own defenses began to build.

Then he unleashed the mental tumult at her hated form. So intense was the power of the blast the air rippled violently as the mental energy forced its way through to her. The crippling Aura blast enveloped the Dire Queen, crushing down on her soul with all of Adalric's mental might.

The Dire Queen staggered back for a moment, as her darkness threatened to dissipate. Then a grating laugh escaped from her, as her eyes regained their luminous strength. "A valiant effort, my old friend," she tormented, "but a vain one, nonetheless. Now it is time for old friendships to pass to new ones." Her eyes began to grow in intensity again.

Adalric felt his shoulders sag as he leaned against the back wall in near exhaustion. His attack drained him considerably and should have destroyed her. For the first time, he understood her words were true. He was no match for her alone. That realization pierced into his soul, more agonizing than a thousand mental attacks. He was suddenly forced to face his inadequacy but refused to accept it. He pulled his electrosword from its sheath and activated it with determination, sending lethal shimmering sparks along the crystal blade.

The Dire Queen's laughter sounded again, more taunting than the last. "Surely you are deluding yourself, Adalric. Why not accept defeat gracefully? I'll make it as painless as possible."

The overlord pushed himself off the wall with his free hand, as he managed his first steps toward his old mistress.

"If this is what you truly want," the sovereign said with a sigh of seeming glee.

"I do," he said, as he tightened his muscles, causing his broad chest to stress the endurance of the uniform tunic. "Let's finish this."

~ * ~

Blaze stared desperately at the cherry red star which was quickly growing in the *Wraith's* bridge windows. Her stomach roped into agonizing knots as her heart pounded to the threat of bursting.

"How much longer?" she asked again, feeling her fingers clenching into tightened fists.

"We are pulling within a planetary diameter of *Sentinel* now," the captain answered, greatly relieved this bizarre run was finally at an end and her severely damaged ship had held together. "Your shuttle is standing ready. You should be on the base in twenty minutes."

Blaze let out a breath of relief, still unsure of why she had done this, though she was positive he was in grave danger. She turned to her Shadowguard and motioned for him to follow. "Come on, Travis, we have to get over there quickly."

Suddenly she felt as if her head imploded, as waves of pain lanced through her mind. Her knees buckled and gave out, barely giving Travis time to catch her before she collapsed.

"Blaze," her Shadowguard asked with confused concern, "what is it?"

"No," she said with a groan as her eyes watered. She then felt her sense of control finally returning, but also suddenly felt terrified past reason. *"He needs me now.* Travis, I *must* get to him…now!"

Her desperate plea made Travis' eyes sadden with the confirmation of his suspicions. Despite the added weight on his heart, Travis pulled Blaze into the omni-lift, signaling for it to take them to the hangar, where her craft lay waiting. "We'll take off immediately," he assured her as she finally stood on her own. "In twenty minutes, you'll be on the *Sentinel*."

"That's twenty minutes too long, Travis," she told him while wiping the moisture out of her eyes. "There must be a way." Suddenly her eyes lit up as she turned to her personal guard. "The transportation units."

Travis shook his head. "Not permitted. No barons use them due to the risks."

"You'll operate the Cosmic Rift unit," she informed him, suddenly sure of her actions. "You're the only one on the *Wraith* I trust with my life, Travis."

She stopped the omni-lift at the transportation chamber level and pulled him out into the corridor. "Come…with the aid of the unit I'll be by his side in a few seconds."

"But if I operate the unit, then I can't come with you," he said, protesting. "You can't go over there alone."

She smiled and tried to quell his fears. "I'm only going to the *Sentinel*."

Travis let out a soft laugh. "Blaze, I'd be a very poor personal guard if I couldn't tell when you were preparing for battle."

Despite herself, she let out a smile and grabbed his armored hand. "I have to get there now, Travis," she insisted, "and you're the one who can send me. The future of the Imperium rests on me getting there *now*."

Travis nodded as they entered the Cosmic Rift transportation room. He crossed to the controls while she stepped onto the platform. "What destination?"

She looked back at her guard in surprise, suddenly realizing she was holding her breath. "The corridor outside the throne room."

"Blaze?"

"Just do it," she commanded, as she mentally prepared herself for what she was sure would be her greatest challenge, with no clue what she would do when she arrived.

"Transporting now," Travis said, while activating the unit, and silently hoping she'd be safe.

Blaze closed her eyes and tried to steady her nerves, as the enveloping waves of energy opened the rift in the Cosmic Aura which allowed these journeys. She stepped into the rift and vanished with a soft flash of light.

~ * ~

The corridor was silent as Blaze felt her body emerging from the subspace fold, but instantly she knew something was dreadfully wrong. The door to the throne room was partially open, and dregs of russet steam seeped out of the entrance clouding the corridor and burying her feet beneath the fog. There were no signs of any guards. She immediately ran to the doorway, hoping she wasn't too late.

The throne room was filled with obscuring red mists with the queen's crimson sphere shimmering through the fog with its intense energy. The lone remaining light revealed the Dire Queen who sat next to her throne, half draped across the arm in visible exhaustion. The Dire Queen's eyes seemed dimly lit, and her ebony dress was torn in many places, exposing her blackened emptiness.

Blaze looked around the throne room, but what her eyes couldn't find, her heart directed her to instantly. He lay half crumpled against the far wall, blackened and covered in his own blood. His electrosword was clutched in his right hand, but the blade was broken halfway down, as scant sparks shot from the gaping hole in the crushed crystal. One of his eyepieces was shattered and his regal cloak was in tatters.

"Tanus," Blaze called, her voice releasing an anguished groan, as she hesitantly stepped in his direction, suddenly cursing herself for arriving too late to prevent this.

"My child," the Dire Queen's cracked voice whispered imploringly.

Blaze turned to her mistress, confusion pounding in her mind. "Regine," she asked, desperate to know the truth, and equally afraid of what that truth would be, "what happened here?"

"He betrayed me," she said softly, her voice regaining the power which had captivated Blaze's attention many times in the past, "as I foresaw that he would." The Dire Queen pulled herself back to a standing position, as she leaned onto the luminous sphere which she had moved next to her throne. "This is what I have warned you of, he must be dispatched."

Blaze's lips parted softly as her worst fears were realized. She knew she rode a fence that she would one day have to cross, and now that moment was here. She turned back to Adalric, feeling his pain almost as surely as if it was her own. For a moment he did not move, and she feared he might be unconscious. His head lifted slowly upward, revealing the darkened bruises and burns which covered his unmasked cheek.

"Blaze," his hoarse voice whispered as he shook his head.

He felt her presence as she arrived but was too drained to warn her away. From the moment he accepted her as an ally, he had planned for the time when she could fight the Dire Queen at his side. Now, all he could do was fear for her life and realize her safety meant more than any other prize he could claim. He struggled to a kneeling position, coughing up blood. "You must leave…this is between the Dire Queen and me."

"No, Blaze," the Dire Queen commanded, having partially regained her strength once more, as liquid energy seeped along the sphere. "You must now fulfill the destiny I told you of… kill Overlord Adalric before he turns on us again!"

"What?" the young woman asked, her head reeling with shock. She felt the pull of her mistress' words, the call to remain loyal, but her love kept tugging her back across the line to his side. "I could no more destroy him than you, Regine," she finally replied, forcing the quiver from her voice. "You are my queen, but he is my overlord and my teacher. There must be some way to solve this—"

"Destroy him!" the Dire Queen screeched. "Now, while he is weakened."

Blaze's eyes stared hollowly at the Dire Queen for what seemed an eternity, tasting the fear which encased the Imperial ruler like a shroud. Suddenly the young noble's mind cleared, allowing her to sift past the internal conflicts; conflicts which were being falsely induced by her mistress' will. The internal walls crumbled, as she finally comprehended how badly she had been used. Adalric had been cruel at times, Blaze reasoned, even to the point of trying to kill her…but he had never falsely befriended her. His plea for her to abandon him, when he needed her most, was final proof of his love. "I can't destroy what I love, Regine," her voice stated coolly, as she braced her stance against the Dire Queen.

The Dire Queen's darkened form solidified as she read the defiance in her new servant, her anger reeling as the horror of what she had allowed to occur sank home. "Child…you would betray me?" she asked, her voice a low hiss. "You *will* destroy him or be destroyed yourself."

"You do not frighten me, Regine," Blaze challenged as her heat shields began to form around her. "You have power, but you are a coward, without the will to complete what you started yourself."

"No," Adalric weakly pleaded as he saw the Dire Queen's eyes flash white, but he was too slow to stop the furnace blast as it crushed Blaze's fiery shields and enveloped her writhing body.

The ferocious attack lifted her off the floor and sent her across the room, skidding out the open doorway back into the corridor.

Adalric's face contorted in rage as he charged the sovereign once more, wielding his destroyed weapon and issuing what little psionic strikes he could, desperate to direct the Dire Queen's hatred back to himself.

Blaze shook the daze from her eyes in time to see Adalric tossed back from the Dire Queen again, violent energy explosions ripping across the overlord's broken frame. The baroness' eyes cooled as she studied the sovereign, her attention somehow riveted to the Dire Queen's right hand, which never left her prized crimson sphere, its rippling energy brighter than she ever remembered seeing it before.

"I need more power," Blaze whispered as she pulled herself off the floor, realizing her pyrokinetic heat shield barely saved her life.

She knew that in moments the sovereign would regain herself enough to attack Adalric again. Turning from the throne room, Blaze darted down the corridor in a motion so fast she seemed to almost blur, as she hoped she could run her errand before Regine struck again, and prayed he was not already dead.

Her old room was not far away, one floor down, and she was there within seconds. Everyone she passed stared blankly at the faintly smoking Imperial noble that streaked by, but she ignored them all, focusing on her immediate goal. She entered her room and ran to the bed, praying that what was long forgotten was still there. Nervously, her dampened hand slid far under the mattress and closed on its warmth, as she let out a breath of relief, happy Tanus never found it there. She pulled it free and bolted back toward the unknown tempest which lay hidden within the throne room of the Imperium.

~ * ~

Adalric coughed more blood, noting its darker color this time. He knew that some time had passed since the last attack against him, and he wondered if he had lost consciousness for a few minutes. He had felt his body flush with relief when Blaze fled…yet still could not believe she abandoned him. He was not sure at first, but he felt a change in her before the sovereign's attack, and knew she had achieved on her own what his training could not complete.

"Still alive, old friend?" the Dire Queen asked as her voice cackled, refreshed by the brief respite. "Your traitor bird has flown, and you are alone once more."

"No, sovereign," he contested, while pushing his injured body up to a half-seated position against the far wall again, "I *was* alone when I served you, more alone than your blackened soul could ever hope to understand. Now I'll never be alone again…even if you kill me."

"*If?*" She laughed cruelly, as a hunter who had finally caught up with the prey she had been tormenting. "No, my servant, there is no *if* in this case. There is but *when*…and the when is now." Her eyes began to build up in intensity again, preparing for the final blow. "So dies the fool who would be king."

"*Regine,*" came the angered call from the doorway, revealing an exhausted Blaze.

The Dire Queen glanced over sharply, furious that her new servant dared to return. Then she felt *its* presence like the first rays of sun on a winter's day, as her eyes were drawn to Blaze's fist, and the pale blue light which was emanating from *it* in brilliant streams. Suddenly the glowing blue crystal in her hand cracked, brilliant red light spilling through the spiderweb fissures in its surface. The Queen instantly knew that not only was it a

Cosmic Nodule in her servant's hand, but one of such intensity and magnitude unlike any she had felt before.

Blaze knew she would have one chance at this as she let the jewel, and the now revealed Nodule within, absorb all her psionic energy. For a moment she became a part of the Cosmic Aura, her and the Nodule as one brilliant glow of red light. The stone lit up like a miniature supernova, as her vision began to blur into numbness. With the last of her effort the young noble raised the jewel. Instead of releasing the energy — energy which might have been mentally deflected — she hurled the miniature sun at the Dire Queen, letting it carry all the power of her lifeforce energy.

The Dire Queen flinched back, never having felt anything like this, while she powered her psionic shields to their fullest. But the sovereign had not been the intended target. The starfire jewel struck the Dire Queen's crimson sphere with a solid crack, imploding instantly as the hidden red negative Cosmic Nodule within erupted against Blaze's positive one. Both luminous forces violently cancelled each other out, as the tremendous conflagration knocked Blaze to her knees, and Adalric stared on in disbelief.

The Dire Queen let out a grave stirring shriek as her precious sphere disintegrated, the source of her link to the Cosmic Aura gone. Both she and the fiery glow collapsed back onto the throne as the last of the implosion died out, leaving the room in practical darkness. By the time Blaze managed to look back up at the throne, the sovereign was already dissipating, her ability to sustain her darkened form quickly dying out.

The Dire Queen glanced down at her sagging dress, as her luminous orbs slowly lost their sight. Then her eyes flashed back at Blaze, already a blurred image in the dark. "I would have given you *everything,*" her fading voice hissed one last time.

Then she was gone, leaving the smoking throne, and an empty obsidian dress.

"He can give me more," Blaze whispered, an exhausted smile crossing her perspiration-drenched face.

Adalric struggled to get up but fell back to the floor again as Blaze stumbled to his side. Already they could hear the distant clanging of running boots far down the hallway.

Without hesitation they fell into each other's arms, fighting back their pain with the joy of having survived. Blaze pulled back to arms' length and gazed over his broken form, hardly believing he was the proud overlord she admired so long ago. "It would seem," she finally said with a light laugh, as tears of relief and happiness misted her eyes, "that the prophecy was true after all...I have ended your life as you knew it, haven't I?"

Despite his pain, Adalric felt himself smile, and pulled her back into his arms. He held her tightly as he stroked her hair with his free hand, reveling in the consuming fires of their love. "Rule this Imperium with me," he asked, his dry voice echoing with new strength.

Blaze pulled back from him again, her eyes trying to penetrate his eyeshields to read what was behind. "What are you asking?"

"I am taking this Imperium, Blaze," he said, while slowly forcing himself to his feet, "and I want you to be my queen." With his powerful hands, he pulled her upward. "Rule with me, side by side. One voice."

Blaze fell into his arms as he held her close. She stood there silently, enjoying the warmth of his body, feeling his psionic bond grow despite his broken state, and knew what her answer had to be. "I would stand by your side, even if you were facing the entire Alliance single-handedly. I would be proud to be your queen...and love to be your wife."

Their lips met as the passions which bonded them together pulled in closely, sealing forever their two lives as one.

Chapter Twenty-eight
Reception

The resilience of the Imperium astounded Blaze, for she expected great turmoil to follow the death of the old sovereign. However, Adalric had many followers, and with Koroqo backing him with the strength of the S'teka, there were few who objected to his coronation as sovereign of the Red Star Imperium, less than a week after the Dire Queen's death.

~ * ~

The view of Nyx's moon was most impressive from the *Sentinel's* main officers club, and so it had become one of Blaze's favorite lounges. It was there that she sat at a small table, going over final details with Admiral Steward. Her brow furrowed, she had no time for this. There were inspections to be made, delegates to be met and more files to be read than she ever thought she could finish. She found it difficult to concentrate on anything with so many people staring at her wherever she went. As usual, her presence in this club was of major interest to all the officers who relaxed here, both senior and junior. Admiral Steward and she ignored the spectators, as they searched for lost details, safe in the knowledge that Travis would keep anyone who was too nosy at a distance.

"They stare like they've never seen me before," Blaze said as she sighed quietly. She absently scanned over some last-minute holographic dress designs, while her mind, in truth, was concentrating on whether or not her colonial expansion plan was feasible, and when would be a good time to discuss it.

"It's difficult for them," Joshua Steward said with a light laugh. "Hell, I've known you the longest and I still can't believe what has happened." He let out a fatherly smile as he reached over and placed his hand over hers. "When I saw you there on the sidewalk, dejected at being turned down as a Legionnaire, I knew even then you were destined for greatness…but I never expected to one day call you Queen."

Blaze's eyes widened as they searched her mentor for the support she needed. Her grip on his hand tightened slightly as her smile broadened.

"I suppose what I'm trying to say is that I'm very proud of you."

"That's why I asked you to give me away at the wedding ceremony. I couldn't imagine anyone else doing it."

A light pink flush colored the admiral's ears, and he looked down for a moment as he tried to control his blush.

Blaze let out a sweet laugh, then she felt her smile melt away. "I still can hardly believe that everything happened less than a month ago."

"The end of an era best forgotten," Joshua reassured. "There is still a war to be won against the Alliance, and soon Lady Drusee-la will be awaiting new orders from the two of you."

She nodded woodenly, as she absorbed his advice. "You are right, Joshua," she consented, trying to sound official, internally calculating what those orders would be.

"But the ceremony is tonight."

"…tonight," she whispered, her skin tingling into rows of unexpected goosebumps.

Admiral Steward read her face and smiled warmly. "Not having second thoughts, are you? After all, being the forerunner of a great Imperial dynasty is no easy task."

"No," she assured him, "no second thoughts. It just seems to me that the most bizarre things happen in my life, and most are not at all what I planned." She inhaled deeply and smiled. "Forerunner of a great dynasty? I don't think so. But this *is* a fantastic Imperium, and I intend to make sure it stays that way." She flashed a tiny wink. "Besides, I hear the new sovereign is in over his head, and needs a strong presence to guide him along, laced with just the right feminine touch to keep him in line."

"It seems you have matters well in hand, Blaze."

"Yes," she agreed, sharing his joy with her new sense of self contentment. "I think I finally do."

~ * ~

Tanus Adalric stood at the far end of the ballroom, overwhelmingly pleased that he finally was being left alone. He hated such affairs, and the fact this one was in his honor made it no less unbearable. As the wedding celebration was but an hour old, the attention had finally been diverted to the other guest of honor.

"Where is she?" he voiced aloud, unaware he had done so.

"The delegates from *Limbo* are talking with her now," Koroqo pointed out as he approached his friend from behind. "Adalric, this reception is supposed to be for you *and* Blaze, and you haven't even danced with her yet."

Adalric flashed a glare at his companion.

"I know," the Proximan said with a quiet laugh, "overlords don't dance. But look at her…"

Both men's attention were drawn across the large hall, to the new young queen as she patiently listened to the incessant pleas and demands of her subjects. Her long scarlet dress complimented her supple tan skin, and her silken hair was regally pulled up to accent the strong yet delicate line of her jaw, as she quietly explained to the delegates the laws of need versus capital the Imperium had to spend.

Adalric felt his lips go dry as he watched the hordes of young men surround his new wife, handsome and dashing officers in full dress uniforms. She smiled back at her admirers and laughed politely at their humor, charming yet never suggestive.

"A most impressive woman," Koroqo said as he observed the tension building in his friend. "Still, she *is* a woman, a woman who needs attention…if you don't provide it…I'm sure some other man will be glad to."

The new sovereign felt his hands form into fists as a cavalier senior officer offered the queen his hand and led her out onto the dance floor. A space was cleared as the two of them began to dance, moving toward the center of the ballroom. Adalric was about to turn away in anger, when he caught Blaze flashing him a smile. It was not much, the briefest glance. When her lips curled gently toward him, his anger drained like light into a

Black Hole. He checked on the ruby broach which held his gold-trimmed, crimson and black cloak in place, then he pushed his friend aside. "I'm going to dance with my wife."

Koroqo's smile spread to a huge grin. "I thought overlords didn't dance."

"They don't," Adalric agreed, the corners of his lips resisting a smile, "but emperors most certainly do."

He left the S'teka master behind as he quickly crossed the ballroom floor with a few powerful strides.

The guests grew silent as the sovereign approached the dancing pair, even the music died to low murmur. He placed his gloved hand on the officer's braided shoulder, gently yet forcefully turning him about.

"I think the first dance should be mine, Commodore," Adalric informed him, his countenance masking his true desires.

Blaze's eyes lit up as the officer bowed and stepped aside, allowing the sovereign to take his new wife into his arms. Everyone remained silent for a few more seconds, then the music began again, as Adalric began to sweep Blaze across the shimmering floor.

"You received my message," Blaze said as she let out a soft chuckle and lovingly pulled him tightly in. "I was hoping you'd dance the first dance with me."

"The first, the second, and all the ones after that," Adalric assured her, breaking his stoic facade to flash her a quick smile. "I love you, and don't ever want to see you in another man's arms again."

"Well then," she responded with a playful grin, "you'll have to keep my attention, I get bored easily."

"You do?" he asked while slowing to the softer music which began filling the grand room. "I will have to strive to keep your life entertaining."

"Knowing you," Blaze said as she caught her breath, "that shouldn't be too difficult." She drew herself close to him, placing her head against his chest. "You know I'll never let another woman touch you."

"I know."

"I also want you to free any *special* prisoners you have left."

"Long since gone," he responded knowingly, then pulled her out to a gentle spin, bringing her back in close again.

"I love you too," she finally said, reveling in the truth which accompanied that sensation. Everything was perfect in her mind, yet somewhere, far in the back, there was still a question to be answered. She achieved more than her wildest dreams, but as she skimmed back across the dance floor, the eyes of the Imperium on her, she began to wonder at what cost.

~ * ~

Drusee-la leaned back on her bed in her suite aboard the flagship. She regretted she was missing the great changes in the heart of the Imperium, both coronations and the wedding, but knew how important keeping the front lines safe was. Already the word came in that the flagship was to be renamed the *Exodus*, since it was to lead the Imperium back across the stars to one day rule the planet Earth. Not that she cared much for the name of the vessel, all that mattered to her was it was hers to command, by decree of the new emperor and empress. She had heard the death of the Dire Queen had been a traumatic battle but was more than impressed by the end results.

Her new Narman bodyguard stood stoically inside the doorway, always prepared to defend her life. She found herself purring as she watched the low lights of the room play delicately across his muscular frame. Such thoughts she forced aside as she rose and checked herself in the mirror. She brushed a stray lock of fur back into place and gave herself a last-minute seal of approval.

"We're going to the bridge," she informed her Shadowguard, then exited the room.

Crew members quickly stepped aside as she strode down the corridors, her white-furred chin held high with a great sense of pride as she walked the length of her ship. Finally, she arrived on the bridge and allowed her smile to grow as the Narman guard stepped in first, making way for her.

"All rise," he commanded the bridge staff, "Drusee-la, Overlord of the Imperium, is entering the bridge."

Chapter Twenty-nine
Repercussions

"How could you do this?" the Dire Queen demanded as Blaze fell to her knees before her, the intense pain growing. "I trusted you. I saved your life when Adalric wanted to destroy it …and this is the way you repay my kindness? I always expect ambition in my servants, but you have *betrayed* me."

"But Regine—"

"Don't call me that," she howled, her blackness intensifying like a growing storm. "I treated you like a friend, a daughter, and you gave that up for the carnal pleasures of a man."

"I love him," Blaze defended herself, confused by the accusations. "I could no more destroy him than myself."

"I loved you also," the Dire Queen said, her hissing voice taking a softer tone, "you were like the daughter I never had."

"No," Blaze yelled, her soul angered by the false emotions she was expected to grieve over. She slowly brought out the blue jewel with the crimson Cosmic Nodule in it, deliberately taunting the Dire Queen with it. "Regine, you are not capable of love."

Her full lips curled into a sadistic smile as she hurled the jewel forward, destroying the former sovereign forever.

"And you think you are?" the Dire Queen's voice hissed one last time as the spectral shape dissipated into nothingness.

"How can you kill without emotion," asked the voice behind her, "like some cruel machine?"

She whirled around at the accusation, to find Travis standing behind her and the burning capitol building on the *April* colony silhouetting his armored body.

"What?" she asked, dazed by the transformation.

"You kill without mercy," Travis continued, each word stinging her flesh, "without compassion, and without hesitation. Beware of Blaze the Executioner."

She glanced over at the collapsed capitol building, remembering the crushed governor inside. "He was too scared to escape when we asked him to. I didn't kill him, he killed himself."

"You could have saved him. His blood is on your hands as surely as if you used your sword. You hated him, and you let him die."

"I didn't hate him," she defended, "he was incompetent."

"He asked you for sex to allow you into the Imperium and still turned you down anyway."

"I never..." she said, her voice growing hoarse.

"He would have turned you down regardless..."

"He was a bastard," she replied, her anger returning with the memory.

"So, you killed him."

"He deserved to die..."

Travis nodded at her sadly.

Blaze's lips parted in fury as she realized what she had said, then felt depression hit her like a hammer. "That's not why he died...I *didn't* kill him."

"You most certainly did," Sloan yelled as she pointed to the still flaming body which lay at the foot of their booth in the bar. "I never would have thought you could be so callous."

Blaze glanced around at the many accusatory faces in the bar, hearing their whispers... *"killer", "butcherer", "sadistic demoness", "she's like the Dire Queen, worse maybe."* She covered her ears as she fell onto the bench, gazing up at the betrayed faces of her former friends.

"He was right," Sloan said, "you used your power, and it consumed you. You've become the thing of evil *he* hoped you never would."

"Who are you talking about?" Blaze asked, feeling a lump form in her throat at the torturous words of her companions.

"You know who," Sloan stated flatly.

"How could you do this to us?" Rabies cried. "I thought you liked us."

Suddenly Blaze remembered why she was here, then reached over and grabbed the rodent by the scruff of the neck and lifted him over the table. "Give me the disk," she demanded, causing Rabies to squeal even more. "Give it to me or I'll fry you like the others."

"You knew we had the disk all this time," Sloan yelled, "but now we're your enemy for trying to use it?"

Blaze's grip on Rabies tightened. "You attacked the *Wraith* and killed hundreds of Legionnaires...*I was a Legionnaire,* and you both knew that."

"You're hurting me," pleaded Rabies with short gasps.

"Shut up, rat," Blaze yelled back at him as she tried to shake the disk loose.

"I'm not a rat," Rabies squeaked, "I'm a Jarbban."

Blaze caught Sloan's movement out of the corner of her eyes, barely summoning her pyrokinetic powers before her old companion could shoot her dead. The explosion barely drowned the horrific screams...

"More blood for me?" Sinclair whispered from behind.

She whirled to face her lost friend, shocked at the blood which trickled down in a slow stream along his chin. He pulled his cloak tightly about him, as his lips parted to reveal the crimson-stained fangs. Her eyes were locked in an icy stare as his image disappeared into a cool mist, smelling of fresh snow.

"We should be more *cooperative,*" Alliance technician Boone taunted as she twisted around and fell back into the chair, straps binding her tightly.

Blaze glanced nervously around at the sterile walls of the "tomb of horrors", pulling frantically as she tried to escape the torture that was to come. "Why couldn't it be you who I killed?" she yelled while shaking her head violently back and forth.

"Is that why you've killed so callously?" asked an unknown voice to her left. "Are you trying to make up for the ones you couldn't kill?"

Blaze glanced over, to stare into Jenkins' lifeless eyes. "What did you say?"

Her former fellow inmate gave no recognition as he turned away and left the room. The energy waves from the "chair" struck her as a scream left her lips.

"Why did I even bother to save you?" the Proximan Alliance cadet accused angrily as she gazed down on Blaze's numb body. "I spared your life so you could slaughter thousands of my people?"

"Zakaja," the exhausted TelSor tried to defend herself as the energy beam faded away, "you don't understand. The Imperium must survive, and the United Star Alliance stands in its way."

"The Alliance is good," Zakaja insisted. "That makes you evil."

"The Alliance killed Sinclair."

"I never wanted you to use that as an excuse to kill in my name," Sinclair stated sadly to her right. "I think you know that, Angel."

"You don't understand," she defended again, but he was gone.

"Angelina Calida Sierra Pagán," came the voice of doom, "you have been found guilty of murder in the second degree, in the case of the deceased Captain Patrick Rand."

"He was a pirate and a killer," Blaze said, as she turned to face the Alliance judge, her mind envisioning the pirate captain who had once held a young girl's infatuation. He was the first man she had ever loved, the first man she ever killed. "He was about to waste an Alliance battleship captain, and I nailed him barely in time to save her life."

"You murdered him in cold blood."

"*He* was the murderer," she protested. "Why do you care about him? He was a two-bit crook, a smuggler, pirate, and bounty hunter who killed in the name of the Red Star Pirates."

"How is that different from what you do now?" accused a tired voice from behind.

Blaze felt her senses reel as she turned toward the voice, falling to her knees in dumb confusion. She opened her eyes to see Sinclair's dying body in her arms, as the hot desert sands blew into her eyes. "They'll pay for this," she swore bitterly, her throat tightening as the memory fully resurfaced.

"No," Sinclair shook his head weakly as he gently stroked her moistened face. "I told you to release the hate."

"It's all I have now," she whispered back, as tears flowed down her cheeks.

"Don't let your power consume you, it will lead to more evil."

"I don't understand," Blaze cried, her whole body screaming out in rage and anguish.

"You will someday," he said as he coughed through a crooked half-grin. "Take care, my little Blaze."

"Don't leave me again," she begged as his body dissipated in her arms, abandoning her in total blackness. For what seemed an eternity she remained kneeling, oblivious to her darkened surroundings, then the slightest red glow caught her attention, dragging her out of her state of self-wallowing. The Imperial throne stood before her, and instantly she recognized the obsidian hooded image which sat there, a hollow cackle issuing from behind the luminous crimson eyes.

"I destroyed you," Blaze said, barely able to rise back to her feet from exhaustion.

"You can't destroy me," the Dire Queen said while laughing cruelly. Her hood fell back, revealing Blaze's own image within the ebony dress. "We are one and the same."

Blaze's scream echoed throughout the darkness, as her senses finally collapsed, and oblivion set in.

~ * ~

Adalric felt the mental shock vibrate through the Cosmic Aura as surely as if another TelSor attacked him psionically. He quickly turned over in his large bed to find his young wife tossing and turning, tears rolling down her slumbering face. He felt his heart ache at the sight of her distress but could easily read the turmoil within her subconscious soul.

He reached out a strong hand and gently brushed a dampened lock of hair off her cheeks as he leaned over and lightly touched his lips to hers. "I went through this also, Blaze," he quietly comforted, even though he knew she could not hear him. "I would help you, but this is a question you must answer for yourself…just as I had to for myself." He lay back down, while letting out a saddened sigh of remembrance. "I love you," he whispered once more, then gently placed his arm over her and returned to sleep.

Chapter Thirty
In the Name of the Imperium

Blaze leaned against the wall in the operation center, rubbing her weary eyes as her husband continued to conduct business with Admiral Steward and the new strike force which was to meet with Drusee-la and the *Exodus* at the Alliance front lines. She hated to back away from the discussion early, but rarely had she felt so exhausted. Glancing down at her bright-red bodysuit, she tried to clear her mind enough to return to the strategic meeting. She had considered changing her look, since she was a sovereign now, and no longer a baroness. However, this was the look which she was comfortable with, and Adalric had not changed much other than to permanently keep the golden trim on his cloak. She forced herself to concentrate on the admiral's assault schedule for the recently repaired and renamed *Wraith*. Wondering if it was too aggressive, as she tried to forget the events that plagued her nightmares. Suddenly she chuckled with soft irony, grateful that at least the horrid nightmares of the night before failed to bring back Reaper's death on Tenebrous, as they most often did. What she did not understand was why her dreams caused her to wake up needing to vomit, or this incessant state of nausea that was finally starting to fade as the morning dwindled into afternoon. Silently she vowed never to eat so much at a celebration again.

She watched Baron Koroqo enter the command center, and cross over to her at the far wall. He gave her his usual warm smile but frowned as he studied her more closely.

"Are you all right, my Queen?"

For an instant Blaze forgot it was she who bore that title, then she smiled at the Proximan. "I had a lousy night," she said with a forced laugh, "so I'm taking a break. Does it show that badly?"

"Of course not," he reassured her with his usual suave charm. "But don't forget your emotions are not as easily hidden. Why was your night lousy, if I may ask?"

Blaze hesitated for an instant, then reconsidered, wondering if a friend was what she needed. "I had a nightmare," she said, "a really bad one. Could we talk about it later?"

Koroqo raised an eyebrow in curiosity. "Of course, how about the officer's club at two. It's usually deserted at that time."

Blaze nodded gratefully. "Thank you, Troy."

Then the S'teka master nodded, signifying his excuse, and turned toward her husband. "Sovereign Adalric," he said as he approached the tight conference. "They are ready for the two of you on the main flight deck."

Adalric turned to Koroqo. "Thank you, we'll head there right away." He glanced back at Joshua. "Admiral, I'm sure you would like to join us."

"For an inspection of the S'teka, I would be honored."

"There are some last-minute details I have to attend to, your majesty," Koroqo explained, "so I will meet you on the flight deck."

Adalric glanced over at his wife, concerned at her quiet and withdrawn behavior. "Blaze, you are coming, aren't you?"

Blaze shook her head. "I think I'm going to go to the observation deck and catch my breath. I'll see you in a little while."

Adalric nodded, understanding fully that she needed time alone, to settle her own accounts. With a wave of his hand, he motioned for the admiral and his guards to follow, as they left the *Sentinel's* command center.

~ * ~

Blaze leaned against the large picture window on the observation deck, grateful that no one else was there to bother her. Even Travis had been kind enough to wait outside, to ensure her solitude. Her stomach pains had subsided, and she was finally relaxing after her long night. She tried to think about the possible meanings of her strange dreams. They had seemed so real, yet already many parts faded from memory. She was looking forward to talking with Koroqo. Not that she couldn't talk with her husband, but she knew he would probably tell her to stay in control of her emotions. There was a sensitivity about the Proximan noble which transcended normal communications. She considered that perhaps it was his empathy, but regardless, he was always helpful in solving her feelings. She supposed it was that quality which made him the one person, besides herself, that Adalric trusted…

Tanus…something is wrong. Her veins froze as the premonition struck her square on. "My love," she whispered, suddenly afraid for him, as she turned and ran from the observation deck.

~ * ~

Tanus Adalric strode along the corridor which led to the main flight deck of the *Sentinel*, where the fighter craft were launched from, each footfall ringing with the pride he felt. Rows of Legionnaires would be standing there like stone statues, awaiting his command, plus all of Koroqo's S'teka. The soldiers had always shown reverence to him, but there was a difference now. He was their ruler and could feel the change within his people. Slowly his lips curled in a smile of self-satisfaction. They had finally won, both he and Blaze together.

"This is quite a change for them," Admiral Steward commented as they moved through the corridors. "They're used to serving a queen who hid from view her entire rule, while you were her eyes, ears, and voice. Perhaps that's why they flocked to your banner so easily."

"Perhaps," Adalric agreed, shocked at the level of informality the Admiral was taking with him. He thought of a time, not so long ago, when such actions would have been cause for his instant reprisal, but not anymore. He glanced over at the man who was chiefly responsible for his wife's introduction into the Imperium, and was glad to have the admiral beside him now. "It is good for people to see their rulers. It gives them a sense of belonging to a proud Imperium. Besides," he added with a grin, "I think our people are infatuated with their new queen."

Suddenly he slowed and his smile vanished, sensing a change in the regular background noise, as they turned down a deserted section of the corridor.

The ceiling above them erupted as six black-garbed warriors in skin-tight uniforms and masks fell to the ground, short laserblades in their outstretched hands.

"Death to Adalric," was said by all six as they struck, killing two of the Shadowguards before they could react.

Admiral Steward pulled his pistol free of its holster but stiffened as the cauterizing blade entered his back from behind. For a moment his face registered the horrified realization of the deadly blow, then he silently fell against the wall and went down.

"S'teka," Adalric whispered in wonder and anguish. He pulled his electrosword free and ignited it, while sending a crippling psionic blast at his closest assailant. The black-garbed warrior's eyes exploded as he shrieked in agony and fell. At the same time, the last of Adalric's Shadowguards managed to send a lethal electrified energy blast searing into another of the assassins with his carbine.

Two of them came at the guard at once, and he barely had time to wound one of them as the laserblade from the other attacker penetrated the Shadowguard's helmet and cauterized his brain.

Adalric swung viciously at the wounded assassin who foolishly turned his back, practically slicing the warrior in two as the rank odor of charred flesh permeated the tight corridor. Then agony flashed white as a laserblade buried into his side from behind, causing searing heat to flush through his system. He started to collapse as he swung his weapon around, decapitating the inflictor of his pain in a spray of scarlet rain.

As the last two assassins closed in on the blood-covered sovereign, they paused as the clattering of boots resounded down the hall. Four more Shadowguards rounded the corner, with Blaze in the lead. Both of the black garbed warriors leapt with swift grace toward the aperture in the ceiling.

"Stop them!" Blaze yelled fiercely as she ran to the side of her fallen husband. She didn't need to see the blackened flesh on his side for her heart to fill with anger and pain. Her eyes locked on the fleeing assassins with fury. *"Die,"* she called after them, her voice a cold low murmur, as she sent forth a brilliant ball of flame from her hand. The superheated blast caught one of the escaping warriors, his intense whelp of pain was his final sound as he fell back to the floor. The second made it into the ceiling, and was gone.

"Get more help," Blaze ordered Travis. "That assassin is not to escape from this base. Bring medical teams here now."

The Shadowguards scattered, leaping over the fallen bodies to carry out her orders. "I want that person brought to me alive," she yelled after them again, "no one is to kill him but me."

Adalric's dry lips twisted into a sour grin, then winced in pain. "The wound went deep," he told her.

"The medics will be here soon, Tanus," she whispered to him as she held him tightly, refusing to allow death to snatch him away from her.

"They were S'teka," he said to her, still in shock. "I thought I could trust him."

Blaze nodded thoughtfully as she surveyed the grisly scene around them. There was no denying it, they seemed exactly like Koroqo's prized warriors. She reached out gingerly to the closest corpse and pulled off his mask, revealing the pale white skin and pointed ears. "Proximans," she whispered. She turned back to her husband. "This proves nothing, love. Koroqo once told me the S'teka were founded on Proxima many centuries ago. That planet is inside the United Star Alliance. Maybe these are Alliance S'teka, and not Koroqo's at all."

Adalric nodded as he fought to stay awake. "Perhaps you are right but stay on guard…and promise me that none of the assassins will survive."

"That is an easy oath to give, Tanus." She held him a moment longer until the medics arrived and began to gently place him on an antigrav stretcher.

The doctor looked him over for a moment and shook his head with grave worry, then turned to the queen. "It's a bad wound…I'll do my best," he informed her, hoping she would understand his curt words.

He glared at his medics. "Let's go!" he commanded, ushering his team quickly along.

Blaze felt a wave of fear course through her body as she watched her husband pushed swiftly down the corridor, then her eyes caught sight of Joshua, still slumped against the wall where he fell. She sped to his side and immediately lifted his limp head into her lap. She looked down into his seemingly lifeless face and felt a tightening in her throat. Then she softly touched his shoulder and pulled in a sharp breath when she heard a slight moan. "Medic, here too."

Medics quickly moved the admiral away also, leaving her reeling with uncertainty as she watched both her adopted father and new husband whisked away to the medical wing. Her anguish was broken by a low groan from the assassin which she had burned while attempting to escape, and she realized he was still alive. She let the remaining medic check the rest of the Shadowguards, as she knelt over the prone S'teka and pulled off his mask. The young Proximan glared at the queen in defiance, then he quickly scanned for his lost weapon.

"Is this what you're looking for?" Blaze asked as she activated the fallen laserblade and held it up to his face. Her voice quivered slightly from her internal rage as she pushed the luminous blade within an inch of the Proximan's nose. His look of bravado faded to fear as he tried to slide away, but he was against a wall, there was nowhere for him to go. "Who sent you?" she demanded.

"Why should I tell the Crimson Queen anything?"

"Crimson Queen?" Blaze asked, a sad smile coming to her lips. "Is that what I am called?"

The Proximan warrior nodded.

"I've never heard that," Blaze stated quietly. "Which means you're from the Alliance, as I suspected...but are there any more of you here?"

He glared up at her with his coal black eyes but said nothing.

She considered torturing him for the information she needed, but her smile turned into an angry grin. Slowly she allowed her mind to force its way into his. Like an electrosword piercing flesh, Blaze's thoughts drove through him with a blinding rage which even his natural Proximan defenses couldn't defy. The young S'teka let out a silent shriek as the desired knowledge was ruthlessly ripped out of his mind. Blaze nodded silently as a satisfied breath was slowly released, then she allowed her psychic probe to sharply twist, tearing the fabric of his brain with such force that cerebral fluid and blood erupted from his ears and nose.

Blaze stood, dropping the weapon on the dead assassin's body. "Get me Baron Koroqo," she ordered her remaining Shadowguard. "If anyone can catch this last assassin, his people can."

~ * ~

Blaze leaned back in her chair in the officer's club, wanting to do anything but relax and discuss her emotional problems. But with Koroqo's S'teka and her Shadowguards scouring the *Sentinel* for the missing Alliance assassin, there was nothing she could do but wait…and she hated waiting. She felt helpless. Without knowing the identity of the assassin, she couldn't even use her powers to pinpoint his thoughts.

"How is Tanus?" Koroqo asked, showing genuine concern as he gazed at the queen from next to the table.

Blaze glanced up, suddenly grateful for the Proximan's presence. "He's sleeping now, but the doctors say he'll be fine."

Koroqo reached out with his pale hand and squeezed her shoulder tightly, as she placed her delicate fingers over his.

"Thank you," she whispered, feeling his tremendous relief, and concern. "Joshua is still in critical condition, they aren't sure about him and even if he lives, he'll possibly never walk again."

"Admiral Steward is strong," Koroqo said as he sat down. "Don't count him out yet."

As the Proximan finally settled into his seat, she glanced around the large dining hall, pausing at the one wall which was open to the stars, covered by a large picture window. "You were right, at this hour no one is down here."

"I often choose this time to dine here," Koroqo said absently, his casual words covering his emotions.

Blaze turned her attention to him, sensing the Proximan's continued unease. "You're still worried about him, aren't you?"

"I'm concerned that he let his guard down so easily," Koroqo explained. "The fact that the assassins were S'teka troubles me tenfold."

"We'll catch the last one," Blaze stated coldly, her eyes frosting over at the memory of her wounded husband, and possibly crippled friend. "When we do, I will quite enjoy what I'm going to do to him."

Koroqo raised an eyebrow at the strong emotions that were projected toward him. "Which brings us to your dreams."

Blaze felt her face flush as she realized how transparent she had been. The memories of the dream came rushing back, accented by her recent butchering of the assassin she caught. She tried to make sense out of her concerns but failed. Finally, her voice found its way to the real question. "Are we the bad guys? Corrupt and evil, like Earth and the Alliance would have everyone believe?"

"That's a strange thing to ask," Koroqo said with surprise. "Do you think we are?"

"I don't know," Blaze admitted. "I know that in the Alliance I've seen chaos and poverty, injustice and inhumanity. In the Alliance I've known terror, grief and betrayal," she continued in a low voice which seemed to come from a great distance. "Here in the Imperium, I've known safety, pride...and love. Yet, the Imperium was founded by greedy, malicious pirates...and ruled by a creature that was barely this side of being a demon."

"Which you played a paramount part in changing," he reminded her. "None of us liked the Dire Queen, but she ruled out of fear...and that was good for a time."

"How so?"

"Fear kept a loose gang of pirates and mercenaries together long enough to establish a military order. Don't be ashamed of our beginnings, Blaze. Some of the greatest empires throughout history were founded on the high spirits of thieves, convicts, and other outcasts. It's what you do once you are there that matters." He paused as he watched her nod her agreement. "But that's not what you really wanted to ask, is it? You love this Imperium as much as any of us could, that's apparent in your every move. The trouble is *you* think you're evil, and that's what strangles your thoughts."

"I see things in my mind which haunt me," she whispered, "people I've killed. It seems that number grows every day. I feel regret for their deaths, but I don't mind killing those who deserve it. I don't know the answer."

"Who was he?" Koroqo asked quietly, reading through the wall of confusion which had previously masked her feelings. "He must have been quite special if his death placed this burden on your soul."

"How did you know?"

"I was not born here," he replied thoughtfully. "I was once a person of great importance on Proxima, with a wife and child that I loved dearly. My wife died in my arms, begging me to give up being a S'teka and take care of our young daughter." He hesitated for a moment as he gazed into Blaze's eyes. "You see, my wife was killed by mistake, the assassination attempt was intended to kill me."

"Who did it?" Blaze asked. "Did you avenge your wife's death?"

"Every day of my life," he responded sadly. "Rather than heeding her request, I started a crusade of vengeance which led to my dismissal from the Alliance Secret Service, and eventually to my instatement here in the Red Star Imperium.

"Instead of taking care of my daughter, my hatred drove her away. Every night I've questioned my actions, and every morning I've come up with the same conclusion…the very conclusions which keep me sane."

"What are they?" Blaze asked quietly, almost afraid of the answer.

"That *I've* chosen the life I lead, and nothing can change that. I don't view my actions as good or evil, but as what is necessary. I've chosen to serve *here* because it's all the Alliance is not, and that's good."

Blaze stared down at the table, then lifted her brandy in silence, half expecting answers to form on its obsidian surface. She swirled the thick red liquid, allowing her abilities to heat it. "His name was Sinclair," she finally spoke. "He was killed by an agent of the Alliance." She sipped from the glass, letting the warm liquid slide down her throat. "He was a harmless soul who never hurt anyone. I can't think of anyone who deserved to die less. He was hit by an energy bolt meant for me," she finally voiced, as her eyes misted over, "and I think I've hated myself for that ever since. With his last breath, he warned me never to use my power, because it would lead to evil. Perhaps he's right, all I've done is kill with it."

"You're wrong, Blaze," Koroqo disagreed, as he reached over the small table and gently placed his hand back on hers. "When you were a Shadowguard, I saw you use your gifts to save Adalric's life, even though you knew that in doing so you would risk death by revealing yourself to him."

"He almost did kill me," she said with an ironic laugh. "The Dire Queen saved me…and I repaid her mercy by betraying and killing her."

"She saved you to *use* you, and nothing more. There was no mercy in her actions," he replied strongly. "Don't you realize that?"

Despite herself, she found she had to nod in agreement. "I suppose I wanted Regine to like me so much I blinded myself to the truth. But in my dream, she said I was no better than her."

"Do you believe that?"

"If I knew the answer to that, I wouldn't need to be talking about this now."

They both gazed at each other in silence, then let out a light laugh.

"It seems every time I get a grip on my feelings, something changes," Blaze finally continued. "Like my old companions doing something to hurt the Imperium, or meeting with a governor who used to be a sergeant I despised."

"Life is adversity," Koroqo said with a warm chuckle. "Otherwise, it would be quite dull."

"So," Blaze asked, suddenly hoping to change the subject, "how long has it been since you saw your daughter?"

"Almost ten years now," he admitted, an almost wistful look settling in his eyes. He suddenly turned his face up to the ceiling and stared at it intently. Then he glanced back at the new queen and smiled. "It's been quite some time."

"What was that all about?" Blaze asked while motioning to the ceiling where he had stared.

"I don't know," Koroqo tried to explain. "Merely a feeling I'd thought I'd forgotten." He glanced down at his wrist chronometer, then back at the ceiling. "I really must get back to the manhunt," he explained as he stood. "I hope I've been of some help."

Blaze judged her companion with some concern, sure he was concealing something which was bothering him. "Yes, you have, though I don't know exactly how."

Baron Koroqo walked over to the doorway, then turned back to the queen. "Blaze, it's simply a question you must ask yourself and no one else can answer. It doesn't rely on promises given to deceased relatives or friends, or even to a sworn code of life. All that matters is how you really feel about yourself. Ask yourself, Blaze, do you think that you're evil?"

Blaze stared blankly at the Proximan noble as she tried to sort through the confusion which still permeated her every thought. In the end, she remained silent, and Koroqo finally left her in the officers' mess hall alone.

It was almost two hours later when Travis burst through the door to find her still sitting where the S'teka master had left her. He patiently waited at her side, remaining silent.

Blaze finally glanced up to recognize him, motioning him to speak.

"My queen," her Shadowguard informed her with pride. "We've caught the last assassin."

~ * ~

Blaze had to exhibit great control not to pace back and forth as she waited in the main detention level's interrogation room. It had been a few minutes since her arrival, but her Shadowguards and Koroqo's S'teka still had not brought the prisoner to her.

"Here they come," Travis informed her quietly as the main doors opened. A team of Koroqo's S'teka entered proudly, wearing their ceremonial red sashes. They were followed by the Shadowguards who led the prisoner before them. From the assassin's stance and shape, Blaze quickly deduced it was a woman, despite the concealing S'teka garb. The prisoner's ebony clothing was covered in soot and grime, causing Blaze to realize that a sterner security system was needed in the *Sentinel's* air ducts.

Blaze's Shadowguards pushed the prisoner up to the queen and forced her to her knees. The captured S'teka tried to rise back to her feet, but the guards forced her roughly back down into submission before their queen.

"Let her rise," Blaze commanded coldly, her voice devoid of emotion.

Her dark eyes were full of anger as she glared at the prisoner, her thoughts dwelling upon the odds that *this* survivor was the one who almost killed her husband or Joshua. Her mouth twisted into a wicked grin, as she contemplated the agonizing death this one would face.

The prisoner met Blaze's eyes, showing no fear as she faced the enemy. Rising silently, she straightened her shoulders and glanced at her numerous captors.

Blaze mentally measured the intruder before her — alone, trapped, surrounded by the enemy. Visions of Tenebrous sprung to her mind, but she extinguished that fire with the memory of Joshua's trauma, and Tanus' last command to her.

Moments of silence hung as they stared at each other, prisoner and Imperial Sovereign, until the captured S'teka finally found her voice. "Aren't you going to ask questions? Demand to know military secrets?"

Blaze shook her head slightly. "I already got everything I needed from your companion before I executed him."

The prisoner's eyes flashed in hatred, and Blaze felt the emotional backlash, causing her to remember her captive was a Proximan.

"I know that feeling too, S'teka," Blaze consoled her without intending to. "The Alliance has cost me as much as I'm sure we have cost you."

"I doubt that," the prisoner replied, allowing her rage to fuel her steadfast resolve. "Your Imperium has cost me *everything* I hold dear. How could you possibly understand that?"

Despite herself, Blaze began to smile. With a slow but steady motion, she reached over and pulled off the prisoner's cowl, revealing the young face beneath. For an instant her thoughts froze as her captive's features set in, then she blinked twice in disbelief. "Zakaja?" she whispered, hoping her memories were wrong, but knowing they were not.

The prisoner lost her angered stance at the recognition of her name, and her lips parted in surprise. "Do I know you?"

The young queen nodded, then turned away from her, feeling the pain of the nightmare return. She was half desperate to remind Zakaja that the Proximan saved her life back on the *Phoenix* rehabilitation colony, and half hoped the young S'teka didn't remember. Finally, Blaze turned back to the prisoner. "I thought you were going into the Alliance Navy, in psychology."

"How did you know that?" Zakaja asked, her voice displaying her shock. "The Navy was an Alliance cover for me while I trained as a S'teka. That's classified information you could never possibly..." Suddenly her voice fell silent as she stopped seeing Blaze as the enemy Imperial sovereign, the feared Crimson Queen, and truly looked at her for the first time. "You're Angel—"

"You're mistaken," Blaze blurted out before she knew it.

"No," Zakaja pursued, her defensive posture momentarily forgotten,

"I'm not. I'd heard the new Imperial queen had risen from nothing, but I never realized how true that statement was."

Blaze felt her anger returning, and realized she should end this now, before it became too intricate. "That was another life, another person. Now you are the enemy, an enemy who almost killed my husband."

"The sovereign *survived*?" Zakaja asked in shock as if struck by a vicious blow as she hung her head in burning shame. A lone tear drifted down her ivory cheek, as she fought to regain her standing.

Blaze's anger faded back into confusion, as she read the mixed emotions of hatred and utter despair within the S'teka. "I don't understand. How could my husband's death mean that much to you? What hold does the Alliance have on you?"

"It's not that," Zakaja replied in outrage, her tears flowing freely now. "Adalric's people *ripped* my family apart and stole the one person who could put it all back together again. Adalric deserves more than death...but I have failed."

Blaze felt a cold flush which sent tingles down her spine, as the curve of Zakaja's jaw, the sharp angle of her tall ears, and the familiar glint in her eyes revealed a now obvious truth. "You're Koroqo's daughter," she said, startled by the realization, and in wonderment of how she had missed it before.

Zakaja wiped away her tears and forced her body to stand proud and tall. "Troivaka Koroqo was a great man, and Adalric turned him into a twisted thing of evil. I'll never forgive the sovereign for that, for stealing my father."

"Or forgive your father for letting it happen? You're wrong about your father, Zakaja," Blaze assured quietly. "...just as I was wrong about myself. We're from two different worlds, but perhaps there's not as much difference between us as I thought." Blaze suddenly knew she would not kill this woman, despite her promise to Tanus. Her vengeance would instead be unleashed on those who gave the orders to this woman...on those who allowed her to believe terrible lies about her father. The United Star Alliance would pay dearly for its mistakes. "Talk to him," Blaze suggested. "Talk to him and listen. You may find that the father you loved is still there."

Zakaja stared in disbelief at the queen. "You're not going to kill me?"

"After you talk with your father, you can decide whether you want to stay here, with him, or return to the Alliance. Either choice is yours to make freely."

The young Proximan woman studied Blaze for a moment, feeling the honesty of the emotions behind the offer, then smiled softly. "I-I thought I knew all about the Crimson Queen of the Red Star Imperium, but I was wrong. Maybe I was wrong about my father also."

"Take Zakaja to her father," Blaze ordered Travis. "She is to be guarded carefully but is to be treated as a guest."

The Shadowguard nodded his compliance, then led the S'teka woman to the doorway, but she paused there and glanced back. "Thank you."

Blaze felt herself smile. "Tell your father that I've asked myself…and the answer is no."

"I don't understand."

"He will."

Zakaja walked out into the corridor, and Travis led her from the detention level. For a moment Blaze watched the empty doorway in silence. A feeling of contentment settled over her which she couldn't explain, and she found that she didn't even care to try. Then she turned toward the back door and left the room as well, eager to check on her adopted father and to be by her husband's side.

About the Author

Born in New York City, Nicholas Samuel Stember spent most of his life in the suburbs of Princeton, NJ. Growing up with a profound love and appreciation of the genres of fantasy, science fiction and horror, the direction his writing took was firmly set. His love of those genres also found him a wife from across the sea, and he ended up marrying her and moving to the Faroe Islands, where he resides today. His works can be found in magazines, anthologies and upcoming novels. He also_joined the Horror Writers Association in 2024. For more information check out his website at https://nsstember.com
https://www.facebook.com/nicholassamuelstember.

VISIT OUR WEBSITE
FOR THE FULL INVENTORY
OF QUALITY BOOKS:
http://www.roguephoenixpress.com

Rogue Phoenix Press

Representing Excellence in Publishing

**Quality trade paperbacks and downloads
in multiple formats,
in genres ranging from historical to contemporary romance,
mystery and science fiction.
Visit the website then bookmark it.
We add new titles each month!**

www.ingramcontent.com/pod-product-compliance
Lightning Source LLC
Chambersburg PA
CBHW070643180626
46817CB00006B/2223